Nate Grisham

Black Mountain Man

WR Benton
Grady Clark

LOOSE CANNON ENTERPRISES
Paradise, CA

2nd Edition
ISBN 978-1-944476-37-3

www.loose-cannon.com

The renowned artist,

K. O. Haberstroh

created the cover art of

the Black Mountain man

for this book.

See more of her fine work at:

http://www.westernartandpoetry.com

She may be contacted by email at:
info@westernartandpoetry.com

Books by W.R. Benton

FICTION

Red Runs the Plain

Missouri in Flames, I Rode with Jesse James

War Paint

James McKay, U. S. Army Scout

Alive and Alone

NON-FICTION

Simple Survival, A Family Outdoors Guide

Impending Disasters

Dedication

W. R. Benton

To Stephen Carrier and Clyde Lowe, I remember Southeast Asia as if it were yesterday. Hang tough, my brothers in arms.

To Shirley Benton Lyons, my sweet cousin, and country girl at heart. May God continue to love you, as I always will.

Grady Clark

To my friends on the Facebook group Women Writing the West, actor Gerry Glenn Jones, Jo Johnstone (Best Selling Author J.A. Johnstone) and John Lockiev, for giving me the inspiration spin yarns.

Table of Contents

Author's Note

While to some readers the thought of Nate Grisham moving west to the shining mountains may seem highly improbable, but a great number of African Americans did in fact go west and very early in our nation's history. Men such as Moses "Black" Harris and James P. Beckwourth (the son of a black woman and a white plantation owner) are just two excellent examples. The mountain man period brought many freed black men, as well as runaways to the area, and the end of the Civil War saw still more moving west seeking a new life.

Writers and historians often ignore the contribution of African Americans, and other minorities, to our great nation's development. We feel it is time history truthfully reflects the contribution of all who moved west, regardless of race, religion, or national origin.

Additionally, Fort Atkinson, which is referred to numerous times in this book, was used to give a central point of civilization west of the Missouri river to assist in making the story flow smoother. Saint Louis is more likely where many mountain men would have gone, for better prices, but there really was a Fort Atkinson and it was located near present day Omaha, Nebraska. Many trappers traded furs at the fort to avoid the long trip to St. Louis, which was a greater distance away.

W. R. Benton and Grady Clark
1 May 2013

Chapter 1

Nate Grisham was a big man, a big black man, who had come to the shining mountains to make a home. His real name was Nathan, but most folks called him Nate because it seemed to fit his deep booming voice better. Standing six foot and six inches in moccasin feet and weighing almost two hundred and thirty pounds, his body enhanced by five years of hard work as a blacksmith, was powerful. Nate was all muscle and brawn, so not only did he look strong—he was. His mind was that of a quiet man, often thinking but speaking only when it was required, because he thought there was no reason to comment or complain about life during the course of a normal day. However, Nate was a deep thinker and while he had no formal education, he was intelligent. All of his learning was of things he'd learn outside of the schoolroom, since Nate had never been to a schoolhouse in his twenty-two years of life.

"So, what do ya think Nate?" Cotton Top asked as he added a log to the small fire and grinned. Cotton Top was not really the older man's given name, that was John, but he'd picked the new name up in the mountains almost instantly, because his hair and beard were completely white. He was an average sized man, of about five foot ten inches tall, and maybe one hundred and sixty pounds. While not nearly as strong as Nate, Cotton had the kind of lean and long body that could walk or run for days without rest. Nate had seen the man do just that and more than once, when the Blackfoot were hard on their back trail.

"'Bout them Injuns?" Nate asked and repositioned the coffee pot on the dancing flames. He thought for a minute and then continued, "Look, Cotton, they've moved on, or I think they have. Injuns are notional folks, and I've learned as long as you don't mess with them, they'll leave you be . . . unless they're pissed off 'bout life in general, then they'll kill anybody they can find. When we left 'em they were happy enough, right?"

Cotton Top gave a big lopsided grin and then replied, "Yep, I guess, but it's hard to tell with a Sioux." He stretched out his legs by the fire and quickly added, "Ya know, I've been 'round Injuns for years, but I still don't trust none of 'em worth a damn."

"Good, because the day you start to trust all Injuns is the day you'll die. Look, let's eat some of this buffalo meat and have some cornbread. We need to be back in the saddle early in the mornin'. I want you on guard the first half of the night and I'll take the second."

Cotton let out a light laugh, scratched his cheek with his right hand and said, "We'll be up and movin' way before the rooster crows and ya know it. I have no problems doing my guard duty, but on this night at least let me get four hours of sleep. The last few nights I no sooner get to my robe than you wake my ass up to move on. I'm a tired old man this night Nate and need me rest."

The fire cracked and popped for a few minutes and then Nate replied, "Cotton, you'll get some sleep this night, because we have a big storm comin' and it's moving in from the west."

Cotton glanced to the west and he could see gray clouds gathering, some darkness at the very bottom of the dreary fluffs, but not a sign of a serious storm. He gave a loud chuckle and said, "Now where in the world do you get the idea we have a storm brewin'? Oh, I see them clouds over there and I suspect some rain, but a big storm? I think not."

Nate grinned, his black face reflecting his good mood, as he spoke, "It'll storm. I know 'cause every single time my nose feels like it does it storms."

It was near midnight as Cotton Top sat by the horses, when the storm hit. At first there were long lances of lightning flashing along the horizon, followed by the loud boom of thunder a few seconds later, and then came the light pelting wetness of raindrops. The rain was gentle at first; almost soft to the mountain man, but then it increased in tempo to the point of being almost brutal. In a matter of minutes, it fell it sheets of wetness, which soaked every inch of the ground and promised to continue for hours. It was then, at that point, Cotton moved to the shelter where Nate was sleeping.

Seeing the man move into the shelter, Nate smiled and asked as he raised his head, "Storm?"

"Yep, raining like a horse pissin' on a flat rock. I come under here 'cause there ain't nothin' movin' out in this weather. Hell, just them raindrops hurt me some and it's starting to hail now."

The thwacking sound of hail striking the taunt canvas cover of the shelter grew louder as the two men watched the storm move quickly toward them from the west. Though it was dark, the storms movement was easily seen with each frequent long and bright flash of lightning. Angry dark black clouds rolled and tumbled overhead as the canvas snapped and popped in the gusting wind. Hail littered the grasses on all sides of the shelter and the fire pit washed away. Both men realized there was little to do but rest, so the two of them rolled up in their wool blankets and were soon fast asleep.

It was near dawn, with a small part of the storm still overhead, when Nate awoke and listened. Something or someone had awakened him, but he was not sure what he'd heard. He'd been sleeping soundly one minute and then he was wide awake the next, with his heart pounding hard in his big chest. Had it been a bad dream? He didn't remember a dream, but he'd had them before and then was unable to remember them the next morning, only this didn't feel like a dream. He'd heard something, but what?

Nate glanced over at Cotton Top and saw the smaller man was moving slightly as well. So, thought Nate, Old Cotton heard it too and he's awake. Well, we ain't got no fire, so if somebody is out there they didn't find us by the light or smoke of our fire.

"Nate, there is somebody or a critter out there. I think I saw some movement on the west side, but I can't be sure because of the rain." Nate heard his partner whisper lightly.

"You keep an eye on our horses. I don't think it's a beast, too wet fer 'em to be out. Most likely it's somebody up to doin' no good on a wet night."

"Injuns?"

Nate gave a light snicker and replied, "Now, Cotton, how in the world would I know who it is? It could be God's angel Gabriel, but I have my doubts. You just keep your head pulled out of your rear until we find out who it is and we'll be ok."

Suddenly from where Cotton Top had seen the movement there come a yell, "Hello the camp! I'm a white man! I have a sick woman and child with me! Can we come in?"

"Come on in, but keep your hands were we can see 'em. If your hands drop sudden like I'll drill you plum center of your meat bag. Do you understand me?" Nate yelled in return, as he pulled the hammer back on his Hawken rifle with a loud snap.

"I hear you and we're coming in!"

Less than a minute later, three faint images of darkness slowly moved toward the shelter. As they came nearer Nate could see a man, woman and a child moving toward his canvas shelter. The man held an old shotgun high in his left hand, the woman had a pistol in her belt, and the child carried a soft cloth toy of some sort in his right hand.

"Oh, thank God, you're white men!" The woman blurted out as she neared the canvas shelter.

Nate chuckled and replied, "Well, at least one of us is, but I ain't. Come on in here, get under the canvas, and tell me what's goin' on out there."

The three dark figures entered the shelter of the canvas, sat in the dirt and glanced around. A few seconds passed before the woman asked, "Then you're a black man?"

"I've been called that."

"We liked to never found you. We saw the light of your fire a long way back last night, but then we lost it in the storm. We've been out on the plains for days now." The man with the small group suddenly spoke.

"Why?" Cotton asked as he pulled the cork from a bottle of trader's whiskey and filled two tin cups. As soon as the cups were full, he handed one to the woman and one to the man.

"Blackfoot hit our wagon train two days ago right at sunup. We were out gathering fire wood, so they didn't see us." The man quickly replied as he took the cup of strong amber alcohol and raised it to his lips.

Nate thought for a second and then said, "Blackfoot? Kind of south for Bug's boys, so are you sure it was them and not another tribe? It doesn't sound like them to be out this time of the year and surely not way down this way. And, why would a civilian wagon train be moving out here?"

The man cleared his throat and replied, "I'm Captain Taylor M. Banks, of the U.S. Army, and this is my wife, Sara. The boy is our son William. I didn't get your names sir."

Nate chuckled and said, "I didn't give our names, but I'm Nate Grisham and this is Cotton Top Thomas. But, you didn't answer my question, why was a wagon train out here in the middle of nowhere?"

"Well, Mister Grisham, as an officer in the cavalry I know my Indians. God knows I've fought them enough times and it was Blackfoot alright. And, to answer your question, we were a small group of wagons on a mission for the United States Army."

The two mountain men glanced at each other, only due to the darkness they could see little but the vague image of each other. Finally, Nate said, "Cotton, get us a small fire going. It looks like most of the storm has passed. Folks, if you'll give us a few minutes we'll have some light, give you some hot food, and then we'll talk some more."

As soon as Cotton Top had the fire burning, Nate glanced over at Sara Banks. The big man watched her grimaced as she took a small sip of the rough trader's whiskey, but it was obvious to the mountain man she was very hungry, tired and not well. Her eyes had the look of a hunted animal, reflecting fear deep in her very being. Sara's hands trembled in the poor light of the fire as she raised the cup to her full lips once more. Nate wondered if her hands shook from fear, fatigue, or illness.

Sara Banks was a small woman, just a tad over five feet tall, but with a large bust, narrow waist, and wide hips. Her hair was a bright red and her eyes were a deep green. Nate would have not guessed her weight to be more than one hundred and ten pounds if she was soaking wet, and she was.

Taylor Banks was not in uniform, but his behavior clearly indicated he was a military man. He was just slightly less than six feet tall, about one hundred and eighty pounds, and not a bit of it fat. His shoulders were wide and his face was square with light blue eyes. His dark brown hair was closely cropped and his beard neatly trimmed.

The young boy had fallen asleep with his head on his mother's lap and seemed to be a smaller image of his momma. William Banks was only six years old, but he'd already traveled over half of the nation and most of that on foot. The last few days had been hard on the young boy and he looked it.

After the little boy awakened long enough to eat with his parents, Nate asked, "So, what's this about a wagon train bein' attacked?"

"It happened two or three days back and about thirty miles west of here. I hid Sara and William, and then I crawled up on a slight rise to watch it all happen. The Blackfoot over-ran the train and from where I was I'd say there were no survivors or captives."

"Nobody else?" Cotton Top asked as he put the heavy lid back on the Dutch oven and turned to meet the Captain's eyes.

"Well, I didn't hang around to check, but it didn't look good. I will admit, I was somewhat startled by the suddenness as well as the brutality of the attack and by the speed of which it ended. By Damn, I'll bet you the fight didn't last five minutes, from first bullet to the last bullet."

"You're a smart man if it scared you a mite. Them Blackfoot don't play around when they go on a killin' spree and it is rare a person gets away from 'em." Cotton spoke once more and glanced quickly at Nate.

Both of the mountain men knew something about the story was not right, but what? It was late fall or early winter, depending on your view, and usually most Indians, except for small groups of hunters out looking for buffalo, were back in the village preparing for the coming bad weather. Also, what would a wagon train be doing out on the open plains with bad weather due to hit at any time? And, besides all of that, where on earth would a wagon train be heading? It just didn't add up and while stranger things had happened, the two mountain men both thought if the Blackfoot were out in force, something had them riled up good.

"My wife has a slight fever and she's not been well since the attack. I guess part of the problem is that she's not been warm since we had to flee. I felt it would be safer not to have a fire due to the threat of the Blackfoot."

"Could be your feelings were right, but them Blackfoot might have moved on right after the attack. And, I've found it's always better to not take a risk than to take one." Cotton Top spoke, added another log to the dying fire, and then quickly added, "You're safe right now, so relax a bit and let us think about what we're gonna do with the three of ya."

"I need to report to the army and determine what they want to do about this and make sure it's not taken lightly," Captain Banks said as he leaned back in the dirt under the shelter.

"There is an army post at Fort Atkinson, but that's the closest one I know of outside of Saint Louis." Nate spoke and then wondered about the man's concern in reporting the killings. Nate felt that most folks would be more worried about surviving, or getting their family to safety, and not so much about reporting the situation. Granted, the killings needed to be reported, but why worry about the dead when you had a sick wife and your child with you. It didn't make sense to him.

"Would you take us there?" Sara asked as she looked over at her husband and then lowered her eyes.

Old Cotton Top gave a loud laugh and then replied, "I don't see no other choice, and besides, ya need a doctor. You're breathing rough and I 'spect ya have a bad cold or mayhap pneumonia. Both of them illnesses can kill and a woman will usually die quicker than a man will if they come down sick with one of 'em."

"We appreciate your concern, but my wife is quite able to continue on and will do so. If you'll take us the fort, we'll all see a doctor and be on the mend fairly quickly, I assure you. I can send a dispatch to the Department of the Army in Saint Louis and we can immediately continue our move westward from there." The Captain then leaned forward to hold his hands open to the flickering flames of the fire.

The Captain's casual comments made Nate wonder if he really wanted to go to Atkinson and that made the big man suspicious as all get out. And, why had Sara raised her right eyebrow when she heard the name Atkinson? There was an army unit there, so why send a dispatch all the way to the Department of the Army back east? Or, he thought, Maybe I'm making more out of this than there is. It could be after the Injun attack and the last few days out on the plains; these folks are just plain worn out. Lord knows that something like that would be hard on any folks from back east.

"I think it'd be smart if y'all get a couple of hours of sleep before we move toward the fort. The weather might clear up in a few hours, but we'll have to wait a spell to allow the trail to clear up a mite. Right now, the runoff has most likely turned the trail into one big mud hole and travel would be too slow. When we leave later today, your wife and child will share a horse, and we men folk will walk. Near as I figure we're just a tad under twenty miles from the fort, so it'll only take us a day of hard walkin' to get there." Cotton spoke as he handed his spare wool blanket to Sara Banks and watched her cover her sleeping child.

Less than an hour later, as the two mountain men stood guard over the horses, Cotton Top looked over at Nate and said, "I cain't put my finger to it, but all ain't as it seems with this Banks feller. I figure he ain't a Captain, or else he don't want the army to know what's a-goin' on just yet. Seems to me a man in his position would want the army to know what is goin' on and the army fort is the closest place to report it. I mean, why would he send out a dispatch with the army right there at the fort? It seems to be like he don't want Fort Atkinson to really know what's goin' on. And, besides, what in the world was a bunch of pilgrims doin' out on the open plains in a wagon train?"

Nate gave out a light sigh and then replied, "It's hard to say Cotton. Lots of men out here aren't what they claim to be, but Banks I suspect is an army officer, or at least was. But, like you just said, I cain't figure out why he doesn't want the army in-volved first hand and the post is the best place to report all of this. Most fellers would report it to the fort and then let them worry about it."

"You reckon he's on the run?"

Nate thought for a minute and then said, "Could be, but I don't think so. I think the Captain was in charge of the wagon trains security and a thing like that could ruin his military career. He's young and if he was in charge when all the folks got killed, hell, he's finished in army, don't ya see? If he sends a dispatch he can write just about any story he wants and get away with it too, well, at least for a long spell."

The older mountain man gave a low laugh, pulled his hat off and ran his fingers through his dirty hair before he said, "Yep, I can see all of that, but still you can't run from a killin' like that, 'cause it's too big. People will find out and they'll know soon enough who was in charge."

"That they will my friend, that they will, if what he told us is the truth."

CHAPTER 2

Dawn arrived cold with the threat of more rain in the air from the dark clouds overhead and a slight breeze from the west. The two mountain men blew the gray ash of the fire alive, added some small pieces of wood, and started breakfast before they woke the sleeping family. Both knew it would be a rough day of travel for a family from back east, but it was a trip that had to be made if they wanted help. After a quick meal of thickly sliced bacon, hot biscuits, and scalding oil Cotton swore was coffee, the small group started for Fort Atkinson.

Nate insisted that Cotton Top ride one horse out in front to scout the way, while Sara and the youngster William rode double. While the distance to the fort wasn't great, the Sioux at times ambushed travelers on their way to the place, so Nate kept his rifle at the ready. Captain Banks held the reins of the big bay in his right hand and his shotgun in his left as he walked beside the huge black man.

"Ma'am, you keep them blankets wrapped tight 'round you and your young-un, 'cause neither one of you are very strong right now. Try your best to stay warm and if things go okay you'll be in town before nightfall," Nate said as he pulled his old briar pipe from his possibles bag and started stuffing the bowl with tobacco. "William has a slight fever and I know I have one. Are you sure, Mister Grisham, this fort has a doctor?" Sara asked as she looked down at the big man.

Nate gave a loud chuckle and replied, "Please call me Nate and, yep, they have a doctor there."

A good hour passed in silence before Captain Banks asked, "So, Nate, what brings a man like you out west?"

Nate was unsure what the man meant by his question, so he asked, "You mean as a black man?"

Banks laughed and replied, "Well, that entered my mind too, but I meant in general."

"Captain, I came out here to build me a new life. I grew up a slave down in Arkansas, where I was beaten, starved, and treated worse than a hog most of the time, so one day I had enough."

"You mean you're a runaway?" Sara asked suddenly.

"Nope, I didn't *run* no place. One night, right in the middle of a big rain storm, I walked off and I ain't never been back."

Banks stopped walking, met the black man's eyes and then said, "By law you're a runaway slave and that means you could be taken back to your old master. You do know that don't you? There's most likely a big reward for your return."

Nate gave a loud laugh, held his Hawken rifled up high and replied, "Then by God, let 'em try! I'm a free man now and I will stay free, no matter what it takes."

"Look, you just get us to Atkinson and we'll forget we ever saw you. You're helping us and that means a great deal to me and my family," Captain Banks said in a voice that hinted of a bit of dishonesty as far as Nate was concerned. *He thinks he can make some big and easy money when we get to town by turnin' me over to some slave hunters,* Nate thought with a blank expression on his black face.

Nate suddenly grinned and replied, "Captain Banks, understand me right now, because I mean this. If I get so much as a hint that you've said anything to anyone, I'll kill you. I meant what I said a minute ago about staying free."

"Well, I never even considered —"

"Bullshit and we both know it. I'm worth over a thousand dollars and I was told that many times by my old master, but you turn on me and I'll get ugly real fast. I'm helping you and your family, and I expect no repayment, so the least you can do is leave me be."

"Then, why did you tell me?" Captain Banks started walking once more.

"You want the truth?"

"But of course I do."

Nate laughed once more and said, "Because I don't believe your story about the Blackfoot and I don't really care much for you. I guess I wanted to shock you is all and judge your reaction as a man. The truth is, I'm helping the woman and the child, 'cause if it was just you alone, I'd do very little."

Banks stopped once more and replied, "The story is true. And, as far as you not liking me, that's fine as well. I don't care much for your kind anyway, but I will say nothing of you being a runaway to anyone."

Nate didn't miss a step as he walked by Captain Banks and said, "Good, because if you say one word about me it'll make killin' you that much easier. And, you know how vicious and mean us black men can be when we turn to spillin' a white man's blood."

"Oh, my God!" Sara said horror from a top of the horse.

"Now, get to walkin' Captain, we ain't got all day to discuss our likes and dislikes, not with the Blackfoot out in force." With that said, Nate gave a loud laugh, threw the barrel of his Hawken up on his right shoulder, and quickened his pace to walk ahead.

A mile after mile steady pace was maintained and just before dark the lights of Fort Atkinson were seen less than a mile to the east. Cotton Top had ridden back just as the lights were seen and said, "There she is and while it ain't much, but it's the biggest place we got right now. And, if y'all will move over to the right a mite, you'll hit a road goin' right into fort. We'll be passin' through a small town that surrounds the fort, but it ain't much."

"It'll do." Nate gave his friend a warm grin as he moved toward the roadway.

Little had been spoken among the small group after Nate's harsh words with Captain Banks, but it didn't bother the big black man much. He didn't care to talk most of the time and to speak with a man who suggested he might turn him in went against his grain. But, one thing for sure, Nate meant what he'd told the Captain about remaining free.

They entered the fort from the west and walked right up the middle of the street. Few people were out, since it was near dinnertime, but loud voices and a few laughs echoed in the still night air from a nearby saloon as well as the faint sounds of an old piano.

"There is the commander's office." Captain Banks spoke suddenly and pointed at an old sign above a small brick build-ing.

After Nate tied the horses to the hitching post in front of the office, the woman and child dismounted. Sara Banks wobbled a little as soon as her feet touched the ground and Nate knew the woman was much sicker than she had been the night before.

"Cotton, you run along and fetch us a doctor. Tell 'em to come to the commander's office." Nate spoke as he stepped up on the oak boardwalk.

"I'll be back directly!" Cotton Top yelled as he turned his horse toward the center of the fort and started at a fast walk.

Nate opened the door to the office, stepped inside, and immediately felt the intense heat of the small room. The Banks family followed him inside and the commander, who'd been leaned over a desk talking to a young private, suddenly looked up.

"Well, now, I'll be damned, iffen it ain't Nate Grisham! How in the hell are you doin'?" A middle-aged man with thinning red hair asked as he moved from his desk to shake the big black man's hand.

As they shook hands, Nate replied, "Doin' fine Patrick. I found this family out on the plains about twenty miles west of here and they claim the Blackfoot killed most of a wagon train. "

The old major sat on the edge of the desk and then asked, "You sure it was the Blackfoot?" Then standing, he added, "I'm Major Patrick O'Brien."

"I'm Captain Banks of the United States Army and this is my wife, Sara, and my son, William, sir. It was the Blackfoot beyond a doubt." Banks gave a quick salute, which O'Brien waved away.

"Well, let me get my pen and some more paper out, because we need to report this right away." The major said as he moved behind his desk, sat down, and started pulling papers from the top drawer of his desk.

It didn't take Captain Banks long to report what had occurred and just as he finished a civilian doctor walked into the small room with Cotton Top. The doctor was a lanky young man, carrying a black leather bag in his right hand. Nate would have guessed him near twenty years of age, but suspected he was older just by his profession. The sawbones quickly evaluated both Sara and William, and then said, "They both need hot baths, some light soup, and plenty of sleep. If you can put them up in the hotel, I'll come by in a little while with some medicine for them both. By rights, they should both have pneumonia, but

I don't think they have at this point. Keep 'em warm, feed 'em lot's of hot soup, and they'll be fine in a few days."

"We'll get a room and when you come by with the medicine I'll pay you." The Captain said as he gave the doctor a big crooked grin.

"Good, the fee is a dollar and the medicine will be another two bits." The doctor spoke as he opened the door to the commander's office and stepped outside into the growing darkness.

"Private Smith, show these fine folks to the hotel, and Nate, if you and Cotton Top are in the saloon in a few minutes, I'll let you both buy me a beer. I have K-Troop out now and our surgeon is with them, or the medical care would have been free." O'Brien said.

Twenty minutes later the three men were in the saloon and seated at a table against the far wall. They discussed friends, fur prices, and the cost of a good horse, when Nate suddenly asked, "Pat, what do you think of this Banks feller and his family?"

Pat O'Brien pushed his hat back on his head, met Nate's eyes and replied, "You know, at first glance they seem like a normal family, but something ain't right about 'em. I'm sure Banks is, or at least was, in the army, but even in the hotel room Private Smith said the wife still seemed scared. Now, to me, after reaching safety she should have shown some relief, right?"

"I'd figure as much. But, she's been sick too," Cotton said as he raised his beer and looked over the rim of his glass at the major.

"What I saw in that woman's eyes in my office was fear Cotton, not relief. Only you might be right, maybe she's just sick, but I'm gonna run some checks on Captain Taylor M. Banks. As a matter of fact," O'Brien said as he stood, "I'll head over and write out a dispatch right now and contact the army. I had Smith check our old dispatches here, but we don't have anything on the man. Then, come morning I'll ask him to show me his written orders."

Cotton laughed and replied, "I bet it's months before you get an answer too. The army works slower than ninety year old man hoein' a field full of corn."

"While you're doin' that, me and Cotton will move out west of town a mite and set up camp. If you need to reach us, we'll be where you got lucky a few years back and killed that big whitetail buck. I suspect we'll spend a couple of days there and then we'll head back out west." Nate stood, no man noticing the scrapping sound his chair made on the wooden floor as it moved away from the table.

Two men mounted and rode west, as the third made his way to his office where he hoped to find Private Smith still awake.

Smith was a very young man, just barely over eighteen, but he could write as fast as any man O'Brien had ever watched on the job and was an excellent speller. The young man was tall, nothing but bones, and had the largest feet the Irishman had ever seen on another human being. O'Brien had seen the type before, most likely the young man would start to spread in a year or two and grow into a big man almost overnight. It just seemed to take some boys longer to grow man size.

"Sir, I was just about to come and get you." Smith spoke as he looked up.

"About what?"

Smith said, "There was a killin' back east."

"So, what does that have to do with us?"

Smith picked up a dispatch and read, "Attention all units. U.S. Army looking for a Captain Taylor M. Banks. Banks maybe out west. Arrest immediately. The real Banks is in Washington. Hold all suspects for U.S. Government. One thousand dollar reward offered for arrest and conviction of impostor Captain Taylor M. Banks. Captain Banks' real name is Taylor Donnelly and he is wanted for murder and desertion from the United States Army as he awaited incarceration. Exercise extreme caution as Donnelly is armed and considered dangerous. Signed, James E. Burke, Colonel, United States Army."

"Holy cow," O'Brien spoke in a loud voice and as he pulled his pistol and brought the hammer back he yelled, "tell the sergeant of the guard Banks is here and tell 'em to get to the hotel now! In the mean time, I'm going after the man!" As he turned and ran toward the door he yelled at the lanky kid, "Do it *now* Smith!"

Patrick O'Brien was used to handling his own problems. Granted, Atkinson was not a big place and the most serious crime committed was usually a drunken soldier shooting a gun in the streets after a few beers on payday, but the Irishman knew how to handle trouble if need be. He ran into the hotel, down the hall to room 102, threw the door open, only to find

Sara Banks and William deep asleep in bed. A lamp burned low on a night table beside them.

Turning the wick to the lamp up, Major O'Brien said in a loud voice, "Mrs. Banks, you need to wake up!"

Sara rolled over, gave a low moan and asked, "What's the matter and what are you doing in my room?"

"Where's your husband, we need to talk?"

Sara sat up, glanced around the room and then said, "I have no idea. The last I remember Taylor was in the chair, sitting by the widow and sipping on a glass of rye as he read the newspaper. Is something wrong, sir?"

Spotting the paper on the floor, Patrick O'Brien walked over, picked it up and read the headlines, 'U.S. Army in Uproar over double Killings in Washington.' O'Brien quickly skimmed over the story and shook his head as he read the details. Meeting Sara's eyes a few seconds later, Pat asked, "Where were you stationed before you came out west?"

"We were in Washington, where Taylor commanded a troop of cavalry, why?"

Meeting her eyes once more, O'Brien asked in a soft voice as his eyes narrowed, "Sara, your real last name is not really Banks, is it?"

Lowering her head, Sara replied just above a whisper, "No, it's not. Our last name is really Donnelly, but Taylor changed our name when the army threw him out. He said we'd never get a fresh start after the way the army had treated him. So we borrowed some money and we came out west to start a new life. I don't understand, people do that sort of thing all the time now. Major O'Brien, this is all very confusing to me, I mean, why all the questions?"

"Why did the army get rid of your husband?"

"Taylor was accused, falsely of course, of taking some missing army funds. I don't understand all of it, but I know the amount was said to be less than two hundred dollars. He ran the officers mess and the money collected for the fund disappeared one evening and Taylor was blamed. He received a military courts martial, was convicted, and asked to resign for the good of the service."

Quickly looking the room over, O'Brien then asked, "You have a place to return to back east?"

A blank look came over the woman's face as she asked, "Now, why would you ask me that? As soon as Taylor returns we'll continue our trip west."

The major gave a low chuckle and then said, "Sara, all of your husband's gear is gone, even his shotgun, and from what I can see he has no intentions of ever returning."

Suddenly, as she too looked around the small room, it dawned on Sara Donnelly, that she was now alone. Tears silently ran down her cheeks as she replied, "I . . . I can go back to my parents, I guess." Then, glancing quickly up at O'Brien, she asked, "Why would he abandon his wife and only child? What kind of man would do that to his family?"

Turning and reaching for the doorknob, O'Brien said, "A scared man Sara, a real scared man."

Chapter 3

A frightened Taylor M. Donnelly was miles out on the plains by the time the commander entered Sara's room. While he loved both his wife and son, he knew the authorities would check his military record and he'd be discovered. He realized he had little choice except to run and his family was too sick to run with him. Any background check would show he was not only a thief, but also a killer and both charges out west could and usually would bring instant hanging. The deep and almost uncontrollable fear he felt deep inside was only for him and not for the two people he'd left back in the hotel room sleeping. He knew Sara could always take William and return to her rich family back east, though he strongly disliked the thought. Her family had never wanted him to marry her to start with, often saying he was beneath her.

Taylor had been the perfect example of a military officer and he'd graduated from the U.S. Military Academy at West Point in 1815, as an engineer, placing second out of a class of forty-five. But, since the army had an overage of engineers at the time, he'd been assigned to the cavalry, which seemed to fit his bold personality better anyway, or so he thought. He'd quickly won his superiors over and his skills as a mounted soldier were borderline genius. Petty theft ruined his career and brought out almost uncontrollable anger and deep rage. Of all wrongs in his small world, Taylor M. Donnelly disliked being denied revenge most and to him to right a wrong was a privilege. Taylor still wanted to preserve the almost perfect image of himself he'd fought so hard to maintain in the army up until his courts martial conviction.

The story of the Blackfoot attack had been true, though it had not happened exactly the way Taylor had said it had. The ex-Captain had convinced three families in Missouri to accompany him to start a new life near Atkinson, but he'd gotten lost and they ended up way north and west of the small fort. Taylor had never said anything to anyone, but he'd suspected days before that he'd somehow missed the fort and had made a serious mistake in navigation. Only, instead of admitting his mistake, the small group had continued moving forward—away from Fort Atkinson.

A few minutes before dawn, on the day of the attack, he'd started a fire, placed a pot of coffee on and then spotted a Blackfoot warrior in the grass. As soon as the warrior moved off at right angles from him, Captain Donnelly had panicked and it took him a few minutes to get himself under control. Then, he'd gone about his business as if everything was normal, but at the last second he had quickly awakened his family and led them to safety in the trees. Once in the heavy brush and forest by the small river, they'd moved quickly over a slight rise and down into the valley below, where he'd hidden his family from the attacking Indians. At no point had he attempted to warn the other members of the wagon train nor had he planned to do such a thing.

From his position on the rise, Donnelly watched the vicious killings and then mutilation of the other members of the wagon train. He was shocked when he discovered he could hear their pitiful screams of pain and fear from where he was hiding on the hill. As soon as the braves had departed, Taylor had returned to the scene of death, collected all the money and gold he could find, and then buried it in an empty coffee can under a huge tree in the woods.

From the money he had on him as he now rode, plus the buried money from the massacred wagon train, Donnelly knew he had enough to make a new start and perhaps to one day send for his family back in Boston. His problem now was the fact that Fort Atkinson was the last known settlement of any size west of the Mississippi River, but he'd moved west after leaving the fort.

The big stolen horse he rode was taken after careful consideration of all the horses in front of the saloon. When Taylor had evaluated the animals, he wanted one that had a rifle, bedroll, and other items, as well as being in excellent physical condition. The horse he now rode was the type of horse that was full of energy and the ex-cavalryman knew the horse under him would run until it dropped. A natural on horseback, Donnelly allowed his body to move with the gentle movements of the horse until they became one with each motion. *This horse is another reason I have to keep moving,* he thought as he scanned the countryside, *if the owner catches me, I'll hang for sure.*

It was well after midnight before Donnelly stopped for a few hours of rest. He knew he had to cover many miles over the next few days to put some distance between him and the U.S. army. They'd come looking for him and he had no doubt about it. His only hope was to cover more miles than they would expect him to cover and then he could blend into a town or city in some way. Once he had money, he'd not worry much about the army catching him, because with cash he could buy safety. *I'll rest a couple of hours, go and get the money from the wagon train, and then head east to a town,* he thought as he made a small fire of buffalo chips.

Off in the distance to his west long fingers of lightning were reaching out of the darkness, as if frantically searching for something, and a few seconds later he heard loud claps of thunder. The night was dark with clouds rolling violently overhead and he suspected rain at any second, but it remained dry. He ate a quick meal of bacon he'd found in the stolen saddlebags along with two stale biscuits. While not the best meal he'd ever eaten, he was so jumpy he didn't give his food much thought.

He had just rolled up in his horse blanket when he heard a slight noise near the horse. Glancing up, Donnelly noticed the bay looking toward the east and his ears were standing straight up. *Shit, looks like something or someone is out there,* he thought as he pulled the hammer back on his stolen Hawken with a loud click.

Suddenly, without any warning, three Indians ran from the darkness toward Donnelly's campsite. The ex-army officer lined up the sights of his Hawken on the man in front and gently squeezed the trigger, grinning as the man went down hard and began thrashing in the tall buffalo grasses. At that point lightning weaved through the night air and he spotted a second man slightly to the right of where he'd shot the first man. Pulling his pistol, he aimed, jerked the trigger, and saw the brave drop, but Donnelly suspected the man was not hit. The third man had gone to ground and Taylor waited for the next flash of lightning. Quickly and with shaking hands, he reloaded both his pistol and rifle. His shotgun was out of reach, still in the sheath and near his horse. He'd not pull his second pistol until things turned rough.

A few minutes later, from the tall buffalo grass behind him, Captain Donnelly heard a slight noise and as he turned, he saw the dark outline of an Indian. Swinging his pistol around he squeezed the trigger and had the satisfaction of seeing the man knocked backward by the impact of the heavy slug as it struck him in the middle of the chest. Sweating and breathing hard, Taylor quickly reloaded.

Many long minutes passed without a single sound, except for the grasses moving with the wind. The storm was moving past and the clouds were starting to thin enough to allow a faint light from the moon to break through. As he glanced around his campsite, Donnelly could not see a soul, nor could he hear any sound out of place. While not especially woods smart, the Captain had been in combat many times and he knew the first man to move might very well be the first man to die. He kept still and waited.

Raising his head Taylor scanned the area once more, but this time before he could lower himself he felt an arrow strike him hard in the upper right shoulder. Immediately the loud scream of a war cry sounded and saw the warrior he had fired at earlier racing toward him armed with a knife in his left hand and tomahawk in his right. Cold fear knotted in Taylor's stomach and he knew he was going to die, but before he could move, the warrior hit him hard. The impact of the charging brave knocked both of them to the ground and Donnelly screeched in pain as the arrow was driven completely through his shoulder.

They rolled and rolled in the grass, until finally the brave ended up sitting on Donnelly's chest with the white man holding tightly to both of his arms. Feeling his strength leaving him, Taylor knew the brave felt it too. When he finally lost his grip on the brave's right arm, he saw the blade falling and then felt the bite of the keen edge of the tomahawk on the right side of his face. In a panic, he pulled his second pistol from his belt with his right hand, stuck the barrel against the warrior's stomach, and squeezed the trigger. He felt the Indian's body jerk violently as the lead slug hit him, felt blood spewed on his legs and stomach, and then the warrior fell to the side.

Donnelly must have passed out, because the next time he opened his eyes it was almost daylight. A light gray veil covered the plains and from the east, he could see the sun just starting its journey across the sky. At first he didn't move. For a while, he laid there listening to the sounds around him and fighting his pain. He could hear his horse moving, birds starting to chirp, and the wind rustling the grasses. It was then, at that point, he knew he was alone.

He attempted to stand, but his legs were too weak and he wasn't sure if it was from the loss of blood or if he'd taken an injury there. Moving very slowly on his hands and knees he crawled slowly to his fire pit, where after a few minutes he had a small fire burning. He heated up some water and then washed his face as well as he could with his shirt. Taylor was shocked when he felt a long flap of skin hanging below his cheek and he wondered what his injury looked like. While he knew his face had taken a serious injury, he was more worried about the bleeding from his right shoulder. He quickly pulled a quart of whiskey from the stolen saddlebags and drank about half of it for the pain, but it helped little. The sun was up and sky was clear overhead when Taylor M. Donnelly finally fainted beside his fire from the loss of blood.

Hearing voices, Taylor opened his eyes. He noticed immediately he was in some sort of a shelter, because he could see tightly stretched gray canvas overhead, but he had no idea where he was, or what he was doing there. His right shoulder ached with each beat of his heart and his face felt almost numb with pain. He raised his head, fought back a dizzy spell, and looked toward the voices.

"By God, he yet lives." A big man with long blond hair said as he noticed Taylor moving and turned toward the injured man.

"You hungry some?" A second man, sitting on a log by the fire asked as he gave a big crooked grin. Taylor saw he was very tall, but as thin, and had dark black hair.

"W . . . water?" Taylor managed to get out before he fell back against his blanket.

The two dirty and smelly mountain men looked at each other, grinned, and then the big man got up and made his way to the supplies. Taking an old tin cup, he poured it half full of raw trader's whiskey and then topped it off with water. He turned and quickly walked to Taylor's side with the drink. Kneeling beside the seriously injured man he said, "Howdy do, I'm Thomas Abington and the feller resting his fat ass on the log is Jonathan Sachell. But, I'm called Doc and Jonathan is called Skeeter."

Taylor attempted to lift his head but he was unable to do so and Doc seeing the man's difficulty placed his left hand behind his head and raised it. The mountain man let just a little of the whiskey slide into the Captain's mouth and then lowered his head. Taylor met the man's eyes and said slowly, "I . . . I'm Taylor . . . Wyer."

"Well, by God, you're a lucky young coon Mister Taylor Wyer. We come up on your campsite jess after dawn and found ya a-layin' in a big puddle of blood. Hell fire, we couldn't tell how much of it was yours or them three Blackfoot you killed." Doc replied as he raised Taylor's head and gave him another sip of the watered down whiskey.

"Yep, I think in 'nother thirty minutes and ya would have gone under on us. But, old Doc, well, he went to school back east to be a doctor, so he know'd how to fix ya up real good." Skeeter said from his log without looking over at the shelter. He added a log to the fire and then continued, "Son, your hurt pretty bad. Now, I 'spect ya'll live, but I gotta be honest with ya, ya don't look none like ya used to look."

Through his pain Taylor heard the tall man's words, but he didn't understand what he meant so he asked in a weak voice, "W . . .what do . . . you mean?"

Doc suddenly grew serious and replied, "Ya took a hatchet strike to your face and I had to sew ya back together. Your lower jaw, on the right side, was cut clean through to the teeth. Son, ya was cut from your right ear all the way to your mouth and when we found ya it was all just a big flap of skin hangin' loose. The arrow in the shoulder was easy to fix, all I had to do was pull some of the shaft the rest of the way out, clean ya up, and then bandage it good. If it don't fester on ya, ya'll live."

"My . . . thanks," Taylor said just before he closed his eyes against a wave of deep pain and arched his back.

"Here, drink the rest of this and then sleep. Right now the best thing for ya is some rest. Hell's bells, a fight with three Blackfoot will take a lot out of any man and you're hurt on top of it." Doc spoke as he once more fed some of the watered whiskey to Taylor. The mountain man watched as the injured man either fell back to sleep or passed out. Then, he stood and made his way to the fire.

"He gonna make it?" Skeeter asked as he pulled out his old briar pipe.

Doc rubbed the right side of his bearded face, turned and met Skeeter's eyes as he replied, "More than likely he'll make it, unless he festers. But, when he sees his face, well, I don't wanna be around then."

Pulling a burning twig from the fire and placing it against the bowl of his pipe, Skeeter didn't answer until he gave it a couple of hard puffs, "Aye, he's a bit on the ugly side right now, but don't ya think most of that is due to swellin'?"

As a white cloud of smoke covered Skeeter's face, Doc said, "Skeeter, the man lost his right ear, the tip of his nose, and about half of his upper lip. The swelling can go all the way down and it won't help his looks much. But, I'll tell ya right now, that man over there has the hair of the bear, he has. Did you see how he took that pain when he woke up? Tough as tree bark he is."

Skeeter thought for a few minutes and then extended his long and lanky legs out in front of himself before he replied, "The sumbitch is lucky to be alive. 'Sides looks don't matter much no ways out heah and you know it. Now, back east the boy might stir up some problems a-lookin' like that, but ya and me both know out heah it don't matter none a-tall."

"Well, we'll see if he goes under or not. I think he has a good chance of livin', but we can't move for a spell or he might start to bleedin' again."

Skeeter laughed, slapped his right knee with his right hand and replied, "Ya got some place to go all of a sudden? Ya got a gal friend ya ain't told me about?"

Doc grinned back and said, "Nope, but I just wanted to warn ya is all. Now, what do ya think this feller was doin' out here alone?"

Skeeter shrugged his narrow shoulders and spoke with a big grin on his face, "It's hard to tell. This place is fillin' up quicker than a whorehouse on payday. I can remember when I could ride for weeks and not see another white man, but hell, I'm lucky to go two weeks now without seein' one. Didn't ya say ya found some army clothes in his stuff?"

"Shirt, and it had a Captains rank on the shoulders. Only we both know that don't mean shit, because he might have bought the shirt used. Then again, he might have been in the army once."

"Well, it don't matter none to me one way or the other. But, there was no way I could leave a white man hurt like that." Skeeter looked into the fire for a moment, raised his head, and continued, "Not after what them red bastards did to my family when I was a kid. I swore then I'd help everybody hurt by 'em and kill every damn Blackfoot I could find."

Doc gave a loud laugh, slapped Skeeter on the back and replied, "Well, you've done a damned good job of keepin' your word old son. I'll bet you've killed over twenty Blackfoot and this is the third man we've helped since we joined up to trap together. Only, go easy on the hate ya have Skeeter, it ain't good for a man to carry too much of it inside."

While Skeeter didn't reply immediately, he bent over and placed the old blackened coffee pot on the flames, and then stood. Reaching down he picked his Hawken up by the barrel, checked his flint, and then walked off toward the rolling plains. As he moved from the fire, he said over his shoulder, "Goin' huntin', so ya keep the coffee hot for me. I 'spect I'll be back in less than an hour. I'll kill us a buff calf and we'll fix a broth that'll help make this Wyer feller stronger, so he heals quick like on us."

Doc waved at his friend and yelled out, "Watch your topknot out there pilgrim. Them damned Blackfoot might still be 'round."

Six days later Taylor was sitting by the fire as Doc applied a new bandage to his shoulder. The face was healing nicely, but the mountain man could see scabs forming on the injured man's face and he'd failed to make eye contact as he looked the injury over. *Damn, he's goin' to take this face injury rough once he sees it,* Doc thought but said, "You're healin' good Wyer and I 'spect you'll be almost back to normal in a couple of weeks. Now, if ya feel up to it, we'll leave in the mornin'."

"That'll be fine. I feel pretty good, except my face feels tight and itches to beat the band at times." Taylor replied.

"To be expected, because the flesh is healin' and scabs are formin'. That's good and there ain't no sign of festerin' at all, so I think ya'll survive this time." Doc said. Then, suddenly thinking of more to say, he quickly added, "Don't forget ya got three horses them Blackfoot was ridin', plus two rifles, a pistol, and three knives. From what I can tell, you've added a considerable amount of wealth to your whole situation. Butterfield will trade ya top dollar for any or all of those things as soon as we get to the tradin' post."

Taylor grinned and asked, "When will we be there?"

Doc chuckled, glanced over at Skeeter, and the skinny man said, "Oh, I'd say in about four days, if the weather stays good. And, let me tell ya right now, Butterfield will drive a hard bargain, but he's a fair man. It's just hard to get the better of him when it comes to a hoss trade."

All three men broke out laughing and after a few minutes Doc said, "Wyer, ya better get some sleep, because we got us a long day tomorrow. Skeeter, ya take the last watch and that means you need to hit your robe too in a few minutes. I want us all up and riding as dawn peaks up over the skyline in the mornin'."

CHAPTER 4

Nate and Cotton were sitting around the campfire enjoying the cracking of the burning wood and making small talk, when they heard a horse approaching. Quickly moving back into the cover of a few stunted trees the two men pulled the hammers back on their Hawken rifles and waited for the rider, only the wait was a short one.

About a hundred feet from the fire the voice of O'Brien rang out loud and clear, "Nate, Cotton, it's me, Major O'Brien!"

"Come to the fire, Pat, and let's talk." Nate yelled out and moved toward the campsite.

O'Brien rode his horse to the picket line, dismounted and tied his horse, and then walked to the fire where he squatted on his heels by the flames.

"Here," Cotton said as he handed the major a tin cup, "pour yerself some coffee, but if ya drink juss one cup of Nate's coffee you won't sleep fer a month."

"Thanks, Cotton." O'Brien spoke and then turning to meet Nate's eyes he added, "You were right about our friend the Captain."

Nate, confused, narrowed his eyes and asked, "What do you mean? Wasn't there a train load of folks killed?"

"Yep, that parts true enough, but Captain Taylor M. Banks ain't out West, he's still in Washington and has no plans to come out this way. Seems our man Banks is really named Donnelly and while he was a Captain, they threw his ass out a few months back for stealing. Then, just after he left the city, the army discovered the bodies of the man who had accused him of the crime, a Colonel Aker, and his wife. Seems they were both butchered if the newspapers are to be believed. The army has a thousand dollar reward for Donnelly dead or alive."

"What a damned fool! Didn't he know that the army would suspect him right off?" Cotton asked.

"Cotton, when some men want revenge they'll do just about anything to have at it. I've seen some strange stuff happen when hate takes over a man's mind." O'Brien said as he pulled out his plug of chewing tobacco and cut off a short piece with his penknife.

For a few minutes, the fire snapped and cracked loudly as the moisture in the wood was exposed to the flames, but finally Nate asked, "So, Pat, what do you want from us?"

O'Brien gave a loud laugh and his eyes sparkled with mirth as he replied, "Actually, Nate, not a damned thing. All I want you to do is to keep your eyes open and if you see this Donnelly feller bring his ass in alive or dead."

"What about his wife and the youngster?" Cotton asked as he pushed his hat back on his head.

"She's going back to Boston and the boy's goin' back with her. Seems her daddy is some rich feller back east, only I'll have to send a troop with her to Saint Louis to get them on a boat. I think the boat trip will cost fifty dollars, but she's got just a little more than that."

"Waugh!" Cotton exclaimed, his eyes grew large at the thought of spending that much money just to travel.

Leaning forward and looking into the dancing flames of the fire, Nate asked, "How could a man just leave his family like that, Pat? What kind of man would do that?"

"I would say a scared man, Nate, but most of the men I know would face the problem and not run from it. He must have known the army was looking for him, so he skedaddled before we could catch 'em. But, you mark my words, one day he'll pay for running, they always do."

Nate Grisham shook his big head and then spoke slowly, "No, he wasn't scared, not in the way you and me know the word. I think Taylor Banks, or Donnelly, is a coward to start with and this killing just brought it all out. I suspect he's a selfish man too, one that is used to having things his way all the time."

"Could be, but the army wants him badly."

"All he means to me now is a reward if I catch his butt." Nate said and then chuckled.

O'Brien said, "That's a lot of money, a thousand dollars."

"Ya ain't goin' lookin' fer 'em are ya, Pat?" Cotton Top asked as he leaned back against a log and pulled the making of a ciga-rette from his shirt pocket. The old mountain man had picked up the habit down south living with the Mexicans.

Pat gave a loud snort and replied, "Nope, not me. I don't have the authority to do so and I can't take the time off to do it as a private citizen either. I just came out here to warn you two to keep your eyes open. If I had the troops, we'd be out looking for him right now."

"Pat, why don't you spend the night out here and ride back to the fort in the mornin'?" Nate asked, already knowing the man wouldn't stay.

Pat O'Brien gave a big grin, stood, and said, "Nope, I can't do that Nate. See, today is payday for my boys. They'll get to drinkin' and whorin' early in the evenings and come midnight they'll be out to raise some hell. That's when I have to be on the street to help keep the peace. Most of 'em are good boys, Nate, but they'll start the night with a pocket full of money and then go back to the barracks broke."

Cotton gave a loud laugh and said, "Hell, that sounds like me at a rendezvous'! I usually trade all my pews in; get me some foofuraw, and then some Taos lightning. Waugh, it's fine doin's when a man's got some arwerdenty deep in his lights!"

Pat, confused, looked over at Nate and saw the humor in his dark black eyes as he asked, "What in the living hell is this old fool talking about?"

Nate snickered, pushed his old felt hat back on his head, and then replied, "Foofuraw is trade goods for the Injuns, like beads, mirrors, needles and whatnot. Taos lightning is alcohol that'll knock a man on his ass in about a minute. Arwerdenty is mountain man's version of a Spanish word, agua ardiente, and it means firewater or fiery water. I ain't sure which, because my Mexican ain't that good."

"And, you know what lights mean, right?" Cotton Top asked with a big goofy grin on his face.

"Yes, guts, you damned fool. That ain't mountain man talk, that's normal talk. Look fellers, I gotta hit the trail and get back to the fort before my boys get out on the streets. You two take care now, heah?" O'Brien spoke as he moved from the fire to-ward his horse. Once mounted, he walked his horse passed the flickering flames of the fire and said in a low voice, "Watch your topknots out there boys and I'll see ya when you come to Atkinson next."

"Take care Pat." Nate said as he stood by the fire.

Cotton, still grinning, yelled out, "Old coon, ya watch them flatlander soldier boys of you'un real close like, 'cause there ain't none of 'em worth a damn drunk!"

O'Brien was still laughing at Cotton Top as darkness of night swallowed him up and the two mountain men sat back down by the fire. A long zigzag of lightning flashed on the western horizon and the wind started to pick up. The canvas shelter started to snap and pop as the two men remained by the fire, both unspeaking. Finally, Cotton broke the silence and asked, "What now Nate?"

Nate grinned and asked, "What do you mean? We'll do what we had planned to do and that's it. If we see this Donnelly feller we'll bring 'em in for Pat, but we ain't goin' lookin' for him, because there is too much country out there Cotton and I ain't in the man huntin' business."

Cotton met Nate's eyes and said, "He's a worthless sumbitch and reckon you know that?"

Nate laughed and then said, "Yep, I know that Cotton, but the west is full of 'em and I've heard tell there more than just a few of his type back east too."

Cotton's eyes suddenly grew serious as he said, "If I see 'em Nate, I'll kill 'em. Oh, not for the robbery or them killin's back east, but fer leavin' his family like that."

There he goes again, Nate thought as he pulled his hat down to cover his eyes, *and now he'll start tellin' me about how his family was killed by the Blackfoot when he was just a kid.*

"When a feller don't have a family no more something deep inside of him dies, and let me tell you, it stays dead. I think God meant for us to have families and to live together, 'cause it ain't natural for us to be alone. The worst hurt in the world is the loss of a family. Why I remember . . .

"John, you and Isaac go out and gather up some firewood. The fire in this stove is about dead and iffen you two want to eat your breakfast, I need wood." Cotton's ma had said to him early one morning in May as soon as he'd dressed.

"Aw, ma, Isaac is big enough to go by his own self. He don't need no help!"

"John, don't you sass me boy! You get your behind out that door right now and gather up as much dry wood as you can find. Try to get oak or hickory, because they both give out the most heat."

John was fourteen and his brother Isaac with twelve. John took after his skinny ma, while Isaac looked more like the boys pa, William. Isaac was okay most of the time as far as brothers went, but like most kids, they fought when there was really no reason. Pulling Isaac roughly out of the cabin door, John said, "Come on, Isaac, let's go and get the wood. I want to hurry so we'll get to eat in a few minutes."

"I'm hungry too and ma said today we're goin' to have some fried sow belly with our grits!" Isaac spoke and then gave a big lopsided grin.

"Who cares about sow belly, I want me some cornbread and milk! That's real manly food. Only sissies like grits!"

Moving through the trees near the cabin, the boys soon had an armload of wood each and it was just as they started home that John heard a loud gunshot. At first there was just one, then two and three more quickly followed, until it sounded like a battle taking place at the cabin. Dropping the wood, the two boys ran to the edge of the clearing that ran around the cabin and what they saw scared the living hell right out of them.

A small group of Indians was pounding on the front door to the cabin with a huge log, obviously attempting to gain entry, and every few seconds a rifle barrel would stick out of a window and fire at the braves. Each time the log struck the door with a loud bang, the two boys in the woods could hear their mother scream in fear. Isaac, unable to control his anger, quickly ran unarmed from the woods toward the warriors. John watched in horror as a brave grabbed his younger brother by the hair, pulled his head back and quickly cut his throat. Blood spurted high into the air and John could hear Isaac choking on his own blood. Temporarily John stopped watching the door to cabin as his brother thrashed and kicked in the grass near the front door. As soon as the young boy lay unmoving, the brave who had killed Isaac leaned over and ran his knife around the young boys head. Grasping the front of his victim's hair, the warrior pulled the hair back toward the nape of the neck until the scalp came loose. Then the brave quickly held the hair high in the air with his left hand as he gave a spine-chilling scream of victory.

Deep down inside John wanted to help, just as Isaac did, but he knew there was nothing he could do against this many Indians. After all, Isaac was killed in the blink of an eye, so all he did was lean over and puke in the grasses.

Noise from the cabin made John raise his head and when he did, he discovered the cabin door was no more. Brave after brave entered the small building and he could hear his mother's screams of fear, as well as his father's loud curses of anger. There was one rifle shot and then suddenly it became very still. Not another sound came from the cabin or the nearby woods.

Long quiet minutes passed as John lay hidden in the brush before he once again heard noises from inside the cabin. The language he did not understand, but the voices alone told him his pa and ma was both dead, except he was wrong. A few seconds later his mother, with the top half of her dress ripped away and breasts exposed, was led from the cabin by a huge brave with a rope around her neck. Other Indians left the cabin with things that his ma and pa had spent a lifetime collecting, pots, pans, knives, guns, and other valuables. The young boy watched as others took foods, alcohol, clothing, and anything they wanted to plunder from the small backwoods cabin.

One warrior held what looked to be the scalp of John's pa in his right hand as he left the cabin and moved quickly toward the woods to the north. The young boy noticed the scalp was still dripping blood as the brave departed. At that point, there was no doubt in John's mind his father was dead.

A short and plump warrior held a firebrand in his right hand and just as he started to throw it into the cabin, a man with many eagle feathers in his hair spoke harshly to the brave and then pointed to the east. Almost immediately, the warrior dropped the burning wood to the ground by his right foot, turned, and walked from the barnyard to the trees to the north.

For almost an hour John stayed hidden in the woods, but finally decided he had to know what had happened inside. *Maybe*, he thought, *pa is still alive! Please God, let my pa still be alive!*

As he walked past the body of Isaac, he saw a big ugly gap under his chin where the warrior had cut his throat. Blood had pooled under the dead boy's head and his unseeing blue eyes were staring at the cloudless sky. John stopped, leaned over, and puked. After retching so hard his eyes watered, the young boy wiped his eyes with the back of his left hand and forced himself to move toward the cabin door. He had to know what had happened inside his home.

His father was in the middle of the room lying on his back. The eyes, like Isaac's, were open and unseeing, but they reflected pain and fear. John noticed two arrows in his father's chest, a severe cut to his forehead, and bullet wound to his right arm. Three dead Indians were scattered on the floor near his father's body and one had a butcher knife buried up to the handle in the middle of his chest. How long he stayed in the cabin John never knew, but it must have been for at least an hour. Eventually, he kneeled by his father's body, closed the man's eyes, and then gently brushed his long hair away from his cut forehead. "Pa," John spoke softly, "I wanted to help you and ma, but I couldn't do a thing. Pa, I hope you can hear me."

It was then he heard a yell near the door, "Sergeant Major, take three men and circle this cabin. If you see the Indians do not attack them, return and let me know."

"Yes sir!" A loud and instant reply was heard.

As John moved toward the door to the cabin still in deep shock of what he'd seen, someone outside screamed, "Somebody's movin' inside that damned cabin!"

"Hold your fire, men, until we see who it is. We might have a survivor of this attack." The first voice John had heard ordered.

Moving closer to the doorway, John felt the warmth of the sun on his face and the brightness from the rays hurt his eyes as he said, "I'm John Thomas and this is my family."

"Mister John Thomas, I'm Captain Alijah Bradley of the third Missouri Home Guard and we're looking for the Injuns that attacked your cabin. You'll be fine now son, we'll take care of you." The Captain spoke to John in a very soft voice, turned, and then ordered, "Corporal Finn, dismount and check that boy out, but make it quick."

"Yes sir." The corporal replied as he unhorsed and made his way to the young boy standing in the doorway. As he moved toward John, the corporal looked around the barnyard and suddenly noticed Isaac's body. Seeing first the blood and then the fatal injury to the young boy, the old soldier fought down the urge to heave.

The rest of the day was lost to John's mind. He lost a complete day in his life and had little memory of anything else except the attack on the cabin. It was not until the next day that he learned a little more about what had happened.

"Son," Captain Bradley said as he sat down on a stump near a small fire, "we found your ma, but she didn't make it. We suspect the Blackfoot killed her after we got hot on their trail, because they knew a white woman would slow 'em down." But, what the Captain didn't say was that John's mother had been raped numerous times and then her throat cut.

John didn't answer; he just stared into the flickering flames of the camp fire.

"John, listen to me boy. Your pa, for what it's worth to you, was a very brave man and that's why the Injun's didn't mutilate his body like they usually do. Plus, they knew we were hot after 'em so they didn't take their own dead or set fire to the cabin, because they knew we'd see the smoke. Now, if you want, I can send some men back to see what we can find that might help you out some."

"Leave it be! I don't want nothin' from there!" John suddenly blurted out in a voice filled with anger as his eyes started to water.

Captain Bradley put his right hand on John's left shoulder and replied, "Son, it's a hard life we live out here, but it's mostly a good life. People die every day and you'd best be rememberin' that. Now, tomorrow let me take you to a family I know down in the Ozark Mountains who are in need of a good strong boy of about your age to help 'em around the farm."

That night Cotton Top had run away from the kind Captain Bradley and never saw him again.

Nate had heard the story countless times and while he could feel his friends hurt and pain, he felt Cotton needed to accept the deaths of his family and move on. Adding a log to the fire, the black man glanced at his white friend and seeing his tear stained cheeks he quickly said, "I'm bushed Cotton, you take the first shift and wake me when you get tired."

Cotton didn't answer but he did nod his head.

As he rolled up in his buffalo robe, Nate said a prayer for his friend, "God, you know I ain't much and ain't never been much. Now me and you both know there is a heap of suffering, killing, and pain goin' on down here. I ain't asking you for nothin' for Nate Grisham, but for my friend Cotton Top out there by the fire. He needs some of your healin' power Lord. I ask ya to look down at Cotton and take some of his pain and sufferin' away. This I ask you in the name of Jesus Christ, our Lord and savior, amen."

The big man gave a big grin as he finished his prayer, covered his shoulders with his robe and was asleep in just a few minutes. Nate never knew if the Lord heard his prayer or not.

CHAPTER 5

Three riders tied their horses to the hitching post outside the door to Butterfield's trading post just as the sun was coming up. The morning air was cool and there was a threat of more rain off to the west, but the night before had been dry. Just as Skeeter reached up to remove his saddlebags, the door to the trading post opened and old man Butterfield stepped out onto the porch. He held a double barrel Greener shotgun in his hands.

While everyone called Butterfield old, he was just a little over twenty-five, but he seemed older and much more mature than most mountain men did, mostly because he had received a good education, though it was hard to tell by his language. He was a big man, well over six feet tall and near two hundred and fifteen pounds, none of it fat. The old man seemed in a good mood most of the time, and mountain men often joked it was because he was nice and snug in his trading post while they were out freezing their balls off wading cold streams for beaver.

"Howdy Doc, Skeeter, I see you both still got your topknots." The big man spoke and then he pulled his pipe from between his teeth with his right hand and gave them a warm smile.

The two mountain men laughed and then Doc replied, "Yep, we're doin' fine, Mister Butterfield. How's business been?"

"About as slow as an old-assed man a-pourin' molasses out of a tin plate durin' the dead of winter. It's been poor doin's this year boys."

"It'll pick up, 'cause it's getting' close to trappin' time." Skeeter spoke as he stepped on the first step leading to the porch.

"Who you got with ya? Must be a new feller, 'cause I don't remember ever seein' 'em before."

"His name is Wyer and he was hurt pretty bad out on the plains. But, hell, he kilt three Blackfoot and that alone show's he's got some tough bark on 'em. Doc fixed 'em up pretty good, so he'll live." Skeeter spoke, pulled off his hat and then asked, "You got any drinkin' whiskey in there?"

Butterfield gave a mighty laugh and replied, "Does a chicken have a pecker? Of course I got whiskey and you damned well know it too. Come on in boys, the first drink is on me."

The three men entered the store right behind Butterfield. An old potbellied stove was glowing bright red in the far corner, with a long stack of firewood nearby in a wood box. There were three roughly made tables in the center of the room, as well as a mixed-matched collection of chairs, stools, and benches scattered around the floor.

"My meatbag's a bit empty, Butterfield; ya got any food in here?" Doc asked as he sat down at the table nearest the door.

"I got some beans, deer meat, and cornbread, if ya want some?"

"That'll do us jess fine."

"Comin' right up." Butterfield spoke as he walked behind the counter and returned with a quart of rye whiskey. Placing it on the table, he said, "But, first I suspect you boys will want something to wash some trail dust from your mouths."

Skeeter gave a big grin and replied, "By God that we surely want to do."

Taylor had been quiet since they entered the store and he was more than just a little uneasy about being somewhere that might know about him. Instead of sitting at the table, he moved around the store looking at the items Butterfield had for sell. He noticed beads, combs, tins of coffee, knives, hatchets, and other things a mountain man would need to trade to the Indians or use just for survival. He was looking a big knife over in the display case when the old trader returned with their food.

Placing the food on the table, Butterfield said, "It ain't much good, or so I've been told often enough in the past, but I never claimed to be much of a damned cook."

"This is fine makin's as far as we're concerned. See, we been eatin' Skeeter's cooking for a hell of a long time and he don't care if he gets fur, bones or whatnot in his cookin'." Doc said and then gave a loud chuckle.

Pouring three glasses of whiskey, Skeeter glanced around and spotting Taylor back by the wool blankets he said, "Wyer, ya better get over heah and eat before Doc eats his and your-un too."

Taylor made his way to the table, pulled a chair out and took a seat. He looked up at Butterfield as he raised the first spoonful of beans and noticed the old man wince. *Now, what in the hell was that all about,* Taylor thought as he lowered his spoon, *I wonder if he knows about me?*

"Wyer, I hope to God you know your one lucky man." Butterfield said a few minutes later and he pulled out a chair and sat down at the table.

Taylor met the old trader's eyes, gave a weak grin and asked, "What do you mean?"

Butterfield's eye grew narrow and he replied in a flat voice, "Son, any time you can get away from the Blackfoot with your hair and balls you've just used up five years of good luck. Ain't many people that would have survived an attack by three of those mean bastards. They're good folks, I guess to their own kind, but they're holy hell on any white men they meet. I figure you're lucky to be alive."

Taylor grinned and responded, "I guess so, and according to Doc here that tomahawk almost killed me."

"I can tell jess by the damage done you was close, real close. You got any idea what that 'hawk did to your face?"

Donnelly laughed and said, "Nope, I ain't seen it yet but if you'll bring me one of them traders mirrors you got behind the counter I'll take a look."

Butterfield glanced over at Doc and saw the man nod slowly and then looking over at Skeeter, he saw the tall man shrug his shoulders, so he got up and went behind the counter. Picking a large eight-inch hand mirror, the trader returned to the table and sat the mirror next to Donnelly's right hand.

Donnelly took a gulp of his rye, refilled the glass, and then picked up the mirror. He took a long look and after a few minutes, he lowered the looking glass to the table, picked up his rye and threw the drink back quickly. He met the eyes of each man at the table for a second or so before he said, "I'm about an ugly sonofabitch, ain't I? Hell, my right ears gone, the tip of my nose has been cut off, half my upper lip is missing, and I'll have a scar that will never go away. Damn me!"

"Listen, son, it ain't that big of a deal." Butterfield quickly spurted out.

"Hell no it ain't no big deal to you, because it's my damned face!" Taylor said in a loud voice filled with anger as his right hand slammed the top of the table hard.

The room was quiet for many long minutes, with no sounds heard except the occasional tinkle of glass as one of the men poured another glass of whiskey. Finally, Skeeter cleared his throat and said, "Look Taylor, you can grow yer hair long to cover the missin' ear and full beard will cover the scar on your face and yer mouth. Hell, it ain't no big deal."

"I'll be damned, I never thought of that." Taylor said as he picked up his glass. Taking a sip, he thought, *By God, that will make it hard for people to find me out here too. I've always been so neat and clean-cut that no one would ever expect me to grow long hair and a beard. They'll be looking for a former army Captain, not a mountain man.*

"Skeeter's right you know, Wyer, it ain't that big of a deal. To tell you the truth, I'm surprised ya lived at all." Doc spoke as he took a swig of his rye and then wiped his mouth off with the back of his left hand.

"I understand what the both of you are saying and I guess you're right, but damn it's hard to be cut up like I am. I used to be a fairly handsome man."

"Nobody wants to be disfigured or scarred, but it happens, and especially out here at times. Why old Hugh Glass passed through here 'bout a year ago and if ya want to see some scars ya look his sorry ass over." Butterfield spoke, leaned back in his chair and gave a big grin.

"Who is Hugh Glass?" Taylor asked as he pulled his pipe from his pocket.

"Well, now, Hugh is a mountain man's mountain man. He shines, Hugh does. He had him a fandango with old Ephraim and almost went under. That damned grizz chewed on him and tore his hide to hell and back. When I saw 'em he'd healed up a lot, but I'm tellin' ya, ya name a body part and Hugh had a scar there."

"How in the world could a man survive an attack by a griz-zly?" Taylor asked halfway expecting the man was pulling his leg.

"Guts, son, plain old guts. His partners ran off and left 'em too, claiming he'd gone under on 'em, but old Hugh crawled miles to safety. Hell, I don't remember how far that old coon crawled, only I know it was one rough and long trip, but if my memory is right is was over 200 miles. He claimed he had to root hog or die, and he didn't want to go under, so he crawled. Tough man, Hugh is."

"I'll be damned." Taylor spoke his thought without realizing it.

"Nope, you ain't damned, unless it's damned lucky!" Skeeter spoke and then gave a loud laugh.

"I have some horses out there and some gear I'd like to trade for some things." Taylor said as soon as the laughter at the table died down.

"That's why I'm here Taylor. I'll give ya top dollar in trade for 'em too, if they're typical Injun ridin' stock." Butterfield replied and then smiled.

"Watch his ass, Wyer, he smilin' at ya and he's horse tradin' at the same time! You're gonna lose yer rear old coon!" Skeeter warned and again the table erupted in loud laughter.

"Tell ya what, let's go and take a look at what ya got outside and then we'll talk it over." Butterfield said as he stood, and Taylor heard the man's chair screeched loudly as it moved out from under the table.

Ten minutes later the two men were back in the store. Taylor took his seat, poured a glass of rye and then gave both Doc and Skeeter a wink. Turning to Butterfield he asked, "So, you agreed on two hundred dollars for the three horses, the guns, knives and other gear?"

"Yep, but that's in trade goods, not cash money. As a matter of fact, if ya'll tell me what ya need I'll get it fer ya right now." Butterfield spoke as he wiped his hands on a dirty brown cloth that at one time might have been white.

"Well, I'll need some buckskins, five pounds of powder and the same in lead, ten pound of salt pork, five of beans, three pounds of chewing tobacco, two big jugs of trader's whiskey, and two big sheet of canvas."

"I got four pairs of Sioux moccasins back here I let you have fer almost nothin', if ya want 'em."

"Add them in too. Also, I'll need me a better gun, so what do you have to offer?"

Butterfield laughed, walked over to his gun rack, and returned with a beautiful rifle before he replied, "I got this big Hawken fifty-eight caliber rifle, with double set triggers and the stock is made of good solid oak. Oh, and it's got a German silver front site. Now, by God, how does that sound?"

Taylor laughed and then asked, "How much?"

"Keep in mind Wyer this is the finest rifle made today and it don't come cheap. I'll tell ya what, ya take what ya've already ordered, I'll throw in the rifle, and we'll call it even. How does that hit ya?" Butterfield asked as he lowered the butt of the gun to the display case and grinned.

Taylor quickly glanced at the two men at the table beside him and when both of them nodded in agreement, he suspected he was getting a good deal. Giving Butterfield a big twisted grin he said, "Deal, but I want a powder horn thrown in with the rifle."

Butterfield gave a loud chuckle and replied, "Ok, I'll add a horn." Then, looking at Doc he asked, "Where'd ya find this man? Sounds to me like ya picked yer ass up a horse trader out on them plains instead of normal feller."

The whole room broke out laughing. When it quieted down Doc said, "Bring us another bottle of rye, Butterfield. That'll be the last of the whiskey tonight. We'll sleep out in your barn tonight and be gone by sunup, if that's okay with you."

Pulling another bottle out from under the counter, Butterfield pulled the cork with a loud pop and said, "Nope, it'll get cold out there tonight and unless I miss my guess she'll rain too. Why don't you feller curl up in here on the floor to sleep? It will at least be dry. My old barn leaks at times."

"I suppose we could do that and thank you for the shelter. It's not often we sleep under a roof." Doc said and then quickly added, "Now, if you'll stop playing hotel manager, bring that damn bottle of rye to the table. I got me a powerful thirst and serious hankerin' for some ass-kickin' Taos lightning!"

"Hell fire, me too since we don't have to stand guard tonight!" Skeeter said in a loud voice and gave Taylor a big grin.

That night as he lay beside the stove Taylor thought long and hard about what he'd seen in the mirror. His face was severely disfigured and he suspected the razor sharp blade of the toma-hawk had almost taken all the skin from his cheek to his chin right off. He gave an involuntary shiver as he realized how much worse the injury might have been. *Skeeter is right,* he thought as he pulled his blanket up around his shoulders, *I can grow a beard and let my hair grow out too. The only thing peo-ple will notice then is the tip missing on the end of my nose, but that ain't really that bad.*

"Wyer, ya awake?" Doc asked in a low voice from near the window.

"Yep, just thinking is all."

"Me and Skeeter talked some this mornin' and, well, we'd like to invite ya to partner up with us this comin' trappin' sea-son."

That would be the perfect place to hide out for a while, Tay-lor thought, so he said, "Sure, Doc, that sounds great. I mean, I don't have any place to go anyway."

A few minutes of silence passed and then Skeeter asked, "Was ya in the army Wyer?"

For a second deep fear grasped at his stomach and Taylor wondered how they knew, but he closed his eyes hard and replied in a steady voice, "I was. I resigned my commission a year ago."

Skeeter gave a low laugh and stated, "By God, I know'd it too! When ya was hurt we was lookin' for some clean clothes fer ya in yer saddlebags and we found an old army shirt."

"It was mine. I was once a Captain in the cavalry." Taylor spoke from the darkness, cursing silently because he had not thrown his old shirt away, but it had been such a strong part of his past.

"Well, Doc, we got us a Captain along with us. But, I don't care much for callin' 'em Captain, do you?"

Doc gave a light snicker and replied, "Nope, too long, so let's shorten it to Cap, how does that make your stick float Wyer?"

"That'd be fine Doc, but it'll take me a few days to get used to the name." Taylor answered, placed his hands behind his head and locked his fingers together. A few seconds later, he was asleep.

Morning dawned wet, with a heavy rain beating a steady rhythm on the roof of Butterfield's trading post. Lightning flashed and thunder boomed as the trader fixed a breakfast of smoked cured bacon, leftover beans, and some fresh biscuits. The wind howled just outside the door, making the men glad they were inside and not out in the weather.

Just as Butterfield placed the meal on the table, the front door suddenly flew open and a wet man stood in the doorway. His hair was long, soaked and matted, and his buckskins were hanging loosely on him from the rain. His eyes were closed tightly, as if in pain. Taylor watched as a puddle of water gathered under him from the water running from his clothing.

"Merser, is that you?" Butterfield asked in surprise as he made his way toward the man and then hesitated.

The man didn't answer, instead he attempted to walk into the room, but after only a couple of wobbly steps he fell to the rough plank floor of the store. Rolling over slowly he said in a thickly accented German voice just before he passed out, "Es var Indianer, Indians. Mein Gott, meine Freunde wurden getötet, dey kilt Cob and Phillips, C . . . Crow . . . it vas."

"Shit, it's Merser and he's got an arrow in his back." Doc said as he quickly moved from the table to kneel beside the injured man.

"He gonna go under?" Skeeter asked as he stood, unsure what to do.

"Not sure yet Skeeter, but Butterfield, I need ya to boil me some water, and Cap, I want ya to go out on the porch and keep an eye on things. Whoever attacked him might have followed, but I doubt it in this rain."

"That's a Crow arrow in 'em Doc." Skeeter said as he pointed at the broken shaft in the man's back. All but about two inches of the arrow shaft had been broken off.

"That it is Skeeter. Now, I want you to get a jug of trader's whisky out from behind the counter and fill up three cups, and hurry." Doc ordered as he pulled his skinning knife and started cutting Merser's shirt off.

"I put the water on to boil. It don't look too bad, does it Doc?" Butterfield asked as he squatted beside the mountain man.

"Nope, don't look bad, only it might be. If it missed his lights, and if he ain't lost too much blood, he'll make out alright. That is, if festering don't set in on 'em and kill 'em."

"Here's the whiskey Doc." Skeeter spoke as he neared holding the filled cups in both hands.

"Good, now you take that whiskey and go over to the table. I want you to sit there and drink 'em all real slow like." Doc commanded as he winked at Butterfield.

"Hell, I can do that!" Skeeter said and gave a big grin as he slowly turned and made his way back to the table.

In a low voice Butterfield asked, "Why'd you do that?"

Chuckling, Doc said with the same low tone, "Skeeter is a good man, Butterfield, but when it comes to seein' the blood of his friends and helpin' those that have been hurt he just goes to pieces. He'll fight and hard too, and kill when it needs to be done, only don't ask the man to doctor a dog. He wouldn't be able to do it. Oh, he knows how, he just don't like to be around hurt people and he turns to tremblin' and such."

Butterfield glanced at Skeeter and saw he was sipping the whiskey as he looked out the window. *Strange feller,* the trader thought, *to be a mountain man. I guess there are all kinds out here, but one that can't take blood is the first I've ever seen.*

Doc cut the arrow out of Merser's back and the man never regained consciousness, which in the mountain man's view was a blessing. As soon as he pulled the arrow head out he poured about a half of cup of alcohol on the injury and then wrapped it up as tightly as he could. Doc knew the bleeding would stop in a few minutes, only it would be later in the day before they'd know if the man would survive or not.

Abruptly the door swung open and Taylor said, "I have movement all around this place. From what I could see it's Crow."

"Oh, shit." Skeeter replied as he looked over the rim of the third cup of strong whiskey and then giggled.

CHAPTER 6

Nate sat next to the fire on a log and held his coffee cup in both of his big hands. It was about an hour before dawn as he sipped his coffee and Cotton was frying bacon in a skillet over some hot coals. There was a hard frost on the ground and while there was little wind, the day would be a cold one to travel.

"So, where are we goin' to get them supplies we need?" Cotton spoke as he turned the bacon with the tip of a big skinning knife. "We need some more coffee, 'baccer, and a few more little things before we head up into the mountains."

Nate place his tin cup down by his right foot, gave a sleepy yawn, and replied, "I thought we'd head over to Butterfield's and get what we need. I don't use traders much, because they charge too damned much, but since we only need a few things the cost won't be too high."

"Butterfield is alright; just a bit high on some of his goods. Hell, most of the fellers I know runnin' a tradin' post ain't worth a horse turd. Every single one of 'em is out to get rich in a year or two, from what I can see. Naw, Butterfield has always treated me right, just stay away from buyin' guns, powder or lead and we'll be ok."

"Waugh! I think you're queersome at times Cotton."

"Hell, I'm not strange in the least. The old trader has been fair to me, but if you want we can find another place to buy our goods. We could head over to Brown's tradin' post, if you think he'd be any cheaper in price." Cotton said and then flipped the bacon over once more with the tip of his knife blade.

Nate gave a mighty laugh, poured another cup of coffee, and then said, "No, Brown is higher than Butterfield. Like I said, we only need a few things, so we'll go to Butterfield's. Besides, he's along the way and after we get our supplies we can head right on up into the high mountains."

No sooner had the two men finished breakfast than they were mounted and moving cautiously down a winding trail that led to Butterfield's trading post. The skies were clear and the wind, while cool, was light. The recent rains had cluttered the trail with rocks, logs, and other debris that forced the two men more than a half a dozen times to go around or to clear a way.

Late in the day, as they rode side by side, Cotton asked, "Did ya hear that?"

"Yep, sounds like gunfire to me." Nate spoke as he stopped and cupped his right hand behind his ear.

"I still hear it off and on. Ya reckon there is a fight goin' on at Butterfield's?"

"Could be," Nate said as he pulled his Hawken and checked the load, "but who in the world would attack a trader? It don't make any sense to me at all. I mean even the Injun's trade with Butterfield."

"Did you hear that shot? That sounded like a big Hawken to me, at least a fifty-eight caliber or bigger." Cotton spoke, met Nate's eyes and then continued, "What do we do now?"

"I figure we're about a mile from the tradin' post, so let's leave the horses here and Injun up to see what is goin' on. I don't know what's happenin', but you can be sure if old Butter-field is in trouble, by God, we'll help 'em." Nate said as he quickly dismounted and led his horse to a thick grove of pines.

"We cain't go down the trail to the post, jess in case them jaspers doin' the attackin' have a feller watchin' the trails." Cotton said as he tied his horse to a big limb and then pulled his Hawken rifle from its buckskin sheath.

"Okay, let's go through the woods and we'll approach from the north side. I want to stop on that rise on that big hill and take a look see before we get into this mess." As soon as he spoke, Nate started a slow trot toward the hill.

Less than thirty minutes later the two men were looking at the trading post, but little could be seen. The weather was still clear, the rain from the night before had moved on to the east, and there were clear skies overhead. Suddenly, the two men saw a warrior run toward the front door to the trading post, only to take a slug that knocked him dead on his ass near the hitching post.

"Sumbitch," Cotton said just above a whisper, "Them's Crow warriors down there."

"How many do you think?"

"Nate, that's impossible to tell. There could be a dozen or maybe two dozen. The only one I've seen so far is the one dead by the hitchin' post, but there's a couple of handfuls at least."

Right then, two braves sprinted toward the building. Both Crow were holding firebrands in their right hands. A shot from inside the trading post knocked one warrior back hard into the dirt, where he screamed and twitched in pain. The second one was almost to the front porch when Nate lined up his sights, took a deep breath, and gently squeezed the trigger. The sound of the Hawken echoed in the valley below, a great cloud of white smoke formed in front of the two men, and Nate said, "Let's move now over to the right. They'll know someone else is in the dance now and I suspect they'll come lookin' too."

As the two men ran to the east, Cotton said between gasps for breath, "Ya got that red bastard plumb center!"

The hill was filled with stunted pines, oaks, and heavy brush, so the two men moved into the dense brush where they could still see the trading post and yet remain concealed. For long minutes nothing was heard and then there came a very slight sound that reminded Nate of leather brushing against leather. *He's comin' up on us and he's close*, the big black man thought as he pulled his Green River knife. Nate was tense, ready to spring forward and yet uneasy. He suspected there would be more than one, unless the others were busy doing something else, but what could that be? And, if there was more than one, where were the others?

The Crow brave bent over to look at a bent stem of grass and as he started to rise, Nate moved up behind the man, threw his left arm around his neck, and plunged his knife deep into the warriors back. Though the big man's arm kept the Crow from screaming, he kicked and thrashed for a few seconds, then his bowels emptied and he went limp. The black mountain man slowly lowered the dead man to the grass and took his scalp.

Nate moved back beside Cotton and man asked just slightly above a whisper, "Why in God's name did you take his scalp? We don't take hair!"

"I took it so them Crow will think another Injun did it. Now, stop your yappin' and let's move, so we can finish this job quickly."

Moving around the trading post they finally spotted a small group of five Crow near the rear of the log structure. After a few minutes of looking the situation over, Cotton whispered, "They're the chiefs."

Nate grinned and mouthed silently, "Kill them."

Nate pulled one of his pistols, as did Cotton, and then lined up his rifle on the man with the most feathers in his hair. The big mountain man figured the man with the most feathers was an important man, thus a dangerous man. Once his breathing was controlled, Nate slowly squeezed the trigger and was rewarded with a slight snap and light pop of the powder exploding, followed almost immediately by the rifles loud discharge. He heard Cotton's rifle go off at almost the same time. Quickly moving over to his left a few feet, he spotted another brave and fired his pistol at the man, watching him go down.

As Nate moved and fired, Cotton reloaded his rifle, quickly targeted a big Crow warrior and shot the man through the head. The remaining brave quickly went to ground, leaving the two mountain men searching for him. Finally, seeing a patch of tanned buckskin, Cotton touched off another shot, missed, and then saw the brave suddenly stand and run right toward him. Pulling his pistol, the mountain man kneeled, aimed at the approaching Crow warrior and waited for him to get closer. When the man was less than ten feet from him, Cotton pulled the trigger—only to have the weapon misfire! Throwing his worthless weapon aside, the skinny mountain man pulled his big razor sharp knife and ran toward his enemy.

The two men struck with such force that Nate actually heard them hit. Locked together, each man holding the others knife hand, they rolled down a slight incline, where the Crow ended up on top. *Damn me, but this feller is a strong sumbitch,* Cotton Top thought as he watched the brave's knife descending slowly toward his chest. There came the loud report of a Hawken, the brave's head exploded in a red mist of blood, bones, and brain tissue, and then the man fell to the side.

Cotton stood on shaky legs, gave a crooked grin at Nate and asked, "What took ya so long?"

"Ya was doin' just fine up until the last minute or three. I thought I'd let you have the honors of killin' the man, but all you wanted to do was play with 'em." Nate said as he reloaded his rifle.

Hearing the sound of running horses, the two men looked toward the noise and saw twelve or thirteen Crow riding hard due north. Two of the warriors appeared to be injured and were riding crooked on their horse blankets as they went over a hill.

"Well, I think them boys done stopped the dance, don't you?" Cotton asked as he walked to his pistol, picked it up and started reloading it. Nate noticed the man's hands were shaking as he poured powder down the barrel.

"Yup, the Crow are gone. Let's give the boys in the trading post a few minutes to simmer down a little and then we'll call out." Nate grinned, patted Cotton on the back and added, "Let's move over by the barn and we'll call 'em from there."

Twenty minutes later Nate stood sheltered by the barn as he yelled out in a deep and loud voice, "Y'all in the tradin' post, it's me, Nate Grisham and I have Cotton Top with me. Are y'all okay?"

Doc, glancing around the small room in the store yelled in return, "Nate, I'm sure glad your black hide showed up when you did. I have three wounded in here and need your help! Come on in!"

"Doc, we're comin' in now, so keep your fingers off the triggers."

The old mountain man in the store laughed and commanded, "Come on in Nate!"

Nate and Cotton Top moved toward the store and just as they stepped up on the steps to the porch there came the abrupt sound of a nearby pistol shot. Nate saw Cotton knocked violent to the right, strike the logs of the roughly made building, and fall to the wood of the porch. Pulling his horse pistol and cocking it at the same time, the big mountain man spun around and saw a Crow brave, the one he had shot from on the hillside, attempting to reload his pistol. Nate fired and hit the man in the center of the chest, knocking him back into the dirt. This time, to make sure the man would stay dead, the big man pulled his keen edged knife and cut the warriors throat.

The door to the store swung open and Doc stepped out onto the porch with a pistol held at the ready in each of his hands. Seeing Nate he asked, "What happened?"

"One of 'em was playin' possum and after we passed he shot Cotton in the back."

"Damn me, I'm sorry Nate, I thought they was all dead."

"Not your fault Doc, it was ours. We should have checked the man as we walked in, but we didn't. Now, if you'll move out of the way I'll pick up Cotton and bring him inside."

Nate gently lifted his partner and carried him inside the trading post. He immediately noticed a bloody Skeeter bandaging Butterfield's head and another man in bed. Walking over near the stove, he placed Cotton down on a buffalo robe Doc quickly brought out from a back room. Glancing around the room, he saw another man watching the rear of the building through a window that had about half of the panes broken and shattered by rifle fire. Though the man's back was to Nate, something about the man was familiar.

"Cap, you see anybody out there?" Doc spoke as he pushed Nate away and began to cut the buckskin shirt from Cotton.

"Nope, not a thing, I think they are gone." Cap spoke, turned, and the second he saw Nate he froze.

Nate already had his pistol in his hand, but he remembered it was unloaded after he'd killed the Crow outside the door. Looking at Taylor he said, "Well now, if it ain't

Captain Taylor M. Donnelly. Drop the gun pilgrim or I'll drill you plum center."

Taylor considered shooting the big black man, but there was something in the man's eyes that told him not to try. Thinking of his chances of being able to raise his rifle in time and killing Nate for only a short second, Donnelly let the weapon fall. *I'd never get the gun raised in time, he's already got me covered with that horse pistol,* Taylor thought as he lowered his head in defeat.

"Skeeter, you get over there and get that rifle." Nate ordered as he stood.

Skeeter quickly went to the window, picked up Taylor's new rifle and asked, "What in the hell is a-goin' on heah?"

"This man is wanted by the army for some killin's he did back east. I know Captain Donnelly or Banks as he once called himself, and as far as I am concerned he's worthless. Bring that rifle to me Cotton."

"He told us his name was Wyer." Doc said as he rolled Cotton over on his back so he could check the wound.

"Nope, he's not Wyer. The army sent a dispatch to Atkinson and told the Major O'Brien to arrest him. Only when Pat went to Donnelly's hotel room he'd already gone, leaving his wife and small boy alone." Nate spoke as he took the rifle from Cotton and checked the load. Then, once he was sure the rifle was loaded, he handed his pistol to the tall mountain man and said, "Reload my pistol Cotton, I forgot to do it after I killed that Crow outside."

"Damn you!" Taylor swore when he realized the black man had tricked him.

"You deserted your family?" Skeeter asked in disbelief.

When Donnelly didn't answer, Doc said, "Nothin' lower in my book than a man that runs off and leaves a family to fend for themselves. Skeeter, ya take that rope over by the door and hog tie his ass up real good and dump him over on the far wall under the window."

As Skeeter secured the man, Doc looked up at Nate and said, "I don't know if Cotton Top will make it or go under on us. He was hit hard Nate and I think it struck his lights."

Nate knew if Cotton took the shot in the lungs he'd be dead by morning, but he also understood it was out of his hands. All he could do was wait and see what the morning would bring. So, kneeling beside Doc he said, "You just do the best you can with him, that's all I expect." Then glancing around the room he said, "I thought you told me you had three wounded in here. I can tell the feller in the bed has been hit and Butterfield, but who is the third?"

"Skeeter took a ball to the left hand and it took most of is little finger off. He'll be okay, but I imagine it hurt like hell when it happened."

Nate laughed and replied, "He'll be all right. Skeeter might look like a rail split ten ways, but he's got bark on 'em and he's tough. Who is that in the bed?"

"Mountain man named Tom Merser, but most of the fellers call him Bear. You know 'em?"

"Yep, I know 'em, good man too, though the last I heard he was a company man." Nate said as he moved toward the bed.

"He was until last year, then he turned free trapper. He was up north with a couple of other fellers named Cob and Phillips. According to him, the Crow attacked them, killed Cob and Phillips and he made a dash for the tradin' post. He come in a couple of nights ago when it was raining bucks of water and had a Crow arrow in his back."

Nate pulled the blanket back, checked Merser, and then brought the covers up and covered the man's face. Turning to Doc, he said in a flat voice, "He's dead."

"What? That can't be! He was fine a couple of hours ago." Doc spoke as he placed his knife blade in the open door of the potbellied stove to heat.

"I don't think the arrow killed 'em Doc, but he took a ball in the head at some point during your battle with the Crow."

Butterfield, who had felt dizzy and sick from his head wound stumbled to the bed, pulled the blanket back and stated, "He's a gone under, Doc. He's dead as hell from the looks of it."

"Nate, I need ya to come over here and hold Cotton down as I cauterize his injury. He'll maybe twist and turn on ya, so hold 'em tight." Doc spoke as he placed a long and wide piece of cotton cloth on the floor beside him.

Nate moved to the injured Cotton, held his shoulders down flat, and watched in fascination as Doc removed the red- hot blade from the stove and immediately placed the flat of the blade against Cotton's lower chest. Cotton gave a terrible scream of agony, arched his back high into the air, and shook his head violently from side to side. The sweet smell burnt flesh filled the small room. Cotton Top stopped moving and entered unconsciousness.

"I'm glad that's done, my God, what a smell!" Butterfield said and then placed his right hand over his mouth and nose.

"Roll him over Nate," Doc said as he placed his knife blade back in the flames of the stove, "we still have to close the entry hole."

Butterfield gagged, moved behind the counter, and pulled out a jug of whiskey. Motioning for Skeeter to join him at the counter, the trader filled two cups with whiskey, and handed one to the thin mountain man. Skeeter grinned, touched his cup against Butterfield's, and said, "I do thank ye Mister Butter-field. That smell kind of gets to a man, don't it?"

Butterfield didn't answer; he simply gulped down his whiskey, wiped his mouth with back of his left hand, and poured himself another drink.

Once more, the process was repeated with Cotton Top, only this time the man didn't move much at all. A couple of times his muscles twitched and jerked involuntarily as the hot blade moved on his lower back, but he was out cold. As soon as Doc placed his knife back in his sheath, he poured a half of cup of al-cohol on each wound, wrapped it tight with the cotton cloth, and then stood. Making his way to Butterfield he asked, "Can I have one of them drinks? I'm feelin' a mite peaked right now."

The rest of the day and most of the night used cleaning up the damage done by the fight with the Crow. Two dead warriors were taken into the woods and left, one horse was so badly in-jured it had to be destroyed, and there was broken glass all over the inside of the store. Butterfield walked around cussing most of the evening about how much the glass had cost him and how difficult it had been to have it brought out to the trading post from Saint Louis.

Donnelly didn't move, not at all. Instead, he thought about his situation. He kept his mind moving as he thought of ways to escape, but Skeeter had tied him so well he knew he would not get away this night. But, Fort Atkinson was a long way off and it would take days to get there. Taylor knew if he was patient enough his chance would come.

Chapter 7

The next day, just as the sun was peeking over the mountains, Nate and Doc stood by their horses. The sky was clear without any hint of bad weather, but the temperature was just a little above freezing. Glancing around, Nate noticed frost on the steps to the trading post and on the roofs of all the buildings. Donnelly was already mounted, with his legs tied loosely under the horse's belly and his hands tied tightly to the saddle horn. Butterfield informed him at breakfast that while Cotton would be sore and hurting for a while, he'd live.

"Doc, the trip back will be rough, so you and I will have to keep our eyes open. With the Crow on the warpath and Donnelly along, it won't be easy. Are you sure you want to come along?"

The older mountain man gave a slight grin and replied quickly, "Skeeter and Butterfield are enough to protect this place for the time being. More and more mountain men will be comin' in fer trade goods within the next few days, so they'll be fine. And, ya need help to get this sumbitch back to the army."

Nate laughed and said, "Well, you're right on the money about needin' help. I suspect Taylor will make a run for it first chance he gets, 'cause he ain't got a damned thing to lose by trying."

Doc mounted, pulled his horse around and spoke with a smile, "I hope he does make a break for it, 'cause I understand the reward is for dead or alive, right."

"That's what Pat O'Brien said and he's a man of his word."

Doc's eyes narrowed, but the smile remained on his lips as he met Donnelly's eyes and said, "Well, it is much easier to take a dead man back than a live one, except fer the stink. Oh, and before I forget, that reward, as far as I'm concerned, belongs to you and Cotton Top. All I want is a drink or three in town and mayhap a good meal."

Nate laughed and replied, "No, my friend, it won't work like that at all. We'll cut the one thousand dollar reward in four pieces, so all of us get a chunk. It's not Skeeter or Cotton's fault they are injured and they both deserve some money in my eyes."

"Okay," Doc said as he started his horse down the trail at a slow walk, "but does your momma know she raised a fool for a son, Nate?"

Nate rode up beside the older mountain man, leading Donnelly's horse by its reigns, and spoke, "I reckon she does Doc, but she also raised me to be an honest and fair man. See, the money this man brings will help the four of us during the coming trapping season. I don't see it as blood money, or even bad money, because this man deserves to be turned in and I'm glad we're doing the job. We just got lucky is all."

"Yep, ya got a point there Nate. I guess those of us out here have to do our own law work and do it fair and square, or this place will fill up quickly with no-goods. Hell, it's rough enough without his kind runnin' free."

Nate chuckled, kicked his big bay in the ribs lightly, and said, "Let's move, we're wasting daylight."

The weather remained clear all day, with the three men riding at a mile after mile eating pace that put them well over twenty miles from the trading post at dusk. Nate knew it would take them just about a week to get to the small army post at Fort Atkinson and knowing Donnelly was growing more and more desperate the closer they got, he insisted that the man be kept tied up at all times. The only exceptions to this rule was when the man ate or relieved himself, then he had one hand loosened just long enough to do the job. Other than those times, Taylor M. Donnelly hog-tied.

That evening, as soon as a small fire was burning, Nate placed a skillet full of bacon to cook on the hot coals as Doc made a pot of coffee. Since Butterfield had given them a dozen biscuits to take along, the meal would not take much time to prepare. Doc had just placed the coffee pot on the fire, when a yell was heard just outside of the campsite, "Hello the camp, we're white and friendly. Can we share yer fire?"

The two men quickly moved back into the brush, leaving a very scared Donnelly bound by the fire. Long minutes passed, during which time the two men pulled the hammers back on their rifles and made ready, before Nate yelled out in return, "Come on in, but keep your rifles held high in your left hands. Any sudden moves and I'll shoot to Kill!"

"We hear ya and we'll do as you say." The voice answered from the semidarkness.

Two dark shapes slowly materialized from the woods and walked to the fire with their rifles held high.   Looking around, but seeing only the bound Donnelly, the bigger of the two said, "We're here, now what?"

"Put your rifles on the log and then move to the other side of the fire." Nate commanded as he lined his sights up on the smaller man and whispered to Doc, "You target the bigger man."

The two men quickly placed their rifles on the log, moved over to the other side of the fire and sat down in the grass. Nate and Doc stepped from the woods and cautiously approached the fire. *Just because there are two in camp doesn't mean there ain't more of 'em out in the dark,* Nate thought as he walked up beside Donnelly.

Doc, sat on the log, kept the barrel of his rifle in the general direction of the two men and asked, "Who in the hell are you two and what are you doin' out this way?"

Nate looked the two men over and if he had met them under different circumstances, he might have laughed. The bigger of the two was dressed in a black suit of rough wool, wore a white shirt with a string tie, and was wearing thick leather boots. While his hair was long and black, his face was cleanly shaven. As near as the black man could tell, the big man was near forty years old or so. The other man was short, just a tab over five feet, fat, and as bald as a baby's butt, except for a filthy brown beard. While he had not opened his mouth yet, Nate knew the man had buckteeth by the way his upper lip stuck out.

The big white man looked over at Nate, gave a big toothy grin and said, "I'm Reverend Moses Matson and this man beside me is Deacon Samuel Waters. We have come to lead the red man into the hands of God."

Doc gave a low chuckle, squatted and started turning his bacon. After a few seconds he said, "Just you two?"

"Yep, it's just us and God. We have been sent by the Lord to deliver the red man from his path of sin." Then looking at the bound up Donnelly he asked, "Why is that man tied up?"

"Well," Nate said without a trace of humor, "it's a good thing you got God with you, because if you run into any Injuns out here you'll be needin' 'em pretty fast. And, Mister Donnelly here is a killer that we are taking back to the army for trial."

"Sir, we are not concerned about our safety, because we are protected during our journey. I had a dream where God spoke to me and he ordered me to leave my church in Illinois, go out west, and preach to the Injuns. I was told I would succeed in my quest to bring religion to the tribes." Moses said, then met Donnelly's eyes and quickly added, "If you are guilty of the crime of murder repent and the Lord will give you ever lasting life."

"Leave me be preacher man. I don't have any use for your kind!" Donnelly spat out in deep disgust.

"Waugh, you must be out of your mind!" Doc spoke suddenly from beside the fire, "First tribe you meet will open you up from crotch to brisket and leave ya to die, if yer lucky. These are not the same tame whiskey drinkin' Injuns you've seen around forts and such, these are real kill ya in a minute Injuns out here."

"I will not be swayed from doing the work of the Lord, sir." The big man named Moses replied quickly.

Nate, hoping to cool things down said, "I am called Nate and the man by the fire is Doc. We have both lived out here for years Mister Matson and we both know fetch from come heah."

"Howdy-do, we'd like to share your fire for the night and then we'll move on come mornin'." Moses said and then added, "I believe in what I am doing, Doc, though you may very well think I am a foolish man."

Doc shook his head slowly and spoke in a very serious tone, "Moses, these Injuns out here already have a religion. They pray each morning and at times they go out to spots in the mountains for visions from God, and they take good care of their old and hungry. What makes you think they'll take to your religion, when they already got one?"

"I have my orders Doc and they're from the highest authority."

Doc gave a low snicker and then replied, "You mean to tell me you'll risk your life as well as the life of Waters because of a dream you had? Right now, Moses, you're deep in Absaroka country and in serious danger."

"I never heard of Absaroka, who or what is that?" Moses asked as he leaned forward and placed both of his hands toward the fire to warm them.

"Crows, Moses, Crows. They're a good people, among their own kind, but purely hell when they are stirred up. Right now they are stirred up really good and most likely not in the mood for a Bible thumper to come visitin'." Nate spoke quickly and then met the eyes of the older man.

"I will journey forward regardless of the danger. I cannot and will not go against an order from God."

Doc turned and looking over his shoulder at Moses, he softly said, "Then you are a fool."

"Perhaps," Moses quickly stated, "but I think not."

Many long minutes of silence passed with no one speaking as the fire cracked and popped and the bacon sizzled in the pan. The biscuits were placed on the rocks surrounding the fire to heat up and the coffee could be heard boiling in the old blackened coffee pot. Finally Nate said, "We'll eat and then move down the trail a ways. It's never smart to sleep where you've cooked in Injun country."

"We have a bit of deer meat we can share as well as a little parched corn." Waters spoke for the first time.

"Why that would go fine, Samuel, we'd be glad to have some real honest to God meat and not this flatlander bacon." Doc replied and then grinned at the fat man.

"I'd prefer the bacon because I don't care much for the gamy taste of deer." Samuel said as he reached into his possibles bag and removed a large piece of venison. Handing it to Doc, who was still squatted by the fire, he continued, "I'm not a woodsman, Doc, and I've never been out of Illinois in my life until this trip."

"Well, this is a first time for everything, but Samuel, I meant what I said to Moses. This is not the best time for you two to try and bring religion to the tribes. If I was you -"

"But, you are not us, Doc." Moses quickly interrupted, gave a weak grin, and unrelentingly said, "We believe in our journey and we will continue. Nothing you say will change our minds gentlemen, nothing."

"So be it, I will not bring the subject up again." Doc spoke as he cut the large piece of deer meat into smaller pieces, pierced them with sharpened sticks, and then stuck the other end into the dirt so the meat was hanging over the hot coals. Almost immediately the meat starting dripping greases and the fire flamed up as the oil struck the red coals.

"Thank you, Doc, we appreciate your concern, but the Lord will protect us."

"Well," Nate spoke just above a whisper as he sat up straight, "I surely hope so. Listen to me, all of you, there is someone movin' just outside this camp right now. Don't go for your guns, don't stand, or don't even move. I think they followed you two here and I suspect it's Sioux, if so we have a good chance of leaving here with our hair."

"Our guns are there beside you!" Waters spoke at a whisper, but Nate could hear the urgency in the man's voice.

"Good, that's where they need to be, now let me try to handle this." The big man replied and then spoke loudly in Sioux, "It is a cold night for my brothers to be away from the warmth of a fire. Come, sit by my fire and share my meat."

Moses looked over at Doc and asked, "What did he say?"

"Keep quiet you damned fool or ya'll end up gettin' all of us killed. Ya sit there with your mouth shut until you're told ya can talk." Doc shot back quickly with a tone filled with frustration.

Long minutes passed before a lone Sioux warrior walk silently from the woods and stood just within the flickering light of the campfire. He did not speak, nor did he threaten. He was a short man of maybe five feet three inches, squat, and with an oval face. The warrior's black and slightly slanted eyes spoke of nothing, giving no hints at all of his thoughts.

"Ma'to Wa kan, is that you my friend?" Nate asked, but still he did not rise from his seat on the log.

"It is Medicine Bear." the brave replied in thickly accented English.

"Come my friend and share the warmth of my fire and eat of my meat."

The short warrior walked to the fire, pulled a stick from those cooking over the flaring coals and began to eat. Moses started to speak, but Doc shook his head when he met the man's eyes and he closed his mouth. The brave ate four of the sticks of meat and then moved over to the log and sat beside Nate.

"So, what brings my friend Medicine Bear out from the village alone?" Nate asked as he pulled his old briar pipe out and started stuffing the bowl.

"I seek my people. Three suns ago I left with a hand of warriors to hunt tatanka, but we had a great battle with the Crow. Now I am all that is left."

"You do not know where your people are?" Doc asked, bewildered that the man could lose a village.

The warrior met Doc's eyes and replied, "I know where my village is, but I now seek the village of Hungry Eagle. I will not return to my village, because to do so will bring great sorrow and pain to my people. The grieving for those who are no more will last for many suns."

"What is he sayin'?" Waters asked as he scratched the right side of his dirty beard.

"Him and five others were out hunting buffalo when they were attacked by Crow. During the battle all the other fellers was killed. Now he's a-lookin' for another group of Sioux so they can get some revenge." Doc quickly explained what was going on to the two Bible thumpers. He then placed more meat on sticks near the flames.

"I saw the light of your fire and came to see who you could be." Medicine Bear said as he lowered his eyes and looked into the dancing flames of the fire.

Nate, unsure what to say or do, simply thought for a few moments and then asked, "What will my friend Medicine Bear do now?"

The braves head came up as he said, "I will find Hungry Eagle and join with his warriors to raid the Crow."

Nate leaned over and rotated the meat on the sticks so it would cook evenly, then looked at the Sioux warrior and said, "It is a good thing you do. Tonight you must eat, drink, and rest, because your travel will not be an easy one. The Crow are a worthy enemy and they are brave in battle."

"What you speak is true Big Raven Man, but a man must do what Wakantanka leads him to do." The Sioux said and then gave a weak grin as Doc handed him a cup of scalding coffee.

"He too is on a trail that God has given him to walk." Doc said to Waters and Matson as he pulled the bacon from the pan and placed it on two tin plates. He quickly added a biscuit to each and handed a plate of food to each man.

"What do you mean by that?" Matson asked as he picked up a crispy slice of pork.

Doc quickly explained what the brave had said, added another log to the fire, and then asked Nate, "We still movin' in a few minutes, right?"

"Yep, I think it would be fairly smart after what Bear has just told us. Let's hurry and eat, then we'll move on." Nate picked up a piece of meat on a stick and took a big bite. The meat was cooked perfectly for him, burnt black on the outside and raw on the inside. As he ate, he'd occasionally reach up and wipe his mouth off with the back of his left hand, not even noticing the blood dripping from his chin.

Hours later, in a cold camp, Moses Matson sat beside Doc as they stood guard over the camp and asked, "What did you mean earlier about that Injun being on a journey for God."

"Well, Injuns think that life is a circle and such. They also believe in revenge when they've been wronged. Hell, in that respect they ain't no different than a white man."

Matson thought for a long time and then said, "An eye for an eye and a tooth for a tooth is what the Good Book says."

Doc gave a low chuckle and then replied, "Kind of like that, but with the Sioux it means a scalp fer a scalp."

"I didn't think these savages believe in God. That's what I was told anyway back east."

The mountain man chuckled once more and said, "Moses, they believe in a God and the Sioux call him Wakantanka, or the creator of all things. Now, since they don't call him God in English, why, most folks think they don't know about him. But, trust me, they do and they are a fairly religious group of people too."

"I don't think I understand this."

"It's fairly simple. The tribes don't speak English, so they use their own words for God. I've lived with the Sioux, Snakes, and the Osage and every single one of them tribes believe in God. See, they are really a good bunch of folks when it comes to the people in the tribe they live with. They'll feed the hungry, take in an orphaned child, make sure the old folks are taken care of, and lots of other things. Just because they don't speak English and have different customs doesn't make 'em animals."

"But they wear skins and hides like a savage."

"I wear skins and hides too, but that don't make me no savage. Besides, I suspect most warriors of any tribe are much more religious than any mountain man. They're raised with religion Moses and its part of their lives. They pray as the sun comes up, they pray before a battle, they pray after a battle, they pray when someone is buried, and they even say a prayer of thanks to the animals they kill. Now, I don't think Injuns are savages, they're just different is all."

"I didn't think Injuns buried their dead."

"No, not like we do in the ground. They put them up high on a scaffold where they are closer to God and they lay weapons, food, and water beside them so they have those things as they crossover to the other side. And, once the dead has been placed up high, and all that other stuff placed beside them, why the living folks pray. They pray just like we do when somebody dies and they grieve hard too."

"What of the teachings of the Bible? They cannot be Christians without guidance from the Holy Book."

Doc gave a light laugh and said, "I never claimed they were Christians. I said they believed in a God. Look, Moses, we can't change people just because they don't think like us. These Injuns out here are some real mean sons of —men, but they have their own way of life. See, most white folks judge 'em against our white society, not theirs, and I don't think that's a smart thing to do. It's jess like them fools back east cryin' about us killin' the noble red man. The folks back east, including you, don't have the foggiest idea how an Injun thinks, or that we're killin' 'em just to stay alive."

The remainder of the shift Moses Matson didn't say a word, but he did some deep thinking.

Near four in the morning, the wind picked up and by six the rain started. At first, the drops were light and far between but within a few minutes they were falling hard. Nate had constructed three crude shelters made of canvas the night before, so at least the men would stay somewhat dry. Medicine Bear and Doc shared one shelter, Moses and Samuel another, and Nate moved in with Donnelly.

It was during a break in the storm, when Doc was handing out pemmican that Medicine Bear asked, "Why do you keep one man so he cannot move?"

"He is a killer." Doc spoke.

"Killing is a good thing if a man kills his enemies, is it not?"

"He is a killer of his own people. That and he left his wife and son with no money." Nate quickly replied and then noticing confusion in the warriors eyes he said, "He left his family with no food, no shelter, and without protection for the years to come."

"Has his wife thrown him out of the lodge to end the marriage?" The Sioux warrior asked.

"No, this man is without honor. He killed his chief and the chief's wife, left his family alone, and ran to the mountains."

Medicine Bear thought for many long minutes then asked, "What will your elders do with him once he has been returned?"

"The hanging death awaits him." Nate said in a flat voice.

"Aaaiieee, that is not a good death for a man. The spirit inside cannot leave from the man's mouth and travel to the other side. The spirit will die inside and the body will die on the outside. He will truly become a dead one."

"So be it." Nate replied and looking down he noticed Taylor grinning. The big black man fought down the urge to kick the white man in the face.

The rain increased in tempo, lightning flashed and the loud *boom* of distant thunder heard. The shelters shook, flapped, and danced on their ropes, but all stood firm against the terrible force of the wind and rain.

It was near nine before the storm blew over, the sun came out, and the men mounted up. Moses and Samuel decided to go with Medicine Bear, and the brave was amused having the two white medicine men accompany him on his search for Hungry Eagle. Nate had pulled the brave aside as soon as the rain stopped and explained the two men to the Sioux. Medicine Bear had grinned and said, "We have Wakantanka and we do not need another creator. I cannot say what will happen when these two Holy men reach a village, but I will speak for them. They will come to no harm."

"Nate thanks for the food, fire and shelter." Moses spoke as he gave a big friendly grin.

"Same here, I want to thank you." Waters spoke and then looking at Doc he said, "And, you, thanks for the talk last night. I think ya learned me a few things."

Doc met the man's eyes and simply nodded in understanding, suspecting the man hadn't learned a damn thing.

"Doc, let's ride, we got a full day in front of us and miles to cover. You two take care and if you have any problems in the village, you go to Medicine Bear. He speaks some English, but he is kind of hard to understand at times." Nate spoke, pulled his bay to the right and started out at a walk with Doc and Donnelly right behind him.

CHAPTER 8

The days in bed were slow for Cotton Top, with him constantly complaining about not being able to get up and move around. He was a tough mountain man and he'd never in his life been in bed or sleeping after the first light of dawn. Even as a young boy his parents had always awakened him an hour before dawn so he could milk the cow and chop some fire wood. The memories of his youth started to come forward, Cotton shook them way, and sat up in bed as he yelled, "Butterfield!"

Butterfield, starting to lose his patience with Cotton stormed to the bedside and said, "Now, what in the hell do ya want? Y remind me of one them damned kings I read 'bout once that never got out of bed and would take to ringin' a bell when he wanted somethin'."

"By God, I want to get up, is what I want. I cain't stay in bed like this, 'cause it ain't normal fer a man to be in bed after dawn."

Butterfield considered the injury and then replied, "Okay, ya can get up and move a bit, but no lifting or bendin' over. Ya tear that damned wound open and I'll have burn ya again."

Cotton gave a big grin, slipped both legs out from under the blankets, and stood beside the bed on wobbly legs. Still grinning he asked, "Do ya think I could have me a small glass of whiskey?"

The old trader couldn't help himself, because he really liked Cotton Top, so he grinned back and replied, "Come on Cotton and take a seat at the table. I'll pour us both a drink. Hell, ya drank up most of my tradin' stock anyway, so one more drink won't make no difference."

Pulling a screeching chair out from the table, Cotton took a seat and winced at the pain in his chest, but he didn't say anything about the hurt to Butterfield. The trader brought a bottle of good rye to the table, poured two cups full of whiskey, and then asked, "Cotton, do ya really think you're strong enough to be up and about?"

"Nope, not really," Cotton said and then quickly added, "but I can't stay in a bed if I can move at all. I'll go crazy if I spend too much time in a bed, 'cause it ain't normal fer a man to do that."

"Hells, bells, son ya was almost hit in the lights! Most fellers I know would be in bed a month."

"I won't and I ain't. While I cain't win no tow sack races right now, I ain't gonna stay in that bed no more." Cotton said and then quickly took a big gulp of his harsh drink.

"Honestly, I don't think I blame ya one iota. I don't like to be laid up my own self, but Cotton, don't reopen that wound or there will be hell to pay fixin' ya back up."

Skeeter came in with an armload of split wood and placed it near the stove. Looking over at Cotton he said, "Well, I knew ya'd be up and movin' in no time. It's hard to keep a good man down fer very long. I was thinkin' on ya as I split this wood. I said, ole Cotton Top needs some fresh meat, he surely does. So, as soon as I bring the rest of this wood in I'm goin' huntin'."

Butterfield's face grew serious and he asked, "Ya sure that's a smart thing to do so quick after them Crows visited here?"

"We need meat, don't we? I mean, ya said last night that deer roast was the last of the fresh meat."

"Yep, we do need meat, but if ya go Skeeter, by God ya keep your eyes open or your hair will end up hangin' in some Crow lodge before the sun goes down."

"I ain't no greenhorn, I've been over the mountain and down the river a few times. I'll keep my eyes out, but we got to eat Butterfield and there ain't no way around it. But, while I'm gone ya two keep your eyes open all the time too."

Picking up his Hawken, Skeeter gave a nod to Butterfield and said, "I'll be back in an hour or two. If I'm not back by dark, somethin' has happened."

"Ya take care of yourself Skeeter." Cotton Top said in a weak voice as he took another sip of the strong whiskey.

Skeeter moved through the woods silently and noticed nothing unusual in the woods that surrounded him. The afternoon was cool, but not cold, and the sky was mostly clear overhead. There was a dark patch of rain clouds off to the west, but Skeeter knew they were miles away from him and not a direct threat. He had just started down a deer trail that meandered off the side of a hill, when a big buck suddenly stood up right in front of him. Quickly bringing his Hawken up to his shoulders, Skeeter squeezed the trigger and through a white cloud of smoke, he saw his intended target go down.

The mountain man approached the deer quickly, with his knife in his right hand and his senses alert for any movement from the downed animal. More than one hunter had been hurt when his downed game turned mean and Skeeter knew the antlers on a buck could cause serious injury to the ignorant. But, one glance told him his deer was down for good.

Skeeter had just opened the animal up to start gutting, when he noticed the noises in the woods stopped. Lifting his head slightly he could no longer hear the birds singing or the squirrels running. *Shit,* he thought, *and I didn't reload after I kilt this deer. What a greenhorn thing to do.*

Quickly grasping his rifle, Skeeter made a mad dash for the cover of some nearby post oak trees and just as he entered them, he felt a severe blow to his lower back. While it didn't hurt, he knew he'd just taken an arrow. *The pain will come,* he thought as he quickly reloaded his Hawken, *soon enough.*

A Crow warrior broke through the woods, on the far side of the deer, and was running right at Skeeter, and then a second man appeared behind the first. Skeeter lined the front sight of his rifle up with the wedged sight at the rear of his rifle, took a deep breath and as he slowly released it he gently squeezed the trigger. There came a light snap of the powder pan firing, a louder crack of the main charge and then a cloud of dense white smoke engulfed him. The mountain man quickly moved over about twenty feet and when he glanced toward the two Crow he noticed one man was down and thrashing violently in the dirt. Lowering his rifle to the ground at this feet Skeeter pulled his horse pistol and aimed at the remaining brave.

The mountain man took another deep breath, but suddenly felt another blow to his back. Turning quickly, he saw a young boy of maybe fifteen rushing at him. Skeeter aimed at the boy, jerked the trigger and saw the young man's face explode in a mist of blood, bone, and gore. He had just started to turn when he felt the impact of the remaining brave as he struck him running at full speed. The two men were thrown to the ground and Skeeter screamed in deep agony as the arrows were pushed deeper into his back, and then snapped off when he landed in the grass.

The warrior was a big man, much bigger than most Crow warriors were and the mountain man could see the deep hate in his dark eyes as he quickly rolled over on top of him. Pulling his skinning knife, Skeeter tried to stab the brave, only to have the man grasp his knife hand in a deathlike grip. *By God*, Skeeter thought as he rolled the brave over onto his back, *this is one strong Injun.*

No sooner was the mountain man on top than the brave rolled once more and at that point, Skeeter broke loose and stood facing the warrior. A round and round they circled, with each man looking for a weakness in the other defenses, but the two were experienced knife fighters and opening were slight or not at all. Finally, Skeeter stepped on a pebble and down he went, landing flat on his back in the grass. Seeing his chance, the brave quickly ran toward him, but the mountain man simply placed both of his feet in the brave's stomach and allowed the Indians own forward motion to propel him into the air. He landed in the dirt behind Skeeter, but before the brave could move, the mountain man quickly buried eight inches of razor sharp cold steel deep into warrior's chest.

As the braves body quivered and twitched in death throes, Skeeter stood over him and said, "Old coon, you got some tough bark on ya, ya surely do. Ya gave me a good fight of it and because of that I won't take yer topknot."

The mountain man fell to his knees, fought the dizziness off, and then stood on weak legs as made his way to his rifle. Quickly reloading the Hawken and his pistol, he made his way to the downed deer. Quartering it, he picked up the two rear quarters and starting on his way back to the trading post. *Stay strong old son, you got less than a mile to go and then you can rest*, he reminded himself as he staggered under the weight of meat on his injured body.

Numerous times the mountain man fell or staggered as he moved down the trail, like a drunken man walking home from a night of heavy drinking in a saloon. He was sure he'd killed all of the Crow that were nearby or they would have an easy time of killing him at the moment. He was weak and dizzy and just as he was about to give up, he saw the clearing that surrounded the trading post. Skeeter stopped for a couple of minutes to get his wind back as he leaned against a huge oak. Then, with a false grin on his face, he walked across the clearing, stepped up on the porch and opened the door. As soon as he entered the trading post, he placed the meat on the first table he saw, sat down in a chair and said, "I had a little trouble out there."

"Ya okay, Skeeter, you're a mite pale?" Butterfield asked.

"Nope, I ain't okay. I know I done took some arrows in my back, but we needed this meat and by God I brung 'er in." And at that point Skeeter passed out, his head hitting the table with a loud bang.

"Sonofabitch! Skeeter!" Butterfield yelled as he ran out from behind his counter toward the table. Quickly seeing the broken shafts of three arrows in the man's back he commanded, "Cotton, ya gotta get up outta bed and help me. Skeeter's hurt and it don't look good!"

"Just a second Butterfield, hell, I ain't as fast as I used to be! Give me a minute and I'll be there. What happened, I was asleep and the next thing I know'd ya was yelling fer me."

"Them damned Crow ambushed Skeeter and he's got three arrows in his back. Can ya believe with him hurt like that he still managed to haul back all of this damned meat?"

"My God, look at all that blood. What are ya goin' to do Butterfield? Do ya know how to doctor up a feller?" Cotton Top asked in a nervous voice as soon as he saw Skeeter's wounds.

"I've done but a little doctorin' Cotton, so I'm goin' to need your help some. Not, much, 'cause I know ya ain't that strong your own self, but ya'll have to fetch some things and hand me things as I try to get these arrows out of 'em. I gotta do something, he's too good a man to jess up and let 'em die."

Cotton's eyes grew large in alarm as he replied, "Hell, Butterfield, we gotta do somethin'. Even if we do the wrong thing, at least we tried to keep 'em alive."

Butterfield reached over, placed his right hand on Cotton Top's shoulder and said, "Ya get me a jug of whiskey, some of that white cotton cloth behind the counter, a big knife and a pair of pliers from in the kitchen. I think I might have to pull one or two of these arrows out."

While Cotton went for the tools, the old trader spread a big bear skin rug out on the floor by the stove, he lighted a lamp and turned the wick up high, so he'd have lots of light. He picked the injured man up from his chair, carried him to the skin, and then slowly lowered him face down on the rug. Finally, taking a penknife from his trouser pocket he cut the bloody shirt from Skeeter and gave a low whistle when he saw the injury.

Cotton Top returned and placed the requested items on the floor next to the rug. Then, looking down at Skeeter's back he asked, "Them look close to the spine to me. Ya gonna have to cut 'em out?"

"Not sure, I'll try to pull 'em out first." Butterfield replied as he picked up the pliers, poured some whiskey on them and then reached over and grasp the shaft of the closest arrow with the metal teeth. The first arrow pulled loose easily with the head still attached. The second arrow was stuck and while it took a few minutes, the old trader was finally able to rock the arrow from side to side enough so he could pull it out. The third one seemed to be completely stuck in bone or at least some tissue.

"I'll have to cut this one out." The old trader said as he picked up a cup of whiskey and knocked it back. His eyes watered, he gave a light cough and said, "Now, let's start the dance. Ya hold him as best ya can Cotton, he might jerk when I start to cut on 'em."

"I'll hold 'em, ya jess do what needs doin'."

Pouring some whiskey on the blade of a big skinning knife, Butterfield then grabbed the shaft with his left hand and ran the knife blade down the side of the shaft. He quickly cut a complete circle around the arrowhead, expecting Skeeter to move at any time, but the skinny man only moaned slightly once. *Thank God he's out*, Butterfield thought as he grasped the arrowhead firmly with the teeth of the pliers and gave a mighty yank. At that second, Skeeter gave a horrendous scream, drummed his toes on the rough pine planking of the floor, and then suddenly laid still.

"Did ya kill the sumbitch, Butterfield?" Cotton asked as he gazed into the old man's eyes.

"Nope, he's still alive. He's just passed out is all. Now, hand me that cotton cloth. As soon as the cloth was in his hand, the old trader poured a cup of alcohol on the wounds, placed the cotton material on the injuries and started wrapping the man up. As soon as he finished he walked to the nearest table, picked up the whiskey bottle in his shaking left hand, poured a full cup, took a long drink, and then said, "We'll have to wait now and see what happens. That last arrow was near his spine, but I ain't sure how deep or if I did any damage when I cut 'er out. But, it had to be done and all we can do now is see what happens."

Suddenly the door to the trading post swung open and in stepped two old mountain men. They looked at each other and then the biggest one said, "Butterfield, what I the hell is goin' on 'round heah. We found three dead Crows 'bout a mile from heah and blood all over the trail leadin' right up to this place.

"Hatch, Skeeter took three arrows in his back and carried back two big rear quarters of deer meat to boot. Hell, I didn't even know he killed them three Crows on top of it all. He's got the bark on 'em, Waugh!" Butterfield responded, still in shock from treating the injured man.

The two men moved to the table, pulled out chairs and sat down. Then, looking over at Cotton Top the biggest man said, "I'm Hatchet Smith and this ugly bastard beside me is Edward Jarvis, more commonly known as Taterhead."

"Howdy-do, I'm Cotton Top and I partner with Nate Grisham"

"I know Nate pretty good and I've trapped some with 'em. He's a hell of a man and if you ride with him that says a lot about the kind of man you are." Taterhead said and then turned his head toward Butterfield, and asked, "Skeeter goin' to live or go under?"

Butterfield wiped his sweaty forehead with the back of his bloody right hand and said, "I'm pretty sure he'll live, unless he festers up. The thing I'm worried about is will he be able to walk when he wakes up. One of them arrows was stuck close to his spine and I ain't sure the arrow did as much damage goin' in as I did takin' 'er out."

Taterhead looked over at Hatchet and said, "Look, you two look like you've been to hell and back. Why don't both of you sip on this whiskey a while? Hatch and I will fix up some grub for all of us. Then, I think it might be a good idea of Cotton Top here gets back in bed before his ass falls over. Hell, son, you're as white as a ghost."

Butterfield gave a snicker and said, "He ought to be, he was shot damned near in the lights a few days back and I thought we'd lose 'em for sure. I'm tellin' you both right now, a half inch lower or to the right and Cotton would have been a gone beaver."

Cotton gave a big grin, lifted his cup and looking over the rim he said, "Close don't count, by God, you're either dead or ya ain't."

The men all laughed and after it quieted down, Butterfield said, "Ok, ya guys cook and take care of the place for a few minutes, while me and Cotton rest a little. I never realized doctorin' somebody up took so much out of a feller."

Hatch smiled, took a long sip of his rye and commented dryly, "I suspect the more doctorin' a feller does the easier it gets to be. I imagine the first few times wear a feller's ass out, because you're scared your patient will die on ya, but after a few times you come to realize they'll either die on ya or live. And, what ya do may or may not really help one way or the other in the long run."

"Well," Butterfield said as he lifted his cup, took a drink, and then continued, "I don't care much fer the job at all. I don't really mind the blood, or cutting, but there is somethin' about doctorin' a real person I don't cotton to. I guess it's the not knowin' if yer doin' the right thing or not."

Hatch gave a grin, nodded his head toward Cotton, and when Butterfield looked over the man was sound asleep at the table. In a low voice he said, "He's a hell of a man fellers. He's got sand in his craw and he's as tough as nails. A lot of men would have died, or at least spend weeks in bed, but Cotton was out of bed within three days. He's a good man to ride the river with."

"Help me get him over to that bed yonder, Butterfield, and then we can talk a bit more. I suspect we need to stay 'round heah for a spell, until them Crow quiet down a little. Something or someone has them all pissed off at the world in general, but I ain't got no idea what's goin' on."

CHAPTER 9

Charging Horse sat by the cracking fire in the middle of the lodge used by the Crow tribe to conduct council meetings. The lodge was dark with only faint outlines seen of each warrior attending the meeting visible to his eyes. *Old fools*, he thought, *why can they not see the danger of allowing the white man to stay on our land? Do they not fear the hunger the white man has for all we call our own? Are they not willing to fight and die for our people?*

"I have seen the white eyes as they come to our lands. They do not cross, they build lodges of trees, they cut the soil, and they make places to live. The white man does not come to stay but a short time, he comes to stay forever." One young war leader named Buffalo Horn said with his voice tinted with anger.

"What is a little land to give the white man in exchange for peace?" Black Bird asked as he looked around the council at the older men.

"Aaieee, the white man is never satisfied with his land. He will take more and more until the land we now sit on will be his. He is like a locus that strikes the fields of corn, he will take it all and leave but a little for us." Buffalo Horn spoke in deep anger as he stood and continued, "I am not an old man to fear battle with the white man. I crave the honor of counting coup and killing as many of them as I can."

"Sit back down Buffalo Horn this is a decision to be made by the elders, not by a war leader." Screaming Falcon, the village chief said with the same soft tone of voice he used to speak to small children.

"I will sit, but only because I wish to show honor to the village elders and to my chief." Buffalo Horn replied in a softer voice and then sat back down on the hard ground.

"My chief, do you think the white man will stay from our lands if we give him a little? Do you think we can have a lasting peace?" Charging Horse spoke for the first time at the meeting.

Minutes of long silence filled the lodge, but finally the old chief replied, "This land is the land of the Absaroke and the spirits of our ancestors walk here. The bones of those who have passed before us are now part of this land and as such, it is sacred to The People. Some of our land we can give, if it will bring a lasting peace to The People."

"Does your heart tell you this is a good thing to do? To me to give one small part of our lands to the white eyes makes my heart heavy in sadness and fills my mind with anger."

Screaming Falcon stood, looked slowly around the lodge, and replied slowly, "Yes, my heart grows sad thinking of giving our lands to the white eyes. From where the sun comes up to where the sun goes down is the land of the Absaroke, and it has been so for many seasons. I want to fight to keep our land, but I do not think in my heart that it is a battle we can win. The white eyes are as many as the blades of buffalo grass and when one is killed four come to take his place in battle against us. I cannot understand why the white man does not stay in his lands to the east where the sun comes up and why he needs our land. Does he not have a village in the land of the sun to live? Does he not have buffalo, deer, and fish to eat when the cold moons come? I am the chief, but I will do as our elders decide, because first I am an Absaroke warrior and this council is the law of The People."

Silence prevailed once again as each elder in the council gave thought to the words spoken by their war leaders and the chief. Every single one of the elders knew the decision was not an easy one and if a mistake was made, The People could end up losing all of their lands to the white man and blood would flow.

Looks to the Sky, the oldest elder of the council, finally spoke, "I say war is the path we must take. The white man is never happy with a little; he must always have it all."

Raven Calling raised his gray head and said, "Peace is the only way we can keep The People alive."

On and on the elders each spoke of what they felt deep inside, until Sees All Things said, "I too think war is the only way. I have no hate for any white man, but I have much hate for any man that wants to take what is not his. This is our land and it must stay our land."

Finally, hours later, Looks to the Sky stood and said solemnly, "It will be war."

The village filled with excitement as each brave thought of the coup he would count, the spoils he would bring back to his lodge, along with the honors and glory won in battle against the white man. The men gathered their gear and warriors went out individually or in pairs to locate the white men, and to bring the information back quickly so the war leaders could plan attacks. The usually quiet and peaceful village turned into a busy place with many men coming and going at all hours.

Buffalo Horn formed a small group of warriors to scout the surrounding area and he asked Charging Horse to join the group. He'd been waiting since the council ended to go out, but a warrior of his standing only rode with the best warriors in the tribe or led his own group. It was just a little after dusk when a small group of ten warriors rode from the village, heading almost due west into the darkness.

As they rode, Charging Horse rode up beside Buffalo Horn and asked, "Do we know if the white men are still where our scouts saw them last?"

"Coyote Barking saw the white men with his own eyes. He counted only three fingers of men and their horses. One of the men is a Sioux and the other two are white men." Buffalo Horn replied as he turned slightly to gaze into the eyes of his friend.

"It is good. The Great Spirit sends our enemies to us and this makes our fight to keep our lands an easy one."

The war leader's eyes narrowed and he replied quickly, "Our fight cannot and will not be an easy fight. Much blood will flow soon, but some of that blood will be the blood of The People. Never forget that our battles with the white men will be many and we will send many of them to the other side, but with each man we lose we will grow weaker."

Charging Horse though of his leader's words and then said, "It is true the white man has many people and killing them does not seem to hurt their numbers. I have killed two and seven suns later returned to the killing spot and found six white men there. Do they not have to wait for their warriors to grow up?"

"I think the white man is many and his warriors are more than the buffalo. We, The People, do not have the great numbers of men that the white eyes have, so we must hit and run when we attack. When we find these men we go for now, we will try to kill them without the loss of a single warrior, except I do not think this will happen. I know in my heart you hate the white man, Charging Horse, but some are good fighters and there is much honor in taking a white man's scalp." Buffalo Horn spoke and then kicked his horse forward to indicate the conversation was finished.

Medicine Bear, Matson, and Waters made camp deep inside a group of oak trees mixed with cedars. The fire was as small as a cup and the dry wood gave off little smoke as the men cooked dinner. It had been a good day to travel and almost twenty miles was behind the small group as they sat around the small fire and started to talk.

"Do you think any Injuns are around us, Medicine Bear?" Matson asked as he poured the coffee dregs from his tin cup into the dirt by his left foot.

"Many." The Sioux warrior replied, as he leaned back against a log near the fire.

"Many? How can that be, I have seen no one?"

"This land is a land of warriors."

"Oh, I see what ya mean; since this land is Injun land, there are lots of Injuns about. Well, that makes sense." Waters spoke as he pulled out his blanket and spread it out near the fire.

"I see tracks of ponies today, many ponies."

"Injun ponies?" Matson asked as he met the brave's eyes.

Medicine Bear nodded.

Matson looked over at Waters and asked, "Well, what do you think Samuel?"

"Ponies don't mean nothin', because they could have been wild."

"Injun ponies, and I think one hand of warriors." The brave spoke suddenly and then added, "Crow or Comanche ponies."

"Dang, not good Waters, that means five warriors. But, I fig-ure we're safe enough traveling with a Sioux brave, don't you?"

Waters gave a loud laugh, slapped his right knee and replied, "Moses, if I didn't think we were safe I'd be riding right now, back to Fort Atkinson."

"Sleep now, I watch. Sun come we leave." The Sioux spoke as he moved off into the brush to keep watch over the camp.

The two white me rolled up in their blankets and were soon fast asleep. The sky was clear and the air was very cold as the stars came out. Looking to the north, Medicine Bear could see the northern lights, only the flickering and moving lights didn't comfort him. *Death will come soon,* the brave thought as he pulled his buffalo robe up around his shoulders, *only who will it caress in its arms?*

Near dawn, the Sioux brave walked into the camp and woke the two white men. He knew he should have had them pull a shift of guarding the camp too, but he didn't trust a white man to stay awake or to do a very good job of keeping watch. Medicine Bear had found most white men, except for mountain men, to be very poor guards and their horses easy to steal.

Waters found a few live coals from the fire and quickly gave them life with his breath. He was adding some small twigs to the fire and Moses was shaving off a few pieces of bacon, when Medicine Bear suddenly stood and gave a bloodcurdling scream. The warrior pulled the string back on his bow and sent an arrow into the woods on the east side of the camp. The arrows flight, though lost in the trees, was followed by a shriek of pain.

Matson had just reached for his Hawken, when Medicine Bear was struck in the middle of his chest by two arrows, and as the preacher turned toward the threat, he saw a small group of Crow warriors break from the trees, running right for the camp. He heard Waters' rifle fire and saw the brave in front collapse, but the Indians still came. Matson quickly lined the sites up on his rifle, squeezed the trigger and watched his target knocked to the ground. Throwing his rifle aside, he pulled his horse pistol and fired once more, again killing a warrior on the right side of the attackers.

Waters had never been so scared in his life, he had just pulled his pistol when he felt a slap on his upper left shoulder and a quick downward glance showed the shaft of an arrow in his homespun shirt. He aimed at the mass of attackers, squeezed his shot off and actually saw the heavy lead slug hit the man. Dust flew from the brave's buckskin shirt, blood flew from his back, and he dropped to the ground where he began to jerk and scream.

Both men were now down to knives and the situation did not look good to either of them. Matson, thinking he could surrender to the braves, as he could a white man, dropped his weapon at his feet and raised his hands high over his head. Waters, however, held his knife firmer and intended to die like a man, fighting.

"What is this?" Buffalo Horn asked as he stopped moving and looked over at Charging Horse. "What does this white man mean by raising his arms? Is he praying?"

"I am not sure, but I think he no longer wants to fight." Charging Horse replied as he quickly added, "What kind of man would kill our warriors and then want to stop the battle?"

"Tie him. We will take him back for the women." Buffalo Horn spoke to the braves now standing around him.

"But, what of the other one? He does not stop the fight and I think he is ready to die." One of the Crow warriors asked.

Pointing his rifle at Waters, Charging Horse said in very thickly accented English, "You no fight. Stop. No Stop, I kill."

Waters seeing he had little choice dropped his knife at his feet. Like Matson, he was tied up and placed against a log by the fire. *Sweet mother of God, I think dropping my knife was a big mistake*, Waters thought as he watched the braves surround the body of Medicine Bear.

Buffalo Horn kneeled beside the dead Sioux warrior and pulled his head up by his long hair. Drawing his sharp skinning knife with his other hand, he quickly cut a complete circle around Medicine Bear's head, at the forehead, and grasping the front of the man's hair he peeled the scalp back. Both Matson and Waters heard the scalp pull loose as it separated from the head. Matson leaned to his right and threw up.

One of the other warriors pulled his knife and began to mutilate the body of the Sioux warrior. Long deep gashes were cut in his legs and arms, he was opened up from his crotch to his breast, and his penis and balls cut off and thrown away. The Crow braves laughed as the mutilation was taking place and one warrior walked over and peed on the dead man's face.

Both of the white men were in deep shock from fear and their minds had shut down. A brave pulled a knife, made his way to the white men and cut the ropes at their feet, leaving their hands tied behind their backs. He then made them stand.

Less than an hour after the battle, with a horsehair rope tied around their necks, the two white men pulled into the trees. Less than a quarter mile from the bloody campsite the Crow had left their horses, so the walk to where they waited was a short one. The two white men were not placed on a horse; instead, a mounted brave held the other end of the rope as the group started back to the Crow village at a walk. Over the next twenty minutes, the two white men fell numerous times and if they did not get up quickly enough the still moving Crow warrior dragged them in the dirt.

"Cain't fall Moses, or they'll drag you to death." Waters warned in a whisper as Matson quickly got to his feet after a fall.

"My God, can this be . . . happening to us? Lord God, save . . . us." The older man prayed.

"You better keep your voice down. Pray if you want, but first chance I get I'm runnin'.'"

"Have you no faith in the Lord?" Matson whispered.

"Yep, I do, but the Bible says the Lord helps them that help themselves and that is something I fully intend to do."

The remainder of the day was rough and exhausting for the two white men. The warriors only stopped for an hour twice the whole day. By the time the braves made an evening camp, Matson was in tears.

"You better stop cryin' Moses, or these fellers will kill ya. I've heard stories how they only respect a brave man."

"Why has the Lord not heard my prayers?"

Waters gave a light dry chuckle and whispered, "Maybe he has. Could be this is what he has planned for us."

The two men received no water or food as the warriors made a small fire and ate a meal of deer meat. As soon as darkness came, the fire went out and all of the warriors except the two guards went to sleep. The white men got no blankets or covers of any kind.

Just after dark, a very light snow started to fall. The big lazy flakes twisted and turned as they fell to the ground and in less than an hour, the ground was white. Matson, who Waters suspected was losing his mind, whispered, "What of my parish? Why do they not come and rescue me from these savages?"

"You left your parish, Moses, and you've come to bring religion to these savages."

"That cannot be. Why would I leave a lifetime of hard work?"

Waters didn't reply, instead he slid his hands down by the top of his boot. Reaching inside the boot top, he felt the handle of a short bladed knife he carried for emergencies. *Well, this is an emergency for sure,* he thought as he pulled the knife from the boot. Twisting the knife blade he quickly cut his hands free and then reaching down slowly he cut his feet free. Quickly glancing around he noticed the snow was falling faster now and in the few minutes, he expected a heavy snowstorm to hit.

Still lying down, he leaned slightly and cut the bonds that held Matson's hands together and then did the same for the man's feet. Whispering softly he said, "When the wind picks up in a few minutes, let's get out of here. Stay down low and crawl until we hit the trees, then run like the devil himself is after you."

Moses didn't respond and Waters wondered if the half crazed man understood what he had said. *Well, it don't matter much. I can't drag him out of here. He'll have to do the job himself or die here, because once I start movin' I ain't stopping for nothin',* he thought as he watched the snow falling and listened to the wind starting to blow harder.

An hour later the full force of the storm had come. The snow was blowing wildly and the temperature dropped to well below zero. Glancing around slowly, Waters saw the guard move into some trees on the other side of the camp for protection from the wind. *It's now or never,* he thought as he whispered to Matson, "Moses, let's move."

As soon as he spoke to Moses, Waters started crawling through the snow. While Waters was cold and wet, he knew this might be the only chance he'd get to escape and he intended to take it. Reaching the tree line, he turned and expected to see Moses right behind him, but the man was not there. Squinting in the darkness, he saw the old man standing in the falling snow, right where he'd been tied.

Suddenly Matson started speaking in a very loud voice, "My red brothers! I bring you word of God, our Lord! Let me show you -" Suddenly his voice was cut short by a spear that struck him in the center of his chest. Glancing down with unbelieving eyes, Moses said in a voice that no one heard, "This cannot be! What of my dream? What of my work?" He first fell to his knees, then his body fell to the ground landing face down, and Crow warriors immediately surrounded him. All were holding large knives as they kneeled.

As Waters stood on weak legs, he heard a horrible scream over the howling winds of the storm and he knew Matson was dead. The young deacon started running through the woods and he continued to run for many long hours, until a faint gray light filled the mountains indicating a new day had come. Stopping near a large pine tree gasping for breath, he noticed the snow was still falling heavily and as he glanced behind him, he saw the snow was quickly filling his tracks.

I gotta have a fire, or I'll freeze to death, he thought as he crawled up under the big pine.

Pulling his flint and steel from his pants pocket with trembling hands, he gathered up some dry leaves and small twigs from around the base of the tree, piled them together, and struck the flit with the steel. A small spark flew from the flint, landed in the dry tinder, and began to smoke. A second or two later a small flame flared up. Gathering all the wood from under the tree and the dead limbs on the lower part of the trunk, Waters knew he had enough wood to keep him alive—but for how long?

Chapter 10

Nate and Doc had no problems with Donnelly on the trip to the fort, but they were always ready and perhaps that alone prevented the man from making an attempt. Donnelly, realizing once he was at Fort Atkinson he still had to be transported all the way back to Washington, decided to wait and try to escape on the trip back east. He knew very well that any escape from the two mountain men would be short lived, and when he did escape he wanted it to be for good. It was more than likely a military escort would be less vigilant than the mountain men were.

Riding into the small army outpost just as dawn was breaking, the three men pulled up in front of a crude building with a sign over the door that indicated it was the post commander's office. Nate dismounted, tied his horse to the hitching post, opened the door and walked in. A sleepy eyed young man with blond hair, blue eyes, and no stripes was working on some paperwork at a battered and beaten old desk.

Looking up the young private said, "We don't need no help from your kind. If you want work, try the saloon down the street, they might need a man like you to empty spittoons."

Nate, placing his big hands on his narrow hips, said in a deep booming voice, "Son, I ain't lookin' for no damned job. I got a job. I hear'd tell y'all are lookin' for a man named Taylor M. Donnelly and if so, I got him outside the door."

The young man stood, looked confused for a second and then replied, "Let me get the Captain. I don't know nothin' 'bout no man named Donnelly."

"Well, you do that son, and one more thing."

The young man was just starting to turn when Nate spoke, so he twisted to look at the big man and asked, "What's that?"

Nate's eyes narrowed, his lips grew tight, as he said in low voice, "Understand me right now white boy, because I ain't going to repeat it. If you ever talk down to me again, I'll tie into you like ugly on a vulture's ass. My name is Nate Grisham, you got that son?"

The young man lowered his eyes, gave a loud gulp, and replied, "I understand."

"Now, go get your Captain."

A few minutes after the young man had entered an office off to the side, the door swung open and out stepped a big man, with dark red hair and neatly trimmed beard, wearing wire-rimmed glasses. His uniform ironed and the creases were sharp enough to cut an apple. Walking up to Nate the man said, "I am Captain Henry Burgess, Major O'Brien is out right now, and I understand you have Donnelly in your custody?"

"I ain't sure I know what custody means, but I got his ass hog-tied on a horse outside, if y'all still want 'em. My name is Nate Grisham." Nate replied with a shallow grin as he realized the white officer had not offered to shake his hand.

Turning to the young blond man beside him the Captain ordered, "Private Burke, go get four men and escort Mister Donnelly to the guard house. Tell the jailer I want him kept shackled at all times, even in his cell, and he is not to be removed from the jail at any time for any reason."

"Yes sir!" Private Burke replied and made his way from the office.

"Well, Mister Nate Grisham," The Captain spoke with a grin on his face, "it looks like you have a good reward coming for this. But, first let's go and talk to this Mister Donnelly, so I can be assured it is the correct man."

The two men walked outside and the Captain pulled an old pipe from his shirt pocket. As he packed it with tobacco, he looked at Donnelly and casually asked, "What is your name, sir?"

"Wyer, Taylor Wyer."

"Strange, this black man seems to think you're a man named Taylor M. Donnelly. Are you sure you're not him?" The Captain struck a match against the hitching post, took a deep drag on his pipe, and waited for a response.

"My name is Wyer."

Through a deep cloud of white smoke from his pipe, the Captain simply said, "Bullshit. I have both a dispatch and reward poster in my office on you. The drawing on the reward poster clearly identifies you as Donnelly. Though neither document mentions the scar to your face, the missing tip of your nose, or the loss of your right ear, I can see it's you. However, even a greenhorn can see those injuries are fresh. You'll be confined to the guardhouse and kept under guard until transportation to Washington can be arranged. Once in Washington you will stand courts martial for the killing of the colonel and his wife."

Right then, Private Burke arrived with a detail and Donnelly was quickly unhorsed and led away.

"And, your name sir?" The Captain asked as he met the eye's of Doc.

"Names Doc, sold'jer boy." The old mountain main replied with a big grin.

"And, your last name?" The Captain asked, obviously upset with being called a soldier boy.

"I ain't got none. I'm a mountain man and we only got one name, and mine is Doc."

The Captain grinned and said, "Ok, come into my office and let's do the paperwork for the reward money. Now, I can't pay you until the army confirms I have Donnelly and that you are authorized payment. Once they confirm he is in my custody and you two are here they'll dispatch me an authorization of payment."

As soon as the paperwork was completed, the Captain sent a rider out with a dispatch to the Department of the Army in Saint Louis. Still sitting at his desk, the Captain reached down, pulled out a bottle of rye and three glasses. Filling them with the rough amber colored alcohol, he handed one to each of the mountain men and said, "Well, gentlemen, I propose a toast for the capture of Taylor M. Donnelly."

Raising their drinks all three men took a quick gulp. Then, Nate asked from his chair in front of the Commander's desk, "So how long do you think it will take for the army to answer your dispatch?'

Captain Burgess gave a loud laugh and replied, "It could be within two weeks, but not likely. The army is slow, Grisham, and I suspect a better guess would be between two to four months."

"Shit!" Doc exclaimed, "Why so damned long?"

"The Department of the Army is swamped with messages, dispatches, and letters, Doc, so they have to separate the wheat from the chaff." As soon as he spoke the Captain threw back the rest of his drink and poured himself another one.

Why is it that every army man I ever met has a drinkin' problem, Nate thought, *I wonder why?* But he said, "We'll wait. We'll be camped about a mile out of town on the Missouri River. We'll be down south a mite. We'll check back in a month and see what you have. Oh, and Captain?"

"Yes?"

"You make sure we're paid in dollars and not your worthless army script. I've been paid in script before and it's not worth a hill of beans. The reward poster stated one thousand dollars and not one thousand dollars in script."

The Captain laughed, gave a big grin and replied, "It will be an authorization for the bank to pay you one thousand dollars in cash —greenbacks. I think your checking back in a month will be fine."

The two mountain men left the office of Captain Burgess as the man was pouring himself another drink. Once outside they mounted and rode southeast toward the meandering Missouri River.

Donnelly was taken to the guardhouse where an old grizzled Sergeant running the guardhouse met him. The old noncommissioned officer was a big man, well over six feet tall and near two hundred and fifty pounds. He grabbed Donnelly and threw him against a wall as he quickly frisked him looking for hidden weapons. Once he was satisfied the man was unarmed the Sergeant placed handcuffs on Donnelly's hands and shackled his legs together. The chain on his legs was about two feet long and made walking very difficult. Taking Donnelly to an empty cell the Sergeant said, "I am Sergeant James Church and I'm your jailer. Ya will remain in your cell at all times, unless called for by Captain Burgess. Ya will be fed twice a day. For breakfast ya will have coffee, a biscuit, and a piece of salt pork. For supper you'll get beans and bacon, along with a slab of cornbread. Now, your stay here can be nice or I can make it rough on you. Ya piss me off and I'll beat your ass, ya got that?"

"Sergeant, I'm a Captain in the cavalry and expect some respect from you. You will address me as sir or Captain at all times, do you understand me?" Donnelly attempted to intimidate the guard in his best command voice.

Well, now—" the Sergeant started speaking and suddenly he swung his right fist, striking Donnelly on the jaw. When the blow landed, Donnelly was knocked back onto his rough mattress and his arms were quickly chained to an iron O-ring on the wall above the bed. Grinning, Sergeant Church said, "Ya might have been a Captain once, but ya ain't no more. You're a damned killer and you'll get little or no respect from me, or my boys."

As the door to the cell door *clanged* shut and the key was turned locking Donnelly in his dark cell he thought, *I get a chance, Sergeant Church, and you're a dead sonofabitch.*

Time passed slowly in the cell and Donnelly was driven almost insane by the lack of something to do. He slept as much as possible, considered ways to escape, and even took to counting the logs in the cell. It was three weeks after he'd been locked up before the Sergeant returned and opening the cell door said, "Come with me, the Captain wants to talk at ya. Ya keep a civil tongue too, or ya'll answer to me when we get back here."

In the Captain's office, Donnelly stood in front of the man's desk as he read, "Captain Donnelly, the army has sent authorization to transport you back to Washington, immediately for trial. You have been charged with two counts of murder and desertion from your assigned post on or about January the sixteenth of this year. You will be taken from your cell tonight at nineteen forty-five and with an army escort of three men, you will board boat heading east. Once on the boat you will stay until you arrive in Washington, at which time the Department of the army will relieve my men and take you into their custody. Do you have any questions sir?"

Taylor gave a serious look as he said, "Captain Burgess, I'm still an officer in the United States Army. I've not been convicted of a crime and I have not given up my commission as an officer. As such, I demand to be treated as an officer and gentleman at all times. I have had no reading material in my cell; I'm eating food from the enlisted men's mess, and not being address by my current military rank." *They must not know of my earlier conviction, but how can that be? They must not have all the paperwork in one place yet.*

Captain Burgess leaned forward at his desk, with his hands resting on the very edge as he looked at Sergeant Church he asked, "Sergeant is what Captain Donnelly saying true?"

"Uh, yes sir it is. I had no idea he was a real Captain like he claimed, so he got no readin' material, and the food he gets is the same food me and you eat. I ain't been callin' him a sir or a Captain, because as a prisoner, according to army confinement regulation one hundred and fifty-five, page twenty-two, paragraph six, it states, 'all prisoners, regardless of rank will eat food from the common mess, be addressed by their current rank, unless convicted, and at that time they will be addressed as prisoner. Also, said enlisted, or unknown prisoners, will not be given items of entertainment.' Since I didn't know his rank, I've been callin' him prisoner, sir."

"Take him back to his cell and," Captain Burgess said as he pulled a Bible from the left top drawer of his desk, "give him this to read. I'm sure a man that will soon be condemned to death by hanging can find some comfort in reading the Bible. Dismissed!"

Back in the cell Sergeant Church shackled Donnelly to the wall once more, leaned close and said in an angry voice, "Look shit head, ya jess made me look bad in the eyes of my commander." The big man quickly punched Donnelly on the side of the head with his big fists and screamed, "Don't piss me off *sir*, because I once served under ya for a week. We were back east and I didn't like ya then and for sure don't like your ass now. I went so far as to make myself sick, so I could be sent to the hospital to get away from your ass. Once there I arranged with a Top Sergeant I knew to weasel a transfer out of your unit. Do ya remember me, *Captain* Donnelly, sir?

Donnelly shook his head quickly, glanced up at the big Sergeant and thought; *I will kill you for this Sergeant. Of that much I'm sure.*

Glancing at the guard beside him holding a rifle with a long bayonet attached, Church ordered, "Private Crawford, you will take your post just outside this door until we need to meet the boat. At which time you, me, and another dumb-ass of a private will escort this worthless piece of shit to Washington."

"Yes, Sergeant Church." The Private answered quickly and moved outside the door to his posting.

As he door swung shut with a loud clank and the key turned to lock him up, Church started to walk away, but hesitated a second. Turning, he said, "*Captain* Donnelly, *sir*, I hope on the trip back east ya make a break for it, because if ya do I'll blow a hole in ya big enough to put a fist through." With that said, the old Sergeant gave a loud horselaugh and left the stockade.

On the same afternoon, Nate and Doc arrive at Captain Burgess' office. The captain gave them a letter that authorized immediate payment of one thousand dollars in cash, drawn from any United States bank. Grinning from ear to ear, the Captain said jokingly from behind his desk, "Don't spend it all in one place."

Nate laughed, pocketed the letter and replied, "We won't. Actually, we'll be heading back to the mountains as soon as I visit the bank."

"Well, you can rest easy and know you've done the army a good turn, Nate Grisham. Captain Donnelly will be on a boat this evening and in Washington by the end of the month. It's not often a colored man is commended by the U.S. army."

Doc gave a loud chuckle and said, "Hell fire Captain, I'll bet ya the army didn't know what color either one of us mountain men was, now did they?"

Burgess gave a loud laugh, slapped his right knee and replied, "Nope, I guess not, but what I said is true. You did a valuable job for us, the both of you, and even the army said 'well done.'"

Less than twenty minutes later the two men were standing in the bank arguing with a teller over the money. The bank was small and had just opened up outside the walls of the fort, as other small business had during the last year.

"I cannot just hand over one thousand dollars to you two, because it would hurt the bank. We are not a big firm and that much money would cripple us. We've not been open a month yet." A weasel of a clerk spoke as he shook his thin bespectacled head.

Nate suspected his being black was part of the problem, only he was unsure how to handle the situation when he suddenly heard Doc explode from beside him.

"Get the damned bank manager, before I wring your neck!" Doc screamed at the thin and little man.

Suddenly a side door in the bank opened and out walked a fat short man with no hair on the very top of his head. What little he had on the right side was combed up and over his bald spot in a poor attempt to cover it. Seeing the two dirty mountain men standing in front of the counter he walked over and asked in a calm voice, "What seems to be the problem here Halley?"

The clerk quickly explained the army authorization, the amount of the reward, and then cautioned his boss on releasing such a large amount. The clerk then handed the letter to the bank president.

Looking the letter over very closely, the man said, "I am Silas Peabody and I will authorize the immediate withdraw of these funds. Your paperwork is in order so it will not pose a problem. We don't get many letters authorizing us to pay such large amounts from the army and Halley was confused. Now, would both, or either, of you like to make a deposit of some of this?"

Both Nate and Doc grinned, but Nate said, "Nope, all in cash. Make it greenbacks, because they are lighter to carry than coin."

Fifteen minutes later the two mountain men were mounted and headed west. The sky had turned dark, the wind had picked up and it was very cold. However, the thought of the money in Nate's saddlebag provided warmth for two of them as they rode and neither seemed to mind the miles they yet had to cover to reach the mountains.

At eight o'clock that night on a boat heading to Saint Louis, Captain Donnelly sat in a rough bench seat shackled at his legs and handcuffed with his arms in front of him. Sergeant Church sat beside him and the two Privates positioned with one in front and one at the rear of a long storage area below deck.

As the boat began to gather up speed, Sergeant Church leaned over and said in a low threatening voice, "Try to escape Donnelly, ya sumbitch, jess try!"

I will Sergeant and when I do you'll be a dead man, Taylor thought as he lowered his head and closed his eyes. He knew he had to wait until the men grew tired and careless, then he would make his move. He also understood he needed to escape within the next twenty-four hours and before they entered the Mississippi River. Donnelly knew once he was in a heavily pop-ulated area he'd be rearrested quickly, especially since his facial injuries would make him easy to spot.

Chapter 11

"Skeeter don't smell too good, does he Butterfield?" Cotton asked as he sat at the table and sipped a cup of what Butterfield called coffee. While still sore, the old mountain man was up and moving around.

"He's festered up on us, Cotton, and this morning we got to clean the man real good." Butterfield spoke as he lifted his cup, took a small sip, and then lowered it to the table.

"What do you mean when ya say clean 'em up. Hell, he ain't no dirtier than me or ya."

Butterfield shook his head, gave a light sigh and replied, "His injury is turning sour and if we don't clean the poison out he'll die on us."

Cotton Top thought for a few minutes wondering how they could clean an injury and remove the poison, confused he asked, "How are we gonna do a thing like that?"

The old trader gave a dry laugh, turned and met Cotton's eyes as he said, "We have to scrape the scab off the wound, clean the holes out real good with a rag, pour some whiskey on the whole shootin' match, and then cauterize the wound again."

"Damn, ya sure?" Cotton asked and then gave a shudder.

"Ain't no other way to do the job. It's messy and since he's wide awake now he won't take to 'er much when we do the job either. But, he's got red and purple streaks running up his back, so the job has to be done." Butterfield pushed his cup away, stood and said, "I might as well get the knife blades heated up."

"Skeeter, you awake over there?" Cotton yelled out as he stood and looked over at the bed.

"Yep and I hear'd every damn word you two jess said. I don't cotton the idea much, but if ya gotta do the job do it right

99

and don't pay me no never mind." The injured man said from his bed.

Ten minutes later two long skinning knives were glowing red hot in the stove, Butterfield was beside the bed, and bloody pus soaked bandages littered the floor. The trader had Skeeter roll over on his stomach and then walked to his potbellied stove. Pulling the smallest of the knives from the stove the old trader allowed it to cool and then walked back to the bedside.

"Skeeter, did you drink that alcohol I gave ya a few minutes ago? I mean all of it?" The trader asked.

"Yep, every drop. Butterfield, don't worry 'bout me. You jess do the job and I'll make out fine."

"Cotton, you hold his shoulders as I clean out the wound. And, Skeeter, this is gonna really hurt ya old son."

Skeeter didn't reply, but he did close his eyes.

Butterfield took the knife in his right hand and with one quick motion; he scrapped most of the scab from Skeeter's back. The mountain man gave a heart-breaking scream, thrashed around violently, and a second later, he muffled a loud groan in his pillow. Twice more Butterfield scrapped the injury and when it started bleeding freely, he pulled a ramrod from a pistol, wrapped a piece of clean cotton cloth on the tip of it and then stuck it in the first hole. As the ramrod entered the injury, the old trader twisted the ramrod to make sure it cleaned the injury well. Skeeter quivered violently, moaned, but to his credit did not cry out. As soon as all entry wounds were cleaned, the trader placed the knife on a stand next to the table, picked up a cup of alcohol and poured in on Skeeter's back. The injured man gave another loud but short yelp of pain and immediately passed out.

"Jesus, is he daid?" Cotton asked leaning forward so he could see a little better.

"Passed out on us and that's good. Seems most fellers do it when pain gets to be too much fer 'em." Butterfield answered and then walked to the stove, pulled a red-hot knife from the crackling flames, and returned to the bedside.

"Gonna burn him 'gain?" Cotton asked with large eyes.

"Yep and I told ya that, now hold 'em down, because I gotta do this fast before the blade cools." Butterfield answered and then leaned over the injured man. Placing the flat of the blade against Skeeter's back, he swirled the blade so the melting flesh would cover the wounds. Skeeter moaned softly but he did not move.

As soon as he finished Butterfield placed a bandage on the injury and wrapped the man up tightly. Turning to Skeeter the old trader said, "Let's have a drink. Now, I know it's early, but our morning has been a rough one already."

At the table once more sipping trader's whiskey Cotton Top asked, "Will he live?"

"Lord I hope so Cotton, but it's really hard to say for sure. I've seen 'em live and I've seen 'em die. Ain't much we can do now except wait and see. I don't know why you ask me that question every single time we do a doctorin' job."

Taterhead and Hatch had not moved from the table as the doctoring was done, but both had watched. Hatch finally looked at Cotton Top and said, "Cotton, you know as well as I do that out here some men die and some men live after gettin' hurt. The mountains are hard on good strong men and they kill weak men quickly. I suspect your man Skeeter will live, but if he dies it was meant to be."

"I wish that old Sioux medicine man Spirit Talker was here. By God, he has the healin' touch, he surely does." Taterhead spoke as he lifted his coffee cup.

"I know the man, they say he can see the future and talk to the dead." Hatch said and then grinned as he added, "Pure horseshit."

"T . . . talk to the d . . .dead?" Cotton barely managed to get out.

"Oh, that's what the Sioux claim, but ain't nobody that can do that." Hatch replied and then laughed.

"I ain't so sure, Hatch, them damned Injuns can do some things us white men wouldn't ever consider doin'." Butterfield spoke, leaned over and poured some whiskey into Taterhead's and Hatch's coffee.

Hatch laughed once more and said, "Hell, if they can see the future, why would they go on a raid that kills a bunch of 'em? Why do they go hungry during poor times, if they know it's comin'? It's just nonsense them medicine men use to keep the people under control."

"I don't like talkin' 'bout this stuff. Let's change the subject." Cotton Top said and then took a big gulp of his whiskey.

Minutes of silence filled the small room and then Hatch said as he stood, "We need more meat, so me and Taterhead will go out and get us a deer. I think it will be safer with the two of us, so don't worry about us a-tall."

"That's a dandy of an idea Hatch; let's do 'er!" Taterhead said and then walked over to his Hawken and picked it up.

Right after the two men left for their hunting trip a group of eight men rode up to the trading post, dismounted and tied their horses to the hitching post. No sooner than the first man's feet touched the ground than Butterfield walked out with a big scat-tergun in his hands.

Glancing around the old trader asked with narrowed eyes, "Who y'all be?"

"I'm the Booshway and we work for the Astor Company out of Saint Louis." A short man wearing filthy buckskins said and then quickly added, "My name is Quinch, James Quinch."

"What brings you to the tradin' post? I thought all of ya comp'nee men got yer supplies and such from back east." Butterfield asked as he walked over and placed the shotgun against the wall near the door.

"We do, usually, but Blackfoot attacked us a few days back, killed two men and took over our camp. We lost every damned thing we owned, except what we had on us at the time or could pick up as we ran."

Butterfield thought for a minute and then asked, "Pretty big group of Blackfoot was it?"

"Nye on a hundred, I'd guess."

"So, what can I do fer ya fellers? And, by the way, I am But-terfield."

"Howdy-do, Mister Butterfield. We need enough supplies to last us the rest of the year. I got a line of credit from Astor, so payin' you ain't a problem." Quinch said as he pulled a soiled let-ter from his pocket and handed it to the old trader.

The old trader read the letter, gave a big grin and said, "Well, now, come on in Mister Quinch and let's get them supplies yer boys need. Ya'll have to give me some time to get it all together, but I'll have most of what ya want I'm pretty sure of it."

The two men entered the store and Quinch simply nodded at Cotton, who he recognized as a free trapper, sitting at the table. He knew company men were not usually well received, so he didn't speak. Mountain men had a poor opinion of those trappers that worked for others and more than one fight had started at the annual rendezvous over the issue. Pulling a list from his pocket, Quinch handed it to Butterfield and asked, "Can you supply all of that?"

The trader looked the list over, grimaced a time or two and replied after a few minutes, "I ain't got that much bacon or salt pork and the lead ya want will about clean me out, but I'll let ya have it anyway. Now, the horses I don't have at all. I usually have some, but I just traded some off and ain't got no new ones in yet. But, I think if y'all headed north ya could trade the Sioux out of a few, especially if you find Old Buffalo Humps band."

"Ok, we'll take what you got and be glad to get it. You know anybody around that knows this Injun Buffalo Hump?"

Butterfield grinned and using his right thumb pointed it at Cotton Top at the table sipping coffee and said, "Just Cotton."

Quinch nodded, turned and walked over to the table. Standing beside the table he asked, "You want to earn fifty dollars? I need someone to take me and my men to see a Sioux chief named Buffalo Hump."

Cotton thought for a few seconds, gave a weak grin and replied, "Normally I'd tell a comp'nee man to go to hell before I'd help 'em out, but the Crow have been raising Holy hell and from what I've just overheard the Blackfoot are out and about again, so I'll do the job."

"Why?" Quinch asked as he pulled out a chair and sat down.

"The more of us out running in the woods the safer it is for the all of us. The way I got it figured is, the Crow need taught a lesson and them damned Blackfoot are always a pain in the ass, so I'll help ya just to get yer group out trappin'. That away them Injuns will mess with ya big groups and leave us small groups of free trappers alone."

Quinch gave a mighty laugh, looked over at Butterfield and said, "Bring me a bottle of your best whiskey and add the cost of it to the supplies."

After the whiskey was on the table, Quinch gave Cotton a weak grin and said, "Cotton Top, I know you're a free trapper, as

I once was, but times turned rough and I had to join the company or leave the mountains."

"Waugh, that's plain bullshit. Ya could have joined up with 'nother feller and trapped. I think ya took the easy way out of a hard problem."

The company man laughed, picked up the bottle of whiskey and pulled the cork. Then, he poured a generous amount into Cotton's cup and filled his own before he said, "Okay, I could have done things different, but I didn't. When do you want to leave for the Sioux village?"

Cotton picked up his cup, took a big gulp of the drink, and replied, "Well, how 'bout in about ten minutes? That away we can have one more drink and hit the trail."

"Sounds good to me." Then turning to Butterfield, Quinch said, "We'll go and get some horses first, then return for the supplies before we go back out. Would that be a problem?"

"Nope," Butterfield said as he wrote in his ledger the items ordered by Quinch, "that will give me time to round this stuff up. It will take me most of the day just to weigh the stuff, then bag it, and I'll still have to figure the cost. So, if ya can get to the Sioux and back by, well, let's say three days, ya'll be ready to go."

"Ok, Cotton, let's hit the trail, son. I want to hurry and get back, so me and the boys can be in the mountains before the first hard weather hits. Butterfield, I'll leave about half of my men here, if that ain't no trouble for you. I don't see where five men should have a problem drivin' less than twenty ponies."

"Huh-uh, let your men stay and actually I'd feel a bit safer. But, before ya go, let me gather ya up some tobacco, a half a dozen old guns, and some other foofuraw for them Sioux, or they won't let ya have a blamed thing." Butterfield spoke as he moved toward his storeroom in back.

"By damn, that's a fine idea, Butterfield." Quinch said as gulp down the rest of his drink and poured himself another one.

Cotton raised his right eyebrow and said, "Go easy on the fire water, or I'll not ride with ya. The last thing I'd do is ride into a Sioux village with a drunken man."

Quinch gave a loud laugh and replied, "Cotton, I've not had a drink in over three months, but if it makes you feel safer that was the last one."

"I appreciate it. Them Sioux are hard to figure in the best of times and with a few belts in a man's belly it could be suicide."

A day and a half later, the five men rode into the Sioux village and though the ride was easy, Cotton's injury bothered him more than just a little and he was glad to finally be with the Sioux. The wolves guarding the village spotted them about a half a day's ride from Butterfield's trading post and since they knew Cotton Top by his white hair, they left the men alone and allowed them to enter the village unchallenged.

"Welcome to my lodge, Snow Head." Buffalo Hump said as Cotton rode up and stopped his horse in front of the chief's lodge. The chief was a short and stocky built man with wide shoulders, narrow waist, and black piercing eyes. His cheeks and face was scarred from a battle with small pox he had survived as a very young child. Also on his chest were four deep scars from the sun dance, which meant as far as Cotton was concerned he was one tough hombre.

"I am honored to be here, Buffalo Hump, and I have brought friends that would like to trade with The People for horses."

The old chief gave a big grin and said, "Enter my lodge and let us eat and smoke, then we will talk."

The lodge was shadowy and the white men had to stop just inside for a few minutes to allow their eyes to adjust to the lack of light. Like most Indian lodges, it smelled of roasting meat, leather, wood smoke, and tobacco. As the men moved to the fire, Buffalo Hump motioned for Cotton to sit on his immediate right—a place of deep honor.

They shared a quick meal of roasted buffalo and then Buffalo Hump pulled out his long stemmed pipe. Pulling a brand from the fire, he lighted the pipe, puffed a few times to get it going well, and then offered it to the four sacred positions, east, west, north and south. Finally, he raised the pipe up and down to symbolize the heavens and earth. As soon as he had finished, he passed the pipe around and each man copied his movements with the pipe. When the smoking was done, Buffalo Hump tapped the bowl of is pipe against his hand and let the sacred tobacco fall into the fire.

Many long minutes passed without a word said, which would have been unheard of in a group of white men. Ultimately, Buffalo Hump spoke, "So, you wish to trade with the Sioux for horses?"

"Yes," Cotton replied, "and we have many things to give you for four hands of horses."

"What things do you have that are worth so many horses?"

Looking over at Quinch, Cotton Top said, "Go and get the trade goods. Buffalo Hump is interested."

Quinch stood and quickly left the lodge with one of his men. Less than five minutes later, he was back and placed all he had brought with him on the ground in front of the chief.

If the old chief was surprised by the small mountain of goods, he didn't show it. His face remained as before, emotion-less. He looked at the goods, raised his eyes to Cotton's and asked, "Do the guns fire?"

"Yes, Buffalo Hump, they work. As you can see we could only get a few pounds of powder and lead to make the balls, but it is difficult to get those things now after the trappers have been to the trading post."

"These trappers, they take most of the good things for them-selves?"

"No," Cotton spoke as he met the old man's eyes, "they take many different things, but they also need powder and lead to live in the mountains. Since they all come to the trading post at pretty much the same time, the good things go quickly."

The old Sioux war chief nodded in understanding and then said, "Come, let us go and pick out twenty horses for you."

The men stood and followed the chief of The People to the pony herd.

CHAPTER 12

Waters was terrified of discovery, even though he knew the snow had filled any tracks he'd left in the snow. At first he worried about the fire and if someone could see it, or smell the smoke. Then he worried about any noises he might make, only to realize a couple of hours later that few people would be out in this weather and the Crow more than likely thought him dead from the storm. He was surprised at how warm his small shelter under the pine was, though he had no coat or cold weather gear with him.

The day passed slowly, with dark clouds rolling overhead and large snowflakes falling, only to be blown in all directions by high winds. The snow piled up against the sides of the pine and this added to the warmth under the tree. Waters knew any smoke from his small fire filtered through the tree branches and while someone might smell his smoke, they'd not see it.

It was near dark when Waters heard faint voices in the howling wind. At first, he could not tell if the voices were white or Indian, so he remained hidden. He knew if the voices belonged to white men, it did not mean they would not kill him. He'd grown up quickly the last few days and knew his views of the Wild West had changed drastically since he'd left the east. He no longer thought all men were good and his trust in his fellow man had disappeared. Waters knew, given a chance, he'd head back home as quickly as he could and never cross the Mississippi River again.

"By God, Nate, I still say I smell smoke." A voice Waters didn't recognize at first spoke, but after a few seconds he realized it was Doc.

"Doc and Nate, I'm over here!" Waters yelled out, greatly relieved he'd found friends.

"Who you be?" The black man's deep voice yelled in return as he swung his big Hawken toward the voice.

"Samuel Waters! We met a while back, when I was traveling with Matson and Medicine Bear!"

"Come on out!" Doc yelled, cocked his rifle with a loud snap, and then added, "If ya got a gun hold it high in yer left hand when ya come out too!"

Waters parted the limbs on the pine, watched snow land on his small fire, and stood as he said, "I ain't got no weapons, except for a small knife in my right boot. Them dang Crows took everything I owned."

Nate gently kicked his horse forward and looking down at Waters he asked, "Waters, what in the hell happened to you?'

"Hell is absolutely right." The man said and then quickly began telling his story of the killing of Medicine Bear and the death of Matson.

"Look," Nate said as soon as the deacon finished speaking, "let's get us a shelter up, a fire goin', and I'm sure you could use some hot grub right about now. I was guests of the Blackfoot once and discovered Injuns don't feed a captive worth a shit. Poor folks to visit, Injuns can be at times."

Within thirty minutes, the camp was established and a big pot of deer stew was on the flickering flames of the popping and snapping fire. Though the mountain men called the dish a stew, it was mostly deer meat, some dried wild onions, and a little flour to thicken it. As the stew cooked, Doc made rough looking biscuits and placed them one by one into his Dutch oven. As soon as the oven was full, he scraped a few red coals to the side and placed his oven on top of them. Reaching over, he picked up a small burning brand from the fire and placed it on top of his oven, knowing the biscuits would now cook evenly. He then made a pot of coffee and placed it on the fire to boil.

The smell of the food caused Waters' stomach to gurgle and growl as he waited. The longer the stew cooked the more impatient he became. Finally, Nate noticed the man and said, half joking, "You'll not be able to eat much. Seems after a feller goes without food for a couple of days his stomach shrinks and while he feels like he could eat a full grown buffalo, he cain't. You should take it slow at first, maybe eat just a half a bowl of stew, then in an hour eat some more. There's plenty there, so you can eat all you want of the nasty mess. Just remember to eat slowly and not gulp it down. I've seen hungry men eat themselves to death and all because they ate to fast."

An hour later Waters discovered Nate was right, because while he finished half a bowl of stew, he could eat no more. He did drink two cups of hot thick coffee as he slowly nibbled on a biscuit as soon as he'd placed the bowl on the ground next to his foot. The deacon discovered he felt as full as he'd ever been in his life, but he had eaten so little.

Nate added a log to the fire, pulled out a plug of chewing to-bacco, and as he cut off a large piece he asked, "So, do you think you could find the place that Moses was killed at? Or, did the storm mess up your sense of direction?"

"I think I can find it. From what I remember I moved straight east toward these hills and woods."

Doc cleared his throat and replied, "Waters, when a man is scared shitless, he often forgets what he's done. I've done it my-self and it's jess' a normal thing. It could be ya are way off on your guess about where ya are."

"Could be," the man confessed and then continued, "but I am pretty sure I headed east. Why?"

Nate and Doc were both quiet for a few moments, and then Nate said, "I can't leave a man of God to feed the wolves. A man like him needs a good Christian burial and I think you could do the job for us."

"I'll do it, if we can find his body." Waters spoke, gazed into the popping fire and watched the flames dance as he thought, *Moses, you were such a fool.*

"We'll find it, unless a critter has already made a meal of it. It'd take a big animal too, but there is painters and grizz both in this area." Doc said as he pulled his blanket up over his shoul-ders to get warmer.

"And, that ain't likely, 'cause all the big beasts are holed up for the winter. Most of 'em are sleepin', or you won't see 'em out much in the cold. Seems like they got more sense than most people I know." Nate spoke and then gave a big warm smile.

"Ya ever seen a man after an Injun gets done with 'em, Wa-ters?" Doc asked.

"Nope, not really, except what they did to Medicine Bear. I hear'd some tales, but figured it was all a bunch of lies."

"I can tell ya right now," Nate spoke as he pulled the blackened coffee pot from the fire and started filling his cup, "he'll be mutilated and scalped for sure. It's ugly as hell, but they do it to almost every person they kill."

Waters taken aback by the thought asked, "I saw them do it to Medicine Bear right after they killed him. But why in God's name do they do that?"

"They think if they don't mutilate a person they fought and killed, why they'll have to fight 'em again once they die. So they cut 'em up pretty badly most of the time, so they won't be whole on the other side. You just be prepared to see it, 'cause it ain't a pretty sight to see." Doc replied as he held his palms out to the flickering fire to warm them.

"But, they don't do it all the time, do they?" Waters asked, finding it hard to believe a person could do that to another.

"Nope, not if you die a brave man, only it ain't easy to die brave with a bunch of Injuns hackin' on yer ass with knives and tomahawks. I've only seen one man not mutilated in all my years in the mountains and that was Ebenezer Grenach. We all called the man Eb, but the day he died, according to the Sioux who fought 'em; old Eb killed nine of them Sioux before he went under. Them Sioux were so impressed, they left him untouched, his weapons beside him, and they still sing of his brave fight with 'em. Ole Eb was as brave as a buffalo bull in the spring and he wasn't scared of nothin'. Ain't nothin' impresses an Injun like a good hard-ass fight."

"This snow is dying off and I think it will be clear in the mornin'. But I know for a fact it'll be as cold as a Yankee banker's heart too. So, I think we should all go to bed and get a good night of rest. Doc, you take the first watch and wake me when you get tired. We'll let Waters relax since he's had a bad time of it come late." Nate spoke and then walked to the shelter for some sleep. Waters followed him a few minutes later.

Morning came very cold, with the tops of the bare oak trees covered with a deep frost from the low temperature, and a light ice fog covered the valley below. As he moved off to make water, Nate noticed it was cold enough that breathing caused his lungs to hurt. He quickly finished his morning toilet and moved back to the fire. Nate had started the fire just about an hour before dawn, to allow his friends to wake up to some warmth. *It'll be cold until at least noon time,* Nate thought as he placed the coffee pot on the fire, *and maybe longer. I suspect we won't get far on this day, but I've got to see that Bible thumper buried proper like as soon as I can. My mama would roll over in her grave iffen she knew I didn't bury a preacher man after he was killed.*

The morning passed slowly with the two mountain men repairing their gear and casting more lead balls for ammunition. As soon as he'd finished pouring three dozen balls, Doc went to the shelter and returned with an old smooth bore rifle, a powder horn, and a handful of lead balls. Handing them to Waters he said, "I can't let ya ride around without no weapons. This gun shoots fair, but a hair to the left, so keep that in mind if ya shoot at a target more than fifty feet out there. I took it off a Blackfoot brave I killed a year back and I meant to give it to ya last night, only I forgot."

Waters gave a big grin and replied, "Why thank ye kindly Doc, I was hopin' one of you fellers might have some sort of extra gun. Since I came out west I feel almost naked without a weapon of some sort on me."

Both Nate and Doc chuckled, and Nate finally said, "We'll move out of here, heading due west, as soon as the temperature goes up a mite. Right now it's cold enough to freeze the balls off a grizzly bear, so we'll stay by the fire. I ain't worried about us movin' so much as I am the horses."

"That's fine with me. Nate, can I ask you a personal question and not make you mad?" Waters asked as he met the man's eyes.

Nate laughed and said, "You gonna ask me a slave question, ain't ya?"

Waters lowered his eyes, his cheeks turned a little redder and he nodded in reply.

"Ask away, 'cause I'm sure you'll ain't gonna ask me nothin' that I ain' been asked before." Nate laughed once more and then said in a serious voice, "I know *what* I am Waters and I know *who* I am too, so ask your question."

Waters raised his head and asked, "Were you ever a real slave?"

"Yes, sir, I was. But one day I walked away and I ain't never been back."

"Was it as rough a life as I think it could be? Nate, I ain't never met no man who was ever a slave and I'm just interested. If you don't want to tell me, I'll shut up."

Nate stared into the dancing flames for a few seconds, with the only sound heard was snapping and cracking of the fire as it ate at the wood. Then he spoke without raising his head, "Samuel, being a slave wasn't rough. What was rough was stayin' a slave. See, any man with a sense of personal honor, well, he don't want to be no slave. I used to get angry, knowing my hard work was puttin' money in my master's pocket and not a dime in mine. Many a day I worked from sunup to way after dark, picking cotton, shuckin' corn, sawin' wood into planks, or cuttin' hay. Then, I'd go to my small cabin behind the master's big white house and have my dinner of sow belly and turnip greens. I'd always sleep like a dead man, but I was just a bit over fourteen years old and lived with my grandma."

"Did ya get enough to eat?"

"We had food, hell; we cost too much to be allowed to starve to death. Only it was usually wormy pork, bits and pieces of beef, turnip tops, or what we could grow. The master he made everyone of us grow a garden, so we had food durin' the warm months. Winters were lean times and more than once, I went to bed hungry after working all day. Usually, during the cold season we ate beans, turnip greens, and cornbread. I would set some rabbit traps and usually, a couple of times a week, I'd get some fresh meat, only there ain't much fat on a rabbit. And, when it gets real cold, like it is now, a person wants fat meat."

Waters thought for a minute, then said, "But the Bible speaks of slaves and the making of slaves."

Nate laughed and replied, "Yep, it does, only it ain't a good thing to do to any man, woman, or child. What I mean is how would you like to be married and have ya some kids, only to see them sold off one at a time, until you're all alone? How do you think it makes you feel inside to hear your youngsters screamin' for you to help them as the new master takes 'em away? Slavery is wrong Samuel Waters and one day the South will pay a high price for the life they are enjoying today."

"What do you mean by that? Do you think God would pun-ish them when it says it's okay in the Bible?"

"Maybe God will, then again maybe not. It might be the North against the South, or mayhap all them black folks down South will rise up and commence to fightin' for their freedom. There is already talk of the North not liking the slave problem and I've heard some fiery talk in some slave quarters about how runaways can head north to freedom."

"Yes, there are free states up north where slavery is not allowed. But, Nate, if all those blacks down South were to rise up at one time, my God can you imagine the blood and deaths that would follow?"

"Anger is just one of the reasons someday something will happen. A man who is a slave is less than a real man and I know what I'm talkin' about. A slave has no hopes, no future, and no desire to work harder than need be to keep a whip off his back. A man who can see a better time comin' will work hard to get to that day, but a slave will only do what he's told to do, and no more or less. Hell, a slave can't even keep his family together, or marry who he wants, or even go to bed at night without wondering if he'll be sold off the next mornin'."

Once again, it grew deathly quiet, with only the fire making any noise. Long minutes passed and then Waters asked, "Those kids crying for help when they were sold, was one of them your child Nate?"

"No, one of those kids was me and I never saw my pa or my ma again. The new master bought my grandma to take care of us kids, but he didn't need no house help and that's what my ma and pa were. The master was a kindly man, who saw I was as sharp as a tack, so he taught me to read and write. Then, after a long spell he taught me how to cipher and do my sums, so I could keep his books. One day, when I was about fifteen, I went into town for him to drop off some papers and I ain't been back since. It was raining that day and I took the biggest horse I could find."

"You're a lucky man, Nate Grisham!" Waters said as he gazed into the black man's eyes once more.

Without blinking and in a flat tone, Nate replied with narrowed eyes, "No, I'm not lucky. I was and still am a very determined man. I wanted freedom, so I got it and I'll keep it. No man will *ever* lay a whip on my back again."

"Praise God you got to freedom."

Nate gave a low chuckle and thought, *No, Samuel, thank my big feet and fact I can run for hours without stopping, not to mention the horse I stole.* But, instead he said,

"We gonna sit here and talk about slavery and such, when we should be eatin' breakfast?"

Doc had listened closely to Nate speak and though he'd never owned a soul he knew he never would. It wasn't that Doc was really against slavery, but a slave would cost him a good year in wages and he just didn't have that kind of money. *There will always be slavery in one form or the other,* Doc thought as he pulled out his cast iron skillet and started shaving off long thin slices of salt pork, *some men are slaves to sex, some to money and some to just being down right lazy.*

By a little after noon, the three men were moving westward and though the temperature was still low, it was not the deep numbing cold that had arrived with dawn.

Nate kept them moving at a slow pace to avoid any injury to their mounts. He had divided the supplies up among the three of them and put Waters on the packhorse. *He's a good man over all, but he don't belong out here. He's got too much learnin' to do and he'd die before he could learn what he needs to know to just stay alive,* the big man thought and then reached up and pulled the brim of his hat down to cover his eyes.

"Samuel, have you thought about what you're goin' to do after we bury Moses?" Doc asked as he moved his horse up beside the deacon.

"I guess go to where I can get back east. And," Waters hesitated a second and then continued, "how are we going to bury Moses with the ground all froze up like this?"

Doc gave a loud laugh and said, "We ain't puttin' 'em in the ground. We'll have to bury 'em Injun style, up in a big oak tree."

"Surely you jest?"

"Nope, I ain't teasin' ya a-tall. We'll put 'em up in a big tree, tie 'em down real good, and say a prayer. Look," Doc leaned over to his right and spat a long thin line of brown tobacco juice to the fresh snow, "this ain't back east. We can't use black blasting powder to blow open a hole in the ground jess to bury a feller. And, besides, I don't think after the Crow got done with 'em Moses Matson is gonna care one way or the other what we do with 'em. Do you?"

Waters gave a weak grin and replied, "No, I don't guess it matters much. God will accept him into his kingdom no matter how we bury him and rightfully so."

Doc thought about what Waters said and then replied, "You don't think me and Nate believe in God, do ya?"

"You're both good men, but sinners."

Doc gave a light chuckle and said, "Could be by your standards we are, but I reckon we ain't. See we both know and believe there is a God, beyond any doubt. All a man has to do is look around out here and he can see the wonderful things God has made with his own hands, the wide rivers, the high mountains, and the critters that live here. No, Samuel, we know there is a God, because we live in his home."

Samuel Waters scanned the countryside, gave a big smile and said, "Yes, this is God's country, but you do not live as the Bible says one should live."

"We don't? I don't see it that way. Sam, the only one of the Ten Commandments we break very often is the one about cussin'. We do and I have to admit, use God's name in vain more than we should, but it's a tough life we live and we are rough men."

"When was the last time you were in a church?"

"Almost twenty years ago, if you mean a real hell fire and brimstone, pulpit pounding church, but look around you. You could get no closer to God in a Baptist church than you are right this minute and I think you know that."

Waters cleared his throat and gently kicked his horse to a slightly faster walk. He had not liked the discussion with the old mountain man, because in some ways he made sense. *Only,* thought Waters, *what he is doing is not right by the Good Book. He is yet a sinner, though he talks a good talk.*

"Hold up, you two. I think I've found the spot where Moses was killed. I want you two to stay here while I check it out." Nate said in a voice barely about a whisper.

CHAPTER 13

Donnelly slept most of the day on the boat, allowing the gentle swaying motion to relax him. He knew when the chance came for him to make a break it would most likely be this night, so he had to stay well rested to cover a lot of ground once free. It was near ten at night when he opened his eyes and quickly looked out the window of the room. The sky was dark, with no moon, and long lances of white moved overhead with a loud crack following a few seconds later. *A storm, just what I need to cover a break,* he thought with a big grin as he wiped the sleep from his eyes and sat up.

A little before ten, the sergeant had turned the lamp down, so the light in the interior of the room was dim but not totally dark. However, it was well after midnight, before the inside of the cabin settled down and the other two guards went to sleep. Donnelly knew the lack of light would help once he made a move against Sergeant Church, who always took the midnight to six in the morning shift guarding him. *He knows,* Donnelly thought, *that when I make my break it will be at night and he's right about that.*

Just before three in the morning a bright flash of lightning suddenly filled the cabin, followed a split second later a loud crack of thunder. Donnelly gave the room ten minutes to settle down, in case the thunder had awakened anyone, and then planned his move. As near as he could determine, the boat was half way across Missouri territory, between Independence and Saint Louis, and the area was rough country with few settlers. *I've got to move tonight, before we get into Saint Louis. If I don't it will be very hard to escape unnoticed east of the Mississippi River,* Donnelly thought as he glanced at the big sergeant, saw the man was catnapping with his head hanging back and his throat exposed.

Donnelly quickly threw the chains from his handcuffs over the sergeant's head and neck, crossed his arms, and jerked as hard as he could. The big man fought for a second, so Donnelly jerked once more, heard something snap and the sergeant started choking. Frightened by the noise, the prisoner jerked hard once more and kept the pressure on the chains until he heard Sergeant Church's bowels empty in death. Then, he removed the keys from the sergeant's shirt pocket, unlocked both his hands and legs, and pulled the dead man's pistol from his belt.

Donnelly pulled the Sergeant's coat off; picked up a blanket he had on the seat between them, and slowly moved forward toward the door to the room. Just as he touched the knob there came the loud report of a pistol shot, the wood beside his head splintered and as he looked back, he saw Private Mumford holding a smoking pistol. Donnelly aimed, gently squeezed the trigger and smiled as he saw the man thrown back against a wall as the heavy slug took him in the center of the chest. Donnelly quickly opened the door, stepped out, and making his way to the top of the boat, he moved to the rail and jumped.

Donnelly struck the water hard, swam away from the boat, and ended up on his back in a small shallow stream feeding into the river. For a second or two he didn't move, but after a while he started checking his body and was surprised nothing was broken. He'd landed much harder than he had expected to land and as he stood on weak legs he discovered nothing was hurting. *The water wasn't deep where I jumped.* The boat was a good half a mile away, but Donnelly watched as it slowed and finally came to a complete stop. *I've got to move now,* he thought as he made sure the gun was still in his belt. He discovered it was, and when he'd killed Sergeant Church, Donnelly had the presence of mind to take a small buckskin bag filled with balls, along with a powder horn. He'd lost nothing during the jump, except for a little skin that had been scraped off his left shin and his hat when he landed. Looking around, he spotted his hat lying near the bank, so he walked over, picked up his hat and put it on. He then crossed through some large trees and moved quickly to the east, knowing he'd head south after a few miles.

It was still raining, plus lightning flashed in anger on the skyline and rain pelted him, he found it growing more difficult to move in the ankle deep mud. But, he knew his only chance of living was to keep going, so while his movements were slow he continued moving east. Donnelly realized that if the mud made his walk difficult the men that would soon be searching for him would have the same problems—even on horseback. Additionally, one advantage he had with the hard rain was the simple fact it would wash away his tracks.

It was near dawn, and hours after he had turned south that he came upon a small log cabin back in some oak trees. The rain was still falling, but lighter now and without the high winds that had been blowing most of the night. *Sure is one hell of a remote spot to make a home*, Taylor thought as he pulled his pistol and checked the load, *but I've got to get a horse, some supplies, and other odds and ends I might need. Hell, I might get lucky and find me a woman at the same time.*

As Taylor approached the house, he kept his eyes open for a dog and soon saw a big mixed breed mutt lying on the front porch, out of the rain. As soon as he saw the dog, he gave a yell, "Hello the house! I've had an accident and I need some help!" The dog stood and suddenly began barking loudly. Many long minutes passed, with the dog remaining on the porch barking, before Donnelly saw the flare of a lamp being turned up and knew someone in the house had awakened to his call.

The door to the cabin slowly opened and an old man holding a lamp in his left hand and big double-barreled shotgun in his right came out. Stopping on the porch the man shouted to be heard in the rain, "Who's there? Did I hear y'all say somethin' 'bout an accident?"

"Yes, my horse slipped in the mud a little after midnight and I've been walking ever since. Seems the fall broke his front right leg and I had to shoot 'em."

"I've had to do that a few times so come on in, but come very slowly. I gotta warn ya though, ya make one false move and I'll fill yer ass full of lead from old Betsy here and she's a good shotgun. Keep your hands up where I can see 'em until I know more 'bout ya."

Taylor gave a grin and moved toward the house. As he stepped up on the porch, the dog growled but did not move toward him. The old farmer had moved off to the side, and as Donnelly stepped into the cabin, the old man moved in behind him. The farmer placed the lamp on a table in the center of the room, aimed the scattergun at Donnelly and said, "Sit and let's talk a bit."

"I do appreciate you giving me shelter, that rain was hard on me after a few hours." Donnelly spoke and gave big warm grin.

"Hell, I reckon so, 'cause it's been raining like a horse pissin' on a flat rock all night. Now, who are ya and what do ya need from us." The old man asked, his eyes watching Taylor closely.

"My name is Captain Thomas Banks and I was in Independence taking care of army business. When I finished late yesterday I started on my way back to Saint Louis, but like I told you outside, my horse slipped in the mud and broke a leg. I'd like to buy a horse or mule from you, if you have an extra one you could let me have."

The old man leaned to his right and spat into a brass spittoon near the wall and replied, "Nope, I cain't let ya have either. I only got one ridin' hoss and one mule to do the plowin' with, and I need 'em both."

"I'll pay you top dollar."

"Not interested a-tall, 'cause I need 'em like I said."

A middle-aged woman entered the room, moved over to her husband's side, and placed her right hand on his left shoulder. For a few moments, it was quiet, but finally the old man said, "My name is Ralf Bamford and this is my wife, Ella."

Taylor notice that Ella Bamford was on the high side of forty, with a big bust, narrow waist, and wide hips. Her hair was blond and her eyes, from what he could tell in the dim light, were blue. Ella was wearing an old cotton gown that suggested there was a lot of woman under the simple cotton material. *She's still one hell of a good lookin' woman even at her age*, Taylor thought as he gave a big warm smile and said, "Sorry to drag you out of bed at this hour, I'm Sergeant Thomas Banks." At the last second he'd remembered he was wearing the coat taken from Sergeant Church.

Ella returned the smile and replied, "I overheard what you told Ralf and I'm sorry we can't help you, but we are poor people Sergeant. Let me put on some coffee and while you have a cup I'll fix us some breakfast. And, Ralf, you put that dang scattergun down a-fore it goes off and you hurt somebody. Can't you see our visitor is a soldier in the army and a gentleman?"

The old man grumbled, placed his shotgun against the wall, and had just pulled out a chair when Ella said, "Ralf you need to go out and get me some firewood so I can get the coffee to boiling and breakfast done."

The old man went out for the wood and as Taylor sat at the table he decided when the old man came back in with his arms full of wood he'd make his move. The place wasn't much to look at inside, but it was clean, and Donnelly doubted they had much besides the horse he desperately needed. *I'll have to kill 'em both*, he thought, *but what have I got to lose? I'll hang if they catch me again, no matter how many killings I do now or in the future.*

The front door opened and Ralf walked in with his arms full of dry firewood saying, "Still raining out there, but the sky looks like it won't last long. I suspect it'll stop before noon."

When the old man reached the wood box beside the fireplace, Taylor pulled his pistol and fired, striking the old man in the middle of his back. Ralf fell hard against the fireplace, blood, and gore slowly dripped down the stones as he fell to the dirt floor of the cabin with his body jerking. Ella gave a loud piercing scream of terror and moved to her husband's side.

Donnelly quickly stood and grasped the big scattergun from the wall, and pointing it at Ella he said in a menacing voice, "Move away from the old man and come sit at the table. And, I mean do it *now*."

Ella, from tough frontier stock, did as ordered but she replied, "You didn't have to kill Ralf. He was a kind old man and I'm sure eventually he would have given or sold you a mount."

"Shut up, I don't want to hear another word from you, or I'll shoot you next."

Ella didn't speak, but her eyes reflected the deep hate she felt for Donnelly. No sooner had she sat in the chair than Taylor had her place her hands behind her back and he tied them with a piece of rope he found near the wood box. He then tied her legs to the chair and once secured, he moved around the house until he found a long piece of rope, which he brought back into the kitchen. He tied a noose on one end of the rope and placed it around her neck, while the other end he secured to a rear chair leg. *Now if she moves too much the noose will tighten and choke her*, he thought as he sat down at the table.

He watched her for a few minutes and grew angry when she did not look scared. If anything her eyes reflected anger and determination, both of which Taylor could not understand, because he expected her to be terrified. Angry, he picked up his horse pistol from the table and reloaded it.

Little did the Captain know that Ella had grown up on the frontier and had been in more than one tight spot during her long life and yet she'd survived. She'd fought Indians, thieves, bandits and others who had attempted at one time or the other to kill her. Ella was no fool and she realized she had to be careful or this one would kill her, he had the look of an insane man in his eyes.

Taylor stood, walked behind her, and reaching over her shoulder he ran his right hand down the side of her neck to her right breast. Ella stiffened, but she did not move at his touch, because she felt the barrel of the loaded pistol at the nape of her neck. He cupped her in his hand and leaned over to kiss the side of her neck. *You might take me, but I'll kill you for it one day*, Ella thought as her body tensed up in anger.

Taylor, feeling excited at the thought of having a woman, walked to the counter and pulled a large butcher knife from a small tub Ella used to wash her dishes. Returning to the woman, he reached down, cut the rope at the chair leg, and then he cut her feet free, leaving only her hands tied behind her back and her neck secured by the loose noose. In a low voice Donnelly said, "Stand up woman. Me and you are going to the bedroom for a little fun. You make one wrong move and I'll blow your head off. Do you understand me?"

"I hear you and I'll do what you tell me to do. But, I got a big family around here and when they find out what you've done to me and mine you'll die for it."

Taylor gave a loud laugh and replied, "They'll have to stand in line to kill my ass. Now come on, I want us to be good friends."

He suddenly jerked the rope around her neck, which caused her to choke and with a loud laugh he reached up and quickly loosened the noose. Taylor led her to the bedroom, made her lay down, and then he secured her neck rope to the headboard of a big brass bed. Returning to the kitchen he quickly returned with more rope and forcing her legs apart, he tied each ankle tightly. Then, he tied the rope from each ankle to the brass footboard of the bed. Reaching over and grasping her gown at the neck with both hands, he slowly ripped it from her.

"Ella, you're a mighty fine looking woman and I'm going to enjoy this very much."

"Go to hell!" Ella quickly spat out in anger and shame.

Taylor lowered his pants and then crawled up in the bed between the woman's legs. As tears rolled down Ella's cheeks, Donnelly ignored her.

A little more than five minutes later, he was finished. Then, standing beside the bed he said, "I'll go and fix me something to eat. Once I finish eating, I'll come back and we can do this again. I expect we'll do this off and on most of the day."

And then you'll kill me, Ella thought and shuddered.

Ella could soon smell the ham frying in the kitchen and at one point, she heard the man leave the house for a few minutes. *He's most likely getting the eggs and milk, so he can have a good breakfast,* she thought and checked her hands once more. She'd been working the bonds on her hands off and on for the better part of an hour, as the man ate and then started ransacking the house. Ella knew he'd find little, because while Ralf and she had worked their asses off, the small rock farm had paid very little. One year it would be a drought, the next year grasshoppers, and then a flood, always something to ruin the crops. They were always just a step away from getting ahead and more than once they had considered moving back east, but now with Ralf dead there would be no move.

Finally, almost two hours after Taylor had raped her, she felt the cloth on her hand slip and she was free. Removing the noose from her neck, she reached over and picked up a pair of scissors she had placed near the bed on a nightstand. The night before she'd been making Ralf a shirt and her sewing equipment was on the stand. She then loosened her feet, and did the same with the neck noose, so the ropes could be pulled off easily, and placed the scissors under her back. She reached up and placed the noose back around her neck.

Three hours after the first assault, Taylor returned with an evil grin on his face and said, "Time for another round, my dear."

Ella didn't reply, but grasped the scissors tightly in her right hand behind her back as Taylor climbed between her legs. She knew the best time to strike would be when the man was distracted. As soon as he lay on top of her, Ella pulled the scissors from behind her back and tried to stab the man in the back. But, Taylor, seeing her arm flash in the light, knocked it aside quickly and laughed. Ella, not to be taken lightly, swung her arm once more and stuck him high in the left shoulder. Screaming in deep pain, Taylor rolled from the bed and landed on the floor.

Ella quickly pulled her feet and head loose from the bed frame, rolled from the bed and ran from the house toward the thick forest of oak trees just behind her cabin. She was as naked as the day she was born and as she ran, she felt disgust that Taylor had used her. At first, she was unsure where to run, but then she remembered her brother's cabin was less than five miles away and she knew she could be there in under an hour.

Taylor felt a horrible rage as Ella ran from him. He followed her for about a mile planning to cut her throat with her own butcher knife, but turned back when his shoulder started to bleed freely and the pain worsened. *I've got to get back, bandage this wound and get the hell out of there*, he thought as he turned around and staggered back to the cabin.

Thirty minutes later, his shoulder bandaged with an old rag, Taylor gathered up fifty dollars in coin he'd found in the house, along with a few pieces of smoked meat, and mounted an old work horse. He glanced back at the cabin, now in flames, as he turned to the north and started out at a walk. He figured he'd ride north a few miles, then turn east for a bit, and then finally turn south once again. Taylor knew if he could reach the Missouri Ozark Mountains he could hide out in a cave for a few weeks to rest up. Once he felt strong enough, he'd head back to the mountains and settle things with that big black man and his sidekick Cotton Top. *Yes*, Taylor thought, *the time is coming when I'll have my revenge. Hell, I might even turn your black ass over to some slave hunters, now wouldn't that be just dandy?*

CHAPTER 14

Butterfield did busy work all morning in the store by placing goods on shelves, dusting, and generally doing work he'd put off for months. Skeeter was doing better, except he was still unable to get around and spent his days in bed. The wounds were healing, but the old trader worried about whether or not the man would ever be able to walk again. The last arrow he had removed from Skeeter's back still had Butterfield worried and he knew there was no place in the mountains for a man who couldn't walk.

Hatch and Taterhead returned from their hunting trip a few hours after Quinch had left for the horses. Immediately noticing the men the company man left behind, the two old trappers had turned the meat of two deer over to Butterfield, loaded up their horses and rode away. According to Hatch, they were headed up into the shining mountains and making a camp, so they could start taking beaver a bit early. But, Butterfield suspected they just wanted to avoid trouble with company men.

Skeeter awoke and suddenly announced, "I'm getting up and out of this bed in a few minutes."

"Well, you can try. Ya just be careful ya don't tear that wound open again or there'll be hell to pay." The old trader said and then thought, *I hope ya can at least stand, because if ya can stand the injury to yer back ain't as bad as I think it might be.*

"Can ya come over heah and give me a hand? My back is stiff and I'll need help to get out bed."

Butterfield made his way to the man's side, helped Skeeter move his legs over the side of the bed, and then placing an arm under him helped him to his feet. The injured man's legs were weak and he wobbled a bit, but he did manage to stand.

"I'm gonna walk to that table and have me a cup of real coffee, but I might fall on my ass, so keep your eyes on me." Skeeter said and then gave a light chuckle.

The old trader stayed beside Skeeter as the mountain man took his first step. His face turned white with pain, but then he took another step. He shuffled his feet like an old man, but eventually he stood by the table. Pulling out a chair with a loud noise, he sat down. Giving a very week grin he asked, "Can I have a cup of coffee?"

"Why sure, I'll bring ya one in a second." Butterfield replied and then thought, *thank God he can walk. There ain't much use for a mountain man out here that can't walk and it scares me to think what a man hurt like that might do to himself.*

Bringing a tin cup filled with hot coffee to the table, the old trader placed it in front of Skeeter, pulled out a chair and sat down. Meeting the injured man's eyes he asked, "Did you have a lot of pain when you moved over here?"

"Fair amount, but nothin' I cain't live with. I figure to be up and about every day until my back gains some strength back." Skeeter replied as he picked up his cup and took a small sip of the hot liquid.

"Good for you," Butterfield said and then quickly added, "Cotton has gone off with some company men to get horses from the Sioux. I half way expect Nate and Doc back by the end of the week, maybe, and then I suspect things will get back to normal. Hell, I ain't had this many visitors in years!"

Skeeter gave a loud laugh, grimaced from a sudden bout of pain, and said, "What are the company men doing around here? I thought they were supplied out of Saint Louie?"

Butterfield quickly explained the attack on the company men by the Indians, the loss of their supplies, and how they'd come to him for more gear and food. "I'll make a pretty penny on their order too, 'cause it looks like the Blackfoot cleaned them boys out. Near as I can tell they've ordered well over two thousand dollars worth of stuff, but I ain't tallied it all up yet. I'll bet you it took me two days just to pull and weigh the dry goods they wanted. Mostly they want powder, lead, tobacco, beans, bacon, and whatnot to get 'em through the winter, but eight men use a lot of supplies.

"That they do, but I ain't never been a company man and don't ever intend to be one either. I'll stay a free trapper for as long as a single pew makes me some money."

At that point one of Quinch's men, a feller Butterfield knew as Hawk, stuck his head in the door and announced, "Riders comin' and it looks to be Quinch."

Picking up his double-barreled scattergun, Butterfield turned to Skeeter and said, "Ya stay right in that chair until I get back. I suspect it's Cotton and Quinch, but I ain't sure."

Skeeter nodded and picked up his cup to take another drink.

Butterfield was standing on the porch when he saw the riders nearing and right off he picked out Cotton's white hair. The old trader walked over to the wall by the door and rested his gun against it.

As the riders rode up, Cotton said, "We're back and these boys got some damned good horses for the trade too."

"Glad to hear that. Quinch, I got your supplies ready to go for ya and I'll tally up the bill in just a little while. Did ya all see anything of the Crow or Blackfoot while moving about?"

Quinch gave a light laugh and replied, "According to the Sioux, the Crow have enough problems right now. Seems they can't seem to agree on what they want to do, fight or make peace. And, of course, if we'd seen the Blackfoot there would be less of us sitting here right now. No, it was quiet for now, but your guess is as good as mine for how long it will stay that way."

"Buffalo Hump said the Crow council has put a stop to the raids on white men for the time bein', but that won't stop a lone brave or two from attackin'." Cotton spoke and then asked, "Ya still got some whiskey in there? I am painin' just a little."

Butterfield laughed and replied, "Quinch ya come in and I'll tally up yer bill. Cotton, I figured ya left too soon with that injury, so come on in and I'll give ya a few shots of whiskey to help kill the pain a mite."

The two men quickly dismounted and as they walked up on the porch Quinch turned and said, "Zachariah you see these horses are taken care of and be ready to move as soon as I finish things in the store."

"I'll get the horses ready and the men too."

As the two men entered the small room of the trading post, they both spotted Skeeter at the table, Quinch nodded, and Cotton walked over and pulled out a chair. Sitting down, Skeeter gave Cotton a big crooked grin and said, "By damn, I'm glad to see ya up and moving around. When I left ya looked near dead, now ya jess look like hell."

Butterfield quickly brought Cotton a cup of trader's whiskey and then walked back to his counter. Pulling out his ledger, he added a few figures and said, "Quinch, the total bill comes to two thousand and twenty dollars."

"Damn, that's a lot of money."

"Don't forget that includes two new Hawkens, three pistols and all of the other supplies and gear you needed. Hell, those traps a lone you need cost almost a third of yer bill."

Quinch reached into his pocket, pulled out the letter of authorization and filled in the amount. Handing it to Butterfield he said, "There you go. All you have to do is get it to a bank or back to Astor in Saint Louis and you'll have your money in cash."

The old trader gave a big grin and then winked at Quinch as he said, "I'll have one of my men take it to Saint Louis and turn it over to the bank there."

Quinch shrugged his shoulders and then said, "Can we start to load the stuff now? I want to be moving toward the mountains as quickly as we can. The weather is turning colder with each new day, so the skins will be prime in a little while."

"Yep, have yer men come in and they can start moving things out." Butterfield spoke as he moved toward a back room in the store to pull the supplies forward to the main area.

Less than twenty minutes later the supplies were loaded, the men mounted, and Quinch said from his saddle, "Butterfield, I do thank you for the support you've give our company. Most traders would not have helped us, so I'll put a good word in with Astor when I see him next.

Butterfield gave a loud laugh and said, "Ya just do that Quinch. Ya fellers take care and keep yer topknots screwed on tight. The Crow or Blackfoot might still be on the warpath."

"Aye, we'll do that!" Quinch yelled as he pulled his horse to the right and started a slow walk toward the mountains.

Looking over at Cotton, who was standing beside him, Butterfield asked, "How many of them do ya think will still be alive come spring?"

Cotton Top put his hands on his hips and replied, "Most of 'em. Quinch runs a tight ship and if they follow his orders few if any of them will go under."

"Let's get back inside, this air has a nip to it." The trader spoke, gave a slight shudder, and re-entered the store.

Each day Skeeter would climb stiffly from the bed and wobble around the inside of the store on weak legs. He spent hours just walking in a circle around the small room, but with each days exercise he felt his body growing stronger. As the days turned into a week, he finally announced at the table over breakfast, "Today I'll go out and chop a little firewood. I need to get out of this place for a while or I'll go crazy."

Butterfield, concerned the man might still tear his injury open, replied, "You can split some kindlin' but don't take on the big wood yet. I don't think yer strong enough to do that right now. By the end of next week though, I suspect you'll be almost back to normal."

Skeeter gave a grin and replied, "Ok, I'll just do the kindlin' until I get tired and I don't think that will take long. I've not had any serious exercise since I was shot, so I'm about as weak as a newborn puppy right now."

"Yer an ugly puppy too!" Cotton joked as he lifted the last piece of fried sow belly to his mouth.

The three men laughed and then Skeeter stood and said, "I'll be back directly. I won't be long."

Staying at the table and sharing coffee, Butterfield and Cotton were quiet for a long time. Both men were thinking about different things and had no urge to make small talk. Finally, after he finished his coffee Butterfield said, "That Skeeter is one tough man. Most of the mountain men I know would still be in bed and them flatlanders back east would be cryin' for their mommas. I think Skeeter knows the best thing for him to do is slowly get some strength back into his body."

"He knows and he's doin' it too. Let's just hope he don't do too much and pull that injury open."

"Well, he might, but I don't think so. He knows if he does that he'll go back to bed for a long spell. As long as he just splits kindlin' he'll be alright. Only the next thing he'll want to do is go huntin' and that'll be in a day or two. When he decides to go you'll have to take 'em." The trader said with a grin.

"I fig'ered as much. That won't be no problem for me and I'll stay close by so he won't tire out on me. We'll start on short hunts and as he gains strength we'll go out further. And, besides, we need the meat."

The next day, the weather was cold with gray clouds overhead and Cotton knew any deer with any sense would be eating as much as possible in the event the weather turned worse. He hoped they'd jump a deer close by the fort, so Skeeter wouldn't wear himself out trying to get fresh meat. It was just after dawn when the two men stepped from the store and moved down a small trail that led to the woods.

As they moved both of the men scanned the woods to avoid ambush and to spot any game in the area. They walked just a little over a mile and then stopped so Skeeter could rest for a few minutes. As they sat under a large pine tree, Cotton suddenly saw movement down the trail from them. Elbowing Skeeter he said in Indian sign language, "Movement on trail. Look closely where we have yet to go."

Skeeter, winded and hurting a little, looked down the trail, saw movement and then quickly signed back, "Deer."

"Are you sure?" Cotton signed.

Grinning, Skeeter signed, "I saw the antlers of a big buck and I saw the head, it's a deer for sure."

"What do we do?" Cotton asked with a quick movement of his hands and fingers.

"Wait. I see more movement!" Skeeter spoke just above a whisper.

Long minutes passed and then the deer suddenly broke and ran into the woods on the far side of the trail. As the two men watched, two Blackfoot braves boldly walked up the trail right at them. The two experienced mountain men moved back further into the branches of the tree. Cotton signed, "They will see our tracks in a few more steps."

"Yes, kill them." Skeeter spoke with his hands.

The two white men were watching the warriors as they moved along the trail when suddenly one stopped, bent down and said something in the Blackfoot tongue. No sooner had the man spoken than the loud report of Cotton's Hawken rifle shattered the air and the brave was knocked ass over tea kettle in the grass beside the trail. The second brave gave a loud war cry and ran right toward the pine tree and the two mountain men.

Skeeter lined up his sights, took a deep breath, and as he let it out he gently squeezed the trigger on his rifle. The only sound was a loud click as the rifle misfired. Cotton stepped from the protective cover of the pine, pointed his horse pistol at the brave and jerked the trigger. The brave spun around and fell to the ground, but in less than a minute, he was back on his feet with blood flowing down his left shoulder. Knowing his bow was useless due to his injury; the Blackfoot warrior cast it aside and pulled his skinning knife.

Cotton, knowing Skeeter was in no shape to fight the Black-foot, moved toward the man with a knife in his right hand and tomahawk in his left. The two men circled each other, each looking for an opening or some weakness in his opponent, but found none. Abruptly the brave gave a horrendous scream and ran right at Cotton, the impact knocking them both to the ground. Around and around they rolled until they stopped with the warrior on top. Giving a big grin, the warrior started down with his knife blade. Cotton, still weak from his earlier back injury could do little against the Blackfoot's strength.

Just before the knife blade touched his chest there was a shot and the warrior's head exploded in a mist of blood and bone. A split second later, he fell to the grass beside Cotton Top. The old mountain man realized Skeeter had just saved his life.

"I didn't mean to interfere with your fight there old coon, but you was cuttin' it too close for comfort." Skeeter said with a grin as he helped Cotton to his feet.

"Thank you kindly, Skeeter, it was touch and go there fer a minute 'er two."

"Waugh! You would have taken him, except I just made things move along a little faster is all. Come on, let's move, I don't feel comfortable out here right now."

The two men slowly made their way back to the trading post, half expecting a fight any minute. Things remained quiet and soon they were stepping up on the porch of the trading post. As they stepped inside Butterfield walked up with a rifle in his hands and asked, "How come I hear all of them shots? It don't take that many shots to down a deer, or did ya run into In-juns?"

"Blackfoot, but there were only two of 'em. Have they been around here this much in the past?" Skeeter asked as he moved toward the table, his back hurting him once more.

"No, not often, but they might have been looking for Crows. Hard to say, but this is the first time I know of that they've been this close to the tradin' post." Butterfield replied as he placed his rifle on the counter.

Pulling the makings of a smoke from his possibles bag, Cotton said, "They were wearin' paint and moving away from the tradin' post, so most likely they were lookin' for Crow or Sioux. We didn't take their hair, 'cause we wasn't sure if more of them were around or not, and didn't want to take the time."

Butterfield gave a light chuckle and said, "No matter if others were around or not, I'll bet you come mornin' them two bodies will be gone."

The next morning, less than an hour after sunrise, Cotton went back to the site of the short battle—and both bodies were gone.

Chapter 15

Nate moved his horse slow toward the site where the Crow had killed Moses, though he kept his eyes moving, constantly surveying his surroundings. He suspected the Indians were long gone, but he'd not assume anything. He pulled his rifle from its scabbard as he neared the spot where a fire had once burned. The big man quickly dismounted and with his rifle in hand, he began a search for the preacher man. Walking toward the east, he soon spotted the remains of Moses hanging head down, the rawhide rope still tied to a limb on a big oak tree. The body of Moses was spinning in the wind as Nate walked up to see how the dead preacher had died. The man'd been lanced in the chest and while the wound itself was most likely fatal, the Crow had made sport of the preacher and it looked like they'd played with him for hours.

From what Nate could tell, the man had been scalped alive and then hung from the tree like a pig at a slaughter. At some point, the warriors had cut long pieces of flesh from the man's legs, arms, and chest, and Nate knew from experience the man had been alive. Then, once they grew bored, the Crow had started a fire under Moses, so his head and brain would cook and then burn. His head was burnt black, face melted, and his shoulders and back showed evidence of terrible burns from the fire. Nate reached up as he pulled his knife and cut the man from the rope. The body fell hard, landing in the long dead fire pit. The mountain man then walked to his horse, removed a spare blanket and then covered the body of preacher Moses Matson.

Riding back to Doc and Waters, Nate slowly shook his head as he met the two men and said, "The spear didn't kill 'em like you thought. He died hard, Moses did."

"They play with him a bit?" Doc asked as he pulled a twist of tobacco out and cut off a long piece with his penknife.

"Yep, they surely did and you know how rough the Crows play when they've a mind to do the job."

"I know them red boys can be purely hell on a live man."

"T . . . they tortured him?" Waters asked in disbelief as his eyes widened.

"That they did Waters and they kept him alive for hours as they did the job too." Nate said as he turned in his saddle to meet the man's eyes. As soon as eye contact was made he said, "We need to get him up in a tree. He's been dead a spell, but most critters won't eat burnt meat, unless they are pretty damned hungry. We're lucky this snow storm passed through too, 'cause most of the serious meat eaters are still holed up. So, what the Crow didn't burn ain't been chewed on. "

Less than an hour later, the body was moved to the base of a big oak tree. Nate wrapped the dead man up better in the old blanket, tied ropes around the body to keep the cover on it, and slowly shook his head at the senseless death of a good man. *He should have stayed back east,* the big man thought, *where his kind need to be.*

Waters sat by a small fire, still sick over the appearance of his friends tortured body. Nate had made him look at Moses and he'd told him, "Take long hard look deacon, because this is what Injuns will do to you if they take you alive. I ain't doin' this to make you sick but you need to know the ways of the people you come out here to preach religion to." Waters had fallen to his knees and puked. He'd puked until he had nothing to come out, except green bile from the very pit of his stomach. Then he sat by the fire for almost an hour, sick, confused, and scared to death.

"Get over here deacon; we need yer help to get Moses up in this tree." Doc said as he moved closer to the tree.

Waters walked to the tree and watched as Doc climbed up to a wide fork in the trunk and lowered a rawhide rope. Nate tied the rope around both of Moses' feet and then motioned for Doc to start pulling. As the body started to rise Nate said, "Help me lift him as high as we can, that'll make it easier on Doc as he pulls the body up."

Waters lifted near the head and as the body rose, his right hand slipped into the blanket and he felt the dry crumbly burnt skin flake off on his fingers. Quickly pulling his hand away, he wiped it on his pant leg, leaned over and puked.

"Damn it Waters, either help or get the hell out of my way!" Nate said brusquely.

Grasping the left shoulder of the dead man, Waters lifted until he felt Doc pulling and the body started to slowly slide up the side of the tree. Once Moses' body was at the fork in the tree, Doc pulled the dead man over and placed him securely in the wide fork of the tree. Then, as Waters watched, Doc ran the rawhide rope around the body a few times to keep it in place and then tied the rope securely. As soon as the job was finished the mountain man climbed down from the tree and said, "Deacon, would you say a few words over Moses?"

Nate and Moses removed their hats as Waters said in a low voice, "Lord, our brother Moses Matson was a good God fearin' man and you know that. He came out this way to bring your word to the same savages that ended up killing him. I don't know why you let a good man like Moses to die like he did, but the Good Book says the Lord works in mysterious ways, and I guess you do. I'll be heading back east Lord, because while Moses had the dream to preach to the Indians I didn't. I came along to help protect him, but I didn't do the job worth a damn. He was my best friend, God, and now he's dead. Ashes to ashes and dust to dust. Amen."

"That was downright nice, Waters." Nate said and then placed his hat back on his head.

"Well, where to now, Nate?" Doc asked as he put his hat on and then lowered the brim a little to shade his eyes.

"Butterfield's trading post, just like we planned all along. We got partners to check on, supplies to get, and Waters here can join a group in the spring headin' back to Saint Louie. From there he can head on back east by himself."

"What am I to do until spring? Is there no way I can return quicker?" Waters asked looking at Nate.

The man gave a loud laugh and replied, "No, you won't be able to leave before spring, because in a little while these mountain passes will fill up with snow so high you'd never get through and no one will be moving east until after the trappin' season is finished and the passes clear. If you spend the winter with Butterfield, he'll put your butt to work choppin' wood, taken care of his stock, and doin' odd jobs around the tradin' post, so you'll earn your keep. He'll feed you and maybe even slip you a few coins when you leave in the spring."

"But, it won't be spring for another five months or so!"

"Smart man we got here Nate, he knows when spring mighten come. Look, Waters, this ain't like back east where ya can jump on a stagecoach, board a train, or even ride yer horse durin' bad weather. When the snow starts to fly here and the temperature drops, well, there ain't nothin' movin' and I mean not a blasted thing. When along comes December you'll be glad you're nice and warm in the store and eatin' good too. So, all I can tell ya is, wait until the weather breaks and then go back home. Some men are made for this type of livin' but I can see right now, you ain't one of 'em. And, I don't mean no disrespect towards you a-tall."

"If that is all I can do, then I'll do it because I have little choice in the matter. Doc, I took your comment about me as the truth and it is. I have no reason to be out here and it's only by the grace of God I didn't die alongside Moses. I see that as a sign or a warning if you will, that I should not be here."

Doc nodded and said, "Mayhap you're right Waters, but right now it's too cold to stand here and talk about what God wants you to do or not do. Let's mount up and head toward Butter-field's place. I want to see how Cotton Top fairs and if he's healed up. If he is, we'll start for the mountains. Those beaver are near prime about now."

Three days later the men spotted the trading post from the side of a low hill and slowly walked their horses toward the place. It wasn't much to look at, but it offered a reasonable amount of safety, hot food, and the chance to share a bottle of rye. Waters was saddle sore and bone tired, because the two mountain men had traveled long, fast, and hard. They rode from sunup to near dusk each day and the deacon had never traveled so quickly. Additionally, he'd gotten very little sleep on the trip, because a horse guard was in place every night and all pulled a shift. But, now that the end was in sight he relaxed in his saddle.

As they rode up to the trading post, Cotton Top stepped out the door with a Hawken in his hands. Seeing Doc and Nate he said with a grin, "Howdy. I guess things went alright when you delivered Donnelly to the army, huh?"

"The trip was smoother than a Yankee horse trader makin' a fast sawbuck. He gave us no trouble at all on the way there." Doc spoke, dismounted and tied his bay to the hitching post.

Followed by Nate and Waters, Doc stepped up on the porch and entered the trading post. Seeing Skeeter at the table sipping coffee the three men went to the table and joined him. Butterfield brought out a large coffee pot and three tin cups. He didn't say a word until the cups were filled and he sat down at the table. Looking at Nate and Doc he said softly, "Army dispatch man showed up here two days ago and said Donnelly escaped on his way back east. According to the man, Donnelly killed two guards on the boat and jumped off in the middle of Missouri territory. He also said the remaining guard heard Donnelly threaten many times to come back here and kill the two of ya."

Nate gave a laugh and said, "Well, let him come and we'll dance a mite."

"Yep," Doc said with a smile on his face and his eyes dancing with mirth, "he knows where we live, except he'll have to find us. These mountains are high and wide, so he'll be lookin' for a long time before he finds us."

"That's if the Injuns don't kill his ass first." Cotton spoke and let out a loud laugh.

"Nate, Doc, this ain't a joke. Accordin' to the army, Donnelly talked constantly about gettin' his revenge on ya two." The trader spoke, picked up his coffee cup and took a sip.

"Butterfield, I've never ran from a man or a fight. While I don't go looking for a fight often, it's never without good cause. I'll not run nor hide from Donnelly, but when he finds me I think he'll find me a hard man to kill." Nate replied with his eyes narrowed to slits and his voice flat.

"I'm the same way and if he starts a dance with me, he'd better be able to pay the band. I won't be so careful to take him alive the next time." Doc spoke in anger as he looked around the table.

"Well, now there's a two thousand dollar reward on the man, dead or alive. Seems the army was notified of a man bein' killed between Independence and Saint Louis, and is wife was raped a couple of times by Donnelly. She identified him from a wanted poster and the injuries to his face."

"Sumbitch!" Doc screamed as his fist hit the table hard, "I can see killin' a man over just about anything from a bottle of rye to a good horse, but there is no cause to ever take a woman against her will. Captain Taylor Donnelly has just signed his death warrant as far as I am concerned, because I'll kill his ass on sight."

"There's always the chance he'll never come back here. I mean he knows we know what he looks like and by now he should have figured out the woman identified him, so maybe he'll head back east to hide." Skeeter said and then leaned back in his chair.

Nate looked over at Skeeter and said, "Nope, he'll be back. See, a man like Donnelly gets revenge in his head and that's all he can think about. It starts to eat at him like a cancer, until is finally consumes his whole being. Besides, now that he has another murder tied to him, along with a rape charge, he must realize he's livin' on borrowed time. He knows he's a dead man once caught again and he's got nothin' to lose by coming back here. Hell, he might even want to die."

"That's foolish talk, 'cause no man wants to die." Butterfield suddenly said as he leaned toward Nate.

"Oh, Donnelly might not realize he wants to die, but see at some point earlier in his life he was decent man and a man like that has a strong sense of right and wrong. Not to mention, I'll bet ya, he regrets the turn his life has taken. He might not even know all of that, but in the back of his mind —he knows it. And, even if he gets away from all of this, he'll find it hard to forget what he has done and sooner or later he'll have to face himself and what he has become."

"I guess so," Butterfield spoke slowly and then added, "only the way things are lookin' now he'll be dead long before he'll ever have to face the fact that he was once a decent man. And, then all of his wrong doin' will be between him and Saint Peter."

Realizing he'd not introduced Waters, Nate quickly explained what had happened and how the man came to be with them. Pushing his hat back to the rear of his head, the big black man asked, "So, do you have the need of a good man until spring, Butterfield?"

"Well, now, I do in fact. But, Samuel Waters, ya have to keep in mind I have a rough bunch of men comin' in here to trade and most of 'em aren't exactly Christians. They're men of sin, just like I am, I guess. I'll let ya stay here and work for yer room and board, and in the end I'll pay ya twenty dollars a month, except no preachin' at the customers or me. How does that sound?"

Waters nodded and replied, "I can do my work and keep my mouth shut. I have seen enough out here to understand why some of these mountain men are so rough and crude in lifestyle and language."

Cotton narrowed his eyes and said, "Ya callin' me crude?"

"W . . . well, I -"Waters started to speak.

Cotton gave a might snort and said, "I guess I am, but I don't know no better!"

The men at the table all laughed and when it quieted down, Butterfield said, "Come with me Samuel and I'll explain yer duties to ya right now. As things come up, ya'll get more work, but these chores will do for the time bein'."

Walking to the back room of the store with Waters the old trader said, "Ya'll sweep in here and the main room each day. I expect ya to start the fire and put the coffee on as soon as ya get up every mornin'."

Waters laughed and replied, "I get up early, near dawn, so that's no problem."

"Good, now follow me outside and we'll cover the rest of yer chores."

Less than thirty minutes later, the two men returned to the table and sat down. Nate looked over at Waters and asked, "Has he got you milkin' the cow, feedin' the chickens, choppin' wood, and bringin' water from the well?"

Waters chuckled and replied, "Yep, he does at that, plus a few more things. But, it's less work than I did on my own farm back east. I don't mind hard work and I'm an early riser, so I'll have most of the things I'm to do finished well before lunch time."

"Good, I'm glad to see you'll be taken care of until time for you to leave. You're a good man, Samuel Waters, and don't feel bad the mountains aren't for you. Many a man has come out here thinking one thing, but finding another. This is a harsh land we live in and very few men are tougher than the land. Hell, if the Injuns don't kill you, why some big critter, illness or accident will. I think you're a smart man to decide to go back and I respect you for being man enough to do what is right. Pride, Samuel, has killed many a good man."

Samuel Waters lowered his eyes and said, "Nate, when I was taken by the Crow, I knew right then and there I was not man enough for this kind of life. I was scared to death and it's hard for me to admit it, but I was a coward."

Nate snorted and replied, "Any man who is not scared when Injuns take him alive is a damned idiot. You had reason to be frightened Samuel and it does not mean you were or are a coward. You saw with your own eyes what the Crow did to Moses and that is what they do to most captives. Sometimes being scared is the only way a man can survive. No, you are no coward in my eyes."

"Nor in mine." Doc quickly said as he leaned over and spat a long brown stream of tobacco juice into an old tarnished brass spittoon beside his chair.

Skeeter, not to be left out of the conversation, said, "I was tooken by the Blackfoot once and I got so damned scared I peed my pants. Since it was at night nobody ever knew, but bein' scared of Injuns is downright healthy in my book. They'll cut on ya, burn ya and poke things out before they kill ya."

"Yep, that's a hard fact and that's why I'll always save one bullet for me." Cotton spoke quickly and looked around the table at the other men.

"I need to change the subject a mite." Butterfield said and then continued, "When ya head back east Waters, would ya carry a letter to the bank for me? I'll see ya are paid to do the job."

"Sure, I'll do it, but why me?"

The trader laughed and replied, "Who else do I know that's headin' east after the snows that I can trust? I figure with ya bein' a man of God, ya'll treat my letter just like it was yer own, so it'll be safe enough. I'd imagine some of the company men will be comin' by here to pick up some extra supplies before they head back to Saint Louis, so ya'll be able to ride with 'em."

"Well," Nate said as he stood, "Cotton, me and you need to get our butts up in the mountains or we'll make no money this year. Doc, you and Skeeter are welcome to join up with us if you want."

Doc looked over at Skeeter and asked, "What do ya think Skeeter? Ya want to join this big-assed black man and trap with 'em?"

Skeeter looked as if he was going to say no, when suddenly he said, "It's okay with me on one condition—he don't do the cookin'. Nate, yer one hell of a good man, only ya cain't cook worth a shit."

The small room erupted in laughter and after a few minutes Nate spoke, "Time to get movin'. Butterfield, thanks for the help and if we need any supplies we'll keep ya in mind. Let's hit the trail fellers the shadows grow long.

CHAPTER 16

One would think the further south you rode the warmer it would get, but that's not always true. Donnelly had been riding south for five days before he discovered this simple fact of nature. Suddenly an ice storm hit him and made him hunt a hole to keep from freezing to death. The weather started as a very gentle rain earlier this morning and then by noon the temperature dropped, and within in less than an hour ice was forming. By late afternoon, the sky had turned a pale gray and it was becoming difficult see the horizon in front of him as he rode. Taylor had noticed no cabins or homes the last few days and suspected he was in the northern part of the Missouri Ozark Mountains, but beyond that he knew little of the area. What scared him the most at the moment, was his horse might slip on the ice and break a leg, leaving him on foot in the middle of nowhere.

Spotting a small cave in the side of a hill that ran along the eastern bank of a small shallow river, he crossed over and slowly made his way to just outside the entrance to the cavern. Pulling the shotgun he'd taken when he killed Ralf, he cautiously made his way into the cave with the scattergun at the ready. Donnelly half expected to meet someone, because the weather was so bad, but the dark hole in the ground appeared empty. Entering, he was surprised by the warmth of the cave and then he remembered the words of an old First Sergeant he'd once known, "Caves make a good shelter fer a man in rough weather, be it winter time or summer. A cave is warm durin' the hardest blizzard and cool durin' the hottest weather. But, if ya get trapped in one by yer enemies, watch out fer bullet ricochets from the rock walls and the roof."

The entrance to the cave was big enough to allow Taylor to bring the horse in and though the animal was a bit skittish at the confined space, he finally succeeded. He quickly removed the saddle, blanket, and his supplies from his tired and cold mount. As soon as his gear was stacked in the rear of the cave, he went back out into the freezing weather and gathered up enough fire-wood to keep him warm over night. Since most of the wood was covered with a thick layer of ice, Donnelly reached under the lower limbs of big trees and broke off the squaw wood. Finding a pine tree and using the butcher knife, he'd stolen from Ella's cabin, he scraped off a large blister of pine pitch and quickly returned to the warmth of the cave.

In less than a minute after his return, the pine pitch was burning brightly and as he added kindling the fire grew in size. He kept his fire small, because he really didn't need a fire to stay warm and also he didn't want the light to be seen by anyone in the area. As his fire snapped and crackled as it burned, Taylor picked up the larger pieces of wood and slammed them violently against the wall of the cave to remove most of the ice. He knew dry wood burned brighter and ice coated wood could very well give off too much smoke, and he knew smoke would be spotted or smelled by anyone traveling near the cave.

Opening a large canvas bag, Donnelly pulled out a cast iron skillet, a large slab of smoked bacon, a can of coffee, some flour, as well as an onion. He placed the frying pan on a small bed of red coals and using the knife, he sliced four thick pieces of the pork, putting them in the skillet to fry. As the meat cooked, he mixed a cup of flour with a little water and then sat it aside as he cut the onion in half. He put the unused half of the onion back in the bag and then filled an old can he used as a coffee pot with water, added a handful of coffee grounds, and placed it on the fire. When the coffee was done, he added a little cold water to the can to help settle the grounds, and poured a cup.

After his bacon fried, he removed the meat with the tip of the knife and then dropped cookie size bits of his mixed flour into the grease from the meat. The crude bread bubbled in his pan like pancakes and after a few minutes, he flipped them over with his knife tip.

"Getting low on grub," Donnelly spoke to his horse as he nibbled on his simple meal, "Gonna have to find some more food in a couple of days. You know, horse, I don't think this storm is goin' to let up today at all, so you can plan on spending the night here." Now, Donnelly had been talking to horses as long as he'd been riding them and he thought nothing of carrying on a complete one-sided conversation with his mount. First, it kept the horse comforted and second, it helped Donnelly fight off loneliness as well. Most of the men he knew talked to their horses and it never seemed strange to the man, and besides he was alone, so who could question the sanity of it?

"We're in one hell of a mess right now, too. I've lost all I ever worked for and all because of the money I borrowed from the Officers Open Mess. Of course, killin' of the Colonel and his wife didn't help things much, and running didn't either. But don't you see, I didn't have much of a choice. If I return to Washington, they'll give me a quick courts martial and then hang me. Nope, horse, I cannot allow that to happen.

Leaning back against the wall of the cave, Taylor continued speaking to his horse, "I'm becoming something I don' like much, but I'm bein' forced into it. Just like Ella and Ralf, I didn't mean to kill him or rape her, only something came over me. I felt such desperation and anger when I did what I did to those folks. I ain't proud of what I did, but I needed supplies and Ella just happened to be there. Don't ya see, I didn't have a choice if I wanted to keep livin'."

The old farm horse looked at Donnelly, blinked her eyes a few times, and then went to sleep. As the man looked out of the cave, he saw the freezing rain had turned to snow and it was falling in big lazy flakes. With little else to do, Taylor gulped down the remainder of his coffee, wrapped up in the horse blanket and went to sleep. He only awoke once during the long night and that was when he rolled over on his still hurting shoulder. He'd cried out softly in pain.

The next morning was bitterly cold, with a heavy snow still falling, as Taylor had a quick breakfast of bacon. Then removing his shirt, he cleaned his injury as well as he could with hot water and dirty red cotton rag. He noticed dark red streaks moving up toward his neck and down his chest as well. After his many years in the military, Taylor M. Donnelly knew the signs of festering, or infection as some folks had taken to calling it recently, and knew he had it. The injury scared him, because he'd seen more than one man die from a simple cut or injury that had festered and it was a slow and painful death. It was a death he did not want to experience, because he knew some deaths were harder than others and festering was a dreadful one.

As he put his shirt back on, he heard voices in the snow outside the cave. Leaving his shirt unbuttoned, he picked up the shotgun and moved to the far wall of the cavern and waited. A few minutes later, he heard a voice yell out, "Hello the cave! I smelled your smoke and vondered if you vould share your fire! I'm freezing to death out hier!"

"How many are with you?" Taylor yelled his reply.

"Yust two of us, me and my cousin!"

"Come in slowly, hold your rifles high over your heads, and if you make any sudden moves I'll shoot to kill."

"Ve'll do as you say, because it's cold enough out here to freeze da balls off a grizzly bear!"

Donnelly saw two dark forms slowly appear from the gray mist of the storm and wade through the deep snow toward him. He pulled the hammer back on the big shotgun and waited, though they seemed friendly enough only a man alone could never be sure.

A few seconds' later two partly frozen men dressed like farmers stood beside the fire trying to warm up. Both of the men had frost on their eyebrows and beards, and their cheeks were a bright red from the numbing cold, but they didn't seem to be much of a threat to Donnelly.

"Meines, I mean my, name ist Thomas Warner and my cousin is Richard Spigeman. We live in the Deutsch village of New Burg, vhich ist about three miles from hier, I mean here. Ve vere out hunting deer und came here to varm up. Please excuse me, I have the trouble vith da English sometime."

Donnelly laughed and then said with a grin, "Meine mutter ist deutsch, deshalb spreche ich die Sprache." Taylor's mother was German, as he'd just told the man, so he'd grown up speaking the language fluently, and from that point the whole conversation was conducted in Deutsch.

"My God, your German is very good! Your mother was a very good teacher." The older looking of the two men said with a big grin.

Spigeman was big and fat, with a long unkempt black beard and his eyebrows had grown together. Taylor guessed his age to be near fifty and he'd had a hard life by looking at his scarred face, but he seemed happy enough. Warner was years younger, had a nicely trimmed blond beard, a thin body, and seemed to have a very good education. His bearing was that of an officer and his eyes were constantly moving, as if he was the untrusting sort.

"It's nice to meet you, Thomas and Richard. I'm afraid my German is a bit rusty, but it'll come back as we talk. I've had an accident and I'm unable to clean my wound properly. I had a fight with Indians and my shoulder was hit with an arrow."

"Let me take a look at it, if you will, because I am a doctor. In the Prussian army I served as chief surgeon and know about injuries." The elder Spigeman said as he moved toward Taylor and pulling the man's shirt back he said, "My God, you have an infection."

"Yes, because it is hard for a man alone to treat an injury."

"I will treat you as Thomas keeps watch." Spigeman replied and turning to Warner he said in French, "Ceci n'est pas de blessure d'une flèche, donc garder l'alerte."

The eyes of Thomas grew large and he replied, "Cet homme est-il menteur ?"

Richard simply shrugged his shoulders and placed a pan of water on the fire to boil. Neither German realized Donnelly also spoke French as well as a few other languages.

So, thought Donnelly, *they know the wound is not from an arrow, but they've not yet decided if I am a liar or a threat to them. I guess learning these languages in school and at home was a good thing to do, but I hated it.*

Giving Spigeman a big grin, Donnelly said in French, "Je suis que je vous ai dit. Je ne suis pas de menace à vous et à je thak vous pour votre assistance. Oh, je parle le français, Italien, es-pagnol, et Russe." The two men paled as Taylor told them he also spoke French, Spanish, Italian, and Russian. His mother had had a natural ability to speak many languages and for days at a time, they spoke one language or the other as he was growing up. He'd grown up with the skill of being able to pick up lan-guages easily and it had helped him as an officer in the army, since so many of his men were new arrivals from Europe.

"Your shoulder is in very bad shape and I think we need to head back to our village so I can treat it, or it may kill you. It is not far and we can be there in less than an hour, even with this bad weather." Spigeman stated slowly still shaking his head over the injury.

"Then we will go there. I have no desire to die from festering or infection as you called it. It is a very bad way to die."

"I think it would be wise, if you can, to walk and lead your horse in the snow. The way is rough and the snow is deep in some places. Do you think you could walk that far?"

"Yes, I will do what I must and my name is Taylor."

"Thomas," Spigeman said as he stood, "come and let's prepare Taylor's gear and load his horse. He has few things, so it will not take long. We must get back to the village so I can treat him."

"I heard the talk, we will go." Thomas replied as he moved from the entrance to the cave and started gathering up Donnelly's scant gear.

The walk to the village was very cold and the three men were forced at times to wade through deep snowdrifts. The snow would stick to their pants and as they walked their body heat would melt the snow, making each man wet. The sky was still gray and to Donnelly it looked like more snow was on the way, but he knew if they could reach the small town he'd have a warm place to wait it out. As they moved, the two Germans took turns leading and breaking through the snow, so the other two would have an easier walk. The horse didn't have any problems traveling at all, mostly because there was little ice, and actually seemed happy to be out of the cave.

About two hours after they had departed the cave the men entered the small German community of New Burg and from what Donnelly could see the citizens were somewhat successful people. Each structure looked painted that year, the buildings were in excellent repair, and the boardwalks cleared of snow. *Typical Germans,* Donnelly thought as he led his horse through town, *everything is clean and it's obvious they are all hard workers.*

Stopping in front of a large building with a sign over the door that read 'Richard Spigeman, Doktor,' the old German said, "This is my home and office. Come, we must treat your injury and then you must rest."

The heat from the small living room was overpowering as the men stepped in from the lung hurting cold. As soon as they entered, a short plump German woman with long braided blond hair entered the room and seeing the men she said, "I will put on a hot drink for all three of you. My God, it is so very cold out there today."

"Hanna-Ilse, we will be in my office, because this man has been badly injured. Please bring our drinks there in about thirty minutes. Until then, do not disturb me as I will be busy."

"I will come in thirty minutes and if you cannot drink at that time let me know."

Entering the office the doctor said in German, "Please, remove your shirt. Now, Taylor, what I am about to do will hurt you, but it must be done or you will die. First, I must reopen the injury, clean it out well, and then sew it closed. Sewing a wound is a new procedure, but we have found less chance for infection than cauterizing it."

"Do what you need to do doctor, I have no wish to die from this." Donnelly spoke and gave a weak smile.

"I will do all that is required, now, climb up on my table there and lay down. I will start the treatment as soon as I clean my tools. I also have a new drug to give you as I prepare."

"What kind of drug?"

"Laudanum, it kills pain and can only be given in very small amounts. It will give you a sense of well being and you should not feel pain as I work. The only problem with the drug is it can be habit forming. It was discovered in 1804 by a German pharmacist named Friedrich Wilhelm Adam Sertürner, but it's not been used much until just a few years ago." Then handing Donnelly a very small glass with the drug mixed with some whiskey in it he continued, "Here, drink this and then relax. You will become sleepy and if you go to sleep that will be fine. Once I have your injury cleaned, you must go to bed for a few days."

Donnelly lifted the glass and drank the drug down all at once, wanting to get the injury cleaned as soon as possible. If the drug would kill the pain, so much the better, because he'd seen men pass out from the pain of cleaning an infection. Almost instantly he felt light headed, relaxed, and then felt sleepy. He closed his eyes and within a couple of minutes, he was in a deep sleep.

A few hours later Donnelly awoke with very little pain and it took him a few minutes to realize where he was. The room was dark, though a lamp burned low on a small table beside the bed, and he was in a large brass bed. A thick feather comforter covered him up to his neck and his head was resting on two pillows. His head felt light and he noticed he had a hard time keeping his thoughts organized and it was even harder to care about his thoughts.

Not long after his eyes opened, Donnelly was visited by Doctor Spigeman. The doctor said, "No more of the drug for you. Just a little quickly put you out and that may mean that you could develop a real liking for the drug with just a few doses. From now on, if you feel pain, I will give you whiskey but not that drug. Besides, the hard part is over and all you have to do now is grow stronger and that will come with good food along with lots of rest."

"Thank you very much doctor, for all you did. As soon as I am able to work I will pay your normal fee for such a job."

"Do not worry about payment; I do much in our town for no money at all. Some they bring me chickens, pork, or vegetables, but real money I see little. If you wish, when you are able, just pay two dollars and that will be enough. I will use the money to buy more of the drug to help others in deep pain."

"I'm tired once more and must sleep." Donnelly said as his eyes started to close slowly.

"Yes, rest and tomorrow you will feel much stronger. Good night and sleep well." The doctor spoke as he walked toward the door, but at the door, he turned and added, "You can sleep as late as you feel like in the morning. If the pain gets too bad tonight or in the morning, just ring the small bell beside your bed and I will bring the whiskey."

CHAPTER 17

Winter passed quietly for Nate and the others, but the weather had turned bad right after Christmas day and stayed that way until the middle of January. Snow had piled up by the foot and the temperature dropped to the point that none of the men dared venture outside of the shelter they had constructed of logs and canvas. The beaver take had been excellent and Nate figured they had well over five hundred pounds of plews stacked up in the small structure they had made for storing the skins. If the price of beaver plews were the same as last year, or better, come spring the men would have between six hundred and a thousand dollars to share among the four of them. Of course, additional skins would be added before rendezvous, but they would be of lesser quality and not prime.

Glancing over at Doc, he asked right after breakfast, "Skeeter still fightin' that auge fit?"

Doc gave a tired smile and replied, "Yep, but his fever broke last night and he should be back to normal in a few days."

"Doc, I know all of us get it from time to time, but what causes it?"

The older mountain man thought for a minute and then said, "Well, they don't know fer sure, but mostly it's just mountain men that get it. I think it has to do with the cold water we're wadin' in all the time to take a few plews. Seems to me, and I could be wrong, that cold water brings on the fever from time to time and I've yet to meet a mountain man that ain't had it. Workin' in ice cold water cain't be good for a man and that's a fact."

"I ain't really thought about it much." Nate admitted and then continued, "Only I don't see no other way I could make a living. The way I see it, I have to stay out here where I can remain free. If I ever go back to the states, why, I'd be back in chains in a month. A big strong runaway like me would bring top dollar on the auction block and I know it too."

"It's a cryin' shame a man can be chained up and worked like a dog, all because of his skin color. But, Nate, I've seen some free black men up north by New York or Boston, only I ain't sure how they got to be free. I know most states north of Kentucky don't hold to slavery much and it's mostly the deep Southern states that welcome it."

Nate laughed and replied, "Two reasons for the South needin' black folks to work the fields. The white owners are too lazy to soil their own hands and the crops they have, cotton and tobacco, take a hell of a lot of men working from can see to can't see just to make a good profit."

"Well, you can thank God that you're out here and not back in the states. If I was you, I'd stay out here."

Suddenly, Cotton Top appeared. Nate knew they had trouble because the man's eyes were large with excitement and he'd been standing guard. Gasping for breath, Cotton said, "I . . . I spotted movement comin' up the trail and it's Injuns. From . . . what . . . I could see it's . . . Blackfoot."

"Shit!" Doc exclaimed in a low voice as he picked up his Hawken rifle and cocked the hammer back with a loud snap, "How many of 'em?"

Nate asked, "How in the hell did they get through all of this snow?"

Cotton having finally caught his breath replied, "They were wearin' snowshoes. I never would've considered snowshoes and there was about a dozen of 'em, Doc."

"Okay, then they know we're here and they've come to surprise us." Nate said and then turning to Skeeter he asked, "Can you move Skeeter? We got Blackfoot guests comin' fer dinner."

Raising his head, Skeeter said in a weak voice, "I'll do better than that; I'll blacken my face against them sonsofbitches and help y'all fight."

If he hadn't so worried about the coming attack Nate would have laughed at the man's grit and the look of determination in his eyes. Instead, he grinned and said, "You get back in the trees there and get ready to count coup. I suspect we'll be up to our asses in Blackfoot in just a few more minutes." Then, quickly looking around, the big man noticed Cotton and Doc were in the woods nearby.

Less than ten minutes later, a lone Blackfoot warrior suddenly materialized from the trees and walked in the center of the camp looking around, obviously confused that the white men were gone. He waved a hand and six more braves entered the camp, all of them puzzled over the disappearance of the four white men they'd expected. At that moment, Nate lined his sights up on the biggest brave, took a deep breath and squeezed his trigger. A split second later his rifle shot echoed in the still morning air and three more shots came instantly from the trees. The shots almost sounded as one because they fired so close together.

When the smoke cleared, Nate noticed four of the Blackfoot down for good and the other three had gone to ground. *If Cotton's countin' was correct, we still have eight of them red buggers to kill,* the big black man thought as he moved silent to a spot about twenty feet of where he'd taken his shot. He'd reloaded immediately after firing is rifle, so he waited patiently to see what the Blackfoot would do. Nate knew they were a fierce group of warriors and most of the mountain men he knew respected the hell out of them as fighters.

Almost an hour passed before the big man saw a small patch of brown move and knew they were getting ready to attack. Thinking like a Blackfoot would, Nate swiftly realized a frontal attack was coming in hopes the Indians could overrun the white men before they had a chance to reload. Pulling his pistol, he placed it by his right foot and waited. *You might get me you red jaspers, but by God I'll take at least two of you with me on the road to hell,* Nate thought in anger as he watched the spot where he'd seen the earlier movement.

Suddenly, as if on signal, a loud war cry echoed and eight Blackfoot broke from the trees and ran right at the four mountain men. Four rifles sounded, three of the brave dropped, with one thrashing violently and spewing red blood on the white snow. The mountain men, each knowing his pistol shot would have to count, waited until the Blackfoot were almost of top of them and then fired.

When the smoke cleared, Nate saw three more bodies on the ground and he could hear the sounds of hand-to-hand combat taking place in the woods near where Doc and Cotton had gone. Quickly reloading both his rifle and pistol, the big man then started running toward the sound, but half way there he heard a scream of anguish and then laughter filled the air.

Leaping over a log, Nate entered the woods going full speed and slightly off to his right he saw a brave aiming a pistol at a target on the ground as he laughed. Quickly pulling his rifle up to his shoulder, the mountain man jerked his trigger and saw the Blackfoot's head explode. The Indian's body dropped instantly, but Nate didn't go over to see who the warrior had been aiming at, instead he moved toward the sound of a battle taking place deeper in the woods.

Less than fifty feet away, in the middle of a bunch of pines, he spotted Skeeter fighting a brave on the snow-covered ground. The men were rolling around in the snow and Nate knew the feverish man would not be able to put up a fight for very long, because he was too weak. Just as the Blackfoot's knife hand came back, the big black man pushed his pistol barrel against the warrior's back and pulled the trigger. The brave's body jerked violently as the big fifty caliber lead slug struck home and he gave a horrendous scream as he fell to the left.

As he fell his legs and arms thrashed around in the snow, as if he was making an effort to run. Nate grabbed the warrior's hair, pulled his head back, and calmly cut his throat. A fountain of red erupted into the air and with each beat of the warrior's heart it would spurt once more, until he began to choke on his own blood. Less than two minutes later the man's arms and legs slowly lost power until his body lay still. One finger twitched on his right hand, and then the man died.

Quickly turning and walking back to Skeeter, he saw the man was bleeding like a stuck hog and it didn't look good. Pulling his own shirt off, ignoring the blistering cold, Nate place it on Skeeter's bleeding stomach and secured it in place with a long blue sash from his waist. Since the white man was light in weight, the big black man simply bent down and scooped him up in his arms. He slowly started back to camp.

Nearing the spot where he'd killed the first brave in the woods, he saw Doc standing and shaking his head as if to clear it of cobwebs. Seeing Nate packing Skeeter, Doc asked in a concerned voice, "Is he hurt bad Nate?"

"It don't look good to me. He took a knife deep in the lights. When I got there, he was already bleeding like a stuck pig. I don't think he'll make it Doc, he'll go under."

"Damn me! My second pistol misfired, or this wouldn't have happened!" Doc said in anger as he bent down, picked up his hat, and dusted the snow off.

"We can discuss that later, right now let's get him back to the fire and see if you can doctor his ass up."

As he walked from the trees into the clearing, Nate saw Cotton Top had his big Green River knife in his right hand as walked from Blackfoot to Blackfoot making sure they were all dead. The tip of the razor sharp blade was dripping fresh blood that left a red trail in the snow from warrior to warrior. Just short of the fire, a loud scream pierced the air and Nate knew one warrior had been playing 'possum. There was always a great deal of danger in leaving any Blackfoot alive, even if they looked near death, because the only way a Blackfoot warrior would stop coming for you was if they died.

Doc quickly spread out a wool blanket beside the fire and Nate lowered Skeeter gently to the cover, noticing the man was unconscious. Then, he added a log to the fire as Doc removed Nate's bloody shirt from Skeeter's belly.

Nate asked a few seconds later, "How's it look?"

"Cain't tell yet, but not good. I think he took a blade deep and it looks like the Blackfoot twisted the blade too. If he did that, Skeeter is a gone beaver."

"You need any help?"

Doc gave a weak smile and said in a low voice, "Heat up some water and stick both of our Green River's in the flames and let 'em heat up real good. When the blades turn bright red, pull one out of the flames, and let it cool to the touch, then hand it to me."

Nate placed the big blades in the flames and watched as the metal started changing colors. Both of the men were quiet, each deep in thought and the only sound was the snapping flames. Finally, the big man pulled one of the knives from the fire and waved it in the air to cool it down, and then asked as a question struck him, "Hell, he's already cut, why you need a knife?"

"I've got to open the top layer of his belly a bit to see how much damage was done deep inside of 'em. If he's cut as badly as I think he is, there won't be much I can do, except to keep 'em comfortable until he goes under."

"Doc, don't sell Skeeter short, he's got some tough bark on 'em. If anyone can survive a cut like this he will."

Doc slowly shook his head as he took the sharp knife from Nate's hand he said, "No one can survive a deep stab wound to the lights and ya damned well know it too. I hope like hell this man lives, I've been ridin' with 'em fer years, but at times things happen we ain't got no control over."

"I know that Doc, but I gotta have hope and I've prayed already for God Almighty to save him, so it's out of our hands. All we can do is fix 'em up good and then see what happens."

Doc sliced upward on Skeeter's belly with the knife tip and then gently pulled the skin apart as he looked inside. After a few minutes, he said, "Pull the second knife and let 'er cool Nate, we won't need it."

"Why? Ain't you gonna cauterize the wound?"

Slowly shaking his head very slowly a few times, the old mountain met Nate's eyes as he replied, "There ain't no use to cause him anymore pain before he goes under. From what I can see in 'em he's cut every which way inside and there ain't no doctor in the world that could keep him alive."

"Sliced up bad, huh?"

"Yep, and we both know a man with a serious wound to his belly won't make it." Doc spoke solemnly and then used the back of his left hand to wipe the tears from his cheeks. As soon as he'd spoken the old mountain man placed a clean piece of cotton cloth on Skeeter's wound and then wrapped him tightly using part of a torn blanket.

Nate allowed the knife from the fire to cool. It was much later, when he realized it was his and placed it back in the sheath. Putting the coffee pot on the flames, he thought for a few minutes and then said, "I'm goin' to help Cotton Top drag the bodies off. We'll give Skeeter some time, so we know one way or the other what will happen, but as soon as we know we have to move. It could be a big bunch of Blackfoot know where we are, or know where these fellers were headed. In either case, they'll come lookin' for 'em and I want to be miles from here when that happens." Standing, Nate looked down at the pale Skeeter and said, "If you need me, just give a yell."

Doc didn't reply, but he did nod.

By nightfall, snow was falling once more, which pleased Nate to no un-end. He knew fresh snow would cover the tracks and body's of the killed Blackfoot braves, and also give his small group some time to prepare to leave. Six sets of snowshoes were saved from the dead warriors, so the big black man knew they could walk out now if they had too, but they'd have to lead the horses. And, no mountain man liked to walk a yard if he could ride instead. Each man would carry an extra set of snow-shoes and the horses could carry the pews. He was also thank-ful for a snow-covered ground and that it was not ice. Ice on the mountain trails would have been dangerous to both the men and the horses, where a broken leg could mean death to either.

The small group sat under the canvas shelter, yet near the fire, sharing a pot of hot coffee. The wind had picked up and al-most as much snow was blowing around at ground level as was falling.

"We got twelve knives, eight tomahawks, four pistols, one Hawken, and two old smooth bore rifles from them dead Black-foot. I didn't look to see how much powder and such they had, I just placed it all in the supply shelter. That Hawken is a fine rifle too, with good German sights, double set triggers, and a big fifty-eight caliber, so I kept it for myself. This old Kentucky long rifle I have is a good gun, but she's a mite on the old side now and too damned heavy when compared to a Hawken. Plus, I like a big bore much better than my forty-fire caliber." Cotton Top spoke as he held his coffee cup in both hands near his lips, not saying what he was actually thinking.

Nate laughed and replied, "Cotton, you keep the rifle and get you a knife and tomahawk out of the supplies. I think every man should have two knives, two pistols and a 'hawk out here."

"I'll do it in a few minutes, before it gets full dark. Nate, I scalped them boys too and I think I can trade the hair to the Sioux come a good break in weather. There ain't much a Sioux likes more than Blackfoot hair. Now, I figured we could trade them scalps for some good horses come spring. But, them scalps belong to all four of us, so I need to know if the idea is a good one or not."

At that exact moment Skeeter's back arched violently, his eyes flew open, and he let out a deep loud rattle from deep inside his throat followed by a loud scream, "Mein Gott!" His body thrashed and kicked violently for a few seconds and then he was still. Hurrying to the man's side, Doc quickly looked into the man's unseeing eyes and said slowly, "Now there are only the three of us now, Skeeter has gone under."

The next mornin', as the sun was attempting to break through the heavy cloud cover; the three men were gathered under a large oak tree. Skeeter's body was in a large fork in the tree. All three of them removed their hats and bowed their heads, as Nate said in his deep voice, "Lord, take our friend Jonathan Sachell, we called 'em Skeeter, into your Kingdom. He was a good man, Lord, and he never drank too much, cussed too much, or sinned a lot that I could see. Jonathan was a man that other men envied because of his strength and courage, and you let him know we all miss him. Ashes to ashes and dust to dust, thy will be done on earth as it is in heaven. Amen."

As they were walking back to the campsite Cotton asked, "What was that German Skeeter said just before he died?"

Doc looked over and said, "What Skeeter said was, my God. See, Cotton, he knew he was dying then and there. He was one hell of a man, German or not, and I respected him."

Cotton Top placed his left hand on Doc's right shoulder and giving it a slight squeeze he replied, "That's all any man could ever want for someone to say about him after he's gone beaver. Let's get the horses and move Doc, I don't like it much here any-more."

Chapter 18

A month after being taken to the small German village, Don-nelly was up and moving around. The wound had healed nicely, though it was still sore as hell at times, the deep pain and infection had gone away. He'd stayed with Spigeman and his wife the whole time and had eaten well. The old German doctor cleaned his wound each day, made him drink lots of hot soup, and fed him whiskey until the serious pain had disappeared. Taylor was just outside the kitchen door chopping wood to get some strength back in his chest and arms.

"Mein Gott, vhat are you doing?" The doctor asked as he stepped out from the house.

"Getting some exercise doc, I can't stay still all the time."

"Ja, und if you open that vound again, we vill have the trou-bles all over."

Donnelly laughed, lowered the ax head to the ground by his right foot and replied, "Okay, I'll stop. But, would it at least be al-right for me to do some walking around town then? I'm bored being in bed most of the time."

"Ja, I t'ink the valking vould be gut for you."

Leaning the handle of the ax against a log, Donnelly picked up his hat, placed it on his head and said, "I'm going for a short walk and I'll be back directly."

"Make it a small valk, nein?" The doctor said with a warm smile and then placed his hands in his pockets against the cool morning air.

"Yes, I will make it a short walk doctor." Taylor replied in German and then turned toward the town. As he walked he thought, *this is a nice town. If I wanted, with the way I speak German, I'll bet I could blend in well here and never be found.*

The town was small, maybe eight hundred people and there were only a few streets. Donnelly walked down the boardwalk of the main street and saw a sign that read, saloon, in very poor English lettering. Entering the bat wing doors, he stopped just inside for a minute to allow his eyes to adjust to the dim interior. Then, clearly seeing the bar he walked up and ordered a beer.

The man behind the bar was huge, maybe four hundred pounds, blond hair, blue eyes, and in a very deep voice he said, as he placed a beer on the top of the bar in front of Taylor, "Dat vill be vun dime."

Taylor paid the man and noticed the barkeeper dropped the dime into a cigar box on a shelf behind the bar. The big man went to polishing beer glasses. Sipping his beer, Taylor thought, *no one in the world makes a better beer than the German's do. This beer is as smooth as a well-oiled gun, but strong.*

In German, Taylor asked the man if he had heard any news. If him speaking fluent German surprised the big bartender, he didn't act like it at all. He shook his big head and said, "No, there is nothing new. They are still looking for a killer that they claim jumped from a boat way up north, but no news that affects me or this village."

"Killer? I just got in town a while back and I've been staying with the doctor, so I've heard nothing of a killing. What happened?" Donnelly asked, then raised his beer to his lips and took a long pull.

"A criminal escaped from the army, killed two guards doing so, and then killed some farmer up north. What bothers me the most is, they say he also raped a woman and that is not a good thing to have happened. I suspect when they catch him they'll just kill him on sight, as they would a mad dog. There is a two thousand dollar reward for him, but I think he's long gone, back east."

Taylor finished his beer, ordered another one and asked as the bartender refilled his glass, "What makes you think he went east?"

"Well," the big man said as he placed the new beer on the bar, "he was being brought from the west, so why would a smart man head back west to where the trouble started? It would make little sense."

"Yes, that is true and I also think he would move east." Taylor said as he raised his glass.

"Or, he might head south, if he was real smart." The bartender said and then shrugging his massive shoulders, he continued, "But, who is to say what a cold blooded killer will do? It is a violent time we live in, so I have seen and heard it all."

Donnelly choked on his beer when the man said south, looked up with a weak grin on his face, and then replied as he gasped for air, "Yes . . . who . . . can say."

"Go easy on the beer, because it is a very strong beer. If you are not used to German beer it will make you drunk quickly."

"I know German beer."

"Maybe you do and maybe you don't. While your German is very good, you are not a German."

Taylor laughed and asked, "How do you know I am not German? I could be you know."

The man shook his head and replied, "A real German would never go into town, or even a bar, without shaving first and having a bath. I can see you have not shaved in a couple of days and you've been working hard at splitting wood. Even your hair has not been combed."

"What? How in the world do you know I've been splitting wood?"

The big man gave a mighty laugh and replied as soon as he'd gained his composure said, "You have chips of wood in your hair."

Taylor quickly brushed the wood from his hair, grinned and said, "One more beer and then that's it for me."

Placing the beer on the bar and taking the money the bartender suddenly asked, "You are a friend of Doctor Spigeman's?"

"You could say that. I took a Sioux arrow in my right shoulder a while back and met the doctor a few days after it happened. It had festered on me, so he brought me to his home to treat the injury."

"That sounds just like Richard, he is a very good man and his wife is good woman too. They've both helped bring other Germans from Germany to New Burg and one day we will be a big city."

Not likely, Taylor thought, but he said, "Could be, if you can get enough people to move here and generate enough hard cash to make a go of it."

"Money we have, though not a great deal, we have all done well. The doctor is by far the richest man in the town and I'll bet you he has over a thousand dollars just lying around the house."

Taylor grinned, picked up his beer and gulped the rest of it down quickly. Wiping his mouth off with the palm of his right hand he said, "I find that hard to believe, but maybe he does. I'm not interested in his money or anyone's, I'm just glad he's a very good doctor. He saved my life you know?"

As he picked up Taylor's empty beer glass he replied, "Yes, he's a very good doctor, so I am not surprised. He trained in Munich at the university. We are very lucky to have a man with his skills living with us and I don't think anyone is respected more than he in this town."

As he walked toward the door, Taylor thought, *a thousand dollars in his home? Now, that is an interesting thought.*

When Taylor returned to the doctor's home, the man was in his kitchen drinking coffee. As Donnelly walked in Spigeman asked in German, "Taylor may we talk for a minute?"

"Sure." Taylor answered, pulled out a chair and sat down.

"How were you really injured? I know the wound was not caused by a knife or arrow, because the blade or weapon used had two tips, almost like a pair of scissors or small pruning shears."

Donnelly gave a loud chuckle and replied, "My good doctor, Indians do not attack white men with scissors or shears. They might use a knife, rifle, tomahawk, lance or bow and arrow, but for sure no sewing or shrub trimming tools."

"Perhaps you were stabbed twice, that would explain the double injury I saw."

"Could be, I have no idea, because I was in a fight to the death and at a time like that a man could be hurt many times and not realize it until later. Now, if you'll excuse me, I need to get a little sleep."

Spigeman sat at his table, sipped his coffee and then got up and went to his bedroom, where his wife was making the bed. Closing the door, he said in a light whisper, "Taylor is not as he seems to be. When I question him about his injury, he still claimed he was attacked by wild savages, but the wound is not of a weapon Indians would use. The injury was definitely caused by a pair of scissors or small shears."

"How can that be?" Hanna-Ilse asked as she gazed into her husband's eyes.

"Hanna, I heard of an escaped killer who was responsible for the deaths of five people and one of those was a woman. This same man, the killer, also raped a woman after he killed her husband. According to the Saint Louis paper, the woman fought him off with a pair of scissors and then made her escape. I honestly think Taylor is that man."

"My God, have you told anyone yet?"

"No, I wanted to speak to him first and judge his reaction. He paled a bit when I asked him and his right eye gave a slight tick, but he could very well be the man they are looking for. Of course, he denied the obvious medical fact that scissors of some sort caused the injury. My dear, I cannot take these facts lightly. Here in a minute, I want you to dress and gather your basket, as if you're going shopping for vegetables as you do each day. Then, walk calmly and slowly to the sheriff's office and ask him to come here immediately. You stay in town until the Sheriff or I come and tell you it's safe to return. And, Hanna-Ilse?"

"Yes, Richard?"

"You must hurry. I think he knows I suspect the story he told me is not the truth and that means he might get very angry or turn dangerous unexpectedly."

Quickly placing her shawl around her shoulders, picking up her wicker basket, she gave her husband a quick kiss on the right cheek and whispered, "Richard, come with me and stay safe."

Richard Spigeman shook his head and said in a low voice, "If we both go, he'll suspect something, because each day you go the market alone. I will go back to the kitchen and have me a beer, as I do every morning at this time. Things must look normal and though you're leaving a little earlier than normal, you do leave every day, so he'll not suspect a thing. I'll be safe, but you must hurry."

His wife quickly left the room, walked from the house and in a slow natural way moved toward the middle of town, straight for the sheriff's office.

Donnelly had returned to his room filled with deep anger over the doctor's words and the realization he'd been found out. As soon as he heard Hanna-Ilse leave the house, he quickly picked up the shotgun and making sure it was loaded, he slowly walked into the kitchen.

The doctor, seeing the big scattergun in Donnelly's hands as he entered said, "Taylor, you are still too weak to go hunting. You must wait a few days and then you may go."

Taylor's eyes grew narrow as he suddenly filled with anger and shouted as he pointed the big gun at the doctor, "I want *all* the money in this house and I want it *now!*"

"There is no money Taylor."

"I know there is money here and I damned well want it, all of it, or I will kill you."

"There is some milk and egg money, maybe ten dollars, but that is all there is."

Feeling his anger rise, Donnelly spotted a large butcher knife lying on the kitchen counter. Keeping his shotgun on the doctor he walked over, picked up the big knife and then moving toward Spigeman he said, "Give me the money, or I'll cut your throat, damn you!"

The doctor knew he had to give Taylor money or the man would kill him, he could see it in the younger man's eyes. Spigeman had seen crazy people often enough in the past, when their families had brought them to him for treatment in Darmstadt, Germany, and he knew he had to go along with Taylor or the man's mind might completely snap any second. Meeting Donnelly's eyes the doctor gave a loud sigh and said, "Yes, of course there is *some* money and if you will come with me I will give it all to you Taylor."

The doctor stood, made his way to bedroom and then reaching under his bed he pulled out a large metal box with a small lock on it. He pulled a key from his right trouser pocket and unlocked the box, swinging the lid open, and Taylor could see the green bills in the container. As he handed the money, well over a thousand dollars to Taylor with his left hand, the doctor's right hand was searching frantically under the bed for his pistol. Suddenly feeling it, he grasped it tightly in his right hand and as Taylor was counting the money the doctor pulled the pistol up, pointed it at Taylor, and fired.

Taylor catching the doctor's quick movement in the corner of his right eye swung his scattergun toward the man and jerked the trigger on the right barrel. The old fat doctor was knocked to the floor where he immediately started to scream in pain. Donnelly swung the butt of his shotgun down hard, striking the old man in the face, and then frantically started ransacking the house. He knew he had to hurry and he did so. Running into the doctor's office he quickly grabbed some bandages, gauze, and one of the pint bottles filled with the laudanum. Donnelly knew if he was injured again, he would need the medication.

Quickly returning to the kitchen he filled three bags with smoked meats, vegetables, bread and other foodstuffs. He then picked up his gear, walked to the barn and saddled the doctor's best horse. Donnelly mounted and as he left the barn, he swung his horse away from town, leaving at a gallop, not realizing he was bleeding until he was miles away and moving south, deeper into the Missouri Ozark Mountains.

Minutes after Donnelly had fled, Hanna-Ilse returned home with Sheriff Sherer in tow. Both the sheriff and Hanna had heard the two distant shots while still in his office, but Sherer didn't respond immediately. The sheriff had to load his shotgun and check his pistols before he could face Donnelly. "Besides," the young lawman said as they hurried to the doctor's home, "what has happened has happened and we cannot change it."

They found Richard Spigeman lying on the bedroom floor with a deep gash on his forehead from the butt of the scattergun and a minor shoulder wound. The doctor was awake and cursing nonstop as his wife and the sheriff entered the room. Seeing the sheriff, Spigeman sat up, leaned back on the side of his bed and said, "He robbed me, shot me, and then stole things from my home! And, after I doctored him and let him use my home as his own as he healed! What kind of country have I moved to? What kind of people are these! I ask you, what kind of people would try to kill a man who has sworn to spend his whole life treating the sick and injured?"

"He is a killer Herr Spigeman, a real killer." Sherer replied as he helped the fat doctor to his wobbly feet.

"Well, don't just stand there, Sheriff Sherer, looking like a fool. I want you to go and get my money back and everything he took from my home! We pay you to protect us, so now go and do your job!"

As the young sheriff turned and walked from the bedroom, he heard Hanna say in a gentle voice, "Richard, you must calm down. You know it is not good for an injured person to get angry, it makes the blood hot and it flows faster."

CHAPTER 19

Nate, Cotton, and Doc didn't have much time to grieve for Skeeter, because as they moved down the side of the mountain the weather worsened. The sky turned a light gray from horizon to horizon and only the dark pine trees prevent a complete whiteout. Large snowflakes filled the air and the wind picked up. All three of the men were tough mountain men, but each realized they would have to seek shelter before too long, or they would end up dead. They stopped frequently to avoid overheating and during one of the short rest periods, they began to talk of the cold.

"Be-jeezus, it's cold!" Cotton suddenly spoke as he opened the top two buttons on his coat to keep from sweating.

"Sure is," Nate replied and then looking over at Cotton said, "and any skin not covered will freeze in less than a minute, while we work up one hell of a sweat walking in these snow-shoes. Lordy, its hard work movin' in this snow."

"Either one of ya jaspers given any thought to huntin' a hole yet? I'd hate to freeze to death out here." Doc asked.

What scared the mountain men was not just the cold, but the danger of sweating as they moved and then having the thin layer of sweat freeze when they stopped to rest. Shortly after the freezing of their sweat, their bodies would start to shut down from what would one day be called hypothermia, the lowering of the body's core temperature.

"We'll travel a couple of more miles to a cave I know of and then call it a day. If some Blackfoot gets on our back trail, there will be hell to pay and you both know it too. Right now what I am more worried about though is one of us coming down with chilblains, because that would really slow us down." When Nate spoke, his breath was seen in the cold arctic air.

"I'm more worried about this sweating and stopping we're doing. But, hell, it's too cold to take a coat off and sooner or later one if us is going to start to freeze." Doc said as he moved up beside Nate.

"Let's move right now and no stopping until we get to the cave, but keep the pace slow and steady." Nate started walking once more.

About an hour later, the big black man pointed off to the right of the trail and the small group move into the trees. A little later, they entered a small hole in the ground, lowered their heavy backs from the horses to the floor and looked around. A large stack of firewood was stored against a wall and the blackened remains of a rock ringed fire pit were near the entrance. None of the mountain men was concerned, because it was normal for anyone using a cave as shelter. Most would leave dry wood inside when they left, so others might use it later. Indians and mountain men saw caves as emergency shelters and kept wood stored inside so it stayed dry.

"I'll care for the horses." Cotton Top spoke as he turned and walked from the cave.

"Real cold doin's out there right now." Doc spoke as he pulled open the pack containing the coffee and food.

"Ain't much to eat, is there? The last I saw, we had a few bites of pemmican, some jerky, and about a pound of beans. What we need is some fresh meat, but with this weather like it is that won't happen until it clears." Nate said as he walked to the wood, pulled some kindling and tinder, and walked to the fire pit. Pulling a small patch of charred cotton cloth, he placed it on the ground. Next, he pulled his flint and steel, and holding the flint in his left hand, he struck it hard with the steel in his right. Sparks flew from the flint, landing on the cotton cloth and immediately burst into flames. As the minute fire flared, Nate added small pieces of tinder. Quickly growing is size, the flames were soon eating hungrily at the wood, giving off cracking sounds. At that point, the man added the rest of his kindling and walking to the woodpile once more he picked up two small logs and placed them on the fire.

"I figured to cook the beans tonight, so we can save the pemmican and jerky for lean times."

"Doc, it we don't get some fresh meat in the next couple of days, it's going to turn into ain't got nothin' to eat times."

Doc shrugged his shoulders and smiled as he picked up the big Dutch oven. Pouring in some water and adding the beans he said, "Hell, we've all seen it before. Ain't a mountain man out here ain't gone hungry for a long stretch or two. The longest I've ever gone without victuals is five days and that was in a big-assed blizzard. I 'spect this weather will break in a day or two."

"I've gone four days, but I don't like doing it much. Eating is a habit I picked up when I was just a young pup and I've grown fairly fond of doing it too. I can go without food and I won't complain, but I won't like it at all."

Doc laughed and replied, "Well, ya could always turn like old Stump. He got snowed in, oh 'bout five years back, and as his trappin' partners died of hunger he et 'em."

Nate stopped working on the fire, turned and looked Doc right in the eyes as he said, "You're teasing me, ain't you?"

"Nope, not one bit. What I told ya is true, but it was real hard on old Stump."

Nate thought for a second or two and then said, "Sounds to me like it was a hell of a lot harder on his partners."

Doc laughed once more and then spoke, "Nate, Stump was a good man. After the weather cleared, he walked out of them mountains, but he was never the same man he once was. No one wanted to winter with him after that and he took to drinkin' pretty hard for a year or so there."

"I imagine a man might turn to whiskey after something like that. But, why did you say Stump was a good man instead of is a good man?"

"Well, early one day me and him went out huntin' fer buffalo. We'd killed a calf and had just put the best meat on one of the horses, when a small group of ten Blackfoot warriors rode up on us. After fightin' for a long spell Stump took a lance to his chest, but he'd already managed to kill three of them warriors before he got hit. We were forced early in the fight to kill our horses, so we could use them as a sort of breastwork against them charging braves.

At this point Doc leaned over, placed the Dutch oven on some red coals and continued, "We both knew Stump was done for and there was no way I could move him fast enough to lose them Blackfoot, especially on foot. So, he said, 'Doc, I'm done fer and won't last much past daylight, no matter what happens. Now, oncet it gets dark I want you to light a shuck out of heah and get back to the tradin' post.' Well, I didn't take to what he had to say and told 'em as much, but he only laughed at me and said, 'I should have died in that big storm a few years back with my partners. I didn't and most of the time I wish I had. I've thought of killin' myself so many times you wouldn't believe it, but I couldn't do the job. See, I et my friends in the mountains to stay alive, so I had to continue to live for them, not me. If I'd killed myself, then eating them would have been a horrible sin.'"

"What happened, Doc?" Nate was engrossed by the horrible tale of mountain man cannibalism.

"When it got dark I snuck out of there and ran for the better part of three days. When I got back to the tradin' post, there was a bunch of free trappers tradin' with Butterfield, so we went back to get Stumps body." At this point Doc stopped talking and stared into the fire for a couple of minutes. Then he said, "When we got there we all expected Stump's body to be all cut up and mutilated like most Injuns would do a man, but there wasn't a mark on 'em no place. When I went through his possibles bag and clothes, hoping to find a name or address I could write to, I found two balls and just enough powder to fire 'em both left."

"You figure they didn't cut 'em up because he put up a brave fight?"

"That's the only thing I know of that would have prevented it from happenin'. We found blood all over the surrounding plains, so Stump must have tapped a few of 'em after I left 'em. He was one hell of a man, ole Stump was."

Cotton Top entered the cave, wiped the snow from his hat and shoulders, and then squatted by the dancing flames of the fire. He opened his palms and extended his arms toward the heat, and said, "Colder than a banker's heart out there right now!"

"Yep, cold doin's it is fer sure." Doc commented as he raked a few more coals around the sides of his Dutch oven so the beans would boil.

Nate stretched his long legs out beside the fire and said, "I've been thinking on our situation and I don't like it none at all. I think it might be best if we headed to the Sioux and spent some time with them, but just until the weather turns a bit nicer."

Doc though about the suggestion and replied, "Well, that might work, only we don't know how they are doin' food wise.

The Sioux don't call this the moon of hunger fer no reason, ya know?"

Nate chuckled and said, "I know, but we got to do something. If we can show up at a village with some fresh meat, they'll take us in quick enough. I just ain't sure which bunch to visit. Now, if old Buffalo Hump is winterin' where he usually does, he'd be the closest to us right this minute. And, since we got some extra guns and knives we took from them Blackfoot, we could do some gift giving after we get there. I know he'd welcome our Hawkens and us, because we can shoot meat a hell of a lot further away than his braves can with their old smoothbores and bows."

"Ain't many of them Sioux got a Hawken, 'less they kilt the white man that once owned it. Most of 'em got smooth bored rifles from the British or an old Pennsylvania long rifle. The long rifle is a good gun, but heavy as hell and too long to carry in heavy brush. And, smooth bores cain't hit shit any further out than fifty feet and not worth the effort it takes to carry 'em." Cotton Top spoke and then leaned back onto the dirt floor of the cave. Taking a twist of tobacco from his possibles bag, he bit off a large chunk and started to chew.

Nate grinned and said, "Okay, as soon as this snow stops and the temperature goes up a bit, we'll head to Hump's village. Right now let's clean our guns and fix some of our gear; we'll need everything in good shape for the trip."

For the next three days, the weather stayed cold, with dark almost black snow clouds rolling overhead. Snow continued to fall and the men, now out of real food, were down to just one handful of greasy pemmican a day. But, not a complaint was heard from any man as the ration was handed out each evening around the fire.

Finally, five days after they had entered the cave and with all of their food now gone, they packed the horses and started north to find the Sioux. The temperature was barely above freezing, but the deep chest hurting cold was gone. The trail was littered with rocks and logs that had moved from the melting snows, and often they had to dismount to clear a way for their mounts. At other times, they were forced to go around obstacles that were too large to be moved.

Near the end of the first day, a big buck stood from the side of the trail and watched the three riders slowly approaching. Finally deciding the men were a threat, the deer started to turn and run, when a big slug from Nate's rifle struck the animal in the chest, killing it immediately. Moving quickly to the downed animal, the big man pulled his knife as he dismounted, and said, "Tonight we'll eat well!"

"By damn, it's about time too! My meatbag was starting to think my throat had run off." Cotton said as he dismounted and made his way to the deer.

"Nate, do ya want to call it a day? We can camp up on the rise off to our left back in those oak trees." Doc asked as he scanned the countryside to see if anyone would respond to the loud report of the Hawken rifle.

"Yep, let's do that and we can eat all we want tonight too! Me and Cotton will be up there in a couple of minutes, with this deer, but you take the horses and go on up.

An hour later, a shelter was up, the horses tied to a rope picket line, and deer meat was roasting on sharp sticks leaning toward the flickering flames of the fire. The smell of the meat cooking caused each of the men to think about how hungry they were and it took all of the willpower Nate had to keep from picking up a stick and eating the meat raw. He'd been hungry before, many times, but only red bloody meat seemed to satisfy his deep hunger after being without for a while.

Soon the men were eating meat as more sticks holding deer meat roasted beside the flames. Grease ran down Nate's chin and he wiped his mouth off with the back of his left hand and then wiped it on his left pants leg. His buckskins were stained with grease and oil from previous meals, so the lightly tanned skins actually had a dark brown color on the legs and front of the shirt. Nonetheless, his clothing was as clean as any mountain man's was and Nate had never given them a second thought.

After eating, the men sat around the fire relaxing and making small talk while a feeling of contentment from the meal filled each man.

"Nate, how much further to Hump's Sioux, do ya think?" Doc asked as he pulled an old log over and positioned in on the flames of the fire.

"Day's ride, maybe less. If they are where they usually are and I don't see no reason they won't be there."

"Naw, Injuns are creatures of habit and they seem to always follow the food trail. If I remember right, in about two more months the buffalo will start moving back north and they'll pass right by where the village will be. I'll bet ya them Sioux been wintering there for a hell of a long time." Doc spoke and then thought, *Damn, I'd sure like a cup of coffee about right now.*

"I fig'er a lot depends on what the Blackfoot and Crow been up to around here. They both get on the war path and things will change, and quick like too." Cotton said from beside the fire.

Nate grinned and stated in a flat voice, "Fellers, we can try to guess if the Sioux are there or not and it won't make a bit of difference. They'll either be there or they won't be. If they're not there, we'll head over to Butterfield's, trade some of our lesser quality plews for some supplies and head back out. Only next time we'll head for Table Rock and try our luck there."

"Table Rock! Nate, have you lost your damned mind? That place is full of Blackfoot and we'd have to fight our way in and out, most likely." Doc exclaimed as his eyes grew large in astonishment at the thought of entering Table Rock.

Nate laughed loudly, glanced at Doc and said, "We'd only be on the mountain for a couple of weeks. I know a back way in and I've used it often enough with old Cotton Top here with me. Ain't we Cotton?"

Cotton had been sucking on a dry pipe, since all the smoking tobacco had gone well over a week ago, and he pulled the pipe from his lips as he replied, "Yep, we've been there a few times, but I don't like it much. It's like bein' a guest at a graveyard, except you're not dead yet, only waiting to die, and iffen them Blackfoot catch us that is exactly what will happen. In all the nights I've spent there, I don't think I ever had a good nights sleep on that mountain."

Nate suddenly grew serious and said, "It is a dangerous spot, no doubt about that, but we can take more beaver in two weeks there than we could any place else in two months. It shines, it surely does."

"Look, old hoss, ya know I ain't no coward, but there are times a man can avoid gettin' killed and stayin' away from that mountain might be one of those times. I'll go back iffen ya two go, but I'm a tellin' ya both right now, I don't take to the idea much." Cotton Top spoke quickly, placed his pipe back in his mouth and then crossed his arms on his chest.

"Well, I'll tell ya what we'll do...we can invite Waters to come along with us, if ya want. I'm sure by now just bein' with Butterfield most of the winter has about drove him mad." Nate said, suspecting both men would not like the idea and he was playing with them.

Doc thought for a moment and then said, "Ya know, that might be a good idea. We all know he'd not be worth a shit trappin', but he could care for the ridin' stock and keep camp for us when we're out gatherin' skins."

"And," Cotton quickly added, "if I remember right, he's a pretty damned good cook too. I say let's go to Butterfield's, get some supplies, and see if Waters wants to join up with us. Hell, what have we got to lose?"

"Our hair," Nate said flatly, "just our hair."

Later that night a warm front moved in as Nate stood guard over the camp. Off in the distance he heard a wolf howl and a few seconds later he heard another one answer from the high side of the mountain behind him. The sky was clear, with millions of stars flashing overhead, and the mountain man knew the morning would bring good weather for traveling. *Just think,* Nate thought as he leaned back against the rough bark of a pine tree, *if I'd stayed a slave I'd never heard or seen the likes I have as a mountain man. By God, to think I almost didn't come here! Thank ye Lord for allowin' me to see your handy work first hand.*

The mountain man was right; the morning dawned warm without a cloud in the sky. Waking his two partners, they had a quick breakfast of deer meat washed down with river water, and then loaded the horses. Less than an hour after eating the simple meal the three men were mounted and slowly moving down the trail toward the Sioux village.

CHAPTER 20

Donnelly kept moving until the loss of blood made him so weak he fell forward on his saddle and he dismounted to make a camp. The area he was in was almost twenty miles south of New Burg, though by looking at the country you could not tell it was even the same state. He was riding beside a small meandering stream and it was in a deep valley, with high bluffs along both sides of the waterway. There was little wind and dusk was coming soon, because the bluff on the west side was casting a shadow that grew larger by the minute. Taylor knew he had less than thirty minutes to get his camp organize or he'd be covered by darkness of the shadow.

His left side was stiff and a sharp pain was throbbing in his left shoulder. He knew the old German doctor had shot him, but he'd been so busy attempting to escape that he had been forced to ignore it until he reached some sort of safety. It was with great difficulty he removed his shirt and was surprised by the bullet hole in the shoulder, as well as the dark purplish bruise that surrounded it. The entry hole was leaking a little blood, so Taylor started a fire and walked to the stream where he collected a pan of water. The pan, like all the gear and food he had with him, was stolen from the doctor's house.

As the water heated, so he could treat his wound, he took the money from his coat pocket and quickly counted it. A big smile came to his face as he realized there was much more than the original one thousand dollars he thought was there. He counted exactly thirty-five hundred and ninety two dollars, more than enough for him to hide out a long while as he rested and healed. He'd had a rough past few months and even the injury from the scissors still ached at times, though he knew a few months of good food, whiskey, and wild women would get him back to normal.

Taylor cleaned his wound, applied a rough bandage, and tied it in place using part of an old saddle blanket he'd added to the gear when he made his break. It wasn't much, but if he could find a small town or even a city he could get a doctor to do him up right. *That damned German was rich as hell!* Donnelly thought as he added some coffee to the boiling water, *If I'd been smart I would have held him hostage and made his fat-assed wife go and get me a few more thousands from the bank. She would have done it too, just to keep his worthless butt alive. Only problem was, I didn't know when the doctor or his wife would turn me in. He was a smart man, him knowing my injury was caused by a pair of scissors and not a knife blade.*

The next morning it was hours after sunup before Donnelly awoke. The shadow from the eastern bluff had blocked the sun as it rose and it was high in the sky before the light reached out far enough into the valley to awaken the tired and weak man. Rubbing sleep from his eyes, Taylor stood on weak legs, and then moved to the side of the camp where he made water. As he felt his bladder empty, the man gave a light moan.

He had just blown a coal alive from his fire of the night before when he heard a slight noise on the trail behind him. Quickly glancing at his horse, he noticed the animals head was turned and it was looking at the back trail. Taylor quickly moved into a small group of stunted pines, pulled the shotgun up close and checked the loads. Just as he finished looking his scattergun over a lone man rode into his camp and dismounted.

The damned fool is just asking to be killed, Donnelly thought as he watched the man carefully to make sure he was alone.

Sheriff Sherer slowly walked around the campsite noticed the empty blankets, the fire burning, and some discarded bloody cloth near the fire. He glanced at the horse and immediately knew it had been stolen from the doctor. *He is very near,* the young German thought as he removed his pistol and pulled the hammer back with a loud snap. Glancing down at the sand beside the fire, Sherer noticed fresh tracks in the dirt heading into the pines. With a small grin on his face, the German started toward the trees cautiously, never knowing he was being watched all the while.

The young lawman had just entered the trees when Taylor pointed the big gun at the young man and squeezed the right trigger. The loud blast of the shotgun echoed through the small valley. Sherer was thrown back hard into the clearing and instantly started screaming as he convulsed violently in the grass. Taylor, slowly walking up to the injured man, saw the shotgun pellets had taken Sherer's right arm off at the elbow and a huge chunk of flesh was missing from his side. Blood from the severed arm was squirting high into the air and he was lying in a pool of bright red blood from the wound to his side.

Kneeling beside the German, Taylor pulled the knife he had taken from the doctor and then stuck it hard under the Sheriff's rib cage, twisting and jerking it as it entered. Sherer gave a horrible scream, his eyes grew large and blood ran like a small stream from the right corner of his mouth. His body shuddered violently once, he gave a loud sigh, and as he met Donnelly's eyes—he died.

Donnelly quickly removed the lawman's knife, picked up the pistol, and made his way back to camp. He found the sheriff had a packhorse that was loaded down with meats, canned goods, ammo, and even clean clothing. Leaving the packhorse loaded, Taylor pulled the saddlebags from Sherer's horse, noticing a rifle in the scabbard, and taking the bags to the fire he sat down and began going though them. He found a book in German, ten dollars in gold coin, both of which he sat aside, and little else he wanted.

Standing, he walked to the dead man's body and went through his pockets, where he found some smoking and chewing tobacco, forty dollars in greenbacks, a pen knife, and a silver watch, all of which he kept. The dead man was about the same size as Taylor and after checking it for fit; he took the sheriff's dark gray hat. Glancing down at the dead man Donnelly said as he shook his head slowly, "You was a damned fool. Why in the hell did you just ride into to my campsite? Did you think I'd go in without a fight?"

Deciding not to eat breakfast, Donnelly mounted up and taking the reins of the packhorse in his left hand, he continued moving south. The weather was warm and the sky was clear, but Taylor kept wondering about the way the sheriff had just ridden into his camp. Finally he thought, *Hell, he wasn't no real lawman, he was just a German used to the German attitude toward absolute compliance with authority. I'll bet you today is the first time in his life he'd ever pulled that gun for a real reason. Well, he learned the hard way that not all folks are puppets when it comes to obeying the laws of the land.* Taylor gave a loud almost insane laugh.

The middle of the day, five days later, he entered a small town with no name as far as he could tell and it was obvious why. The place consisted of four buildings, one of which was a saloon, one a store, and the other two seemed to be private homes. Riding up to the saloon Donnelly dismounted, walked through the bat wing doors and up to the bar. A tall skinny man with large hawk-like nose was wiping the bar down with a dirty rag when Taylor said, "Beer."

Placing a beer in front of Taylor the bartender said, "That'll be a dime."

Pulling a dime from his right coat pocket, he handed it to the bartender. As the money exchange hands Donnelly asked, "This place got a name?"

"I call it the Bluebird Saloon."

"No, not the saloon, I mean this town."

The bartenders eyes glimmered in mirth as he smiled and replied, "Nope, not yet. It's all new and a name ain't been decided on. Hell, it ain't much to look at right now anyways, but it might be some day."

Taylor chuckled and replied, "All towns start small, but you're going to need some other businesses to move here if you want more folks to settle nearby. I'd try to find a doctor, livery stable, school and for sure a church of some kind. Ain't nobody going to live in a town that don't have those things as a minimum."

"I hear ya, beer for the mind, doctor for the body, and a church for the soul. We'll get 'em all someday, but it takes time."

"Yep, that it does. Do you know where I can stable my horses and find a place to sleep? Actually a good meal would be nice too, if I can round one up around here." Taylor asked as he pointed at his near empty beer glass and nodded. His shoulder was hurting him, but he was unsure of how much to tell the friendly bartender.

As he refilled the glass the bartender said, "I let rooms out back for a dollar a night, you can stable your hosses out back as well, and it's only two bits for both horses. Now I got the best and only food in town and my cook starts serving right at five this afternoon. If you want to eat something now, you'll have walk over to the general store and get ya something small to chaw on until supper time. Hank's got pickles, crackers, canned goods and whatnot, but not a whole lot more than that in yet. He just opened up a month ago, so all of his stock ain't arrived yet."

Placing a dollar fifty on the bar Taylor asked, "How much is a quart of good rye whiskey here?"

"Two dollars and its good stuff too, come all the way from Kentucky. I'll tell ya what, there ain't nobody in the world that can make better whiskey than them folks over in Kentucky."

Taylor added another two dollars to the money on the bar and said, "Give me a bottle and if you'll tell me where my room is I might just take me a nap until supper time."

Taking the money and placing it in his right trouser pocket, the bartender reached under the bar, pulled out a quart of whiskey and said, "Hell, I'll do better than that, I'll take ya to your room. Business is slow and standing behind this bar gets old when nobody is around, so the break will do me good. Come on, I'll take ya to the room, it's dry and warm, and the roof don't leak much, unless it rains.

An hour later Taylor was in the room going through the gear and supplies the sheriff had been carrying. Besides the man's gear, he now had a good Hawken rifle and another pistol, so even without counting the big scattergun he was well armed. But, it surprised Donnelly to discover the man had enough equipment with him to stay on the trail for a month, which meant he'd been determined to bring Taylor to justice. Donnelly felt no remorse at all over the killing, after all the man had been looking for him, so as far as he was concerned the lawman got what he had coming.

In one of the packs, he found two blankets, a heavy sheepskin coat, some more clothing, and a mountain of canned foods and a few pounds of dried meat. In the other, he found cooking utensils, canvas for a shelter, a hand ax, and the normal supplies a man on a long trip would usually carry. Donnelly gave a slight grin when he discovered a sheriff's badge in the bottom of the second bag. As a joke, he put it on his shirt, right above his right breast pocket and then took a long gander in the mirror.

He was still wearing the badge a few minutes later when there was a loud knock at the door. Pulling the pistol, he cocked the hammer back as he grimaced in pain from his shoulder wound and asked, "Who's there?"

"The bartender," a loud reply came almost instantly.

Still holding the gun in his right hand, Taylor opened the door a crack and asked, "What do you want? I was taking a nap."

"I didn't mean to wake you, but I came by to tell ya that my cook is fixin' up some beef steaks fer dinner and the whole meal will only cost ya fifty cents. Good cook too, so you'll not want to miss out on it." The bartender said and then seeing fresh blood on Donnelly's shirt he asked, "Are ya alright? I see a lot of blood on the front yer shirt, sheriff."

Sheriff? Has he lost his mind? Donnelly thought and then remembered the badge over his pocket, so he replied, "I was trailing a feller earlier today and while I got 'em, well, he put some lead into my shoulder."

"We ain't got no doctor as such, but old Hank at the store has a gentle touch when it comes to healin'. Do you want me to fetch 'em for ya?"

Donnelly, not wanting the man to know he had much money on him asked, "What do you think he'd charge me to take a look at it? A lawman doesn't make much money and this ain't my town, so my funds are a bit low."

The tall bartender replied, "Hell, nothin' probably with you bein' a lawman and all. Oh, I guess he might have to charge ya fer medicine or bandages, but I'd figure less than a dollar. I'd better get him, because if that festers up there'll be hell to pay."

"Ok, go get him and let him take a look. The bullet went all the way through, so he ain't going to have to dig it out or nothing."

As soon as the bartender left, Taylor reached into his saddlebag and took out the pint bottle of laudanum. Adding just a little of the powerful drug to his glass, he filled the remainder with Kentucky rye. He was still sipping the drink when Hank arrived with the bartender less than twenty minutes later.

"Sorry it took me so long," Hank said, "but I had to close and lock up the store."

Donnelly threw back the remainder of his rye and laudanum, gave a glassy eyed grin and said, "It's not a problem as far as I'm concerned. I've stopped the bleeding, so all you really need to do it clean it out real good and cover it with a bandage."

"Well, take off your shirt and let me take a look at it. You've lost a lot of blood and I'd imagine you feel pretty weak about now."

"Yep, I do, so let's get the job done so I can get back to sleep." Donnelly said as he fought hard to keep his eyes open.

The storekeeper had Taylor lay down on his back in the bed and within minutes, the man was asleep from the affects of the alcohol and drug. Hank, taking his time, gently cleaned pieces of Donnelly's shirt and other debris from the wound. With the assistance of the bartender, he rolled the injured man over and repeated the process on the exit hole. Satisfied with his work, he then poured whiskey on both the entrance and exit wound, expecting Taylor to wake up screaming in pain, but the man only gave a very weak moan.

"How come he didn't scream or jerk all over the place when ya poured that whiskey on 'em? Every man I've ever seen goes ape shit when ya pour whiskey on 'em like that." The bartender asked as he stood beside the bed looking at Hank.

"Not sure, but I suspect it's due to all the blood he lost and the fact he's so weak. He's a lucky man, because if that bullet had been an inch lower it would have shattered his collar bone. But, I can tell you one thing, he's had that injury for a while." Hank said as he wrapped a long piece of clean white cotton cloth around Donnelly's shoulder.

"How do you know that, Hank?"

"There was not much of a bruise there anymore and a fresh wound always has a bruise, so his story 'bout bein' shot today is pure horse shit."

The bartender thought for a minute or two and then replied, "He is the law, so maybe he has a reason for not telling us the truth. Could be he's on a trail and don't want the man he's after to know he's been hit."

Hank shrugged and replied, "Hell, it don't matter none to me what his reason is. You just tell 'em when he wakes up he owes me two bits for the bandages and that's it. But, don't make no mention of the bruise or how we know he lied to us. I fig'er since he's a lawman he has his reasons and I don't need to become a part of any of it."

Donnelly slept until near six that evening and when he awoke his head was pounding and his shoulder was hurting him badly. Slowly, very sluggishly, he stood on wobbly legs and put his hat on, he needed to use the outhouse for a few minutes and then get some hot food in him. But, first, he poured a quarter inch of the laudanum in his glass and two fingers of whiskey. He knocked the drink back quickly and as he left the room a few minutes later he could already feel the pain disappearing.

Entering the saloon a little later, he noticed the bartender behind his bar polishing some glasses.   Seeing Donnelly the man said in a cheery voice, "Well, sheriff, nice to see you up and movin' around. Ya was pretty much out of it when Hank patched up yer bullet hole. Oh, by the way, my name is Ephraim Henderson, but my friends call me Hen. Hell ain't nobody that much likes the name Ephraim, including me, so I'd appreciate it if you'd call me Hen too."

Taylor gave a low laugh and replied, "Sure, Hen it is then. I'm Sheriff John Downey, out of Saint Louis." Taylor had quickly selected the name Downey, because it was close enough to his real name that he'd most likely respond if called. He'd added the common first name of John, though he knew no one would call him that. He'd be addressed as Sheriff Downey by all in the small town, mostly out of respect for his position.

"Ya 'bout ready to eat?" Hen asked with a smile as he put the glass he had been polishing on the bar.

"Not yet, I need a double shot of rye first. I still got the bottle in my room, though your man Hank must have poured half or more of it on my injury."

Placing a shot glass on the bar top, Hen poured Taylor a double as he said, "Yep, that he did and ya know as well as I do that alcohol is about all we can use to fight against festerin'. Hell, sheriff, festerin' ya don't want. I see'd a man die like that once, back in the war of 1812, and it's a hard death, it surely is. That drinks on the house sheriff, but the next one will cost ya."

Taylor threw the drink back, wiped his mouth with the back of his hand and said, "Let's go and see how that steak goes down. I need a couple of days of rest and then I have to move on. I got some jaspers that I need to have some serious talking with."

CHAPTER 21

Nate and his small group made excellent time as they rode north toward the Sioux, mainly due the fact that the weather had cleared and it had turned down right warm. It was early morning just as the sun was just starting its journey across the sky, when Cotton Top spoke in a low voice from the fire without looking up, "We got comp'nee and it's the Sioux."

Doc didn't move at all, but asked just above a whisper, "Did you see 'em or hear 'em?"

"Saw one of 'em move toward us a minute ago, but just a flash and then he went to ground on me."

Nate stood slowly, leaving his Hawken lying on the blanket he had slept in, and said in Sioux with loud voice, "My brothers, come share my morning fire! It is a good time to eat and talk with my Sioux friends."

No sounds and or movement was noticed for many long tense minutes, with Doc silently praying it was the Sioux Cotton Top had seen and not the Blackfoot. Finally, a lone brave stood and without speaking. He watched the two white men and one black man for some time.

Nate, recognizing the warrior said, "Pis ko, come and share my simple meal! Bring the others as well, for we have meat for all."

"I'll be damned, it's ole Night Hawk, ain't it?" Cotton asked.

"Yep, it's him, and I suspect a few others. As a leader of the Dog Soldier Clan he's not often out like this, unless they suspect some serious trouble is coming." Nate replied as he watched the brave slowly move toward him. Soon, ten more warriors stood from the tall grasses and then walked over to stand by the fire.

"Sit my friends and let us eat. Once we have eaten we will speak of many things." Nate said as the warriors sat around the fire.

Large portions of meat from a deer Cotton had killed the day before was skewered and place near the fire to cook. The mountain men knew each of the braves would eat a lot of meat and once the meal was finished there would be little left of the animal. Well over an hour passed without much being side by either group as they ate, and while that would've bothered most white men, the mountain men knew Indian's rarely spoke as they ate. The serious talk would start once the meal was finished.

Wiping his greasy hands on his buckskin leggings, Pis ko, or Night Hawk as he was called said in thick English, "I am glad to see my friend Buffalo Head is well."

Nate, who the Sioux often called either Raven Man, due to his black color, or Buffalo Head, because his curly hair resembled that of a buffalo, simply nodded. Then, pushing his hat back to the rear of his head, the big man met the warrior's eyes and said in Sioux, "What brings my friends the Sioux to my camp?"

"We are returning from a raid to steal horses from the Crow, when Many Tongues saw the light of your cooking fire last night. This morning we came to see who was on Sioux land."

"I see no horses with you, so your raid did not go well?"

The warrior gave a shy grin and replied, "We have them and they are many. Our young boys are now watching them less than five arrow shots from this camp."

"Is Buffalo Hump wintering by the sparkling waters?"

"Yes, it is our winter camp. Do you seek Hump or The People?"

"I have need to rest and want to visit my friends once more. Will I be made welcome?"

The warrior's dark eyes constricted and he replied, "Buffalo Head you are one of The People, as you know. You will be made welcome and given much to eat when you return with us."

"I thank The People for honoring me and my friends. Let us pack and we will join you on your journey to the village." Nate spoke as he stood, which to the warrior meant the conversation was finished.

For two days, the group moved toward the Sioux village, but instead of taking the fastest and most direct route, the warriors headed west and a day later they moved north. Nate knew the braves didn't want to lead the Crow right back to their village, but as he glanced around the moving group the black man thought, *A child could follow these tracks and the Crow are a long way from being children. This false trail won't fool them at all, or at least not for long.*

An hour after breaking camp this morning the sky off to the west suddenly darkened and the loud crack of thunder was heard. *I'll be damned, I wonder if these fellers knew it was going to rain,* Nate thought as he glanced at Cotton Top and said, "Strange, I was just wondering how the tracks we are leaving could be covered up, but now I see. Do you think they knew this storm was coming?"

Cotton chuckled, turned in his saddle to meet Nate's eyes and replied, "Night Hawk told me the village shaman told him not to worry about the Crow following him because God, or Wakantanka as they call him, would protect him during the return trip."

"Do you believe that will happen Cotton?"

Cotton broke out in a loud laugh, pointed to the west with his right hand and said, "Well, it's gonna rain like hell in less than an hour, so how's that fer an answer?"

Nate, confused over the Sioux Holy man's knowledge, pulled his hat down lower and thought, *It just can't be. Ain't no man that know's what God is goin' to do or not do. It's just plain good luck for the Sioux is all.*

Less than an hour after the dark clouds had fist appeared on the horizon the rain started to fall, gently at first and then slowly increasing in force. The Sioux feeling safer from pursuit, never considered stopping to get out of the weather. Nate knew the Indians would keep moving as long as the rain fell to wash away their tracks. Pulling his blanket tighter around himself and lowering his hat still more, he rode in the rain. He allowed the gentle swaying of his horse to comfort him. At times long white streaks of lightning sped along the horizon always followed a few seconds later by the deep boom or sharp crack of thunder. *Piss poor weather for man or beast to be out in,* Nate thought with an inward chuckle, *but it'll sure enough wash our tracks away.*

The rain continued to fall the next day and it was still falling when the small group approached the Sioux village beside a slow meandering stream. The trip had been almost nonstop once the rain started. The braves suddenly turned the horses straight for the village and at that point made no efforts to hide their destination, knowing the rain and runoff would wash away all sign of tracks.

Guards from the camp quickly rode toward the group to determine who they were and once they saw Night Hawk and his men they started firing their rifles in the air, screaming loud war cries, and generally raising a lot of noise in celebration of the taking of so many horses from the Crow.

Entering the village, the young boys in the raiding party took the stolen horses to add them to the main horse herd, but the warriors rode straight to the lodge of Buffalo Hump. The old man stood by the entrance to his lodge and waited for them to approach. As he watched them ride up his heart filled with pride in his warriors. As a Sioux chief, he was proud of his warriors when they did well against their enemies, just as he grew sad at the death of a single one of his braves. But, as a Sioux he knew it was better to die in battle fighting ones enemies than to live to be old and useless to The People.

"I see you have done well against the Crow, Night Hawk." The old man spoke with deep satisfaction in his voice, while his face showed no emotion at all. Buffalo Hump was in his mid-fifties, old for a warrior, short and squat, with an oval face. His eyes were a piercing black and they had a light upward slant to them. On his chest, above both nipples were deep scars, the results of a Sun Dance ceremony many years before.

"Yes, we took six hands and three fingers of horses from the Crow, without the loss of a single man."

"Songs will be sung of your leadership, Night Hawk, and the Sioux people will praise your bravery."

"So be it." The leader of the raiders stated flatly, but inside he was very glad the raid had gone so smoothly and no one had died, because the Crow were not an easy group to steal horses from in the best of times.

Buffalo Hump noticed the white men and Nate as they neared, but he waited until he'd praised Night Hawk before acknowledging them, "I see Night Hawk has brought Buffalo Head, Snow Top, and Medicine Man to visit The People. It is good to have you visit our lodges. Come, we must eat, smoke and then we will speak."

Two hours later, after a big stew of buffalo and wild potatoes, a long ceremonial pipe was pulled from a blanket beside Buffalo Hump. The old man stuffed the bowl, picked up a flaming brand from the fire, and as the flames of the twig met the bowl of the pipe, the old chief puffed a few times to get the tobacco burning well. As soon as the pipe was burning freely, the old man moved the pipe in the four sacred directions to symbolize the north, south, east, and west. Finally, he raised the pipe to signify the heavens and then lowered the pipe to symbolize the earth. He immediately handed the pipe to the man sitting on his left, who repeated the performance. It was not until the pipe returned to him that Hump spoke as he looked at Nate, "Have you come to visit The People for a moon or just for a few suns?"

"We will stay only for a few suns or perhaps less. We must soon leave and visit the trader Butterfield before we return to the mountains." Nate spoke as he met the old chief's eyes.

"This is a good thing to visit But-er-feel the trader is known among us as a man who speaks with one tongue and is fair when he trades with us." The chief leaned forward and moved a small log on the fire so it would give off more light.

"The trader has had much trouble with the Crow."

The old chief didn't speak for a few minutes and then said, "The Crow are a mighty people and their warriors are good enemies. A real man is measured by the strength of his enemies, so the trader and the Sioux are made greater because we both are enemies to the Crow."

"This is true, Buffalo Hump, but why have the Crow started attacking the trader? Do not all Indian's need the things the trader sells them or gives them in trade?" Nate asked.

Once again, the old man grew quiet and the only sound was of the windblown rain striking the stretched buffalo hide that covered the lodge, but at last he said, "Maybe the Crow, like the Sioux, are thinking of the great numbers of white eyes that flood onto our land. I cannot speak for the Crow, only for The People, but we too have many young men who want to kill all white men and force them from our lands."

Nate considered the comment from the chief and then replied, "The men from the east, the ones you call white men come in many different colors, and their number are greater than the grasses on the open plains. If you kill one man, five more will take his place. One day they will come and the Sioux will be no more. I think you feel this in your heart and it is part of your thoughts."

This time the chief spoke slowly, "The only white men we have not had trouble with have been those like you, the takers of beaver's skins. I grow old and I fear a fight between my people and yours, because I know your words of the white man's numbers are true and it is a battle we will not win in the end. But, in my heart I am a Sioux war chief and if I must fight for my land, I will do so, as I have done many times in the past.

To the white men the land is here to be pulled apart and the golden rock found, or food is grown in the torn soil, and that is not the way of the Sioux. We live as one with all things and do not understand the actions of the whites. Why is the yellow rock so precious to a white eye? Can he hunt or kill his enemies with it? Can he make love to it as he might a warm woman on a cold night? Can he not find enough plants to eat without tearing the heart out of the land to grow them? The whites are a difficult people to understand."

Lordy, thought Nate, *how do I explain money to a man that has no idea of what it is?* But he said, "The yellow rock is used by the white man to trade for many things, guns, horses, food, shelter, and women."

"I hear, but do not understand these words you speak. Why a rock? Are not all rocks the same? If a white man wants a woman, does he not give her father horses or gifts to take her as his wife? Cannot a white man steal horses from his enemies? Cannot a white man hunt for food, or make a shelter with his own two hands? I cannot understand why we fear a people who cannot do the simple things a Sioux child can do."

Cotton leaned close to Nate and whispered, "By God, he done backed your ass into a pretty corner."

"Chief Buffalo Hump, our peoples are different and our ways are not your ways. The golden rock has value to the white man, value like a good strong horse, so he desires to own the rock. Our customs are different too, so we do not give gifts for a woman or steal horses from anyone. Most of our people trade for food, shelter, or other things they need and do not know how to do otherwise."

The old chief blinked rapidly a few times, but the stony expression on his face did not change one iota. He considered Nate's words and thought long before he replied, "The whites are a strange people, of which I do not understand any more now than when we started speaking. I know you speak with one tongue, but your words are meaningless to me. But, I think the Crows are tired of having the white man trespass on his land, steal his land, and kill his game. Maybe the Crow have taken the path of war. For the Sioux there is peace with the white man now, but who knows what the next moon will bring?"

Little more than small talk was made the rest of the evening. The Sioux and their visitors knew the real conversation had died earlier when Buffalo Hump and Nate had spoke of white men. It was hours later, as they lay in the lodge provided for them that Doc said, "The red man just don't understand us and his lack of understanding will be the end for all of 'em. There ain't no way they'll ever keep the white man from this place, not once the word gets out about how good and rich this land is out here. And, I'm just talking about the dirt farmers. Hell, the sad part of it all is, that don't even count the gold seekers or other no goods that will one day flow over this land from horizon to horizon, just looking for something, anything to make a dollar."

"There will be a war one day," Nate added, "but let's hope it don't come for a few years yet. Now, get some sleep, I think we'll leave for Butterfield's early in the morning. There was something about the way Hump said some of his boys have been killing whites that grabbed my attention tonight. Suddenly I don't feel so safe here no more."

By dawn the next day, the small group was miles away from Buffalo Hump and the Sioux village. The rising sun brought broken gray clouds and off to the west rain was clearly seen falling in a long grove of oaks that ran in front of a dark purple snowcapped mountain. Nonetheless, Nate wanted some miles between him and the Sioux, if for no other reason than the chief's comment about the braves killing whites. Times were turning mean and it was getting to where even the friendly tribes were no longer as friendly as they once had been. Nate knew it was all due to change and it was a change no Indian would ever understand. As a nomad, the Indian called no single spot home. He traveled to stay near his food source, usually the buffalo or he moved to where he knew certain foods would be at a given time each year. The concept of staying in one spot and calling it home would never enter the mind of a red man. If his food moved, he moved with it. But, a white man would take an acre of land, plow it, plant his crops, grow some pigs, along with a cow or two, and live on the same spot his whole life. And Nate knew there were thousands upon thousands of people east of the Mississippi River that were just waiting for the right time to come west for free land.

"What are ya thinkin' on so hard there Nate?" Doc asked as he rode up beside him.

"Aw, hell, the death of the Injuns, I guess. You know, I don't care much for most of them red devils, but that's only because they are usually out to kill me. I guess as a people, they have a way of life and customs that work fine for 'em most of time, except more and more of us are starting to come out here to make a living. Sooner or later there'll be one hell of a fight."

"Can ya blame either of 'em? I mean, as far as most whites are concerned, these red men are just a bunch of savages that ain't doin' nothin' to improve the land. All those dirt farmers can see is corn and cabbages growing where some Sioux village now has a horse heard. And, we both know the Injuns ain't got even a basic understandin' of how a white man thinks about ownin' land."

"Yep, I once told a Snake Indian about a man I knew who owned a farm with lots of land and ya know he could not understand that. He wanted to know how a man could own what was not his. He considered the land as land and thought no one could own it. He asked if a man could own the waters, the air, or the sky."

"What in the hell did you tell 'em then?" Doc asked with a crooked grin.

"I told him the waters, sky, and air belonged to no one, but I thought a different story. You and me both know if a man owns the land he owns the water on it, but there was just no way I could explain that to an Injun."

"Yep," Doc replied with a dry chuckle, "I tried to explain that to an Osage Injun once over in Missouri and he looked at me like I was crazy. He told me the land belong to the Great Spirit and could not be owned by a single man."

"Well, the way folks are moving into Missouri territory right now I'm sure your Osage friend has a much deeper understanding of what owning land means to a white man."

The two men rode beside each other for another mile or so and then Nate suddenly said, "It's kind of sad our two people can't live together, but it would never work out. The white man is too greedy for land, money and material things, while the Injun is always on the move looking for food, fighting, or stealing horses. Hell, horse stealing alone is a hanging offense among white people, so we both know how well a horse raid would go over with white folks, don't we? And an Injun boy can't be a real man until he takes his first scalp, so that would cause a hell of a lot of trouble as well."

"I see the day comin' when most of the red people go under. I think somethin' will happen that will kill 'em off, and it might be the illnesses they are gettin' all of a sudden too. I visited some Comanche up north about five years back and then I visited the same group last year, and let me tell ya things had changed. On my first visit, there was well over a thousand of them red folks, but when I returned less than two hundred where still alive. I found out from the chief that small pox had hit 'em hard and killed off over eight hundred of 'em in two months."

"I ain't no Doctor, like you are, so what do you think is causing them to get sick like that all of a sudden? It don't make no sense to me, I mean they've lived out here for years."

"There is no way to know for sure, Nate, but before the comin' of big bunches of whites there were no serious diseases or illnesses among the Injuns. I can't prove it, but I think they are catching some of those sicknesses from us. I don't know that for sure, but take small pox for example, if you've been exposed to it at some point in your life you'll never get the disease if it hits your town. Now, most whites have been exposed to a variety of sicknesses by the time they are grown up, so maybe that's important to keep in mind for some reason. Maybe, just maybe, growing up with all of those diseases around us protects us in some way. And, remember, most serious white diseases these Injuns ain't never had or been around before, so maybe there is a link there. Honesty I don't know and I don't think any-one does for sure."

"Ain't there no way to keep a person for catching some of those diseases?" Nate asked, as his eyes grew large at the thought of a sickness that could kill hundreds of people at one time.

"The only one I know of that can for certain be prevented is small pox. A doctor over in England, oh way back in 1796 or so, came up with a way to keep a person healthy by inoculation. That means by scrapping the skin with a needle to put a medicine made from a cow inside the body of a healthy person before they are exposed to the real disease. How some ever, once they get sick with the real disease then it's too late."

"And we both know why the Injuns don't get any of that medicine, don't we?" Nate asked.

"Yup, we do." Doc gave a short reply and the gently kicked his horse forward.

Doc's a strange feller. He talks like a mountain man most of the time, unless he gets to talkin' about medicine or hurts, then he talks like one of them professor's at one of them big schools I heard tell of once. He's a learned man, and I wonder why he's out here? Nate thought, but knew he'd never ask the man, be-cause out west there were certain things you never asked a man, and that question was one of them.

CHAPTER 22

Donnelly rarely left his room in the back of the saloon, except to eat his meals or to buy a shot of rye whiskey. Two days had passed since he'd been fixed up by Hank the grocer and to kill the ache in his shoulder at night Donnelly had taken to mixing the laudanum with whiskey. He realized he needed to quit using the powerful drug, but each time he couldn't sleep due to pain, he'd mix a little of the drug with some rye, quickly gulp it down, and be asleep in minutes. This morning he was in the saloon having a breakfast of eggs, biscuits and gravy, when he saw Doctor's cousin Thomas Warner enter the saloon through the bat-wing doors. Knowing the interior of the saloon was dark and Warner would have to stand for a minute to allow his eyes to adjust to the dim light, Donnelly pulled the pistol from his belt, cocked it, and held it in his lap, but his eyes never left Warner standing at the door.

As the German made his way to the bar, Taylor lowered his head, hoping the man wouldn't notice him, but suspecting he would eventually. Warner was carrying two pistols in his wide leather belt and the man looked like he knew how to use them. Unlike before, the German was now wearing buckskins, moccasins, and a big felt hat. What bothered Donnelly the most was a big knife in a sheath on the man's right side, just behind a pistol. The sheath was hanging low and tied to his thigh, as if it would be the first weapon drawn and after the damage done by the Blackfoot tomahawk, Donnelly had an unnatural fear of edged weapons.

"Haben, I mean, *have* you seen a stranger? The English I have the troubles with." Warner asked Hen as the bartender looked up from behind the bar where he'd been stacking whiskey bottles.

"Nope, sorry, ain't been no strangers come to town in a coon's age, except ya." Hen replied as he stood and gave the German a warm smile.

The German pushed his hat back on his head, ordered and beer as he muttered, "Scheiße!"

"What's that ya said, Fritz?" Hen asked as he placed the cold beer on the bar top and took a dime from the German's right hand.

"It is nothing. I vas talking to meines, my-self ist all, und my name is Warner."

Hen gave a loud laugh and replied, "I do that all the time myself and sometimes it's the only way to have an intelligent conversation in this town."

As the two men were laughing, Donnelly quickly stood, put his right index finger to his lips and shook his head. Silently and as fast as he could, he left the saloon through the back door and went to his room.

Warner, catching a slight glimpse of the Donnelly's back as he left the saloon asked, "Who vas dat man?"

Hen laughed and said, "Our sheriff and he fer sure ain't no stranger around these parts. He's been feeling poorly, since he got into a gunfight with a horse thief here in town and took some lead in 'em."

Warner laughed and then asked, "Vat about the utter man?"

Hen's eyes grew narrow and when they were just slits he said, "Why our sheriff tied his neck to the short end of a long rope and gave his ass a ride right through the gates of hell."

The German looked confused for a second and then asked, "He vas hanged?"

Hen nodded and said, "When you want another beer, just let me know. I got some work to do at the far end of the bar." *There is a good reason the sheriff didn't want this man to see him and I'll bet this feller is either the man or one of the men he wants,* Hen thought as he moved his shotgun closer to the front of the bar without drawing attention from the German. *By God, if push comes to shove I'll side with the sheriff in a heartbeat.*

In his room, Donnelly was unsure what to do about Warner and as he thought, his shoulder began to ache severely once more. He added a little of the laudanum to his glass, poured in some rye, and took a sip, noticing his pain almost instantly disappeared. *I don't think I have to worry about Hen spilling the beans,* Donnelly thought, *he'll keep his mouth shut, I'm sure of it. But, how long will Warner stay in town? Shit, what if he takes a room here for a day or two? If that happens, I'll have to kill him sooner or later. I'd better go out right now and face 'em, at least I can kill him before he can learn very much from the bartender or talk too much either.*

Donnelly checked the load in his pistol, put his hat on and walked from his room toward the bar with the gun tucked in his belt. Entering by the back door, he walked into the saloon, noticed Hen behind the bar, and quickly glanced around the saloon, it was empty.

"Where'd that jasper go that was just in here?" Donnelly asked Hen as he walked toward the bar.

"Gone sheriff, and he said he had to leave right now. He was in such a hurry he didn't even spend the time to have another beer, and that's rare for a German. He told me he was heading south, deep into the Ozark Mountains."

"By God, that's good to know! He's one of the men I am looking for, but I knew with my shoulder the way it is I couldn't take 'em in a gunfight right now. Hell, I can hardly raise my fork, much less a pistol. But, since you know where he's headed, I'll pull out in the mornin' and follow him, but hang back until my shoulder gets some strength back. I ain't no coward, but I ain't no fool either." Donnelly spoke and then asked for a double rye.

Hen gave him a serious look and replied, "I was hopin' ya'd not get into a shootout with him, not hurt the way ya are. But, if ya did, well, I got a big scattergun back here that would have ended the fight pronto."

Donnelly smiled and said, "Thanks for the backup Hen, it's good know there are still some honest law abiding folks around."

"That I am sheriff and I'll always be. I can't stand a thief or a killer, because they both piss me off to no end. I guess because they both take what is not theirs, one takes property and the other takes lives."

Slamming his empty rye glass on the bar top, Taylor said, "Give me another double."

As he poured the drink, Hen gave Taylor a worried look and asked, "That shoulder of yers still hurtin' pretty bad? From what I could see, ole Hank he pulled a lot of stuff from that wound.

You want him to come by and take another look at it before you head out?"

"He looked at it earlier today, before he opened the store and said it was healin' nicely and the danger of festering is about over. Hank told me it should be back to normal in a couple of weeks or so."

Hen nodded and then spoke, "Ya go after that man was just in here, ya better keep your eyes peeled real good like. I didn't like the way he wore that Arkansas Toothpick low on his right side. I've seen knife fighters before and they are pure hell with a sharp blade in hand."

Donnelly gave a loud chuckle and replied, "I won't have to worry about. I'll sneak into is camp one night and take 'em, if I can, without a fight at all. I do it all the time, except with men real experienced on the owl hoot trail, then I just brace 'em." As soon as he'd spoken, he felt an involuntary shudder go through his body at the thought of the big edged weapon.

"Sheriff, I wouldn't have your job for a thousand dollars a month. That German Warner is looking for a man and from what I could tell he's got the look of death all over 'em."

Donnelly grew serious and stated in a flat voice, "It's death he'll find, only it will be his death not mine. I never take a chance with a knife man; they're too sneaky and dangerous."

"So, when are ya goin' after that Warner feller again?"

"Like I said, I'll leave in the morning right after sunup. If you're open that early I'll come by for breakfast, if not I'll say my goodbyes tonight at supper time."

Hen shook his head slowly and replied, "I'll be open, but my cook don't come in until six, so ya'll have eat my cookin'. I can fix ya up some scrambled eggs and deer steak, so at least ya won't ride out on an empty stomach."

Turning slowly, over reacting to his shoulder injury, Taylor replied as he grimaced in false pain, "Eggs will be just fine in the mornin', but I've got to get on that jaspers tail, or I'll lose him."

Taylor didn't do much the remainder of the day except read a month old newspaper, drink a little rye, and repacked his gear for the journey. At one point, he walked over to the store, picked up a jug of trader's whiskey, some chewing tobacco, and a rubber poncho, all of which he added to his supplies.

By the time dawn came the next morning, Taylor had his packhorse loaded and had already eaten a quick meal in the saloon. Offering to pay Hen for the meal, the bartender laughed and said, "Nope, the meals on the house sheriff. Ya know, we ain't got no law here and don't have the need a full time lawman, but if we ever do I hope we get a man just like ya. You're a good man, but ya watch yer ass when ya get on Warner's trail, ya heah me?"

"Thanks for the kind words Hen and I appreciate the meal too. I'll keep my eyes wide open when I trail Warner, and on my way back this way I might stop and spend a day or two with you again." Donnelly stated as he grabbed the saddle horn and swung up in the saddle.

"Ya do that and we'll have a drink together sheriff."

Pulling his horse around, Donnelly spoke over his shoulder, "See you in a week or less Hen, you take care."

The sky was overcast as Donnelly rode from the small no name town and while he had left heading south, he only rode about a mile on a southerly heading and then quickly swung to the east. *I'll head into Saint Louie for a spell and rest a bit. Damn, seems I've not really had any peace since I jumped from that damned boat,* he thought as he glanced upward and noticing no threat of rain or snow, he continued moving his mount at a slow walk.

Less than seven days later, a little before noon, Taylor sat on his horse at the top of a hill overlooking the rapidly expanding town of Saint Louis. Compared to most towns out west, Saint Louis was a major city and built right next to the mighty Mississippi River. The river trade, from both up and down the river, was making many men in Saint Louis very wealthy. From the city, trade was conducted to the north, with the Indian's and mountain men, and down river New Orleans and points in between generated enormous funds for those with business contacts.

Taylor M. Donnelly had been in the city before, as a liaison with a Colonel that represented the United States to the French government, who no longer controlled the land. At the time of his two-year assignment, the U.S. was allowing the French to keep a presence in the city, primarily due to the large number of French citizens that called Saint Louis home. Though the French had sold the land in 1803, twenty years before, they still held much of the cities wealth and had strong political influence in both countries. Being fluent in French, Taylor realized, would be a great advantage to him during his stay here.

Slowly walking his horse into the city, Taylor found the saloon he was looking for in just a matter of a few minutes. The saloon, which also doubled as a hotel, was on the west side of town near the gentle slopes of nearby hills. While just a short walk from main street, it was close enough to a thick forest of oak trees to make a fast getaway if need be, and which is a prime consideration for a hunted man.

Donnelly continued a short distance from the saloon and pulled up in front of a livery stable. Tying his horses to the hitching post, he walked inside and immediately noticed a big mountain of a man pulling a red-hot horse shoe from his glowing forge. Before the man could place the shoe on the anvil, Taylor asked, "You got room for two horses for a few days?"

The blacksmith pushed the shoe back into the red coals of his forge, turned and gave a big warm smile he replied, "Sure I do, but it'll cost ya two bits a day for each critter. I charge so much because I only feed 'em corn or oats and what hay they want."

Donnelly returned the smile, walked up to the big man and said, "I'm Sheriff John Downey and I'm in town on business."

The blacksmith extended this massive right hand and as they shook he said, "Well, sheriff, you'll find I'll treat ya fair and square when it comes to takin' good care yer ridin' stock. Ya need anythin' ya jess let me know, ok?"

Pulling the left side of his coat back, as if he was fishing for money, Donnelly made sure the man could see the badge over his shirt pocket. Finally, pulling out two dollars he handed to the blacksmith and said, "That's pay up front for a few days, but I need a favor from you too."

Taking the money, the big man asked, "Sure, if I can do it fer ya."

Donnelly moved close, as if he wanted to share a deep secret and said in a voice just above a whisper, "I might have some pretty nasty fellers on my back trail and I'd appreciate it you'd not tell anyone I've been here. I think they are already in town, but then again, they could have doubled back on me. Savvy?"

The smith laughed and replied, "Don't ya worry none, 'cause I'll not tell a soul. Hell, I'm a man for the law, so if this helps ya any I'll keep my mouth shut tight."

Reaching over and patting the big man on the shoulder Donnelly asked, "Thanks. Oh, would it be ok for me to leave my supplies from the packhorse here until I get a hotel room? I don't suspect I'll be very long."

"Tell ya what, ya unload yer gear and put it in the tack room I got off to the left over there and I'll keep an eye on it until ya come back and fetch it."

Less than twenty minutes later Taylor M. Donnelly entered the Western Vista Saloon and made his way to the bar. Quickly glancing around he noticed the place was almost empty and that pleased him greatly. Though his hair had grown longer and his beard now covered his face, Taylor was still concerned about being recognized by someone. Glancing at the big mirror behind the bar the reflection Donnelly saw of himself was no longer that of an immaculately groomed military officer, but rather a down on his luck saddle tramp or backwoodsman. He smiled as he met his own eyes in the reflection.

"Whot's the matter, you ain't neveh see'd a lookin' glass afore?" The bartender asked with a laugh as he neared with a soiled white cloth in his left hand.

"I've seen 'em lot's of times, but I just came in from out west. Been a while and I've thinned out a might." Taylor replied as he glanced at the big dirty bartender and didn't like what he saw right off. The man must have been three hundred pounds, with long greasy brown hair, and huge jowls that hung low from his fat cheeks. *This bastard is used to pushing people around because of his size*, Taylor thought as his eyes took the big man in.

"You want a drink, or just stand there and look at yer self?"

Suddenly angry at the man's earlier comment Taylor said, "Give me a rye with a beer chaser and, as long as I pay for my drinks in here, you've nothing to say to me ever again, unless it's to ask if I want another drink."

The big bartender laughed and leaning over the bar, almost right in Taylor's face, he said in a very low voice, "Mister, I could snap yer spine like a damned piece of kindlin' fer a fire."

In one lightning fast move, Taylor brought his pistol up, cocked it and stuck the end of the barrel right against the man's nose. As soon as the man's eyes grew huge, Taylor said, "Yep, you might be able to snap my spine, but you'll have to do the job with a bullet in the head. Now, I'm going to lower my pistol, you're gonna get me my drinks, and then you're going to keep your damned mouth shut. Do you understand me?"

"I . . . do! Yes, I honestly do, Mister. I was jess teasin' ya is all and I didn't mean nothin' by it."

"That's pure bullshit, but it doesn't matter much because I don't take much to teasing and you'd best be remembering that fact." Taylor said as he pulled his pistol from the man's face and put in back in his belt.

A minute later Taylor stood at the bar with a short glass of rye in his right hand. Quickly throwing the drink back, he placed the empty glass on the bar top, picked up his beer and took a healthy gulp. Wiping his mouth off with his right hand he asked, "You still have rooms here bartender?"

"Yep, we got 'em and they are a dollar a night."

"I want a good room for a week, but I'll warn you right now, if anything turns up missing I'm coming right for your fat ass."

The bartender gave a low gulp and replied, "Hell, ain't nothin' gonna happen in yer room, 'cause we run a safe place here."

"You'd better see for the next seven days it stays real damn safe. Here's ten dollars, give me a key to the room and a bottle of rye." Donnelly ordered as he handed the man the money and then when change was given he counted it slowly.

"Room three, that's the last one down the hall on the left side." The bartender said as he reached under the counter and pulled out a bottle of rye, handing it to Donnelly.

"Oh, and bartender?"

"Yes suh?"

"I don't like to be disturbed, so no visitors. None at all, understand?"

"No problem suh, ya enjoy yer stay." The big bartender said as he thought, *you sumbitch.*

CHAPTER 23

The same day that Donnelly entered Saint Louis, Nate and his small group entered Butterfield's trading post near dawn. Noticing Waters out gathering up wood for the breakfast fire, Nate yelled, "Howdy-do, Samuel!"

"Doin' just fine Nate and you?"

"Fine as frog hair! I'm meaner than a bear with a toothache, tougher than a hickory tree, and I can out shoot, out fornicate any man in the shining mountains! I'm Nate Grisham, a mountain man!"

The whole group gave a loud laugh at Nate's teasing of the city man and then dismounted. As Cotton Top was tying his horse to the hitching post, Samuel walked by with his arms full of wood. When the man had entered the trading post, Cotton glanced over at Nate and said in a serious voice, "By God, he's up early and workin' already, so we know he ain't lazy!"

Nate chuckled and replied, "Cotton, not all corncrackers are lazy. Hell, most of 'em are farmers, so they're used to getting up at the crack of dawn and starting right to work. Come on and let's go in, I'll buy you a drink."

Taking a table in the trading post the men were welcomed by Butterfield, who explained that business picked up as a few independent trappers bought supplies. "Not no big bunches yet, but a few at a time. And, my luck turned good just before that last big snow and I got a lot of supplies in from Saint Louis that I sorely needed for this spring. Thanks to Sam, well, I was able to inventory it and put it all up in no time. I'm a-tellin' ya right now, that man is one hell of a hard worker."

"Mister Butterfield, I'll be out in the barn if ya need me for anything." Waters said as he walked past the table.

Butterfield smiled and replied, "Sure Sam, then you come in and eat some breakfast."

As soon as the man left, Nate asked, "He still plannin' on goin' back east come spring?"

The trader shrugged his shoulders and said, "Hell, I don't know if he changed his mind or not. Why?"

Before Nate could say a word, Cotton Top said, "We're headin' up to Table Rock to finish out the season and we need a fourth man to go with us."

Butterfield shook his head slowly and replied, "Fellers, Waters is a good man, but he ain't no damned mountain man, no matter how ya look at it. Hell, he couldn't pour piss out of a moccasin if ya told him to turn it up-side-down to do the job. And, Table Rock is a rough mountain and it could be the death of him, and y'all know it."

Nate grew serious and said, "We know he don't know the mountains and he for sure don't know dumpling dust from Du Pont, but we only need him to keep camp so the rest of us can trap."

Now all of the mountain men at the table knew Du Pont was black powder, or actually the name of the company that made it, but Doc had never heard of dumpling dust so he asked, "What in the hell is dumplin' dust. Now, my greens worn off and it's been off for a long spell, but I've never heard that term before."

Butterfield laughed and replied, "It is flour dust. See, way back in the real old days, just about the time Nate came out here, fellers would add water to a small bag of flour to make bread or dumplings. When the water hits the dry flour in the bag it gives off a flour dust, thus the name. Only the old timers use the name much around here anymore."

Nate gave a stern look and asked with a slight grin, "You calling me old Butterfield?"

The trader laughed and replied, "Yep, old and worthless, but I still love your black hide!"

The men were still laughing when Samuel Waters walked in the room with a pail of fresh milk. As he walked past the men, he was grinning and shaking his head at their humor. He had no idea what they were laughing at, but he knew when Nate and his group came around laughter soon filled the place. Placing the milk on the table in the kitchen he covered the pail with a piece of cotton cloth and went out to where the men sat.

Waters had no sooner sat down than Nate asked, "You still dead set on going back east as soon as possible?"

"I was thinking on it. I would have gone back with the men that brought Butterfield's supplies, but they weren't going back. I could not have made the trip on my own, even though the weather broke and those men had a few weeks of good weather to get here. The last heavy snow I was in taught me a valuable lesson, Nate."

"Well, how would you like to make maybe two hundred dollars in two weeks time, maybe?"

Waters' eyes grew large and he asked, "How in the world can I make that kind of money so quickly?"

Butterfield laughed and spurted out, "Hell, ya know it's either dishonest or as dangerous as all get out fer damned sure!"

The men all laughed but then Nate said, "We need a fourth man to go with us into the mountains for maybe a month or less. Now, I won't lie to you, Sam, the job is dangerous and it could get you killed, but the money will be big if things go right."

"Nate," Waters spoke as he met the big man's eyes, "I don't know a thing about trapping beaver. I'd be more of a problem than a helper, or so I think."

"Not true. We're looking for someone to stay in camp, cook, clean, and care for the horses. From what Butterfield tells us you can do those jobs pretty good, so we'd like to invite you to go into cahoots with us for the trip."

Waters ran the idea through his head and realized he was bored stiff at the trading post, but he also considered the incredible danger associated with trapping in the mountains. *But, he thought, if I can return home with some money it'll make my return easier,* so he said, "Well, I came out here a fool to begin with and I see no reason to change now!"

All of the men laughed and once it quieted down Doc suddenly said seriously, "Sam, just so ya understand the lay of the land, we're not going into Crow country, but into Blackfoot country. And, the Blackfoot make the Crow look like young whippersnappers instead of the skilled warriors they really are."

"I don't really have any gear to take into the woods with me though."

Butterfield suddenly stood, walked behind the counter and quickly returned holding a big Hawken rifle in his hands. "Take this rifle with ya Sam, it's already been bought and paid for by a no account jasper named Taylor Donnelly. I guess I could sell it, but I've done made money on it once and I don't like the idea of making money off of something I've already sold once. Besides, Donnelly was a worthless sumbitch, so at least a good man will hold it in his hands now."

Waters took the gun from Butterfield, looked it over closely and then said, "Mister Butterfield, I don't know what to say."

Cotton Top gave a big tooth gaped grin and said, "Waugh! That gun shines, it surely does Sam. Just tell the man, 'thank ya kindly,' and let it go. Donnelly was a killer and ya'll put the gun to better use than he ever would have."

"Now," Nate said as he leaned his elbows on the tabletop and placed his palms on his cheeks, "we need some supplies before we leave. We got some plews outside right this minute that are in pretty good shape, but I'll be paying in greenbacks for what we need right now. The skins we will have ya keep for us, if you will, until we get back in a couple of weeks or a month."

Butterfield's eyes grew large at sound of greenbacks, so he asked, "Ya mean ya got real honest to God foldin' money?"

"Yep, from the reward for Donnelly, or did you forget?"

"No, I knew there was a reward, but I thought they'd pay ya in that worthless script they're always passin' around. And, I'm here to tell ya all, I won't take a dime in script. Hell, they only pay script off if ya take it to an army post and that has to be on the day the paymaster arrives. But," the trader grinned and then continued, "for greenbacks I'll give ya good price for anything I got in the store!"

Once again everyone laughed.

Nate pulled the reward money from his saddlebags and said, "Since Skeeter has gone beaver on us, we each get three hundred thirty-three dollars and thirty-three cents. But, we'll buy our supplies first and then divide this money up. Waters, we'll loan you fifty dollars for powder, lead, a powder horn, and whatever else you need for the trip. You'll pay us back when we come out with the plews."

"Sound fair to me." Doc stated with a grin.

"That's some, it surely is." Cotton spoke grinning also.

"Huh?" Waters asked confused.

The big black man gave a laugh and said, "Cotton means that's good or nice. I think you'll be learning more than just how to live like a mountain man Sam, you'll have to learn our language too!"

Everyone laughed and then Cotton Top said in a loud voice, "Butterfield, get us a jug of whiskey, 'cause we need to celebrate our new partner, Deacon."

Nate, still grinning, suddenly turned serious and said, "By God, now Cotton, that's a good mountain man name for the man. We cain't go around callin' 'em Mister Samuel Waters all the time, now can we?"

From that day forward, Samuel Waters was no more in the shining mountains, and in his stead was Deacon.

Two days later the morning was cold and the wind had a sharp knife like edge to it as the four men moved slowly toward the distant mountains. The sky overhead was gray, but other than the cold, there was nothing to slow the men down, except for caution. The day before Nate had pulled Deacon aside and said, "We just entered Blackfoot country a couple of miles back. Keep your rifle out of its case and in your hands at all times. If you shoot it, immediately reload it, no matter what happens around you. We will keep our fires small and two of us will always stand guard at the same time. That means we'll all have to pull watch for about seven hours a night, since the days are short now."

"Nate, if you're trying to scare me, you're doing a good job of it right now."

"Deacon, I'm just being honest with you is all. Now, none of this means we'll see a single Blackfoot feather, but if we all want to come back alive, we have to be prepared to fight like hell with less than a seconds notice. Bugs boys are not to be taken lightly at any time we are in their mountains."

"Ok, I'll fight if push comes to shove." Deacon replied as he reached over his saddle and pulled his Hawken from its sheath.

Nate nodded and then moved his horse forward. As the gentle swaying of the horse calmed the big man, he wondered if bringing Deacon along might not have been a serious mistake. Oh, Nate liked the man well enough, but the sky pilot was having a hard time adjusting to traveling with mountain men. The men were up an hour or so before sunrise, packed, breakfast eaten and on the trail before the light of day. The small group rode until an hour before dusk, stopping only long enough every few hours to rest the horses, and once stopped at dusk they'd eat a quick meal and then move a mile or so further down the trail to spend the night. Additionally, each man would stand his allotted time guarding the camp each night, which left little time for serious sleeping. Mountain men took the routine as nothing unusual or even pushing hard, it was just the way they traveled, but for a flatlander from back east the normal day of mountain man travel wore them out quickly. But, to Deacon's credit, he not once complained.

The small group arrived at the spot Nate had in his mind on Table Rock Mountain early one morning about two hours after sunrise. The selected camp was about two miles from the nearest trail of any sort and hidden back in a large and thick forest of pines and cedars. The weather was still cold, but the trees blocked most of the wind, so Nate knew they would have an easy go of it even if the temperature dropped to well below freezing. He knew snow would stack up by the foot. He wasn't worried about food, because he'd bought fifty pounds of pemmican and a hundred in buffalo jerky from Butterfield, so while the simple food might get monotonous after a few weeks, it would keep them alive.

This night as they sat around a very small campfire to fight off the cold, Nate asked, "You having any second thoughts about this trip Deacon?"

Deacon laughed and replied, "I'd be a liar if I said no, but I'll get used to it. You fellers travel fast and hard, and I have to admit I'm more than just a little saddle sore. What bothers me the most though, is the lack of sleep."

Cotton choked on his coffee and once he settled back down he replied, "We travel hard and fast? Hell, Deacon, this trip wasn't rough at all. Now, if we get some Blackfoot on our hindends then you'll see us ride hard and fast."

Nate grinned and said, "I can understand about the lack of sleep, but it's normal for us to only get a couple of hours of sleep a night and after a few months you won't think much about it either. You can catch up on your sleep if the weather turns bad or when we get back to Butterfield. And, what Cotton Top said is true, we'll travel a hell of a lot faster if the Blackfoot get after us."

The first three weeks were uneventful as the three mountain men would leave each morning and return in the afternoon loaded down with prime beaver skins. The simple meals prepared by Deacon were a great improvement over anything the mountain men could cook, and in less than two days, they all agreed that bringing Deacon had been a smart move. The farmer worked hard each day gathering a good supply of firewood, packing water from a nearby stream, taking care of the horses, cooking hot meals, and overall taking charge of the camp. While he might never be called a mountain man, Deacon had proved he was a valuable asset to the men.

One evening, after returning as usual wet and cold, Cotton walked up to the fire and stated, "I saw Blackfoot sign today. I was running my trap line over by Cold Creek when I found a campsite them red boys used in the last day or so."

"Any sign they saw yer traps?" Doc asked as he leaned forward toward the fire.

"Nope, but not much gets by their eyes."

"How many in the group?" Nate asked, wondering if they should take what they had and make a hard ride of it that night.

"Hard to tell, but I'd guess nye on eight of 'em."

Handing Cotton a tin plate filled with hot beans and bacon, Deacon asked, "Do you think they suspect we're around?"

Pulling the coffee pot from the fire, Cotton spoke as he filled his cup, "Now, that is a good question. Damned good question, only I wish I had ya an answer."

Offering Cotton a thick slice of cornbread the farmer asked, "What will we do now?"

"Well," Nate spoke in a serious tone as he turned and met the bible thumpers eyes, "I suggest you say a few prayers. Now, it's possible, but not very likely those Blackfoot have no idea we are anyplace around here."

At that moment, there came a loud war cry and when Nate turned to look toward the noise, he saw a small group of Blackfoot running straight for his camp. The big man raised his rifle, sighted in on the runner in front and squeezed the trigger, knowing before he fired he'd hit his target solidly. The heavy lead ball struck the brave in the chest and threw him back hard against two others right behind him, causing them to fall as well.

Cotton dropped his plate of food, raised his Hawken and fired, watching one brave fall to the ground. Cursing, he said as he pulled his ramrod and immediately started reloading, "Blackfoot won't even let a man eat without startin' some shit! They could've let me eat my beans first!"

"They followed ya back here, ya dunderhead," Doc spoke calmly as he aimed and fired his first shot. His ball struck a brave knocking the man down, but he was quickly on his feet and running once more.

Deacon, unsure of what to do, sighted in on a warrior in the middle of the pack, squeezed his trigger and was surprised when two men went down hard. As he reloaded, he heard Nate say, "Good shootin' Deacon, a two fer one bullet is mighty fine in anybody's book."

Casually the mountain men spoke as the remaining group of running Blackfoot neared, until Cotton Top suddenly said in a voice slight higher, "Gonna be dancin' time in a few seconds, these boys are gettin' a mite close."

Deacon was so engrossed in loading his rifle that he didn't see the brave running straight for him until the last minute. The Blackfoot had a tomahawk in his right hand and long bladed skinning knife in his left. As the warriors hand with the toma-hawk swung downward, Deacon raised his rifle and took the blow from the sharp blade on the steel of his barrel. Then, dropping his empty rifle, the farmer pulled his pistol from his leather belt and with his hands shaking; he pushed the barrel against the braves belly and pulled the trigger. The Blackfoot was blown back by the force of the heavy fifty-caliber ball strik-ing him and was dead before he hit the ground.

Nate had his hands full with a huge Blackfoot that seemed to know what hand-to-hand combat was all about. Both of the big men circled but neither could see a weakness in the other man's defenses. Suddenly there was the loud report of a rifle shot from nearby and Nate saw blood fly from the rear of the Indian's right shoulder. Struck hard and spinning from the impact of the rifle ball the brave tripped and fell into the flames of the fire.

Instantly the warrior's freshly oiled hair flashed up in flames and as he attempted to climb from the burning fire pit, his greasy buckskins flared up. When he finally stood the big Blackfoot warrior was a human torch. Deafening screams came from deep inside the flames as the man began to walk, seeking what even he knew not. After but a few short steps he fell to the dirt on his knees, as the flames continued to consume his greasy clothing. Giving a dreadful scream the brave's body began to jerk violently. Nate walked to the man's side the shot him in the head.

At the sound of Nate's pistol shot, the battle ended. Looking around, as he attempted to keep from gagging from the smell of the burnt Blackfoot, Deacon noticed Nate was holding his left thigh, Cotton was on the ground bleeding from his head, and Doc was holding his left arm as blood seeped through his fingers. Of the four men, only the farmer was unscathed.

"Where'd they all go?" Deacon asked in shock from the brutality of the short battle.

"Most likely back fer help." Cotton spoke as he stood on weak legs and wiped the blood from the graze to the left side of his head.

"Break camp and let's do 'er now boys! We ain't got much time and I think this is going to turn into a ball buster of a rush to get out of these damned mountains with our hair!"

"What about the gear?" Doc asked as he moved over to help Nate to a horse.

"Take the skins and leave the rest! We gotta get the hell out of here and I mean now!"

"Leave it all?" Deacon asked in surprise.

"Deacon, in a few minutes all the damned Blackfoot in the world are going to come visiting us. Now, if you want, your ass can stay here and pack the supplies, but I'm forking a horse and getting the hell out while the getting is good." Nate spoke as he climbed up in the saddle Doc had quickly placed on his horse.

Moving quickly, with packhorses loaded with skins behind them, the small group of white men started down the side of the mountain as fast as they could and still keep their mounts at a walk. Deacon had been surprised at how quickly the men secured the bales of plews to the packhorses, saddles placed on the horses, and all done by men who were injured in battle. Granted the men all felt a desperate need to move quickly, but it was the speed which amazed the farmer. *These are not scared men fleeing in uncontainable panic. These are men well in control of their fears and well trained to do things quickly, need be,* Deacon thought as he rode up beside Nate.

Nate, glancing at Deacon, said in a low voice, "Now you will see just how hard a mountain man can travel when need be. You'll likely not sleep another minute Deacon until we reach safety at Butterfield's. Poor doin's and lean times are comin', and they'll stay with us until we reach the trading post.

CHAPTER 24

Donnelly entered his room and was not the least bit upset by the lack of furnishings, the peeling wallpaper, or the cracked mirror mounted over an ancient chest of drawers. It was typical for most western towns, but usually in Saint Louis, the accommodations were much better but a man paid for what he wanted. Taylor didn't want anyone to know that he had money, so he'd come to this saloon to look the part of a man down on his luck from the frontier. Besides, the ex-army officer had an idea on how to make some serious money and get his hands on that big Nate Grisham. It was in this very place, the Western Vista Saloon, a few years earlier where he had made a lot of important contacts.

When Taylor had been in Saint Louis before, he used his many contacts from the saloon to move stolen gear from the army and at times a horse or two. Once, because the money offered was so good, he'd even given information about a military payroll that was heading west toward Omaha. Taylor had given his contact the number of men going with the gold to protect it, the route they would follow, as well as specific dates, times, and locations where the army would stop along the way. He'd learned later that every man in the escort had been killed and the money stolen, but his information had netted him well over five hundred dollars. It had been in the city by the muddy Mississippi that Taylor M. Donnelly had started his slow slide to being a thief and a murderer.

After having a shot of rye with a little laudanum in it, Donnelly went back to the livery and picked up his gear. As he was bringing it in the saloon, he noticed the bartender give him a glance and then look away. *So, he's learned a few new things today,* Donnelly thought with a light chuckle.

Storing his gear in a far corner, away from his bed, he left the room and went back to the saloon. As he bellied up to the bar he ordered a double rye and as the bartender brought his drink, Donnelly asked, "You know of any soiled doves around?"

The filthy bartender laughed and said, "Mister, about I know in this world is whiskey, beer, and whores."

Donnelly gave a low chuckle and replied, "Of that much I'm certain. How much would it cost me to get a good whore for a day or two?"

"Well," the big man said as he thought, "Ella is good, but all she'll do fer a man is screw his eyes out and nothin' else. Now, if yer lookin' fer a woman that'll do damned near anything you can think of, then you want Victoria. Only, I'll warn ya right now, she don't come cheap, but she'll do any damn thing fer a man if the price is right."

"She all worn out and ugly?"

"Hell no, she's right off the farm. She walked in here less than a month ago and said she was from Illinois, but I don't care where she's from as long as she's good in bed and makes money. The house gets twenty percent of her fees."

Donnelly threw back his drink, grinned and said, "Send her to my room in an hour or so and we'll see if we can make this place some money tonight. If the cost is low enough I might keep her for a couple of days even."

The bartender, more relaxed with Taylor now, laughed and replied, "I'll give her special orders to keep the price low. A good man like ya should get a break while he's stayin' with us."

As he turned from the bar Taylor said, "Bullshit."

An hour later, after he'd had a hot bath, Taylor was dressed and in his room sipping on two fingers of rye as he read the Saint Louis Monitor newspaper. There was a small article about his escape, the killing of Ralf and the brutal rape of his wife, but little else as far as details went. Finally, on the last page of the paper near the bottom, he read about the sheriff of New Burg being found killed and robbed, but his name was being withheld until his immediate family was notified. The article stated there were no suspects in the killing, but it was being investigated by a Federal Marshall out of Chicago. He had just dropped the paper to the floor beside the bed when there was a light knock at his door.

Pulling his pistol and cocking it, Taylor asked, "Who's there?"

There came the sound of a light laugh and then a female reply, "A workin' woman, sugah."

It's the whore, Donnelly thought as he opened the door just a couple of inches and looked out into the dimly lighted hallway. The woman was tall, with long blond hair, big blue eyes, and her lips puckered in a way that he found to be deeply sensual. Looking closer, he noticed she had wide hips, narrow waist, and big breasts with more than just a little cleavage showing. Still holding the cocked pistol, Donnelly said, "I'm stepping back from the door now. You count to four, very slowly and then enter. Once inside I want the door closed and locked immediately. Do you understand me?"

"However you want to play the game honey." She replied instantly and a few seconds later she entered, closed the door and locked it. Turning to face Donnelly she said, "I hope you're as loaded as that big horse pistol is."

"Sit on the bed and let me tell you a few rules I have with whores in my room."

Victoria moved to the bed, but instead of sitting she laid down and then stated, "You set the rules and then we'll talk price. I don't come cheap, but I'll do what it takes to leave you a very happy feller."

"First, no stealin' from me. If I catch you doing it or even suspect you have taken so much as a nickel from me, I'll kill you. Second, you keep your visit with me a secret and you'll tell no one you were ever here. Now, what are your prices?"

The whore laughed and said, "Not yet, 'cause ya ain't seen what I've got to offer ya." Standing, she reached down and grabbed the hem of her dress, and slowly pulled it up over her head. She was complete naked underneath and Taylor was stunned by the perfection of her body. Grinning at him, she asked, "Like what ya see? Wait until ya get a small taste of what I can do with what I got here."

Suddenly turning a complete circle she turned her head slightly she said, "It looks good, doesn't it? You can have all of this, if you have want to pay the money I ask for it."

"How much?"

"Three dollars for just a quicky, five dollars for four hours of the same, or for seven dollars we can spend the night and I will do *anything* you want and for as long as you want." As soon as she spoke, the young whore ran her tongue over her pouting lips slowly and smiled.

Taylor grew angry at his loss of control, but knew he had to have this woman. Maintaining his composure, he walked to the dresser, picked up the bottle of rye and poured two drinks into glasses. Handing one of the glasses to the whore and keeping the other, he asked, "How much for a week?"

"Ya feed me, or give me money to eat on every day, keep me in rye whiskey, and I'll do the job fer thirty dollars even. But, ya have to keep the food and whiskey available or the deals off and it's fifty bucks for the week." As soon as she had made her offer, she leaned back on the bed.

"Deal," Taylor replied.

An hour later Taylor stood, quickly dressed and said as he handed the whore four dollars, "Victoria, I want you to get dressed and go to the nearest restaurant, and find us some good food. Roast beef, steaks, or maybe some fried chicken would be good, along with all of the trimmings. Then, on your way back, stop in the saloon and pick us up another bottle of rye. I suspect this will be a long night and we might as well prepare for it."

Almost jumping from the bed, Victoria gave a big wide grin and replied as she pulled the dress over her head, "Sure and I know just the place fer the food. It ain't nothin' fancy, but it's real good home cookin' and I eat there all the time. I'll be back directly."

No sooner had the woman left the room, than Taylor thought with a grin, *a woman like you could grow on a man. You have the kind of looks and a body most men would kill for, plus you have all the sexual skills a man could ever dream of. When I leave Saint Louis, my sweet Victoria, you may very well leave with me. I could grow very fond of you my dear, very fond.*

Pouring the last of the rye into his glass, Taylor looked around the room and suddenly realized he could still smell heavy lust in the air. He could also clearly smell her cheap perfume, as well as the musky female odor of her deep animal like arousal, and his grin grew larger when he thought of her pas-sion. Victoria had been a woman with a deep primal need for sex and Taylor had enjoyed the simple fact that the young soiled dove enjoyed her sex rough and fast. *If she wasn't a whore and had a few important connections with folks with some money,* he thought, *she'd make a perfect wife.*

The week passed very quickly for Taylor M. Donnelly, with Victoria keeping her promise to him by making herself available to him at any hour of the day. It was early on the morning on the day he was to leave, as Taylor lay beside her in bed, that he asked, "You like being with me?"

"Yer nice enough," the young woman replied.

"How would you like to go out west with me?"

"Have you lost yer damn mind, Taylor? Hell, there ain't nothin' out there, but Injuns and wolves. But, if ya was headin' east I'd go along fer the ride and I mean that in more ways than jess one." Victoria replied and instantly gave a lusty laugh.

"You sure you won't head west?"

"No chance in hell. Look, Taylor, yer a nice man and ya know how to make a woman happy, but I'm a workin' lady and I ain't hear'd of no whores workin' past Fort Atkinson. I'll stay here, if ya don't mind."

She knows about my missing ear and she's questioned me about the scar on my upper lip and cheek, and she's even talked about the tip of my nose missing, he thought as he smiled warmly at her, *and she'd tell all she knows about me for the right kind of money.*

"Well, I have to get up and get dressed in a minute. I want to be on the trail to Atkinson way before sunup and I'll not do that if I spend too much time in bed with you."

"Let's have some fun one more time before ya leave Taylor." Victoria pleaded.

Rolling on top of the woman, he kissed her, and without her noticing, he pulled a long skinning knife from the sheath that had been hanging on the bedpost for a week. Grasping Victoria's hair he pulled her head back and she moaned enjoying the rough treatment.

Moonlight coming through the window flashed briefly on the blade of the knife as Taylor leaned forward, covering her body with his, and quickly ran the keen edge under her chin from left to right, cutting her throat from ear to ear. Her body jerked and twisted in fear and pain as the bed under her head was quickly covered in blood. Climbing from the bed Taylor watched fascinated as she rolled over onto her back, met his eyes, and seem to be asking why? With each heartbeat blood spurted from her severed throat and as she ferociously shook her head violently in both terror and disbelief the walls were soon dripping blood. Finally, less than two minutes after he had cut her throat, Victoria started choking on her own blood and less than a minute later she was dead.

Leaning over, Taylor wiped the bloody blade of his knife clean on her right leg, and said, "What a waste of good woman. Sorry my dear, but you knew too much and I could not allow you to live any longer."

Quickly Donnelly dressed, gathered up his gear and left the room as if nothing had happened. The bartender had arrived earlier than normal this morning and he looked at Taylor as he walked by the bar and asked, "What about Victoria, she still sleepin'?"

"Hell, yes, you know how whores sleep when they get the chance. But, the rooms paid until noon, so wake her up then." Taylor replied with a loud laugh as he walked through the bat-wing doors and out into the fresh night air.

The big smith was already up and working the fire in his forge when Taylor arrived a few minutes after he'd left the sa-loon. Noticing Donnelly, the blacksmith asked, "Ya need yer mounts this mornin' like ya said ya would yesterday afternoon sheriff?"

"Yep, ya got 'em ready to ride?"

"All ready to go except fer what extra gear ya want to add to yer packhorse."

Taking his time, Donnelly added the odds and ends he'd brought with him from his room to the loaded packhorse, paid the smith, and said, "I tell all of my lawman friends about the ex-cellent service I got from you during my stay here. You run a fine business and when I come back this way I'll use you again."

As Donnelly mounted, the smith replied, "Thank ya kindly sheriff and ya have a safe trip."

Moving his horse east, toward the Mississippi River, Taylor waited until he rode over the crest of a big hill, still on the road toward the river, and then suddenly cut due south. *So*, Donnelly thought, *as far as the smith knows I was heading east the last time he saw me.*

The next six days were days with many miles covered and Donnelly figured on the morning of the seventh day he'd already covered more than a hundred and fifty miles since Saint Louis. As he was placing his coffee pot on the flames of the fire to boil, he noticed wetness at his groin, but gave it little thought, assuming he'd spilled some water on himself. He ate a quick meal of fried smoked ham and sliced bread he'd picked up in Saint Louie, and then relaxed as he drank four cups of coffee. It was after he smoked three cigarettes that he suddenly knew he had to make water. Standing as he rubbed the tiredness from his eyes he made his way to the far side of camp and noticed the whole front of his canvas trousers were wet on the inside. Taylor suddenly felt sheer terror run through his body as he realized he'd caught something from Victoria. As he peed, a deep burning pain ran through his member and it took all the willpower he had not to cry out.

Like most military men, Taylor M. Donnelly knew there were some forms of the illness that could be treated, but as far as he knew, none of the illnesses could be cured. Once a week as an officer, he'd been forced by his Commander to have all of his men line up and drop their pants. Then, Donnelly and his First Sergeant would go down the rows of men, looking for the tell tale signs of the French Pox as most of the men called it. He knew well the signs, the treatment and results of some of the diseases, and that very knowledge made him shiver in fear.

For the next six days, Donnelly lived with the pain each time he relieved himself and more than once he had to dry the tears in his eyes from the deep burning ache. The only way he seemed to be able to empty his bladder without any pain was by sipping just a little of the laudanum a few minutes before he made water. What Donnelly knew, but refuse to admit, was he was now dependent on the strong pain killing liquid for almost any minor pain he experienced.

It was midday, seven days after he'd become ill, that he entered a small backwoods town named Cold Creek. It wasn't much to look at and as he rode down the only street in town he was looking for a doctor's office. Finally seeing the sign of a doctor's office mounted above the door of a rough pine planked building, he quickly dismounted, tied his horse to the hitching post, and almost ran up the stairs to the man's office.

As he opened the door a small bell tinkled overhead and he immediately noticed a middle-aged man of average size sitting behind a big wooden desk with his glasses perched low on his long nose. The doctor looked up, gave a smile as he pushed his glasses up, and asked, "How may I help you sir?"

"My name is Taylor, William Taylor, and I think I've caught the French Pox." Donnelly quickly replied and then lowered his head in shame.

"Son, come over here and climb up on my table. We'll not do anything now until we get a few questions answered, ok?"

Donnelly nodded, moved to the table and climbed on top of the doctor's table. Still sitting, he asked, "Do you want me to sit up or lay down?"

The doctor chuckled good-naturedly and replied, "Which ever will help you think better to answer some questions. I won't check you until we do the questions, so relax a little."

Twenty minutes later, the doctor had the answers to his questions, examined Donnelly, and slowly shook his head as he said, "Mister Taylor, from what I am able to tell you have contacted syphilis, of which there is no known cure. However—"

"Good God, syphilis!" Taylor suddenly blurted out in deep fear and anger.

"As I was saying, however, there is a form of treatment for the disease using mercury."

Turning angry Taylor replied with a sharp bite to his tongue, "Mercury? The army tried that shit and it doesn't work."

"No, it doesn't cure the disease, but it does reduce the severity of painful urination when taken orally and once the lesions begin to appear it will make them dry up and heal faster if applied directly on the sore. I'm afraid there is not much we currently know about the French Pox, as you called it, and the best I can do is give you mercury."

Donnelly felt his face turned red in anger and wished he had killed Victoria a thousand times instead of just once. His hands trembled and his voice cracked as he asked, "How long before this shit kills me?"

"It's hard to tell actually. Some die in just a few years, while others live more than twenty years, except remember during the last stage you'll go blind. But, as of this minute there can be no form of sex for you at all, because it would spread the disease and that could kill a lot of folks, especially if you continue to use soiled doves."

"You forgot to tell me I'll go insane before I go blind doctor and I know that from the army! If I'm insane, you worthless damned idiot, do you honestly think I will realize when I start to go blind! What kind of a dumb-assed saw bones are you?"

The doctor lowered his eyes and then replied, "I was keeping it from you because there was no need for you to know all the facts of the last stages of the disease. Why should I cause you needless worry?"

Reaching into his coat pocket Taylor pulled out a twenty-dollar gold piece and asked, "Do you carry that new drug laudanum?"

"Yes, of course, but it will have no affect on curing your illness. It is a painkiller used for surgery or to reduce severe pain from an injury."

"Can you sell me the medication or not?"

"Yes, there are no laws to prevent it, but it is a waste of good money and research has shown it can be habit forming." The doctor spoke as he opened the top drawer of his desk, pulled out two pints of laudanum and placed them on his desktop. Reaching into the same drawer once more, he pulled out a small bottle of mercury and sat it next to the tincture of opium.

Taylor laughed and replied, "Doc, you're one dumb sonofabitch, do you know that? You just told me five minutes ago, I'll eventually die of syphilis and now you're worried about me developing a habit of taking laudanum? What in the living hell have I got to lose by taking any damned drug or drinking my ass off, I'm already a dead man!"

Picking up the three bottles of medicine, Taylor quickly put them in his coat pockets, and gave a loud insane laugh as he said, "You're a real hoot doc, a real live fool!"

And, you, the doctor thought, *will soon be a dead man.*

Chapter 25

Nate and his small group didn't rest for one minute the night they broke camp and fled the Blackfoot warriors. A little after midnight a light rain started to fall and still Nate kept the group moving forward with only short breaks for the horses every few hours. By noon the next day Deacon's eyes felt like they were filled with sand, his rear was saddle sore and raw, and yet there was no hope of getting even the slightest rest.

"Nate, we keep movin' like this and we'll start losin' the horses before too long." Doc warned as he dropped back to ride by the big man.

"Just a few more hours and then we'll stop for three hours, but not a minute more."

"That'll do the job; only I'd hate to get rubbed out by a bunch of pissed off Blackfoot warriors just over some beaver plews and if we wear these horses out we'll lose it all."

Cotton Top gave a dry humorless chuckle and said, "Hell, it still might happen even if we rest. I agree with Nate, we push hard and we keep pushing until we're safe at Butterfield's."

At that point, Deacon leaned far to the right from his saddle and it was only Nate's big hand, which suddenly grabbed him, that kept the man from falling. Giving Deacon a rough shake Nate said as the man's eye's slowly opened, "Deacon, you fall asleep out here and the Blackfoot might get your ass. Now, I want you to remember how Moses looked when we found him. Do you remember how he was all butchered up?"

Deacon felt a sudden rush of adrenaline and replied, "I'm awake Nate and yes, I remember what the Crow did to Moses. It's just that I'm so tired and this moving is killing me."

Cotton gave another dry chuckle and said, "Them damned Blackfoot get their hands on yer ass alive and ya'll wake up fast enough, especially when they start cuttin' on ya. There is something about a sharp knife edge that wakes a man up pronto."

"I'll stay awake now, but I'm not sure how much longer I can keep up this pace. The last time we slept was two nights ago and I've been awake for over thirty hours."

"You'll do what needs doin' and that's a fact. Now, let's ride." Nate spoke with an unusual harshness in his voice.

Two hours later Doc's horse stumbled and then slowly fell to its knees. It took over ten minutes to get the horse back up on its feet and the small group new they could no longer ride, so Nate said, "We'll walk an hour, then ride for thirty minutes, and then walk another hour if need be. I figure it's less than two hours to the spot I have in mind, but we'll do like I just said until we get there."

"Ya thinkin' of stoppin' at the Big Piney River?" Cotton Top asked as he walked beside Nate leading his horse with his reigns.

"Yup, and with this rain we might want to hole up in that cave on the side of the hill to the north. You know where it is, on this side of the river, and near where Jug got killed last year by them Crow."

Stumbling along in the mud, Deacon suddenly asked through the deep fatigue that fogged his mind, "Don't sound so good to me, if another man got killed there."

Cotton laughed and replied, "Jug was drunk at the time and so were his partners. As far as I'm concerned they was askin' to be killed, 'cause only a fool gets drunk in Blackfoot country."

"And, before you ask," Nate quickly said, "the Crow were here in Blackfoot country on a horse raid against them. They just had the good luck of finding Jug first."

Deacon felt a shudder go through his whole body as he thought of how dangerous this beautiful country was. Finally, a few minutes later he asked, "You know, everything from the critters to the people out here are standing in line to kill a man. I don't see why you stay here or how you keep your scalps on."

Doc spoke quietly and in a sincere voice as he said, "Hell, Deacon, it's the pure beauty of the place that keeps most of us here. See, the men out here aren't in large numbers, or at least not like back east, so a man can live for months out here and never see another man—red or white."

"I'm here because it's my home." Nate replied as he stepped over a large mud hole in the middle of the trail.

"Not me," Cotton Top said with a grin, "I love the excitement and adventure found in these shinin' mountains!"

Nate laughed lightly and replied, "Then you should be a *real* happy man right now, because I'm plumb full of excitement and adventure at the moment."

As the laughter died down, the group started walking as quickly as the muddy trail would allow. More than one man fell on his ass as he slipped in the mud and Deacon fell so many times he lost count. The rain grew harder, though there was very little thunder or lightning, and Nate almost constantly reminded the men that the rain would wash away their tracks. As far as the tired Deacon was concerned, the words were wasted because he was so exhausted he no longer listened.

It was a little over two hours after the Doc's horse stumbled and fell, before the men finally reached the small cave. It was not large enough to bring the horses in out of the rain, so Nate and Deacon constructed some overhead shelters for the animals using a couple of large sheets of canvas. While the two men were busy outside with the horses, Doc started a fire, as Cotton Top sliced some bacon and mixed some corn meal with a little water, so he could fry some bread in the grease from the bacon.

Just as the bacon started to quiver in the hot skillet, Deacon and Nate walked into the cave soaking wet. "Gonna come a belly washer here pretty soon," Nate said as he pulled his wet hat off and beat it against his right thigh to knock most of the water off.

Without looking up from the pan of frying bacon Cotton Top replied, "I fig'ered as much by the way them clouds grew dark and the thunder started right before we got here."

"Do you think those Blackfoot are still on our back trail?" Deacon asked to no one in particular.

Nate gave a loud booming laugh, narrowed his eyes, and with a slight grin on his big face said, "Yep."

"Hain't no way they'd quit this soon Deacon. Blackfoot, if they act like they normally do, will still be on our asses when we get to Butterfields." Doc said as he stacked some wood near the fire.

"Look, Deacon, you're still a green hand and don't know no better, but when Bugs boys get on a man's ass they ain't got no quit in 'em at all." Cotton then started turning his bacon.

"As soon as we eat, I want one man on watch and the other three sleepin'. Then after about an hour, I want the guard to wake up one of us to take his place. You feel you can pull your share Deacon? And, tell me the truth, because all of our lives will be in your hands." Nate said as he met the farmer's eyes.

"I'll do my share, but it won't be easy."

Nate chuckled and replied, "No it won't be easy, but I didn't say nothin' about easy in my question. Just remember, if you get tired to the point you can't stay awake then you wake one of us and don't let your damned pride get us killed. Ok?"

"I'll do that and I give you my word." Deacon said as he wondered if he was being honest or just hardheaded.

Two hours later the rain had grown into a full-blown storm and as Deacon was keeping watch from near the entrance to the cave, he heard a slight noise near the horses. Raising his tired head, he cupped his right hand behind his right ear and listened, but he heard nothing more. The heavy rains pelted the hillside and wind continued to blow with gale force just outside the entrance, so after a few minutes of intense listening Deacon convinced himself he'd only heard the noises of the storm.

Suddenly Deacon heard a small sound that reminded him of a pebble rolling down a hill and realized what was happening. He raised his big Hawken rifle and as he snapped the hammer back, the image of a dripping wet Blackfoot warrior stood in the entrance to the cave. The brave held a tomahawk in his right hand. A sudden bright flash of lightning quickly confirmed what he saw was not his imagination. The farmer lined up his sights, squeezed the trigger, and was instantly rewarded with a loud explosion from his rifle, followed by a scream of pain from the brave.

"Blackfoot!" Deacon yelled as he pulled his pistol and killed another brave entering the cave. Dropping his pistol, the man pulled his long skinning knife and stood waiting for the next brave to try entering. His wait was a short one as a large brave wearing a headdress full of eagle feathers in his wet hair ran right at the Deacon, and what scared him the most was that he saw at least four more braves behind the large warrior.

Rifles and pistols suddenly started to pop and Blackfoot warriors began to fall, but Deacon was rolling against the damp walls of the cave with the big warrior and he knew his strength was no match for the Indian. When the two men struck, Deacon lost his grip on the knife and it had fallen to the dirt floor of the cave. *Think! Think of a way to end this now!* Deacon screamed in his mind as he saw the deeply rooted hatred the Blackfoot felt for him in his dark eyes. Pushing himself off the wall and away from the warrior, Deacon assumed a boxers stance. The Blackfoot, having no knowledge of boxing stopped for a second and looked at Deacon as if he'd just lost his mind. Before the brave could react, Deacon punched the man hard in the face with his right hand and then quickly followed it with a left to his jaw. His blow knocked the warrior back against the wall of the cave. Moving quickly, the farmer walked into the brave with his fists hammering the man's belly and face, doing as much damage as his tired body would allow. The warrior suddenly went limp and started sliding down the wall of the cave, coming to rest with his rump on the floor. Deacon reached over with his right hand, grabbed the warrior's scalp lock and began pounding the back of the Indian's head against the wall of the cave with all of his might.

"Deacon, he's a gone beaver! Deacon the man is dead!" Deacon heard Cotton Top yell from off in the distance minutes later. Slowing his pounding of the warriors head and then stopping a second or two later, the tired farmer turned and noticed Cotton giving him a crooked grin.

Looking around, Deacon noticed all of the mountain men were alive and standing, with Nate the only one hurt. The bodies of six Indians littered the floor of the cave and he knew the one he'd killed first had been blown outside. Deacon's heart was pounding hard and his body had never been so tense in his whole life, though he knew the battle was over, he remained on edge. His every sense was keener than ever and he knew he'd done his job of guarding the group properly.

"By God, when ya blacken yer face against a Injun, why ya do one hell of job child." Cotton Top said as he walked over to Deacon and slapped the man on his back.

"That Deacon was some, he surely was!" Doc exclaimed in glee at being alive.

Nate walked over to the farmer and asked, "Do you have any idea what these two old beaver tails are saying to you Deacon?"

Deacon shook his head and replied with a tired grin, "Not sure, but I think I done my job pretty good. I didn't have but a seconds notice before the entrance to the cave was filled with Blackfoot."

"Cotton meant when you go to war against the Injuns you do the job right and Doc means you were, I guess the closed way to describe it would be, unbelievable. Anyhoo, I'm proud of you old coon, you got some tough bark on you and you already know what that means." Nate spoke and then laughed.

Bending down over the Blackfoot Deacon had killed, Cotton Top asked, "You want the hair?"

"N . . . No, I couldn't scalp a man." Deacon stated as he fought down the urge to be sick.

"Waugh! Here yer stick floats, a deadly killer of Blackfoot and ya don't take hair?" Cotton spoke with a slight smile and then quickly added, "We don't usually take it either, Deacon, but ya can do the nasty job if ya want."

Deacon shook his head and replied, "No, I'll pass on the hair. You seem to forget Cotton that I am a man of God. I only fight to protect me and mine, and I kill for the same reasons."

"The Bible clearly states, 'thou shalt not kill', does it not?" Doc asked as he cleaned a small cut over Nate's eye.

"Yes, it says that, but it also goes into great deal about Christian soldiers of the past and the great battles that were fought by those men of God. Doc, in the Ten Commandments I think kill really means murder. But, some folks think it means not to kill at all and as a result I know many folks who won't even eat meat, because the animal is killed."

"Queersome group then, 'cause out here they'd last about as long as a bottle of John Barleycorn at a fur roonyvoo! Hell, out here ya to have to kill to stay alive long enough to eat and that's the truth." Cotton spoke so seriously that the men broke out laughing.

About an hour later, after the dead Blackfoot had been dragged outside the cave and a fire started, Deacon suddenly asked from beside the cracking flames, "How come them injuns didn't just shoot into this cave? Looks to me they would have killed or hurt some of us."

Abruptly, a loud boom of thunder echoed across the land and Nate pointed up as he replied, "The powder in their guns was wet and since a bowstring is useless when it's soaked, they had to take us by force. What I suspect was they thought we'd be asleep and they could just sneak in here and cut our throats, only it didn't happen that way."

"Nate, I didn't hear much at all, just a very small sound and it was as dark as all get out, so I didn't see anything at first. Even when I saw the outline of the brave in the entrance, I waited until a flash of lightning showed me what it was."

"Good thinking on yer part Deacon, because it might have been a white man." Doc spoke as he pushed the coffee pot closer to the fire.

"It could have been, but to be honest with you that thought never entered my head. I thought I was imagining things and didn't want to shoot at shadows and have to take the teasing from you fellers afterward. I was bone tired at the time too and I discovered a tired man sees and hears a lot of things that ain't there."

"Well, I can tell ya right now, there's not a man in this cave that could have done a better job, but Deacon?" Nate spoke as he leaned back against his blanket.

"Yep?"

"Where in the hell did you learn to box like that? I've not seen but a few men that know the moves and punches of boxing."

Deacon laughed, scratched the left side of his face, and replied, "I had a feller in my church that was from England and after church on some Sundays he'd come over and teach me a few things."

"He did a good job of teaching ya too! But, I got to admit, in all my years in the shinnin' mountains yer the first man I ever knew to kill a man with a cave." Cotton spoke as he sat by the entrance of the cavern guarding.

The small group shared a light laugh and then Nate said, "The river will be up come mornin', so in a few minutes we have to light a shuck out of here. There could be other Blackfoot around, or some might to start missing the bunch we just killed, so we've got to move."

"Nate," Deacon said as he glanced around the cave at the other men, "if I die out here bury me real high up in a big oak tree if ya can, because I don't think my tired feet ever want to tough the earth again."

Once again the cave erupted in laughter as Nate stood and said, "Let's move, times a-wastin' and we've got a many mile to cover before we are safe."

The remainder of that night and well into the next day the small group moved in the pouring rain. Thunder sounded as lightning flashed white streaks in the sky and each man cursed as he endured the wetness as best he could. Though each of them felt miserable and cold, none of them would be the first to admit it. Mile after wet mile was covered slowly, especially the night they had left the comfort of the cave, and Nate only allowed short breaks for the horse every couple of hours. Once again, Deacon was in deep pain, but from the chaffing on the insides of both thighs, but he kept his mouth shut and kept up with the others without complaint. The rain completely stopped just at dusk.

Three days later the group arrived at Butterfield's trading post and they had not lost a single man or plew during their flight from the Blackfoot. As usual, old Butterfield met them by the front door to his store holding his scattergun in his hands. Glancing at the men he asked in a serious voice with a confused look on his face, "Now, who in Sam's hell are ya people? I seem to know ya, but the jaspers I know don't look like they've been shot at and missed, and then shit at and hit! Ya boys look the sight, ya surely do!"

The small group laughed at the trader, knowing he was glad they were back and he knew they'd survived hard times. Squinting in the sunlight, Butterfield said, "Well, unfork them cayuses and come on in, so I can fill your meatbags. I don't know why, but ever since I was a young pup I can't let a critter go hungry, even ones as ugly and no good as ya sumbitches look to be right now. Waugh!"

Chapter 26

Donnelly was less than a hundred miles from Butterfield's trading post and he was moving slowly over the mountain passes. In Big Spring, Missouri, which would one day be known as Independence, Taylor had used some of the money he had stolen from the German doctor to hire four men. One of them, a Crow half breed by the name of Talks Loudly, claimed he could speak fluent Crow as well as use sign. The breed was short, about five feet and two inches tall, but grossly overweight from living around whites. Taylor thought the man was just a big mouth drunk, but he hired him with a warning that if he could not speak Crow or use sign he'd kill him when the time came. The remainder of the money he used to purchase guns, powder, lead, whiskey, laudanum, and knifes, because Taylor M. Donnelly had a plan.

"How much further we gotta go to do this business ya got with the Crow?" A short bald man asked for the sixth time that day. Taylor disliked the man immensely, because Foubert was a constant whiner with small beady eyes, long dirty black hair that hung on the sides of his head, and what teeth remained in his mouth were either rotted or broken.

"Until we get there, so shut the hell up and ride!" Taylor replied in frustration as he turned in his saddle to look at the ugly man.

"We are close, less than one sun to the village of my people." Talks Loudly spoke and then grinned.

"Speak English like you usually do and not that damned Injun bullshit." A tall thin man named Randell said in disgust at the half-breed. Randell was a very plain looking man, but his manners and speech indicated to Taylor that he had once been a man with money, or at some point in his young life received an excellent education. He was not a huge man like many tall men, but of average size for his height, and Taylor liked Randell because he was quiet and usually spoke only when asked a question.

"Leave off the breed! Times will come and soon too that you'll be glad his red ass is a-ridin' with us. He's the only thang that might save our white asses if need be, and I know what I'm about." The last man of the group, an old has been of a mountain man named Yates, spoke as he leaned to the right from his horse and spat tobacco juice to the grass. He'd once been a successful trapper, but after a Blackfoot raid that saw his four partners taken captive and then burned to death, he turned to the bottle. Not once had he spoken of his escape or what happened that day to anyone but he remembered. He would always remember. At night when he tried to sleep, he often heard the screams and shrieks of pain or vividly smelled burning human flesh. Like Donnelly, he knew had only a little time left to live, but while Yates was dying due to his drinking, he didn't care.

"All of you quiet down! My God, you men all claimed to be experienced woodsmen and I ended up with a fool of a Crow half breed, a tall idiot that doesn't know enough to keep his mouth shut deep in Sioux country, and damned whiner!" Donnelly spoke in anger once more and realized he wanted some more laudanum for the pain from his injury.

"What about the old assed mountain man?" Foubert asked and then suddenly grew quiet as he saw the old man pull the hammer back on his Hawken.

"Hell," Donnelly replied, hoping to defuse the situation before it turned ugly, "he's the only one of the four of ya that ain't ridin' with his head up his ass! Pull up into those cedar trees over there and let's take a break. And, keep the noise down too!"

A couple cans peaches, a pot of hot coffee, and a few slices of smoked ham made a quick meal, and as the other men ate, Taylor walked off a ways, pulled his bottle of laudanum from his coat pocket and added a small amount to his coffee cup. He returned to the small fire a few minutes later, glassy eyed, but during the entire meal, not a word was spoken.

The going was slow moving over the next few days as the countryside turned more rugged and many difficult miles passed under the hooves of their horses and mules. There were six mules and all were loaded with old guns and trinkets Taylor had bought at Independence to give to the Crow. As a result of the heavy loads, the group was forced to stop more often than Donnelly wanted, but the old mountain man had warned him one morning early into the trip, "Ya go to them Crow and ya ain't got these goods to give 'em, they'll jess up and kill ya, unless they decide to eat ya first. I ain't sure what ya got planned in the future with all this shit on them mules, but once the Crow are happy my ass is headin' back. Ya can be damned sure I'll leave a-fore they get into the whiskey. Now, I suggest ya stop more often and let these critters rest some, or we'll be packin' the guns and whatnot on our backs."

One morning, just as the small group had gathered around the fire for breakfast, Talks Loudly spoke in a very low voice just above a whisper, "The Crow are here and don't anybody move. They will make themselves known in a few minutes, one way or the other."

Long tense minutes passed, until Donnelly spoke to Talks Loudly, "Call out to them, for God's sake man, before they kill us."

Not moving, Talks Loud said in the Crow tongue, "Welcome my brothers, I am called Talks Loudly and have brought you many gifts and presents."

The area remained as quiet as death and Donnelly could feel sweat running down between his shoulder blades to the crack of his ass. He knew it was a sweat from fear, because the morning was cool and dry, and just moments before he'd been chilled as he sat by the small fire.

Suddenly, a lone brave stood near a stunted pine and said, "I am called Charging Horse. Why is a man of the Crow with the white eyes?"

"Come, sit by our fire, eat and then we will speak. That is the way of The People." Talks Loudly spoke in Crow and then whispered in English, "He's pissed about somethin' and I think he wants a fight."

Charging Horse gave a loud laugh of contempt and replied, "You, Talks Loudly, were thrown from The People and told never to return. And on this day you return with white men and ask me to join your fire? The fire burns with wood taken from the lands of the Crow, the water you drink is from Crow streams, and even the grasses your horses eat belong to the Absaroka!"

"We come as friends, Charging Horse, and we have many gifts to give The People. We bring guns, powder, lead, whiskey, and more!" Talks Loudly spoke and then again whispered in English, "Don't nobody move toward a gun, but by God know where it is at all times. If we can keep him talkin' for a few more minutes we have a chance to pull this off, if not we'll have to fight our way out."

"Talks Loudly, what is to keep me and my warriors from killing you and your white friends, and then taking all of your presents?"

Standing slowly, with his hands hanging loosely by his sides, Talks Loudly replied, "Yes, you can kill us, but when your gun no longer has powder to make it shoot or the lead balls to kill with, where will you get more? I bring friends of the Crow who want to help The People become great!"

"The Crow are already a great and feared people, and we need no white man to make us what we are." Charging Horse replied, but thought, *as much as I do not like the white eyes, we can never get enough powder and lead to fight with, so I will listen to the white man and see what I can get to help The People. It is of my people I must think and not my hatred of the white man deep in my heart.*

"You speak with one tongue, Charging Horse, and your words are true, but let your mind rule your thoughts and not your heart." Talks Loudly spoke from the camp.

The Crow warrior walked into the camp and sat by the fire. As he glanced at the white men, his eyes reflected his deep contempt for them, though he did not speak a single word.

"Ask him if he'd like to have many guns and all of our gifts, just for the killing of a few white men." Donnelly said to Talks Loudly, and then pointing to the coffee pot he added, "And let him know our food and coffee is his as well."

The half-breed spoke quickly to the Crow warrior, waited for his response, and then said, "He wants to know why, you a white man, would give him guns and gifts to kill other white men."

"Explain to him that not all white men are the same, just as all Indians are not the same. The Crow are enemies to the Sioux, just as I am enemies to the men I want killed."

Once again, the Crow tongue was spoken between the two men and few seconds later Talks Loudly stated, "This he can understand, but he wants to know how many men he has to kill for these gifts and why you do not kill these men yourself."

"Four, maybe five men at the most and he can have many things if he kills them where I want them killed. Also, tell him that the ones I want killed are mountain men and difficult to kill."

"Five men or ten, it makes no difference to the Crow and Charging Horse says he cannot speak for his warriors, only for himself. And, he added that the men of the mountains are good enemies to have, but are difficult to kill. I think you just got his attention, because I think he'd like to get his hands on a few mountain man scalps."

Donnelly picked up the coffee pot, poured himself a cup and then offered the pot to the Crow war leader. As the brave took the coffee, he spoke a single word that Donnelly didn't understand, so the white man looked at Talks Loudly with questioning eyes.

"He is asking if you have sugar."

Yates picked up a small buckskin bag, handed it to the warrior and in sign language he said, "Here is the white powder that tastes like honey."

Charging Horse didn't reply, but his eyes closely evaluated the old mountain man and he thought, *this man knows the ways of the Crow people and of the mountains. He must be an old taker of beaver skins and he will have knowledge these other white men do not have.*

Pointing to a deer hanging from a nearby tree that Randell had killed the day before, Donnelly said, "Have your braves come to our fire and eat of our meat."

As soon as Talks Loudly had spoken, Charging Horse stood and called out to his men. A few minutes' later twenty braves were sitting by the fire as the Crow leader explained what the whites wanted and why they were in the land of the Absaroka. There were few questions from the braves and Donnelly suspected then the Crow wanted his supplies bad enough not to kill his small group.

It was not until after the braves had finished off most of the deer meat and sat by the fire that Donnelly asked, "Will the Crow warriors join me in my fight against the other white men?"

The war chief of the Crow sat silently for many long minutes. He made no acknowledgement of having heard the question and his facial expression did not change. Finally, Donnelly leaned close to Talks Loudly whispered, "Did he hear you?"

"For God's sake man, don't rush this man. Of course, he heard me and right now he thinks you have no respect for him, or you would not be speaking. It takes time for a warrior to consider things, so let him think this over." The half-breed replied in a low whisper.

Hell, all I want to know is if he'll do the job or not. How long should it take a man to think on something like that? Taylor thought, but held his tongue.

Finally, the warrior asked, "Where are these white men you wish for me to kill?"

Just as the warrior had done, Donnelly did not reply immediately, but sat as if he was giving the question thought. Finally, he replied, "They will be at the trader's post, not far from here."

"Of this place all of the Crow know, but it will not be an easy place to kill the white men. Charging Horse says there are easier places out in the open where the white men can be killed, so why the lodge of the man who trades?"

Donnelly gave a big smile and said, "Because that is where many guns, powder, whiskey and other good things to have are kept. Tell Charging Horse once the white men are dead, all of the trader's goods will be his to keep."

Again a long period of silence passed with only the occasional pop or crack from the fire heard. Finally, the Crow stood and said, "Let us take your gifts to our people and we will return in one hand of suns. When we return we will go and kill your white men."

Donnelly met the warrior's eyes as he asked Talks Loudly, "Can we trust him to keep his word?"

"For God's sake, the man is a war leader of the Crow people and his word will be kept beyond any doubt. Unlike a white man, if an Injun gives you his word he'll for damn sure keep it unless he gets his ass killed. He jess said he'll be back in five days and he'll be here come hell or high water, you can bet your last dollar on that."

Donnelly, giving a big smile replied, "Come and let us look at the gifts I have brought for the mighty Crow people."

Chapter 27

The Blackfoot continued to follow Nate's small group until they reached the relative safety of the traders post before they turned back. Doc had gone out hunting the day after they had arrived at Butterfield's and had found all kinds of sign of the Blackfoot. It looked to the mountain man as if they'd just reach safety in time and Doc suspected if Butterfield's had been a mile further they might not have made it without one hell of big fight.

"So, ya got some of yer green wore'd off of ya on this last trip, didn't ya Deacon?" Butterfield asked over coffee two days after the group had arrived.

"It was a rough trip and I'm glad it's over."

"Well, when them Blackfoot get on a man's ass they don't ever quit and that's why most mountain men hate 'em so much. The only reason they didn't try to get at ya here is they knew it would cost 'em too many men to take this place. But, if they wanted ya bad enough to pay the price, they could have taken this store."

"Yep, they could take this place, but the price would be high." Nate quickly added as he looked over the rim of his cup he was holding in his big hands.

"Hell, with five men in here that shoot like we do, it'd be plumb stupid for the Blackfoot to try to take this place." Cotton Top spoke and then grinned like a fool.

Nate grinned back and said, "Cotton, the thought is plum foolish and we both know it, but if anybody wanted to take this place bad enough they could, only it would cost them in blood and lives."

"Hell," Butterfield said as he lifted his coffee cup towards his lips and then hesitated as he continued, "there ain't nobody goin' to attack a tradin' post because even with jess two or three men in this placed it would take 'em a long time. Just like them Crow did a while back, they'll fight a bit and try a little, but as long as I'm not alone there ain't no problem. 'Sides, all the Injuns out here, includin' them damned thievin' Blackfoot benefit from me bein' here and they all know it too. The only reason them Crow attacked was to show us they're out there and that was about it."

Nate thought of Butterfield's words and then asked, "You ever been attacked before them Crow?"

"N . . . No, why?"

"Just wonderin' is all. You know, I think it might be safer if ya planned as if some Injuns was gonna attack you every day, if you understand what I mean? Hell, they did it once they can do it again when the urge hits 'em."

Butterfield considered Nate's suggestion very carefully and then said, "There ain't much I can do, not really, except to rig some powder to blow if the bastards get in the store. There ain't no way I'd leave powder and guns to fall into the hands of any red man that attacks this place, my God, just think of the deaths I'd be responsible for."

"Alright," Nate said as he stood, "let's rig the powder charge then. The key here, or so I think, is to use the powder at the last second, but that might not be possible if they come in the windows and doors too fast on ya."

"Somebody will do 'er if need be and I'll show every mountain man that comes in this place where it is too, just so we can do the job if we have to." Butterfield commented, stood, and went into the storeroom with Nate.

When they returned, Butterfield looked over at Deacon and asked, "You need to get your stuff ready in a few days, because I heard from a couple of pork eaters that come through here about a week ago that they are heading to Saint Louis come the end of the month."

Deacon grinned and looked around the table as he said, "I ain't sure I'm goin' back. I've give 'er some thought and I like it out here, but not sure if I have enough bark on me to last."

"Ya still have some green on ya, but by God, you can trap with me any time old coon." Doc replied.

"Yup," Cotton Top said with a nod, "fer a sky pilot you'll do to walk the river with any day."

The group looked at Nate, expecting him to accept Deacon, but the big man said in his deep voice, "Samuel, you need to give this decision a lot of serious thought. You're a good man, and I'm proud to call you my friend, but the decision you have to make is not to be made too quickly, or you might regret it later. So, think on it some and then decide."

Deacon grinned and replied, "Nate, I'll stay if it's ok with you. I've been thinkin' on this since that night in the cave, so this ain't something new. You know, there was something about that fight that made me realize I belong out here, and I've not been the same meek man I was before."

"Ya was some and that's fer sure!" Cotton quickly said.

Nate extended his hand and said, "Welcome to the mountains Deacon. The life you have chosen will be rough and hard, but I know you can do what is needed and you'll do the job well."

"Thanks Nate, I have made this decision on my own and with considerable thought."

"Deacon, you're welcome here, but you know we are a rough lot. Only I think it would be smart if you'd not do much Bible thumbin' while out here, but the choice is yours."

Deacon gave a loud laugh and replied, "Nate, I can do marriages, funerals, and whatnot fer all of ya, and still not get in yer way. Waugh, I'm a bossloper that loves me mountains! I can out drink, out fornicate and out eat any man in the mountains!"

Nate gave a loud chuckle and replied, "You might be a hunter, but you're still a bit wet behind both ears. But, I love the way you've picked up on the language, so you'll do."

Butterfield had been quiet, at least compared to his usual chatter, so he finally asked the question that no one had asked, "What of your family back east? If ya got family, you'll want to send 'em a letter or somethin'."

Deacon lowered his head and closed his eyes before he replied with, "I ain't got a family any more. Just a few months before I come out here with Moses, my wife and two little sons burned to death when our chimney caught fire one cold winter's night. You all know how dangerous those wood and clay chinked chimneys are. I was able to get one of my sons out but my wife—she ran back in to save the other boy. I never saw her or my other son, James, again. Frank died on me the next day, so when Moses was looking through the parish for a traveling partner, well, I joined up with him. See, I had no reason to stay."

Nate put his right hand on Deacons left shoulder and said, "You've got a family now. We're a bit rough and pretty crude, but deep inside we're all good men Deacon."

The night was cold with a full moon and the old potbelly stove was working over time keeping the store warm. The inside of the store was dark, except for a slightly red glow produced by the sides of the stove and small finger of light coming from a partially open grate, when Nate heard a noise just outside the main door. Quickly reaching over, he touched the three me beside him lightly and whispered to Doc as the man sat up, "Get Butterfield."

Minutes later Butterfield was squatting beside Nate as the big man explained, "I heard a noise outside and I think our horses are gone. Now, I ain't sure, because I was asleep, but the sound I heard sounded a lot like a horse."

"Do you think its them Blackfoot?" Deacon asked from the darkness.

"Most likely it's them Blackfoot, but hard to tell who it is really. Doc saw lots of Blackfoot sign the other day, so they know we are here and it's just like them red skins to pull a stunt like this. If nothing else just to show us they can do the job." Nate said from near his sleeping spot in the dark room and then quietly made his way to a window that looked out to the stables. Earlier the moon had been hidden by some clouds but it'd moved, allowing the areas around the trading post to light up almost as bright as day.

"I want one man to each compass headin', right now!" Butterfield ordered as he moved toward the main window near the door.

"I'll help load rifles, need be." Deacon said as he moved to the table nearest the door.

There came the loud report of Nate's rifle, a scream of pain and the black man said casually, "I got one of the bastards, as he strutted out of the barn with something in his hands, only he'll strut no more."

Doc fired and replied, "That's two of 'em down then, 'cause mine was movin' toward the door to the store."

"Holy cow, look at all the damned Injuns. I'm tell ya, I must be lookin' at a hundred of 'em." Cotton Top spoke suddenly and with a touch of fear in his voice.

"What tribe?" Doc asked as he pulled his ramrod from the barrel of his rifle.

"Crow, they're Crow, and more of 'em than ya can shake a stick at too."

"Crow?" Nate asked from beside his window, "You sure?"

"Nate, it's Crow, I know my Injuns and ya know I do."

"Hell," Butterfield said, "I would've thought Blackfoot."

Cotton Top turned, gave a wicked grin and replied, "Nobody seems to believe my ass and if not, y'all come over here and take long look. It's the Crow out there and nobody else and let me tell ya, they're all wearin' paint."

Butterfield's scattergun suddenly boomed loudly, he gave a laugh and said, "Shit, Bugs boys would have done a better job than this! If it had been Blackfoot we'd all be dead already. I'll just take all of these Crow on my own self, iffen there's only a hun'ert of 'em!"

"Nate?" Deacon asked from the table as he loaded spare guns from the shelves.

"yep?"

"How many are really out there, ya reckon?"

Nate gave a loud laugh and said, "Well, old son, at least a hundred, if Cotton Top can count worth a damn and usually he can. And, that makes it about twenty of them red fellers to one of us, so there will be more than enough to go around."

Deacon thought for a minute and then asked, "Why are they attacking us at night? I'd heard Injuns never attacked at night."

Nate gave a dry laugh and replied, "Son, an Injun will attack anytime he thinks he can win a fight. The stuff about them not fighting at night is just some malarkey made up back east."

Before any man could say another word there come a loud voice from outside, "You in the trader's post! Send out the big black man and we'll leave!"

"I know that voice!" Cotton Top spoke with surprise.

"Donnelly! You want me, you sonofabitch, come and get me!" Nate yelled out in his deep voice.

From the darkness there was heard a loud laugh, followed by Donnelly's reply, "Have it your way Grisham, but your friends will die for nothing!"

Nate looked around the inside of the trading post, meeting each man's eyes as he asked, "What do you think fellers? Maybe I should just step out the door and let him have me."

Butterfield laughed and replied, "Nate, they'll kill us if you go or not. They want this store too, I suspect, or why else would the Crow be with Donnelly?"

"I agree with Butterfield here and we all know Donnelly wants his revenge against you, Butterfield and Cotton Top, for turning him over to the army." Deacon spoke as he looked over at Nate.

"Yep, whether ya walk out the door or not, we're all dead men and ya know it. Hell, Nate, stay with us and let's take some of 'em with us when we go under." Cotton said.

"I got movement on the porch!" Butterfield almost screamed out.

Before anyone could react, there came a loud explosion and the door was blown off of its hinges and inward, striking the trader as it did so. Butterfield was knocked to the floor as one Crow warrior stepped inside along with a large dense cloud of white smoke. Nate raised his Hawken and fired, not taking the time to aim, and was pleased to see his man go down immediately. Deacon, still near the table fired his Hawken and horse pistol, killing one brave and forcing the other to beat a retreat.

"Quick," Nate yelled inside the smoke filled room, "Deacon, help me slide the bar over in front of the door! Cotton, you move over here and keep your eyes on the rear of the building. Hurry Deacon, before they make another try for the open door!"

The two men moved the heavy oak bar to the door and blocked the gaping hole, and then placed Butterfield's desk on top of it to almost completely seal the entrance. As he turned, Nate heard Deacon say, "Black powder was used on this door!"

"Yep, and there was a lot of it too." Nate replied as he moved to Butterfield's side, kneeled and checked the man over closely.

From the window where he was keeping watch, Cotton Top asked a few minutes later, "Butterfield gonna make it?"

"He'll live. The door knocked his butt out, but I don't see no bleeding and he's breathing fine."

At that point, Butterfield gave a low moan, opened his eyes and asked, "What hit me? Feels like a mule kicked me hard between the eyes!"

"Crow used powder on the door and when it blew it knocked you on your ass." Nate said, grinned and then asked, "Butterfield, you got some extra powder, right?"

"A bunch in the storeroom, why?"

"Come with me, Cotton, we're gonna fix some of these Crows real good!" Nate ordered, chuckled, and then added, "I got me one hell of an idea all of the sudden."

From outside the building a rifle spat flame and single lead ball flew through the store smacking loudly into a far wall as the two men moved toward the powder. Returning a few minutes later, Nate said, "Butterfield, I need some buckskin bags like you use to put balls in, some kerosene, a couple hundred lead balls, and some small glass jars, if you have any."

"Have you lost your mind? What in the hell you gonna do?" Butterfield asked as he moved behind his counter and started pulling the items for Nate.

"During the war of 1812 the British army had what they called grenades. They were made with powder and balls, placed in a container. A man would light a small fuse, throw the grenade, and it would explode."

"Hell, Nate, I even got some blasting fuses in the storeroom that I cain't even give away, would they help?"

"Damn tootin' they would! Get them too and let's get to work."

As the men worked building the grenades, an occasional bullet would fly through a pane of glass or broken window to strike a log that made up the walls inside the structure. Working on the floor in front of the stove with the door open, the men soon had two dozen grenades made. Nate had each man add a handful of power and a dozen lead balls inside each bag, and then insert a six-inch fuse. Once the fuse was inserted, the bag was tied tightly at the top with string to hold the explosive contents and fuse in place.

"Now for my real nasty surprise." Nate said with a big grin.

Butterfield had given the man twelve empty one-quart mason jars. The big man filled each jar with kerosene and put it into a larger buckskin bag that he had added two handfuls of power and a good two dozen lead balls. He inserted a fuse, just like with the grenades and tied it at the top with the string. Next, Nate took a dozen empty quart whiskey bottles, filled them with kerosene, and stuck a cotton rag tightly in the top.

Turning to the small group of men in the building, Nate said, "We've got six grenades and three of the kerosene grenades each. The bottles of kerosene I'll throw when the time comes. Now, a word of warnin' here, these things are as dangerous to the thrower as to the enemy. Once you light the fuse, throw the damned thing and do it fast. They've been known to go off early and let me tell you, from what I heard they can do some real damage. The idea behind the kerosene is when the grenade explodes it will cause one hell of big explosion—with a fire. Though I ain't ever heard of kerosene being used before, it's worth a try."

"These gree-nades work pretty good?" Cotton asked from his window without turning his head.

"From what I hear the homemade ones work about fifty percent of the time, so we can't depend on them to work every time. Once you throw a grenade bring your rifle up on your target quickly."

"I got a lot of movement in the courtyard, but ain't sure what it is. Might be some Crow trying to Injun up on us." Doc said as he quickly glanced at Nate.

"Well, it sure as hell ain't Sandy Claws." Cotton said and gave a loud laugh.

Nate pulled one of the grenades made with kerosene and moved to the window Doc was watching. Holding a small brand from the stove under the window the big man watched until he spotted a very slight movement. Nate quickly checked the window and noticed all of the glass was missing from the frame and there was nothing in his way, so he raised the brand, ignited the fuse and tossed the grenade toward where he'd seen the movement. There was a loud yip in Crow, followed a few seconds later by a loud earth-shattering explosion that echoed through the stillness. One brave stood, entirely engulfed in flames, while another quickly rose with his left shoulder and whole arm burning from the kerosene. Loud screams fill the cool night air.

Both Nate and Doc quickly fired their rifles at dark forms running from the courtyard, completely ignoring the two burning men. The courtyard was lighted up as if it was full daylight and a good half a dozen men were twisting and jerking in the grass, as loud hideous screams pierced the night.

Suddenly there was a second explosion, more screams, and then Butterfield yelled out, "Eat them lead beans ya Crow sumbitches and I'll feed ya some more later!"

At that point, the Crow pulled back and no movement was seen, though a sporadic crack or pop of burning kerosene was heard outside the window.

CHAPTER 28

"What is this weapon the white men have? How can they make fire come from the ground to kill and injure my men?" Charging Horse asked in anger.

"Grenades, I've seen them before, but I have no idea how they got them." Donnelly replied and then asked Talks Loudly, "What is going on?"

The breed met Donnelly's eyes in the moonlight and said, "The Crow think your medicine is bad and they should go home. Already they have more than ten men dead and many more wounded."

"Damn me! And we are so close too!" Donnelly cursed as he walked around in a small circle thinking of a way to keep the Crow at the attack.

"They're a superstitious lot, Injuns is, and always have been." Yates said from the darkness.

Donnelly gave the situation some thought and then ordered, "Foubert, I want you and Randell to move close to the building and place a couple barrels of powder against the door once more, just like you did the last time. Only, double the amount of power."

"Are you crazy? We won't get near that door!" Foubert complained as he shook his head.

Donnelly pulled his horse pistol, placed the barrel against the man's head and ordered, "You will go, because I did not ask you if you wanted to do the job, I gave you an order."

"I found a wheelbarrow in the barn, so we can move the powder in that and only make one trip. If we do it fast, they'll never know what hit 'em." Randell said with a grin and then added, "I'd like to see that powder blow too!"

"Then do it and take Foubert with you. If he hesitates to do as you ask him at any point, kill him."

"You'd kill a man for not wanting to do something stupid like this? Hell, them old mountain men in there can hit a fly's ass at a hundred yards! I'll go, but when this is all said and done, me and you will settle this between us." Foubert replied as he moved toward Randell and said, "Let's get this over with."

"What are the white men doing?" The Crow war leader asked Talks Loudly in a voice barely above a whisper.

"They are taking much powder to the door and will open a hole for all of us to enter the building. Have your braves ready to end this battle."

The Crow moved into position in just a few minutes and waited for the explosion to come. As Donnelly watched in the moonlight, he saw Kendell pushing the heavily loaded wheelbarrow toward the door, with Foubert in front guarding the man with his Hawken.

"Tell Charging Horse to move some of his braves to the rear and to shoot at the building. Tell him to have his warriors hit the building and not to shoot inside. If so much as one stray bullet hits that wheelbarrow the whole thing will go up. I think he can draw some men inside to the rear of the building to return fire and that will allow Randell to place the charge at the door." Donnelly spoke in an anxious voice, knowing the end was near one way or the other.

The Crow leader gave an order in the grunt-like Crow tongue and a good dozen warriors moved to the rear of the trading post. As soon as the braves started shooting, Donnelly noticed Randell moving faster toward the door of the structure. *He knows he has covering fire,* Taylor thought as he grinned, *and it'll all be over in just a few more minutes!*

From inside the trading post, Nate watched as Kendell and Foubert moved closer to the barricaded door. Pulling a grenade filled with kerosene, the big man waited until the two men were near the porch and then said, "Cotton move over here and when I tell you to do it, take the short fat guy plumb center with a ball. I'll take care of the man with the wheelbarrow."

The two men were less than ten feet from the step to the porch when Nate yelled, "Now."

Cottons Hawken went off just as a kerosene grenade flew through the air and landed on the powder in the wheelbarrow.

Foubert quickly dropped to the ground, as dead as he'd ever get, and Randell's eyes grew huge in fear as he attempted to turn and run from the burning liquid. The tall man only covered two steps when the splattering kerosene landed on his back and head, followed almost immediately by a loud *whomp* as it exploded in flames. Now burning, but knowing he had to get away from the burning powder, Randell began to run faster toward the cover of the trees, but to no avail.

The powder exploded with such force that all of the windows in the trading post were knocked out, the bar was pushed two feet back from the door, and a good third of the pine shingles on the building were blown off. The ground shook violently and branches from trees in the nearby woods were ripped from their trunks, causing injuries among the Crow warriors who had been waiting for the door to be blown wide open. Both Foubert and Randell simply disappeared in a fine mist of blood and smoke, leaving nothing that resembled a human being behind.

Charging Horse turned to Donnelly and said, "Your medicine is no good. This is enough! The Crow will return to our village!" Turing to his men, the war leader gave a loud order and the Crow quickly started to retreat toward the horses.

Talks Loudly explained what was happening and a deep panic filled Donnelly' very soul. He had no more money to make another attempt at killing or taking Nate Grisham alive and he wanted his revenge. He grasped the right arm of Charging Horse and pleaded, but the warrior simply shook the white man's hand off and said, "Touch me once more, white man, and I will kill you."

As the Crow disappeared into the darkness of night, Yates walked over to Donnelly and said, "We'd best be movin' our own asses. Once them mountain men know the Crow are gone they'll come fer us and they'll come hard."

"Where? Where can we go?" Donnelly asked in almost uncontrollable fear.

"Well, I think it'd be a good idea to go east, but right now it don't matter jess as long as we make some tracks in any direction and do 'er fast too. I guaran-damn-tee ya, once the sun rises the men inside will be on our trails. We've damp powder and no way to dry 'er."

The remainder of the night passed slowly in the store, even after the men realized the Crow had gone. Butterfield had one hell of headache and sat at the table sipping on a large glass whiskey to kill the pain. Nate watched the front of the building as Cotton covered the rear. Deacon, seated in the middle of the small room, was ready to rush to either side to help if an attack came, but nothing stirred outside.

Just as the sun came up, Butterfield looked around the inside of his store and moaned, "Damn it, look at this mess! I ain't got one piece of glass that ain't broke, the door is destroyed, and I got bullet holes all over the place." Then looking around at the shelves behind his display case he added, "Awww, shit! It looks like a bullet or two put a hole in my molasses keg and that'll be hell to clean up."

Nate stood, glanced around the place and as he looked up at the roof he said, "And, half of your shingles are gone too. You'll be a while cleaning and fixing this place up. Cotton, I want you to stay here with Deacon and help Butterfield as much as you can. While all of you work on this place, me and Doc will trail who was behind this mess."

"Nate, how are you going to find out who was really behind this attack? I mean, other than Donnelly." Deacon asked.

"Pretty simple, Deacon, the men will still be with him and you can be sure they didn't return with the Crow to the village. Most likely the Crow are upset over the number of dead and wounded they have, so they'll want nothing to do with the Captain."

Cotton stood, picked up his Hawken that was leaning on the table and said, "Deacon, let's go outside and see what we've got. Once we take a look and come back Nate and Doc can be on the trail."

Butterfield moved toward his counter and said, "I'll put a good sized feedbag together for ya two, so when ya hit the trail ya'll have some good grub. I'll put about half of these grenades in a possibles bag for ya too, 'cause ya might jess need 'em in a few days."

Stepping from the trading post Cotton Top shook his head at the damage done to the structure by the exploding black powder. Many of the shingles were missing, the porch was sitting crooked, and the hitching post was completely gone. Where the wheelbarrow had been all that remained was deep hole in the scorched ground. Of Foubert, Cotton found nothing and all that reminded of Randell was one arm still attached to a shoulder with the neck and head intact. Nothing else remained of the two men, not a thing. *Hell, bells,* Cotton thought, *how much damned powder did that boy have in that wheelbarrow?*

As the two men moved in a circle around the trading post they found numerous pools of blood, a severed arm and two Crow warriors so badly burned they were black. *Them Crow must have failed to find these two in the darkness, because they don't usually leave their dead like this,* Deacon thought and then quickly leaned to the right to puke from the smell of the bodies.

"Burnin's a rough way to go under son." Cotton Top said as he neared Deacon.

Fighting back a gag, Deacon said, "Yup, a real rough way as far as I am concerned and not one I'd pick."

"I counted twelve big pools of blood, how 'bout you?"

"Ten, but that don't mean those men died, does it?"

"No, some of 'em lived, but not many because the pools I saw had a lot of blood in 'em."

Deacon thought for a few minutes, wiped the tears from his eyes from gagging and said, "Just think Cotton, all of this death and because of one man wanting revenge."

Cotton gave a low chuckle and replied, "Nope, the Crow were greedy too, wanting the goods in the tradin' post, so there's more to it than just Donnelly's revenge."

"Let's get back, Nate and Doc will want to be on the trail as soon as they can."

No sooner had the two men reported what they had found to Nate than the man said, "Doc, let's go, this has to end and I want to end it as soon as we can. I don't usually go after trouble, but if we don't stop Donnelly he'll be back one day. So, if we don't end it now, we'll have to do it in the future."

"Let's move! I don't like this fighting in buildin's and such and I don't like to have a man ridin' my ass that might try to kill me some day. It's time to start the dance."

Hours later, near noon, Nate spotted a trail that moved off away from the retreating Crow warriors. Dismounting, he looked the sign over closely and said, "Four riders and all mounted on horses wearing shoes. It's my guess these are Donnelly and his bunch and you'll notice they moving east."

Doc leaned over from his saddle and spat a stream of to-bacco juice, wiped his mouth off with his right hand and replied,

"Atkinson is where I think they're headed, or mayhap all the way to Saint Louie."

Mounting quickly Nate said, "That's my guess too, so we'll take a short cut I know of through the mountains and meet up with 'em out on the plains."

"Why the plains, Nate?"

"The way I got it figured, once they get out in the open they'll start to feeling safe enough, thinking they can see trouble coming for miles. But, me and you both know there are enough gullies and such out there to hide an army."

Two days later, as they waited in a small stream, the only stream with good water for miles, Nate grinned and elbowed Doc as he pointed west. Moving slowly toward the stream were three mounted men and even at a great distance the two mountain men could hear them talking in loud voices. Seeing the stream, the small group of men stopped on a slight incline, as one older man wearing buckskins rode forward to check for an ambush. As the single rider neared, Nate recognized the man, moved closer to the water, and waited.

Just as Yates dismounted and moved toward the water Nate said in a low voice, "Howdy Yates, since when did you take to ridin' with skunks?"

"Howdy Nate, good to see ya 'gain. I guess yer the man Donnelly wanted killed back at the tradin' post. I didn't know it was ya he wanted, but I've seen lean times Nate and needed me a grub stake."

The sound of Nate cocking his Hawken was loud and he replied, "Yep, I'm the man he wanted. Now Yates, you have two choices the way I got it figured. You can pull your shootin' iron and if you do I'll drill your ass plumb center with my Hawken, or you can fork that bay you're riding and keep movin' east."

"Nate, I'll ride, but I never knew it was you he was after and that's the truth." The old mountain man said as he moved toward his horse.

"Get the hell out of here and do it now, Yates, before my good humor leaves me and I just drill you. And, Yates?"

The old man had just mounted his horse as he asked, "Yep?"

"If I ever see you again during this lifetime I'll kill you on sight. Do you understand me?"

"I'm leavin' Nate and I hear Missouri is a pretty good spot fer a feller like me to make a livin'. Ya keep yer topknot screwed on tight, time fer me to make tracks." As soon as he'd spoken, Yates kicked his horse hard in the ribs, crossed the stream in three jumps and rode like the devil himself was on his ass over the nest hill, heading due east.

From his position on the hill, Donnelly cursed loudly as he saw Yates desert and turning to Talks Loudly he commanded, "Move! Let's get down to that stream and make camp."

As they rode toward the stream, Talks Loudly suddenly asked, "Why did Yates leave us?"

"He's been waiting to leave would be my guess. How far are we from Atkinson right now?"

"Two, maybe three days of easy riding would be my guess."

"Well, as soon as we eat and rest the horses we're going to start out and we'll stop only long enough to rest the horses a little each hour. We'll not rest until we reach the town.

In the bushes along the sides of the river, Doc leaned toward Nate and whispered, "How do you want to do this?"

"Lay low, until they start to eat, then we'll attack them, but remember Donnelly is mine."

Moving further back into the brush, the two mountain men waited, both men noticing the approaching riders had cocked their Hawken rifles and were prepared for a fight.

Just as the two men on horseback neared the river, Doc's horse, which was tied back in the trees, gave a low whinny and stamped the ground with his left foreleg. Talks Loudly turned suddenly and brought his rifle up to his shoulder, just as Doc stood up from his spot in the brush. There was the loud report of the breed's weapon and the mountain man's head exploded as a heavy fifty-caliber ball struck him between the eyes.

Nate aimed at Donnelly and pulled the trigger, only to have Talks Loudly suddenly move forward into the bullets path. The breed took the lead ball in the left side of his chest, gave a loud scream of deep pain and twisting in his saddle fell to ground. Donnelly quickly grabbed the reins of the breeds mount, kicked his own horse hard and moved across the river, but unlike Yates he turned north.

"Damn me!" Nate screamed as he pulled his big skinning knife and moved toward the down breed.

Donnelly at the top of a small hill, pulled back reins of his horse, lined the sights of his Hawken up, and as he released a deep breath, he gently squeezed the trigger. He gave an evil grin as he watched the big black man by the stream collapse to the ground. Without looking any longer than to see his target fall, he moved over the hill and then cut east toward Atkinson. *I got the big bastard!* Donnelly thought as he rode at a gentle run.

Nate had been hit hard and knew he'd made a mistake by not waiting until Donnelly was long gone to enter the small clearing. Grimacing in pain, he noticed he'd take the ball low in his left side and though it hurt like hell, it was not likely to kill him. Finding his knife in the grass where he'd thrown it when the bullet struck him, he made his way on weak legs to where Talks Loudly lay in the grass.

The breed was in deep pain; Nate's bullet had gone all the way through his chest from left to right. Blood was seeping from his open mouth and his eyes were large in either fear or pain.

Kneeling beside the severely wounded man, Nate said, "Sing your death song Crow, because you'll cross over shortly."

Spitting blood, Talks Loudly said, "It is a good . . . day to . . . die. He left . . . me!"

Nate shook his big head and replied, "Now what did you expect from a no account jasper like that?"

The breed began his death song in a weak voice and Nate waited until the man had finished and then asked, "You done?"

Talks Loudly didn't answer, he just nodded his head.

Nate reached over and quickly cut the man's throat and as Talks Loudly choked on his blood, the big black man walked over to Doc's body, picked it up and started for the horses.

Once he had Doc securely tied to his horse, belly down, Nate pulled his possibles bag and bandaged his injured side. After the bandage was firmly in place, the big man mounted his horse and taking the reins of Doc's mount he slowly moved across the river, pulled west and started following Donnelly's trail. *I'm comin' for ya son and there ain't nothin' on this earth that will stop me,* Nate thought as his eyes narrowed and he gave a wicked grin.

Chapter 29

Donnelly moved at almost a leisurely pace, assuming his rifle shot killed Nate. He was laughing deep inside at how easily the big black man had been to kill and from a long distance too. At times as he rode, he gave a low groan in pain as the sores on his penis would ache and more than once that afternoon he'd take a drink of the powerful Laudanum to kill the pain. Just before dusk he pulled into a group of trees along a small stream, pulling his sore member from his trousers he applied the mercury on the bleeding lesions. He had to grit his teeth against the burning pain, and once the ache had gone down a few minutes later he remounted, only this time on the horse that had belonged to Talks Loudly. He still intended to keep riding until he reached Fort Atkinson and figured by trading horse every few hours, he'd make the trip with less breaks.

The day gradually turned to night and while the wind was light, it was cold and from the west. Donnelly pulled his thick sheepskin coat from where it was tied behind him and quickly put it on, pulling his hat down lower to protect his face from the wind. A little after nine that night the moon came up and lighted the trail well enough that Donnelly actually chuckled at how easy the trip was going. However, if he'd been able to see Nate Grisham less than five miles behind him, his blood would have frozen instantly.

Nate was very weak from the loss of blood and his side was throbbing with a dull ache as he slowly followed Donnelly's trail. *I've got to find a place to rest over night. I know my side is still bleeding and me dying won't help bring Doc back to life or put a stop to Donnelly,* he thought as he pulled up in a very small group of trees along side a minute stream, no wider than a foot and about six inches deep.

Removing Doc's body, he noticed the man had stiffened and was now permanently bent at the waist from being tied to the horse. He gently lowered Doc to the grass and covered him with a horse blanket, made a small fire, and placed a pot of coffee on to boil. As the water heated, he changed the bandage on his side, pulled a long strip of buffalo jerky and had dinner. *Got one hell of a bruise where that ball struck me and I'm lucky it didn't hit a bit more to the right or I'd be a dead man about now,* he thought as he pulled a small jug of trader's whiskey from his supplies and poured two fingers worth into his tin cup. Sipping the whiskey, Nate fell asleep.

Donnelly continued to ride all the night through and it was mid-afternoon the next day before he saw Atkinson off in the distance. Chuckling loudly, Donnelly kicked his horse to a faster walk and made his way to the young town. While he was bone tired, his eyes ached, and he needed a bath, Taylor felt sure he'd escaped the threat of the big black mountain man. *I want a bath, hot meal, and a few hours of sleep, then catch a boat back east, only this time I'll stay there for a while,* he thought as he entered the town. Instead of stopping at the first hotel he saw, Taylor rode almost all the way through the small town before he finally stopped.

Quickly dismounting he walked into the hotel lobby, got a room from a weasel of a small man, and placed his gear against the far wall. Without much thought, he picked up some of his clean clothes and went to the bathhouse, where he spent an hour relaxing in the hot water. He noticed the water seemed to relieve some of the pain from his manhood, or maybe the mercury had actually started to work. Drying off and quickly dressing he went to the hotel restaurant, ate a big meal and then returned to his room for a few hours of sleep.

After two days in the town beside the fort, Donnelly had relaxed completely, thinking he'd finally taken care of Nate Grisham. He also noticed the sores on him had disappeared and his member no longer leaked as it once had. Though he still felt a slight burning when he peed, the laudanum he sipped almost constantly usually killed most of the deep pain. It was late in the afternoon when Taylor purchased two more of bottles of the powerful painkiller from a local doctor and as he walked by the front desk in the hotel he asked the clerk to send him up a woman.

"I don't know any soiled doves that I can remember." The weasel replied as soon as Donnelly had asked.

Sliding a dollar coin over the counter Taylor asked, "You sure?"

The clerk quickly picked up the coin and as he placed it in his pocket he said, "Well, now, I just remembered one and she's a looker too."

"Have her in my room in two hours, along with a bottle of rye." Donnelly spoke, placed two dollars on the counter for the rye and then made his way to his room.

Taylor had been taking a short nap when he heard a low knock at his door. Pulling his pistol he moved to the side of the door and asked, "Who's there?"

"It's just a young girl out fer some fun." A soft female voice announced.

If Donnelly had known Nate Grisham was less than two miles from his hotel he'd been gone from his room in a second, instead of enjoying young soiled dove's sexual talents.

Because of the smell, Nate had been forced to bury Doc out on the plains, near the small stream where he first stopped, and it pained him deeply to do the job. All the while as he'd covered is friends body with soil, Nate had sworn revenge and deep down inside the big man knew he'd have it and soon.

As he entered the town, Nate knew he'd have to take it slow and easy, for no other reason that his color. He rode up to Patrick O'Brien's office, unforked his horse and walked in. Pat, who had been looking at a map on the wall, turned and said in a surprised voice, "Nate, you look like holy hell! That's blood on your side, you okay? Do I need to send for the doc?"

Nate wobbled over to a chair in front of a desk, plopped down and replied in a tired voice, "Donnelly is back in this town or your fort some place."

Turning his head toward a back room Pat yelled, "Private Peterson, get the doc and hurry!"

As Private Peterson ran past the door, he said, "Be back directly, sir."

Looking at the injured Nate, Pat asked, "Now what is this about Donnelly being back in town?"

For the next five minutes, Nate told all he knew and then added, "He might have just passed right on through your place, but I doubt it. He'll be tired, hungry, and I'm pretty sure he thinks he killed me with his last shot."

As Nate was speaking the same young doctor he'd seen treat Sara Donnelly entered the office and asked, "What's this about a gunshot wound?"

Pat pointed at Nate.

"I'll not treat a N—!" The doctor started in a loud voice, only to be silenced as O'Brien's gun suddenly appeared in his right hand.

The hammer snapped back with a noticeable click as it locked into position and Pat O'Brien said, "I think you will doctor and you'll do it with nice gentle hands too. You have no choice, since my surgeon is not here and you are the only doctor around. "

"I'll do the job, but I won't like it." The young doctor replied as he moved toward Nate.

Ten minutes later Nate's injured side was clean, had a fresh bandage, and the wrapping was complete. As the doctor stood he said, "That'll be two dollars."

"Hell doc," Pat said with a chuckle, "we both know you only charge a dollar and if you come by at the end of the week I'll see the army pays you for the job."

Mumbling the young doctor picked up his small black bag and made his way from the office.

"Sorry about that Nate, but you know how some folks are."

Nate gave a light laugh and replied, "Hell, don't I know. There will come a day in the future Pat when a man's color won't matter a bit, but me and you'll never live to see it. There is still a lot of learning to be done on both sides of the fence. I know blacks that don't trust none of y'all and of course we know most whites don't care much for us."

Private Peterson, who'd been standing near the maps hadn't said a word, but noticing him, Pat O'Brien said, "Peterson, go to both hotels and see if a man looking tired and worn out has check in the last few days. Tell 'em the man would look like he'd just come from out of the wilderness and not dressed like a tin-horn. Oh," Pat spoke, reached inside of his desk and pulled out a wanted poster for Donnelly, "and see if this picture jar's their memory a little."

Peterson gave a big grin, took the poster from Pat and replied, "Be back as soon as the jobs done, sir."

As the young private left the office Pat said, "He's still wet behind the ears, but overall a good man to have around. He's lightning fast with those guns of his and he got the sense to know when to not pull 'em as well as when he needs to."

"That's important for a soldier boy, so innocents don't get killed or maybe some drunk soldier that's just lookin' for a fist fight." Nate said and then grinned.

"Nate, I hate like hell to say this, but I don't know of a hotel in town you can stay at. But, I can give you a cell in the guard-house if you just want a place to rest and sleep a little."

"Not a problem Pat, the cell will be fine, just leave the door open a mite, or I might think you've turned on me."

Pat laughed, pulled a small pint of whiskey from the top drawer of his desk and as he handed the bottle to Nate, he said, "Take this with you too, because it'll kill the pain a little when you try to sleep."

Nate was soon asleep on the hard mattress in a cell and didn't know when Peterson returned an hour later. The young private walked up in front of O'Brien's desk, saluted and then said with a big grin, "Sir, I found your man down at the Dew Drop Inn and right now he's up stairs entertainin' a soiled dove."

Pat stood, pulled his pistol and as he checked the load he said, "Pull the shotgun as a back up and let's go."

"What about that feller in the cell, the black man? Or, do you want the sergeant of the guard with a detail?" Peterson asked as he unlocked the guns on the wall and pulled a big ten gauge double-barreled shotgun from the rack.

"Hell, let Nate sleep. If we work this right, we'll be back be-fore he misses us. As for the sergeant, he's more than likely asleep as well, because no one is in the guardhouse, except Nate. You and I can do this job, private."

Ten minutes later the two soldiers stood outside of the door to Donnelly's room. Pat raised three fingers, indicating they would enter the room on three. One, two, three, his fingers quickly lowered the Pat kicked the door in with his right foot and entered the room. Donnelly quickly rolled from top of the whore and fell to the floor, coming up with a scattergun he'd place there earlier. Aiming the gun in the direction of the door he pulled one trigger and heard a scream of pain, then heard the sound of two pistols shots close together. The whore rolled from the bed and landed on the floor beside Donnelly and quick glance at her showed the whole right side of her head missing.

Suddenly jumping up Donnelly saw a young man wearing a blue uniform holding a scattergun and as he started to turn the gun toward him, Taylor squeezed the trigger and saw dust fly from the front of the soldier's shirt. The wall behind the man spattered with blood and bits of gore.

Pulling his pistol from the night table, Donnelly checked the two soldiers. The younger man was as dead a hell, while the older one was still alive though his injury looked fatal. The whore was quietly dying and large pool of blood covered the floor beside the bed under her head. Quickly dressing, picking up his weapons and gear, Donnelly left the room through a window and jumped to the ground. Ten minutes later, he was moving east, as fast as his horse would take him.

Nate slept for three hours before being awakened by an old sergeant going through desk drawers out front. Standing slowly, due to the pain in his side, the big man moved slowly into the office and asked, "You got a good reason to be going through that stuff?"

The sergeant turned quickly, obviously surprised to find someone in the jail. Giving Nate a weak grin he replied, "The commander is at the doctor's office and has a chest full of buck-shot bein' dug out right now. Young Pete, well, the undertaker has him. I thought it might be best if I filed a report on this and send a dispatch rider."

"What happened and who are you?"

"I'm Sergeant Major John Appleton and I keep the enlisted men straight on this post bend run odd jobs fer the commander at times. Seem's him and Pete had a feller cornered over in a hotel room they wanted to arrest, only that feller made a fight of it. I'm worried about Major O'Brien, 'cause it don't look good, but young Pete had a wife a youngster he left behind."

Nate adjusted his gun in his belt, picked his hat from a peg on the coat rack and as he put his hat on he said, "If Pat comes around you tell 'em Nate Grisham is on that jaspers tail and you let him know I'll be bring him back—dead or alive."

John's eyes gave Nate a close looking over and then the old man said with a loud cackle, "By God, yer a big enough sumbitch to do the job too! Best of luck to ya mister, 'cause any man that can kill Pete and shoot the old man is one mean bastard."

Nate had been heading toward the door when the man spoke, so he stopped, turned and replied, "I'll do the job and he'll find I take a heap of killin' to stay killed."

"By God," the old man said, still laughing, "I'll just bet ya do old son, I'll bet ya do."

Nate was on the trail of Donnelly within an hour. He'd discovered the man had not left by boat and he'd not taken a stage, both of which were not due out until early the next morning. He'd spoken to the owner at the livery who said Donnelly had claimed his horses in a rush and moved east as fast as he could. Though he'd not known of the shootings at the time, the livery man knew Donnelly was running from something by the fear in his eyes and he'd said as much, "It wasn't none of my business right then and I've learned to keep my mouth shut in this job. But, if I'd known he'd shot Pat and killed young Pete, why I would have taken a hammer to his ass fast like."

He's goin' to kill one of those horses if he don't slow down some, Nate thought as he slowly followed Taylor's trail.

Two hours later Nate rode up on a horse that was struggling to stand, but the animal was heavily lathered up and bleeding from its mouth and nose. Pulling his pistol as he dismounted, Nate slowly walked to the downed animal and shot it behind the left ear. The animal fell to its side and quivered briefly before it stopped moving. *What kind of man would leave an animal to suffer like this?* Nate wondered as he kicked his horse into a faster walk, easily following Donnelly's tracks in the moonlight.

Donnelly had no idea Nate was behind him, but he figured a fort like Atkinson and the town would have a large posse on his ass in very little time after they learned he'd killed two of their military men. He suspected it would take the army time to get organized, so his biggest fear was of the small town. He also suspected if the town caught him he'd stretch hemp and never spend a minute in a courtroom either, because Western towns were famous for administering justice quickly and efficiently to those who broke the laws of the land.

Nate had stopped to rest his horse and grab a small bite to eat, when he saw movement on his back trail, so he melted back into the shadows. A large group of twenty men rode up, one dismounted and walked to Nate's horse. Looking the big animal over closely he said in a loud voice, "This ain't the critter we been trailing."

"Nope it ain't." Nate spoke as he stepped from the brush with his Hawken held in his hands ready.

"You see a man come by here?" A big man wearing garters on his shirtsleeves asked as he moved his horse toward Nate.

Nate cocked his rifle and said, "That's close enough Mister, who are you men?"

"Posse out of the town beside Fort Atkinson and we're looking for a white man named Donnelly who killed a soldier and shot the fort commander earlier today."

Nate gave a loud chuckle and said, "Well, it for sure wasn't me, but I know the man you're looking for and I know Major Pat O'Brien."

"Hey, you're that real big feller who was in Pat's office when I came in to get some papers from his desk." John spoke from the back of the group of riders.

"Pat okay, John?" Nate asked as he tried to see the old sergeant's face in the dim light.

"He'll live, but he ain't goin' to no square dances fer a spell."

"Look fellers, what are we goin' to do? We can see that Donnelly feller ain't far ahead of us and we're wastin' time talkin' to this jasper." The big man with the garters spoke with a hint of frustration in his voice.

"I don't know 'bout you fellers, but this posse ridin's done tuckered my butt out. I'm headin' back to the fort." The sergeant major said as he dismounted. He made his way to Nate's small fire and at the fire he said, "C Troop is leavin' in the mornin' but I don't think they'll find much.

"Well, you head on back top sergeant," garters said as he pulled his horse around, "come on boys we got a hangin' to attend to."

No sooner had the men rode off than Nate said, "John, ya know they'll never catch 'em don't you? They'll wear their horses out first. See, Donnelly done killed one horse running and the one he's on now is fresh. So, they think his horse will be tired in a few more miles, but it won't happen. They'll start droppin' out way before he does."

John gave a laugh and replied, "I didn't know about the fresh horse at all. I dropped out because they won't catch Donnelly, but I suspect you will and I want to be along when it happens."

"What makes you think they won't catch Donnelly?"

"Hell, Nate, they couldn't find their own asses, even if they started with their hands in their back pockets. They mean well, but they're as dumb as a box of horse turds."

Nate gave a loud laugh and said, "Okay, let's eat, sleep for a two hours and then hit the trail. You take the first watch and I'll take the second, alright?"

"Nate, I am an old army Sergeant Major, so you can sleep the whole time and not worry none about me son. I know how to hunt a man, kill a man, and stay awake when need be."

Two days later, as Nate and John trailed Donnelly they came to a spot where the old man recognized a dead horse from the posse. But, more importantly they noticed where the posse had kept moving east and the ex-army Captain had turned north, toward some open country. Donnelly had attempted to cover up his movements and he'd done a good job of it, but John spotted horse droppings on the trail moving away from the others. Less than a mile north, they ran into clear tracks of the horse they were following and both men set the image of the clear tracks of the animal in their minds. Like most men who rode in wild or open country, once they saw a track they very rarely forgot it.

Riding up beside Nate, John asked, "Where in the hell is he headed? There ain't shit north of Missouri but Iowa country and nobody lives there that I know of."

"John, he'll turn west in a few miles. He's doubling back on us and since he lost the posse, odds are he has no idea we're on his tail."

"Now, why in the world would he head back to the place where he raised so much stink? That's pretty dumb ain't it?"

Nate laughed, met John's eyes and replied, "He's about as dumb as a coon with a passel of dogs on his trail. Hell, the posse will think he's heading east until they come to the first large city, then they'll turn back thinking they've lost him, but in the mean time the boy will be hundreds of miles behind them."

"I still don't understand Nate, but then again, I ain't the smartest man around neither."

"All he has to do John is go west and hide for a spell. If he can get his hands on some money, or make some big promises to some lazy men, he'll be back on his revenge trail again. This man is becoming a hard man to nail down."

John laughed and then said, "Well, now, won't his ass be surprised when we show up and knock on his door!"

CHAPTER 30

Dog Barking had been watching the lone white man for over two days. The Sioux warrior knew he could kill the man with ease, but like most Indians he was a curious why a white man would be alone on the plains. The warrior had moved in close during the nights and had watched the white man as he ate his meals, drank from a small bottle that the brave thought contained firewater, and then did a very strange thing. Each night and morning, the white man would pull his manhood from his pants and then put something from a small bottle on his member. *Aiiiieee,* thought Dog Barking, *it must be medicine from a shaman to make him a great lover of women! Just think how he must make the women howl with joy!*

Dog Barking considered killing Donnelly just for the special manhood medicine, but then decided to wait and see what other things he could learn from the white man. If a man had medicine to make him a stronger lover, he might have other things the brave would want. While pleasing a woman was one of the things the Sioux warrior enjoyed, he also craved powered and respect that might be gained from this white man. *I will wait two more suns to see what other medicine this white man has. Then, on the morning of the third day, I will kill him and take all he owns for myself,* the warrior thought as he watched Donnelly fry a skillet full of bacon.

As the pork fried in the cast iron skillet Donnelly had no idea he was watched. He made some rough batter by mixing flour and water and fried them in a smaller skillet with some hot bacon grease from the larger pan. As the crude bread cooked, he removed them from the pan with a fork and placed them on a large rock beside the fire to cool. Pouring a cup of hot coffee, he turned is meat with the tip of his knife and then leaned back as a false dawn started from the east. The darkness first turned from black to gray and then finally a very light whiteness filled the small valley. Shadows from the trees overlapped his sleeping area like latticework or wicker, creating squares of light and dark. Donnelly always enjoyed this part of a new day as the sun came up, when a man could stretch and feel alive.

The air was cold with dark gray clouds moving in quickly from the west and as soon as he noticed the weather coming Taylor removed his bacon from the pan, placed it on his tin plate, and then walked over to his supplies to remove his rubber poncho. *I'll have to tie that behind my saddle today, looks like a hard rain coming,* he thought as he returned to his fire, picked up a piece of fried bread, wrapped a slab of bacon in it and started eating.

Before he mounted up, Donnelly walked to the edge of his camp and made water. He no longer ached when he peed and he was not sure if it was due to the mercury or the laudanum, but didn't care as long as the pain was gone. The mercury seemed to work well on the sores and usually dried them up in a few days, except they always came back when he least expected them. He laughed as he remembered the whore was killed in his room near the fort, hell, *she would have died eventually anyway,* he thought, *she would have got what I got and it would've taught her the evil of her ways in the end! Let all whores and women die of the French pox!*

Dog Barking was less than ten feet from Taylor as he relieved himself and as he watched the white man, he wondered, *why does this one laugh aloud when there is no one to share the laughter? Have I found one who is touched in the head by the Great Spirit? I cannot kill a touched one, because it would make The Creator mad.*

Feeling a slight cramp deep in his belly and a slight sweat, Taylor knew he needed more of the laudanum. Removing the small bottle, he added a little of the medication to the last of the coffee in his cup and quickly drank it, noticing almost immediately a change. Loading his gear on his horse, he mounted, and rode west hoping to cover a few miles before the rains came.

That night as a light rain fell, Dog Barking who had been circling Taylor's camp, noticed a second fire behind the white man. The Sioux warrior thought it might be another wolf of the Sioux, because the flames were small and hidden, so he moved toward the small light. He had gone without fresh meat or the heat of a fire for days, ever since he'd spotted the lone white man, and had the desire to warm by the flames and to eat a hot meal with a brother.

It was not until he neared the fire that he saw a white man and a buffalo man sitting by the small fire talking in low voices. *These are men who know the ways of the people and who step silently when they travel,* Dog Barking thought as he watched the two men cautiously. It was not until he had moved very close to the fire that the warrior recognized Nate Grisham and with a grin, he moved away.

"Can a warrior of the Sioux come and warm by the fire of the Raven Man?" Dog Barking spoke from the darkness a few minutes later.

Hearing the voice and recognizing it, Nate spoke first to John very quickly, "It's a Sioux warrior I know, so leave your hand away from your guns." And, then to Dog Barking he replied, "Come my friend and share my fire and simple meal with me, because the night grows cold."

The warrior walked to the fire and sat on the bare ground and as he met Nate's eyes, "You still live my friend."

"As do you Dog Barking. What brings a wolf of the Sioux out on a cold night to the open plains?"

"I follow a lone white man that I do not know."

"As do we, but to us this one is well known."

The warrior didn't speak for a few minutes and then asked, "Why do you follow this white man? I follow him to watch and learn."

"This is a white man without honor, one who kills his own people without reason."

"Waugh! This is not a good thing to do. Has he been touched by the Great Spirit?"

"No." Nate spoke, pointed at a large piece of buffalo roasting on a stick near the fire and continued, "eat of my meat as I tell you of the man you are following."

When Nate had finished his story of Taylor M. Donnelly, Dog Barking stared into the flames of the fire and said, "We, The People, have heard of great sorrow among the Crow. We have heard of many deaths of our enemies and know much crying is filling the lodges of the Sparrow Hawk people as they mourn for those who have passed on."

Nate picked up the coffee pot, poured a cup and as he handed it to the Sioux scout he said, "Dog Barking, this man is an enemy to all people, red, white or black. But, since you have found him first, what is your wish to do with him?"

"I could kill him, but that would be too easy, or I could give him to you. I am unsure what will be done, so I must think long before I make my decision."

"It is a wise man who thinks before he acts, it shows wisdom."

The warrior gave a light chuckle and replied, "I, Dog Barking, am known as a brave man and a good warrior, but I am not known for having great wisdom."

"You are yet a young warrior, my friend, and as all people know, wisdom comes with age."

The warrior simply nodded his head in understanding and then took a big bite of his meat. As he ate his meat, Nate explained to John what had just been said. The white man never said a word until the big man finished speaking, "What do you think this man will do?"

"Hard to say John, he might let us have him or he might want to kill him just for his guns, but we have to act according to his decision. By Injun law, Dog Barking has the right to kill Donnelly, let him leave alive, or give him to us."

Wiping his dirty hands on his leggings, the Sioux scout turned to Nate and said, "I have thought of this lone white man as I ate of your meat. He has killed a friend of yours and a friend's death must be avenged, as a Sioux warrior would do. I have a great desire to see the Raven man and a white man in battle, because that would be something to speak of late at night around the fires of my lodge."

"You will give him to me?" Nate asked as he moved a small log on the fire to adjust the flames.

"Yes, but I want first claim to his belongings."

Nate thought for a minute or two and then replied, "So be it then. I get the man and you can have his belongings, along with his hair."

Dog Barking nodded and then asked, "When will you make battle against this man with no honor?"

"In the morning just as the sun peeks over the hills."

"That is time the Sioux do battle as well. It gives a new soul time to journey to the other side."

"Well," Nate spoke to John, "we'll confront Donnelly in the morning, at sunrise."

Donnelly slept well and awoke with a cleared head and for the first time in months, he was not concerned about being followed. He had just bent over to add some wood to his almost dead fire when he heard a voice behind him say, "Stand slowly and keep your hands away from that pistol in your belt. Twitch and I'll blow you in two pieces."

Taylor kept his hands well out to his sides and slowly stood as he asked, "How have you been Nate Grisham?"

"Better than you have. You've got a serious problem with the laudanum old coon, not that it matters much. Taylor, you have a choice, you can come in with me right now and end it, or I'll lower my rifle and you can see if you're faster than I am. But either way it ends this mornin'."

Donnelly gave a loud insane laugh and said, "Hell, drop the rifle Nate. Then you can count to three and we'll both go for our guns, or can a damned slave count that high."

Nate, knowing Taylor was attempting to make him mad gave a grin and replied, "Nice try Donnelly, but it won't work on me. See, I'm going to kill you and that makes me happy, so nothing you say will piss me off."

"Drop the rifle and let's put an end to all of this Nate. One of us will walk away from here today and it will be me."

Damn me, Nate thought as he looked at Donnelly, *he's moved slightly and the rising sun is in my eyes. But, I can't back down now, not with Dog Barking watching us.*

Nate suddenly dropped his Hawken on the grass at his feet, glanced at the silhouette of Donnelly in the new sun, and said, "One"

Taylor felt a slight fear start in his stomach and realized he had not had time to drink his laudanum yet. He felt his gun hand sweating and since the morning was cool, he knew it was from fear. His fingers began to tremble slightly and suddenly he had an idea.

"Two." Nate spoke in the clear morning air, confident he could out draw Donnelly.

At the count of two, Taylor pulled his pistol and cocked it in one motion, and as he fired, he saw the bullet strike Nate in the right side of the chest. The big man, knocked back by the blow of the slug, fell to the ground hard.

Taylor ran toward Nate's fallen form, picked up the black man's pistol where it had fallen nearby as he fell, and walking to him pointed it at his head. There was an evil, almost insane look in Donnelly's eyes as he said, "You're a dead man Nate Grisham. I'm going to kill you now."

Nate, knowing Taylor meant every word just spoken, slowly reached behind his back, pulled a long skinning knife from his belt and threw it with all of his might at the ex-army Captain. Nate grinned as the knife sunk up to its handle in Donnelly's belly.

A loud animal like scream came from Donnelly as he slowly dropped to his knees and released his grip on Nate's pistol. As the pistol fell to the grass, his fingers wrapped around the wooden handle of the long sharp knife and his eyes had a look of total disbelief in them as he looked at Nate and said, "Damn. . . damn you . . . Nate . . . Gris . . .ham."

Suddenly from the brush behind the two men, ran John and Dog Barking. The Sioux, intent of counting first coup ran right at Donnelly and touched him on the head with his coup stick. John, more concerned about his big friend picked up Nate's still loaded pistol from the grass and as he watched Donnelly closely he asked, "You ok Nate? I saw ya take a ball."

"I'll live." Nate replied swiftly.

Taylor M. Donnelly suddenly fell to the right and his body quivered in pain as his life's blood leaked from his belly. His hands were both cover in bright red blood and his feet drummed softly in the grass with the pain.

Dog Barking approached from the fire where he'd picked up Donnelly's rifle and shotgun, gave Nate a grin and asked, "You do not take his scalp?"

"It is not my custom. I have promised the Maker of all Things I would never take scalps."

Pulling his knife the Sioux warrior stated flatly, "I made no promises to the Great Spirit. Are you finished with this man, or do you want to play with him?"

Nate slowly shook his head as he replied, "I am finished and he now belongs to you."

Grabbing Donnelly's long and dirty hair, Dog Barking quickly ran his knife around the white man's head and peeled the scalp back slowly. A hideous scream came from Taylor as his scalp pulled lose with a loud sucking sound and the brave held it high in the air as he gave an earsplitting Sioux war cry. Donnelly's body jerked violently and twisted in pain as the warrior starting going through his shirt pockets, and Dog Barking grew impatient with the man's constant moving, so his knife flashed once more in the early morning light.

Nate turned his head as the knife entered under Donnelly's rib cage and the warrior twisted and jerked the knife from side to side. Taylor screamed once more and the warrior, growing frustrated and angry that the white man would not die, leaned over and cut his throat.

Moving away from the blood spurting from Donnelly's throat, Dog Barking said, "He is a worthy enemy, because he does not die easily."

CHAPTER 31

Ten days later as the sun was coming up, a very tired John and Nate Grisham arrived in Fort Atkinson with Taylor M. Donnelly's body tied to his horse. The body, wrapped up in canvas Nate found among the dead man's gear, was starting to stink. The rest of the gear from the dead man he'd given the Sioux warrior. Dog Barking took all of Donnelly's belongings, but when he smelled the laudanum, thinking it was whiskey, he'd poured it out. The small bottle of mercury had pleased the warrior and right in front of Nate and John, he'd pulled his member out and smeared the liquid on himself.

At the time, John had looked at Nate and said, "That's mercury in the bottle. The way Dog Barking just used it he must has seen Donnelly using it on himself. Our man Taylor Donnelly had the French Pox."

"I've seen the treatment often enough in the mountains. But, it doesn't work."

Riding up to the Pat O'Brien's office, they were surprised to see the man walk out and greet them before they could even dismount, "It's finally over, huh?"

Like most small army posts and towns out west, there were folks coming and going on the boardwalk early in the mornings, because most were early risers. Some were farmers moving products, some were city folks on their way to eat breakfast, and still others were soldiers on their way to work. A small crowd gathered around the three men as soon as a body was seen tied to the horse, as all were curious as to what had happened. Unlike he'd usually do, Pat O'Brien did not force the crowd to move away. The commander wanted the folks at Fort Atkinson to know who had brought Taylor M. Donnelly to justice.

"Yep, that's Captain Donnelly on the horse, Major."

"Nate, I'll take care of the paperwork and if you come back in a week or so I'll see the authorization to pay you the reward is ready."

The big black man slowly shook his head and replied as he dropped the reins to Donnelly's horse, "No keep it this time, because I was already paid once to bring 'em in and I don't cotton to the idea of being paid for doing the same job twice."

As Nate pulled his horse around to head back to his shining mountains, John dismounted and waved to the big man as he slowly started to ride from town. Someone from the group asked, "Who was that big black jasper that brought Donnelly in dead?"

John turned, gave a great laugh and replied, "You dim-witted fool, that was a real man's man. That was Nate Grisham, a black mountain man!"

A Special Thanks to:

The American Mountain Men (AMM) is an outdoor organization with a serious interest in the history, skills, clothing and accoutrements of the Rocky Mountain Fur Trade period (1800-1840). By default of that unique combination it is often viewed as one of the best 'living history' groups reflecting the original mountain men of the American West.

More information about the organization can be found at http://user.xmission.com/-drudy/amm/gateway.html

A Glossary of American Mountain Men Terms, Words & Expressions

Compiled by Walt Hayward & Brad McDade

© 1997 The American Mountain Men and used with permission

A

AIRLINE
> The shortest and straightest line between two points. This term was in use long before the invention of aircraft.

APAREJO
> A large, padded packsaddle designed to handle awkward, heavy loads. Very likely the first type of packsaddle, Unlike the sawbuck, panniers cannot be handled with this saddle.

APISHEMORE
> A saddle pad, often made of hair.

APPALOS
> An early camp food made by skewering alternate pieces of lean meat and fat on a sharpened stick and roasting over a low fire. When it was possible to get them, pieces of potato or vegetable, were intermixed with the fat and the meat. This method of cooking was much used by many tribes of Indians, as well as the Mountain Men.

ARKANSAS TOOTHPICK
> A large, pointed dagger used mostly by river men.

AS THE CROW FLIES
> See "Airline"

AUX ALIMENTS DU PAYS
> French for "nourishment of the land'. All the free trappers and many engages were required to live "aux aliments du pays", surviving by using the provisions of nature.

AVANT COURIER
> A French word meaning "scout". This word was used by both voyageurs and mountain men.

AWERDENTY
> Whiskey.

B

BALL
> Bullet. (The actual projectile.)

BARK ON, HE HAS THE
> Said of a courageous person.

BARK TO
> To skin an animal. To scalp a man. a squirrel by shooting the tree bark from under him.

BIG FIFTY
> The .50 caliber Sharps rifle used by the buffalo hunter.

BEAM
> A fallen tree used for fleshing hides. This was also called a graining beam or a fleshing beam.

BEAR PEN
> A type of trap in which the fall acts as a lid over a pen, thereby catching the animal alive.

BEE LINE
> See "Airline".

BITCH
> A lamp made by filling a tin cup with bear or other animal fat, then inserting a twisted rag or piece of cotton rope to act as a wick.

BLACKBIRD STORM
> An unexpected cold storm in late spring.

BLANC BEC
> A term used by voyageurs for a new man who had yet to travel the Missouri past the Platte River. As with many voyageur terms, this was later adopted by some Mountain Men with much the same meaning.

BOIS DE VACHE
> Buffalo chips used as fuel.

BONE PICKER
> A despised human scavenger who hunted for, and sold, the bones of dead animals, mostly buffalo.

BOOSHWAY
> The leader of a party of mountain men. The word comes from the French "bourgeois", used by the voyageurs.

BOSCHLOPER
> See "Bossloper".

BOSSLOPER
> A trapper or hunter

BOUDINS

The real treat of the mountain man. A buffalo gut containing chyme, which was cut into lengths about 24 inches long and roasted before a fire until crisp and sizzling.

BREED
A person of Indian and White blood. A half-breed.

BRIGADE
A keelboat crew.

BUCKSKIN
Tanned deerskin from which much of the clothing of the Indian and mountain man was made. If Indian tanned, buckskin was usually a very light dolor, often almost white. Darker color was usually obtained by smoking the skin over an open fire.

BUFFALO BOAT
A boat made of raw buffalo skins, much used by traders. This boat differed from the Bull Boat in that it was larger and had a normal boat shape.

BUFFALO CHIP
Buffalo manure, dried and used as fuel.

BUFFALO CIDER
The fluid found in the stomach of the buffalo. Used by both mountain men and Indians to quench thirst.

BUFFALO DANCE
An Indian dance used to insure success on a buffalo hunt.

BUFFALOED
Confused.

BUFFALO GUN
See "Big Fifty".

BUFFALO LICK
A natural saltlick used by buffalo and other game animals. Usually a very good place to find game.

BUFFALO RANGE
Any wide-open feeding area used by buffalo.

BUFFALO ROBE
The skin of the buffalo, tanned with the hair on. Used by traders, Indians, and mountain men as ground covers, robes and blankets,

BUFFALO WALLOW

The depression made by buffalo rolling and dusting
themselves. The same wallows were used year after year
often becoming quite deep.

BUFFALO WOLF

A large, gray wolf found around buffalo herds. Young
buffalo calves were the natural food of this animal.

BUG'S BOYS

The Blackfoot Indians.

BUG-TIT

A derisive term used to mean any company official who
tended to think that he was more important than he actually was.

BULL BOAT

A bowl-shaped boat having a willow frame-work covered with green hide. Easy and quick to make; but very
difficult to handle.

BULL CHEESE

Buffalo jerky.

C

CACHE

A safe place, often hidden, for storage of food and other
supplies.

CACHE, TO

To put or store something in a safe place.

CAHOOTS, TO GO IN

To go into partnership.

CALABOOSE

Jail.

CALZONERAS

A form of Mexican trousers often worn by traders.

CANOT DU MAITRE

A 35- to 40-foot long canoe propelled by fourteen men,
(voyageur)

CANOT DU NORD

A 25-foot long canoe propelled by eight men. (Voyageur)

CAROT

See "Carrot"

CARROT

A bundle of tobacco, wrapped in linen, then whip-
wrapped with cords thus forming a crescent-shaped

bundle. An early method of packaging and selling tobacco.

CAYUSE
A horse. Also a tribe of Indians in Oregon.

CHAFF, TO
To make fun of someone. To rub someone the wrong way.

CHAFFER, TO
To haggle over prices or trade goods.

CHAPARRAL
A thicket of scrub oak and other brush.

CHEF DE VOYAGE
A party leader. (Voyageur)

CHILD
See "Coon".

CHINOOK
A warm wind, usually in the spring. This is a common term in the Northwest.

COCK, THE
The hammer of a rifle or pistol.

COLD FEET, HE HAS
He is a coward. Someone who seeks shelter when the going gets tough.

CONE, THE
The nipple on a percussion rifle or pistol.

COON
A raccoon. Also a friendly name early mountain men called each other.

COUNT COUP
To show bravery and receive honor by touching an enemy, usually with a special stick used for that purpose only. In some tribes, touching a living enemy had more honor than touching a dead enemy. Touching a man had more honor than touching a woman. The first to touch received more honor than the second or third. Credit was seldom if ever, given after the third. When feathers were awarded for coup, they were sometimes depending on the tribe, cut or painted to indicate the type and amount of honor they represented. Oddly enough, killing the enemy did not count for coup the first to touch took the honor, be he the killer or not. When used by the mountain man, the expression "I'll count coup on

him" usually meant "I'll kill him", after which, the taking of the dead man's scalp was normal.

COUREURS DE BOIS

A woods runner or hunter an early French trapper, (Voyageur)

COURIER

A messenger, A term used mostly by traders.

CRIMPY DAY

A very cold day.

CROOKED RIVER

Any river which is filled with sand bars reefs, or actual bends.

CURLY WOLF

A man who can brag and is willing to back his talk with his fists or other means.

CUT FOR SIGN, TO

To walk or ride back and forth across an area looking for evidence of a man or animal passing.

D

DEAD FALL

A tree blown down by the wind or other force of nature. Also, a trap which utilizes a falling log or stone as the actual trapping mechanism.

DEAD MEAT

Carrion.

DIAMOND HITCH

A hitch (knot) used to fasten cargo to a pack saddle.

DIG UP THE TOMAHAWK

Start a war. Often the word "hatchet" was substituted for "tomahawk".

DRY, I AM

I am thirst, likely for something stronger than water.

DUMPLING DUST

Flour. This term originated from the early practice of mixing dough by pouring water in a depression made in the flour while it was still in the sack, causing small puffs of dust. Both the term and practice are still used by north woodsmen.

DU PONT

Gunpowder.

DUTCHMAN

Any type of temporary prop or support.
DUTCH OVEN
> A large kettle with three feet and a dished lid. It can be
> used for both cooking and baking.

E

EASY WATER
> Calm, smooth water on a river or lake.

ENGAGEMENT
> A 3-year agreement between a trapper and a fur com-
> pany.

ENGAGES
> Company trappers bound for 3 years to sell all they trap
> to only one company.

F

FACTOR
> Chief of a trading post or trading party, authorized by the
> company to sell or trade company merchandise.

FATHER OF ALL WATERS
> Mississippi River. An Indian term.

FAT PINE
> Pitch pine, very good for starting fires.

FEAST CAKES
> Pancakes.

FILLY
> A young, female horse; although just as likely to be ap-
> plied to a young, shapely, good-looking woman.

FIRE WATER
> Whiskey. This term comes from the Indian practice of
> throwing a cup of whiskey into a fire to see if it would
> burn. If it would not flame up, it would not be accepted.

FIZZ-POP
> A very early soda pop made by mixing a little vinegar
> and a spoon of sugar in a glass of fresh water. Just before
> drinking mix in about a quarter of a spoon of soda.

FLASH IN THE PAN
> A misfire. Also a man who spends a great deal of time
> bragging, but never seems to be around when it comes
> to proving himself.

FLESHED

Any skin or hide which had the flesh and fat scraped off before it was dried.

FLESHING

The process of removing the excess flesh and fat from a skin or hide.

FLAT BOAT

A large scow used to float up to three tons of fur and skins to St. Louis.

FLOAT STICK

A stick attached to a steel trap used to show the location of the trap and the trapped animal. From this comes the expression, "That's the way my stick floats" , meaning , " That's the way I feel about it."

FOOFARRAW

Any fancy clothing or anything fancy on clothing. Just about anything used for decoration

FORK A HORSE (or MULE)

Mount the animal.

FORT UP

Get ready to fight a defensive battle.

FREE TRAPPER

A trapper who worked for himself, trapping and selling where he wanted and to whom he wanted. As free a man as the elements would allow.

FUR COUNTRY

As the mountain men used the expression, The Rocky Mountains.

FUSEES

A fusil or trade musket

G

GALENA

Lead.

GALENA PILLS

Lead balls (bullets).

GALETTE

A basic flour and water bread made into flat, round cakes and fried in fat or baked before the open fire. (Voyageur)

GALLUS'S

Suspenders.

GANT UP

Tighten up on a rope or belt.
GET YER BRISTLES UP, TO
> To get angry.

GEWGAWS
> Beads, bells, small mirrors, etc. used for decoration.

GONE, HE'S
> He's dead.

GORDOS
> Flapjacks (hotcake, pancakes whatever).

GO UNDER, TO
> To die.

GONE BEAVER
> Said of someone who has been dead some time. He's about to go under; but once dead, he's a gone beaver.

GRAINED
> See "Fleshed".

GRAS
> Animal fat.

GRAS LAMP
> See "Bitch".

GREASE HUNGER, I HAVE
> An expression meaning "I am hungry for meat."*

GREASE AND BEANS
> An expression meaning "Food".

GREEN HAND
> A term used by early traders meaning an inexperienced man,

GREEN MEAT
> Meat which still had the animal heat in it.

GREEN RIVER
> A western river (see any good map). The hilt of a knife (from the old GR trade mark up near the hilt). A knife made by Russell Green River Works. A copy of a Russell Green River Works knife,

GREEN RIVER, UP TO
> Anything of quality was said to be "up to Green River".

GRUB
> Food. This very old term is still widely used.

GULLY WASHER
> A very hard downpour of rain.

H

HAIR OF THE BEAR, HE HAS
>The greatest praise a mountain man can say of another.

HALF BREED
>A person of mixed blood, Indian and White.

HALF-FACED CAMP
>A floor less shed, closed with poles on the back and sides, closed with skins and blankets on the front. The roof sloped from the rear of the shed to the front. This form of house or shed was greatly used by settlers until they had time to construct a log structure.

HAWK
>Short for "Tomahawk".

HEFT, TO
>A very old term meaning "to lift and feel the weight of".

HELLO THE CAMP
>A traditional greeting given before entering any strange camp. Better given at a slight distance or the visitor may not leave in the same manner that he entered,

HIDE HUNTER
>A rather low breed of man who killed buffalo for the hides only. Usually despised by all who came into contact with him. "Buffalo skins for the belts of industry."

HIVERANNO
>An experienced mountain man. One who had lived many years in Indian country. (First Voyageur, later Mountain Man)

HOGSHEAD
>A large wooden barrel or cask capable of holding from 100 gallons up.

HOGAN
>A stick and earth lodge used by the Navaho Indians,

HOLLER CALF ROPE
>Give up, surrender. An expression used by river boatmen.

HORRORS
>Delirium Tremans. After the first night or two at the Rocky Mountain Rendezvous many a mountain man faced the horrors.

HUMP RIBS
>The small ribs which support the buffalo's hump. Roasted they were another favorite of the mountain men.

I

INDIAN ANNUITY
Payment given to Indians as part of a treaty agreement. More often than not, a sizeable portion went into the pocket of some bureaucrat.
INDIAN BREAD
Corn meal bread.
INDIAN DOCTOR
Medicine man. Also, a White man well versed in natural medicine,
INDIAN FILE
Single file.
INDIAN GOODS
Trade goods. Often just trinkets of little value to the White man, but of great value to the Indian.
INDIAN HATCHET
Tomahawk.
INDIAN SCOUT
An Indian on scouting duty with the U.S. Amy.
INDIAN SIGN
Evidence of Indians in the area.
INDIAN UP
To sneak up on someone or something.

J

JERKY
Dried meat made by cutting meat into strips about one inch wide, 1/4 inch thick, and as long as possible. This was then sun-dried on racks often with a small hard-wood fire under the meat to smoke it and to keep in-sects off it. In good, hot weather the meat would be dry and ready to use in 3 to 4 days.
JORNADA
A day's journey. A journey between pre-determined points.

K

KEEL BOAT
A 60- to 80-foot long flat-bottomed boat about 16 feet wide. In wide use before steamboats.
KEENER

A man who is an exceptional shot.
KINNIKINNICK
A firm of smoking tobbaco made from the leaves of the tobacco plant plus the leaves and bark of other plants, the actual formula depending on the tribe making it.
KYACK
A rawhide box designed to be strapped to a pack saddle.

L

LARRUPT TO
To eat in a hasty and sloppy manner
LARRUPING GOOD
Anything which has an extra fine flavor.
LASH ROPE
The rope used to tie a load to a pack saddle.
LAVE HOI
Time to roll out of bed. This expression, usually given in a good, loud voice, was used to awaken a partner or a whole party.
LEGGINGS
The buckskin, later blanket, trousers of the Indian.
LIGHTS WENT OUT, THE
He died.
LOBO
Timber wolf.
LOCK, STOCK, AND BARREL
In total; the whole thing. For examples "He sold his shop, lock, stock, and barrel". This expression comes from the 3 major parts needed to construct a muzzle loading rifle or pistol.
LOCO
Crazy.
LODGE
The living quarters be it house, cabin, tipi, hogan, tent, or lean-to, of the Indian or mountain man.
LODGEPOLE
The main cross-supporting pole of a lodge.
LODGEPOLE PINE
(Pinus contorta) Once one of the most valued trees in the Rocky Mountains, due to its many uses. Also known as "Screw pine" and "Tamarack pine".
LONG FORM

A crude bench long enough to seat three or more people.
LUMPY DICK
An early pudding made by stirring dry flour into boiling
milk until thick, then serving with sweet milk and molasses or sugar.

M

MACKINAW
A boat approximately 40 feet long, 10 feet across the
beam, and 4 feet deep, pointed at both ends. This boat,
widely used on the Mississippi, Missouri, and Ohio River
systems, was capable of holding a cargo of approxi-
mately 10 tons. Often these were used for downstream
travel only.
MADE WOLF MEAT, HE WAS
A dead man left where he fell, for the wolves to dine on.
An act of contempt.
MAKE BEAVER, TO
To get a move on, to travel in a hurry.
MAKE MEAT, TO
To hunt for and lay in a good store of meat.
MAKE MEDICINE, TO
To hold a pow-wow or meeting. To pray for spiritual
guidance. To hold a religious service. To actually look for
and find herbs, etc. to be used as medicine.
MAL DE VANCHE
An illness common to the mountain man and voyageur,
It was caused by eating too much fat or fatty meat and
not enough vegetable matter.
MANGEUR DE LARD
Voyageur term for a fur company recruit. These men,
considered useful for common labor only, were usually
fed salted pork, hence the name. The term was later
adopted by the mountain men to mean any man new to
the fur trade.
MANTILLA
A shawl used as a trade item with the Indians,
MEAT BAG, THE
The human stomach.
MEDICINE

The magic, secret charms of the Indian. Also the bait used in trapping.

MEDICINE BAG
The small bag, used to carry the medicine of the Indian. Adopted by the mountain man and used to carry anything small, especially the "secret" bait he used near his traps.

MEDICINE PIPE
The sacred pipe of the Indian. This pipe was used only during special ceremonies, was kept in a special, sacred bundle, and was NEVER allowed to touch the ground.

MEDICINE LODGE
A sacred lodge used only for religious ceremonies. In some tribes it could also be used as a meeting place for the secret societies of braves. The sweat lodge (an early American form of sauna bath) used by many tribes was also considered a "medicine lodge".

MESA
A table-top (flat) mountain or hill.

METATE
The stone mortar used for grinding corn and other grains. The word is Spanish, not Indian.

MOCCASIN
The buckskin or moose hide shoe of the Indian and mountain man. Light, quiet, and comfortable.

MOCCASIN MAIL
A postal system devised by the mountain man. It consisted of leaving messages concerning the condition of the trail ahead, time and place of a rendezvous, etc, in trees, hollow logs, etc. Such messages were quite often put in an old moccasin so they would be easy to see.

MUD HOOKS
Human feet. This expression is still often heard among country people.

MULA
Mule.

N

NEAR SIDE
Left side

NOON IT, TO
To stop for the mid-day meal and rest.

NO-SEE-UM
>Buffalo gnat.

NUTRIA
>Although actually the common name of the myocaster coypusv many mountain men used it to mean "beaver".

O

OFF SIDE
>Right side.

OL' COON
>A friendly nickname used between mountain men.

OL' EPHRAIM
>Grizzly bear.

OL' HOSS
>See "Ol' Coon".

ON HIS OWN HOOK, HE IS
>A free trapper.

P

PAGAMOGGON
>A very effective Indian weapon made by attaching a 2-foot long leather-covered handle to a 3-pound stone. Used as a club.

PALAVER
>Talk.

PANNIER
>See "Kyack".

PAPOOSE
>An Indian word used by many frontiersmen and mountain men to mean any Indian child.

PARFLECHE
>Rawhide made from buffalo hide. It is exceedingly tough. In fact, its name (French) comes from the fact that it could not be pierced by arrows or spears. The word also refers to a carrying case or envelope made of dried buffalo hide and widely used by both Indians and mountain men in place of a trunk.

PASS
>A passage through a range of mountains.

PEMMICAN
>Indian food made by mixing powdered jerky with dried berries and hot tallow, then packed and stored in skin or

gut bags. Used by Indians and mountain men. This is a high energy survival food.

PENOLE

Flour made from parched corn.

PILGRIM

Usually immigrants, people moving west. The term was also sometimes used by the mountain men to mean any man new to the fur trade.

PINCE

The pointed bow and stern of a canoe. (voyageur)

PIPE

The jornada of the voyageur. The distance between rest stops, which were the only times his pipe could be lit up and enjoyed.

PLEW

Beaver pelt (skin).

PONCHE

Trade tobacco.

POO-DER-FE

A destructive, frigid west wind. (Crow Indian word)

POOR BULL FROM FAT COW TO KNOW

To know good times from bad. Either term could also be used alone, such as: "Them days war Poor Bull and that be a sure fact", meaning, "those days food and plews were hard to get and that is a fact".

PORTAGE

A trip between waterways or around a waterway obstruction, carrying everything along with you.

PORTAGE TRAIL

The trail used to carry a canoe and supplies between waterways or around a waterway obstruction.

POSSIBLES

The personal property of the mountain man, Such items as a bullet mold, an awl, knives, a tin cup, his buffalo robe or a blanket capote, his pipe and tobacco, flint and steel, sometimes a small sheet-metal fry-pan, and other accouterments he considered necessary. Firearms were considered "pieces" or guns" and not possibles.

POSSIBLES BAG

The leather bag in which the mountain man carried his possibles. everything from his pipe and tobacco to his patches and balls. What could not be carried in the bag

were hung on the bags shoulder strap. Shooting needs
were given first priority, kept where they could be found
with ease and speed.
POUDRERIE
Dry snow driven through the air by a violent wind.
POW-WOW
An Indian word meaning a meeting followed by dancing
and feasting. The mountain man's term for any discus-
sion between two men, or for a planned meeting.
PRO-PELLE-CUTEM
The motto of the Hudson's Bay Company, meaning "for a
pelt, a skin".
PSALM SINGER
A very religious person.
PULL FOOT
To turn tail and run.

R

READ HIM A PAGE FROM THE GOOD BOOK
To give someone a tongue, lashing, or perhaps some-
thing a little more forceful.
RAISE, TO
To steal from another's cache. Any man found doing this
was likely to become wolf meat.
RAISE HAIR
To scalp an enemy.
RAWHIDE
The dried, dehaired but untanned hide of any animal,
usually cattle or buffalo. Very strong and useful.
READING SIGN
Interpreting the tracks, etc. when tracking.
REDSTICK
Indian.
ROBE HIDE
The winter-killed hide of the buffalo. usually used to
make buffalo robes.
RUBBED OUT
Dead or killed. This expression comes from the early at-
tempts of the Indian to learn English. To erase is to rub
out, anything rubbed out no longer exists, so must be
dead. Adopted by the mountain man with the same
meaning.

S

SANTA FE TRAIL
A well-used route between Independence, Missouri and Santa Fe, New Mexico.

SAW BUCK
A cross-frame used for cutting wood. Also a pack saddle.

SCALP FEAST
A time for counting coup, feasting dancing, and chanting over battles won.

SCALP LOCK
A challenging lock of hair grown on the crown of the heads of the warriors of some Indian tribes.

SCALP POLE
The pole used to display scalps taken from enemies.

SEGUNDO
The second-in-command of a large party or company

SHARPS
A breechloading percussion rifle invented by Christian Sharps.

SHINING
Splendid. To shine means to be extra good at something,

SHINING MOUNTAINS
An early name for the Rocky Mountains.

SHONGSASHA
A form of tobacco made from the bark of the red willow, sometimes mixed with Indian tobacco plant leaves.

SKIN TRADE, THE
The fur trade.

SKOOKUM
Good. An Indian word much used in mountain man slang.

SLEDGE
A flat-decked sled used for transporting provisions.

SLINGING
A method of securing provisions to the back of a mule.

SLUSH LAMP
See "Bitch".

SNAG
A dead tree in a river. Capable of sinking a canoe.

SNOW EATER, A
A chinook.

SOURDOUGH
>Fermented dough used for making bread, biscuits flap-jacks, etc.

SPUDS
>Potatoes.

SQUARE
>A term of respect. Any man of courage, honesty, self- reliance, and devotion to what he believed to be right was " square " and darn proud of-it.

SQUARE SHOOTER, A
>See "Square".

SQUAW CAMP
>A camp for women and children while the men were away hunting or at war.

SQUAW HITCH
>A simple hitch used in place of the Diamond Hitch.

SQUAW MAN
>A White man married to an Indian woman.

SQUAW WIND
>An unexpected warm wind in the middle of a very cold spell. Like a chinook, but in the dead of winter.

SQUAW WOOD
>Small dry sticks used for starting a fire or tending a very small. hard-to-see fire for cooking.

STIRRUP
>Bread made from flour, fat, and water. It was baked in a Dutch oven or on a stick placed over or near a fire.

SWEEP
>The steering oar on keel boats, rafts, etc.

T

TANGLE FOOT
>Whiskey.

TAOS LIGHTNING
>A whiskey made near Taos New Mexico.

TERRAPIN
>Dog meat.

TINDER
>Fine, shredded Birch bark or other highly combustible wood. Used for starting fire with flint and steel, or with a fire drill. Charred cotton was also used as tender.

THERE GO HORSE AND BEAVER

An expression meaning "I just lost everything I owned or had with me".

THRUMS

The fringe on buckskin or leather clothing.

THROW IN WITH, TO

To join a group or party. To go into partnership with someone.

THROW SMOKE, TO

To shoot a firearm

TIMBER WOLF

A large, gray wolf found at one time throughout the United States, now found only in the far north.

TOMAHAWK

A small hatchet used by the Indians and mountain men for fighting and woodcraft.

TOMAHAWK TALKS

Councils of war. Treaty councils. The tomahawk was an important symbol in both war and peace.

TIPI

The conical lodge used by the Plains Indians. (Teepee)

TOW

Unspun flax used for cleaning firearms. Also used as tinder.

TRACE, A

A trail.

TRADE GUN

See " Fusees".

TRAPPER'S BUTTER

Marrow from the leg bones of large animals.

TRAPPINGS

Accouterments, especially for a horse.

TRAVEE

A travois, a form of sled made by fastening two long poles together over the back of A horse or dog, then building a platform near where they drag to support a pack or cargo of some sort.

U

UP TO BEAVER

An expression meaning a very cunning persons one who can hold his own in any situation.

V

VALLEY TAN

Mormon whiskey.

VARA

The Spanish yard (33 inches); the unit of measurement used by many early traders.

VOYAGEUR

A trapper for one of the very early fur companies. Most voyageurs were French-Canadian.

W

WAGH

An exclamation, used by both Mountain Men and Indians, usually denoting admiration or surprise. This grunt-like sound is supposed to resemble that made by a bear. It is, in fact, believed to have ordinate from the sound made by a bear when mildly surprised.

WAMPUM

An Indian term for belts of small beads or shells that were used as money. Many mountain men adopted this term to mean all money.

WAR PATH. ON THE

A person spoiling for a good fight is said to be "on the war path,"

WASNA

Pemmican. (Dahcotah word)

WATTAPE

The fine root of a coniferous tree, used as thread or twisted into rope. (Voyageur)

WAUGH

See "Wagh "

WENT UNDER

To die.

WHITE INDIAN

A White man who went native and joined a tribe of Indians. Many captured White children became White Indians.

WICKIUP

The lodge of some southwestern Indian tribes.

WIGWAM

The dome-shaped lodge of some eastern Indian tribes.

WILLOW KILLER

The first real cold spell of Fall. When the leaves all fall off of the willows due to the cold, it is a sure sign that winter has arrived.

WIPE OUT, A
A massacre. Many a so-called "massacre" was not really one at all, as both sides had weapons and were able to and did fight.

WOLFER
A man who made his living hunting wolves for bounty. The wolfer was only considered a degree or two better than the hide hunter. Neither were ever considered a part of the skin (fur) trade.

WOLFISH, I'M
I am hungry.

Y

YELLOW LEGS
Dragoons.
YUNKS
Children.

The series continues in Books 2-5

Book 2 - Renegade Trapper

Book 3 - Revenge

Book 4 - The Seer

Book 5 - Whispers the Wind

About the Authors

W.R Benton, a pen name, is a retired U.S. military senior Non-commissioned Officer with over twenty-six years of active duty service. He grew up in the Missouri Ozark Mtns., where hunting, trapping, camping, and other outdoor activities were the norm. Additionally, he spent more than twelve years teaching survival and parachuting procedures to U.S. Air Force personnel as a Life Support instructor. Mister  Benton has an Associate's Degree in Search and Rescue, Survival Operations, a Bachelors Degree in Occupational Safety and Health, and a Masters Degree in Psychology near completion.

Mister Benton is a member of the America Authors Association (AAA). You can visit W.R. Benton online http://www.wr-benton.net or his War Paint Site at http://www.warpaint.info.

Visit him on Facebook at
www.facebook.com/wrbenton01

Grady Clark, a pen name, is an avid outdoors person, who prefers the smell of wood smoke and chirping birds to the smell of smog and horns honking. Grady spent many early years on a farm, where work ethics and honesty were taught as a way of life, never to be compromised. Grady spent many years in the medical profession before retiring and starting a professional photography business. This is Grady's third book. You'll often find Grady camping, hunting or walking in the woods of Mississippi, where his deep love for nature was born. Grady is married, with two adult daughters and two sons, and lives near Jackson, Mississippi, with three dogs and two cats. Grady may be contacted through W.R. Benton.